SOUTHERN CROSSFIRE

Southern Crossfire

A Novel of the Civil Rights Era

Don Weathington

iUniverse, Inc.
New York Lincoln Shanghai

Southern Crossfire

A Novel of the Civil Rights Era

iUniverse books may be ordered through booksellers or by contacting:

iUniverse
2021 Pine Lake Road, Suite 100
Lincoln, NE 68512
www.iuniverse.com
1-800-Authors (1-800-288-4677)

Because of the dynamic nature of the Internet, any Web addresses or links contained in this book may have changed since publication and may no longer be valid.

Certain characters in this work are historical figures, and certain events portrayed did take place. However, this is a work of fiction. All of the other characters, names, and events as well as all places, incidents, organizations, and dialogue in this novel are either the products of the author's imagination or are used fictitiously.

ISBN: 978-0-595-46525-5 (pbk)

ISBN: 978-0-595-90824-0 (ebk)

Printed in the United States of America

Acknowledgments

I want to acknowledge my gratitude to my dear late friend Dr. Ron Stegall for nursemaiding me through the writing of this story. His loss is a profound sorrow to me.

I am grateful to Marsha Van Hecke for teaching me so much during the initial editing and re-writing of the manuscript.

I appreciate the time and efforts of my friend Jeff Koob in helping me persevere in this undertaking.

Finally, a big Thank You to my wife Faith for her constant encouragement and support.

Introduction

This story is set in Alabama of the 1960s. The language and attitudes of that era are recorded faithfully here. Gratefully, time and exposure have brought changes in these areas of southern life, although vestiges still remain in certain corners.

Some of the landmarks mentioned in the story no longer exist or have changed their names, others can still be found in the Auburn/Tuskegee area–e.g. Tuskegee Institute is now Tuskegee University. I took certain liberties with parts of the setting in order to make the story work better–e.g. there is no square in Tuskegee, so I created one to hold the action described in those scenes.

Although it was uncommon and unpopular, many southern whites favored ending the strict segregation practices that existed in that time. Some, as is suggested here, participated in the struggle to enfranchise African Americans, and tried to break down other barriers that excluded African Americans from access to the benefits of society. Others, of course, opposed these changes–often violently.

I attempted to tell this story for several points of view, even though that practice is frowned upon by the literati. I did this to give the reader insight into the thoughts and motivations of several elements of the culture at that time, while attempting to maintain the linear storyline. You, the reader, may judge the result of that effort for yourself.

Finally, although one character is the central figure, the heroism of this tale is spread across the efforts of many. Change has come and though there is still much work to do, in general, things are better for a greater number of the citizens of the south.

CHAPTER 1

▼

Auburn University, July 1965

Day by day delicious. The thought washes over Duke, like the sun breaking out from behind a cloud, bringing with it a smile and warmth. He watches as Claire, the redhead, stands at the jukebox, hipshot and concentrating. Something in his chest reaches out to her through his eyes.

For a couple of months he has hung around the student union building, observing the bridge players. Mostly this has been a way to escape the insistent 95/95 days of summer in the Southland—ninety-five degrees and ninety-five per cent humidity; but as he has understood more and more the complexities of the game, the challenge of participating is too much to pass up. When the guy known as Pax gets up to leave, Duke takes the plunge and asks if he might take his place.

At first the game was a mystery, but slowly he put together the fundamentals. Partners sit across from each other and bid for the "contract" in an auction. The winning bidders name the "trump suit" in the auction, the first to name it playing the hand as "declarer". The partner, as "dummy", spreads his cards on the table after the first lead, and plays them as directed. Play of the cards is clockwise, beginning with the player before the dummy. High card wins each trick, unless someone doesn't have a card of the suit led (is "void"). That eventuality produces a situation where a "trump" card may be played and even a deuce of the trump suit will win the trick, unless of course someone else is also void and "over-trumps". The object is to take six tricks plus the number bid in the auction.

Once he grasped the process and the math, the strategies of play became intriguing. And, of course there was Claire.

At the four tables in front of the jukebox, the heavy hitters play. In that small niche of a very southern corner of the country, changes are taking place that will fit with those shaping up elsewhere, and which, when the dust settles, will leave society transformed. Many think for the worse, others for the better ... No matter. The changes will happen. How could Duke even begin to imagine that the voices heard at these tables, when added to those in the larger culture, will influence a generation? In that space on most weekdays, sometime after ten a.m., Paxton "Pax" O'Reilly shows up. Without knowing even that it is happening, his ideas will wreak upheaval that will shape a society.

Pax came to Auburn University from Boston. His uncle graduated here many years ago and offered Pax the incentive of a free ride if he maintains a "B" average. This free ride includes not just tuition, books, and fees, but also room and board (in an apartment), a car, and an allowance. Many envy him. More to the point, however, many hear him. He is emulated by some, and derided by many others.

The civil rights struggle has crested all over the south. Attitudes are mixed (though heavily tilted against the process) and hotly debated in all quadrants. Desegregation was forced upon an unwilling public and to their surprise; it has not hurt as much as had been feared.

Pax is the co-founder of the Auburn Human Rights Forum, a barely visible and somewhat mysterious organization that worked with the first black student to begin studying at the university. After the spectacle of Governor George Wallace "standing in the school house door" in a vain show of protest of the integration of the University of Alabama, the desegregation of Auburn University was a total non-event. Pax and other Forum members had met with this student before his enrollment and by the time he actually arrived, he was known to many—students and faculty alike.

Pax does not lead this effort from a position of defiance, but rather from a posture of fair play. He is a six-footer, a somewhat overweight, pale-looking guy. He wears the uniform of the day: madras shirts, khakis or Bermuda shorts, weejuns without socks. He always seems to be smiling. He is an above average bridge player, which makes him very good at the level played on campus.

The jukebox just about always sets the varied mood at the Union. People compete to keep their favorites playing to the exclusion of others, so for long sets the Beatles and the Beach Boys, and recently the Rolling Stones play. Then Motown will spin for a while. Sometimes even country, but those guys don't have money to spend or just won't spend it on "foolishness".

When the music stops, a dozen voices call out, whistle, and hiss, until someone gives up, feeds the jukebox beast, and, thusly, the crowd. If all else fails, Claire will get up and wander around, going to people she knows or does not know, scrounging up money. Naturally, then everyone has to listen to what *she* wants to hear. She's made her rounds today. The jukebox is stoked with twenty-plus tunes. She sits down there across from the new kid, Duke. And he's got no idea what's about to happen.

As a bridge player, Claire is sometimes brilliant, sometimes obtuse—forgetting the count on cards and missing easy contracts. But whatever else she is at any given moment, she is fascinating to every man within viewing distance. Her hair is that deep red that suggests passion, straight and cut long. Her eyes are cobalt blue and can see through walls. Tee shirts and short—really short—skirts that flash just the right amount of thigh, and sometimes even a little more. She has a great body and she's comfortable in it—always seeming completely unafraid. That is the greater part of her appeal to the guys surrounding her. Of course, she doesn't know that. All those guys don't know it either; they're just slack-jawed, watching and hoping that she gets up to collect more money for the jukebox … She can have it all—just ask them, speak to them, show a little more thigh.

But right now she's holding cards in front of her. The bidding is over. She's to play the hand as declarer at a contract of "Three—No Trump". And old Duke is spreading his meager offerings on the table as dummy. At first, she just smolders. Of course, those who know her and know her game begin spilling small smiles and looking at each other in anticipation. They're expecting a Vesuvian eruption. They won't have to wait long.

"What the hell," she sputters. "What's your name? Duke? What the hell is that supposed to be? For Chrissakes how do you bid 'Two—No Trump' with seven lousy points? Have you ever played this game before?"

By now of course, her voice has risen in volume roughly equivalent to the emergency siren that they still test at noon on the second Wednesday every month. And so every bridge player in the area looks over at poor Duke, thankful that it is he, not they, on the receiving end of this opening salvo from Claire.

"Uh. Well, I thought that if you open 'One No Trump', and I don't have many points but my cards are evenly distributed, that I'm supposed to simply raise your bid; and that tells you that I'm basically a bust. Is that not right? And no, I haven't ever played this game before." Duke—an unknown here. Brown hair cut in a flat top. Long pleasant face. Brown eyes that women say you can swim in. Thin yet somehow powerful looking, he shows no fear in rejoining this eruption by Claire. And although it catches her off-guard, she likes it.

Claire stares open-mouthed, then, "What? You really mean it? You've never played before?"

"Right."

"And you come to *my* table to try out your homespun ideas? How the hell did you get into that seat anyway?"

"Well, that guy Pax? He said that he had to go while you were up feeding the jukebox, and I asked him if I could take his place, and he said 'Sure', so here I am. Is this a closed game or something? I mean, I thought that anyone could play."

Claire rolling her eyes at the crowd. Everyone waits, mouths open. This is new: Claire at a loss for words. She and the crowd wonder who this guy is anyway. Duke—no one has ever heard of him. Then Claire seems to realize that everyone is looking and waiting and expecting, so she says, "No. It's an open game. But do you always just insinuate yourself into heavy action to learn how to do something? I mean, people who play in here are playing *tournament* bridge. How could you expect to compete? Why would you subject yourself to this when you'll almost certainly embarrass yourself?"

Duke flashes this big, open, toothful smile. He's so relaxed that everyone at the other tables just lays back with him, and waits for something to happen. When it does, it's almost anticlimactic. He just ducks his head a little with that smile on his face, never taking his eyes off hers. She's swimming. He's through the wall. They're *seeing* each other. And he says, "Damn, you ask a lot of questions before you give a guy a chance to start answering ... Now let's see, first of all, if my 'insinuating' myself into the game is offensive I'm sorry. But then again since I'm here, we might as well deal with it.

"I've watched these games for weeks now from out there on the fringes and I agree that *some* of the people who play here are pretty sharp, but certainly not *all* of them. I figured that I had learned all I was gonna learn by watching and that the next step is to play ... As to 'heavy action'? C'mon, it's a card game. Gimme a break. It's pretty complicated, but I'll figure it out; and then maybe you won't be so upset at having me as a partner. I figure to be competitive in a few days, *if* I get to play. I'm not embarrassed if I made a mistake here. I'll learn from it. And by the way, with the lead he just made, the contract should make, if you bid correctly."

At least twenty people lean with Claire as she attends for the first time to a possible strategy for the actual play of the hand. A few "wows". Claire squints. Clearly, she hasn't put it together yet; but, also clearly, she's having a little trouble concentrating. Eyes flit from card to card and face to face. She hesitates. She isn't exactly embarrassed, but there's something going on between these two. Something smoldering.

With him it's, *You miss 100 per cent of the shots you don't take.* With her it's, *Who the hell is this guy? He's so calm—not like the rest of these bozos. I wonder if Pax even talked to him.*

She can only think to say, "OK wise guy, come around here and let' see it. You've got my concentration pretty well shot now, so I'll let you do your stuff."

He gives her an enthusiastic smile. Rising, he rounds the table to sit not just next to her, but right up against her. And she doesn't even flinch. Lots of hungry eyes in this place right now. Nobody knows if his enthusiasm is for the game or because he gets to sit that close to *her.* Both look intently at the cards. They seem to whisper though nobody hears. He plays the first cards and loses the trick, but smiles as if he's just scored the triumph of a lifetime. He looks at the right-hand opponent, who now must lead. When that lead is made, he proceeds to take eight consecutive tricks leaving the lead across the table at the "dummy" position. Says to Claire, "So, what do you think? An overtrick, or just make it on the nose? Try the hook or just be conservative?"

Claire looks incredulous. "Why try the finesse? You know that you make the contract without it. I say take the trick and punt. It's just not worth it".

Claire taking the conservative approach borders on the absurd to the bridge crowd. This isn't like her. She's protecting him. And everyone around the tables, all of whom are now watching not just the bridge hand but the larger game being played, knows that this is happening—everyone but Claire.

Duke half-whispers, "I may be wrong about all this, but I think that when you get to those tournaments that you were talking about earlier, if you take this kind of calculated risk and win, you make valuable points. Now remember the bidding and tell me that it doesn't suggest that …" Turns to his right-hand opponent—a guy with long-hair, thin lips, a thin body. Pleasant, non-threatening face with flat gray eyes, looking back with a neutral expression.

"I'm sorry. I don't know your name. I'm Duke." Extending his hand.

"I'm Judd. You gonna play 'em or talk 'em to death?" Said with a smile—just a friendly gibe. He shakes the offered hand. "You know, you're in my French class. And I'm guessing that you'll do OK."

Duke nods and continues to Claire, "So. I say that there's reason to bet that Judd's got the heart Jack or he couldn't have bid at all. So we'll take the hook and just see what happens." And he proceeds to make that extra trick. On his very first competitive hand he not only makes a tough contract, he makes an overtrick. Some people want to cheer. Others think he's lucky. A few others think, *What a jerk.*

Judd says, "That's a top board in any tourney. But it *was* a risk just based on the bidding. Pretty good reasoning though. Like I said, You'll do OK."

"Actually, I knew that it would work—I mean 100 percent sure. No doubt whatsoever." A whimsical little grin now. He's kind of rocking in his chair. His leg slides against Claire's. She's smiling, but looking a little uncertain. Maybe he's getting *too* damn cocky. He realizes this, but keeps rocking and grinning—looking at Judd, waiting for him to ask.

Finally, when the tension is just about to burst in the building, Judd says, "Really? This I've gotta hear. OK. How did you know for 100 percent certain that I had the Jack?"

"Well when I came over here to play the hand, I looked at your cards on the way by. In fact, you had them hidden so well that the only one I actually saw was the Jack of Hearts." People are smiling and squirming now. They're looking at each other the way people look when something unusual has happened and they're not sure what the right response should be. A little shocked that he's *admitting* that he cheated. Everybody knows that you don't cheat, but if you do, you sure as hell don't admit it in front of a bunch of people that you don't even *know*.

Then again he has pulled off a pretty smooth coup here, and doesn't really seem all that boastful about it. He made the contract without the subterfuge—announced that it was a done deal while still seated across the table. Still—cheating? They're all a tad confused. Meanwhile Judd's grinning from ear to ear and finally says, "Well, I had to ask, huh? That's pretty good. Did you enjoy the drama?"

Drama it is. Nobody really wants it to end.

The focus of energy is now between Duke and Judd—a visible, exciting thing. It's almost like fireworks. While they're connecting and really seeing each other for the first time, the truth suddenly dawns on Claire and with an open hand she smacks Duke's shoulder. "You're a real jokester aren't you? Well we'll see how well you do in the future. Now get your ass back over there and try to remember the correct bidding conventions. Christ, how do I end up having to train all the new people?"

She's mumbling this false bluster while he's making his way back to the chair opposite. When he's seated again, Judd looks over and says, "By the way that's Elizabeth ..." nodding toward his partner ... "and if you'd like to come over sometime, we'd like that."

Looking at Claire, Duke says, "You wanna go over sometime? Maybe we could play, and I could learn some more about the real way to play the game."

He's just casual-like. That's about the last thing that Claire's expecting to hear, so she's all muddled up again. This time she hides it from all but a few. Almost without pause she says, "Sure. I'll give you my number. And it's your deal. I gotta go to class sometime, so let's play if we're gonna."

*   *   *   *

A little over a week later, six people sit around in a spacious garage/studio apartment. Duke and Judd are talking bridge conventions. Claire and Elizabeth talk with Aurelia back in the kitchen area. Eddie "Teddy Bear" Baron sits on the couch looking intently at the cards and the problem presented by the arrangement.

A banging on the door—loud, but somehow friendly. Judd sings out, "Come on in." And in walks Pax.

"Oh. Hey, Judd. Sorry. Didn't know that you had company."

He eyes Duke and Teddy Bear—thinking, *Now where have I seen those guys before.* Sees the cards strewn across the coffee table, and asks, "Are you playing or practicing?" Knowing now why he should remember the other two.

Judd says, "Well, practicing; but since you're here we can play a little if you want." He gathers up the cards and shapes them into a neat rectangle, preparing to shuffle. He glances up inquiringly at Pax, who looks at his watch and says, "I can't. Look I've got a meeting in a little while. Come out here and talk to me for a minute will you? Sorry, guys. Personal matter."

Through the open screen, Duke hears a reference to "getting drunk tonight after the meeting" and wonders about it. He also wonders about the unnamed meeting, knowing only vaguely that Pax is involved with controversial matters, and is variously admired and hated. When Judd comes back, Duke comments, "He's pretty cool, huh?"

Judd surprises him by responding, "He's probably the smartest guy I know. Some of the things he does are just completely scary, though." Duke thinks of Judd as pretty smart himself, always seeming to have the answer even to esoteric questions about French literature. He never seems to study, just knows the stuff.

Teddy Bear is an engineering student—very conservative, a numbers man, quiet, always seems to be analyzing something. His name is Eddie Baron and Elizabeth dubbed him "Teddy Bear" about five seconds after she heard that. With his round face and the little mustache that he's sprouted, he even looks a little like a teddy bear. He asks, "What kind of scary stuff?"

Judd launches into the story of the Auburn Human Rights Forum, and their work at easing the whole desegregation scene at Auburn. And then, on into the latest project that includes voter registration in nearby Macon County. Duke has a tie to that place, but isn't ready to reveal that yet. He just listens and remembers.

The bottle of Chianti comes and goes fairly quickly. Lots of laughs, then all too soon they begin winding down toward the ending of the evening. As he's leaving, Duke says quietly to Judd, "Can I come back by for a few minutes after I take Claire home? I need to ask you some things." Being assured that it's OK, he adds, "See ya in a few minutes." Claire hears that and wonders, but keeps her peace until the ride home. Teddy Bear and Aurelia laugh and wave as they crawl into Teddy Bear's bug-eyed Sprite.

Claire seems far too quiet as she glides into the front seat of the '58 T'Bird. Duke has traded around the world to get this ride—other cars, shotguns, dogs, all kinds of dealing to arrive at that car. White panties flash nonchalantly as she gets in, distracting him from the troublesome possibility that there's social upheaval in store for his people in Macon County. Hard to concentrate on anything but those gorgeous legs and that flash of white. He grins as he thinks that the real reason southern men hold the door for their women has just played out before his eyes. He circles the car and enters, keying the engine into a quiet roar—aah yes, lots of power there. As he turns to back out, his glance crosses Claire, who is looking intense and maybe a little angry. Stopping the backward arc of the car's path, he asks, "You OK?"

After reassurances, they are driving along Magnolia Ave. and he asks, "Do Judd and Pax drink a lot?" In his periphery sees her go a little rigid—not much, just a momentary thing, but something that he notices and files away.

She eventually responds, "I don't think that they drink as much as people think that they do. They might do other things though." That piques his curiosity and at the same time he senses that there is a connection lodging itself somewhere in the back of his mind. He waits for her to say more; but she doesn't.

She does get around to asking him why he's going back to Judd's. He tells her that it's about class; but neither of them believes it. She lets it go. It's late anyway and she has that eight o'clock quiz tomorrow. But in front of her dorm, in the shadow cast by the rays of the streetlight intersecting the oak trees, she shows him that she's caring a little more than he had expected. Sweet mouth on his. Hint of tongue at his lips. Just the right amount of suction to cause pressure. And he feels it—right down to his ankles. As she walks toward the door alone, he has to admit that he liked it. And this, too, worries him a little.

The trip back to Judd's takes less than five minutes; but in that space of time his mind has wandered over a complicated landscape of ideas. Vague impulses become crystallized thoughts: *Voter registration? What did "getting drunk" mean? Claire's sensual kiss was spectacular … and that marvelous flash of white. Who is this Pax character anyway? Are the Tuskegee people going to be hurt by all this? Am I missing something obvious here, right in my own backyard? I mean right there in Macon County?—Man that's some shit there. This Pax guy seems nice. He's a thinker, but is he OK? This is likely gonna get hard before it's gets over with.*

There's accidental prophecy in that idea, all right. It will get hard.

Back at Judd's place in the parking area that's enclosed on three sides by buildings and covered with gravel, the T'Bird rumbles softly to a stop, sounding like only those big V-8s can. With the top down, he can hear the bluesy sounds of a Paul Butterfield album coming down from Judd's front window upstairs. There is calmness in the air that isn't always there. The smell of burning leaves somewhere. Crickets creaking in the trees. Climbing these stairs again for the second time tonight, the music gets louder. Still a thousand thoughts play at him from the ambushes of his subconscious.

The door is closed. *Huh?* He knocks and waits and knocks again. Finally, he hears Elizabeth giggling, "Oh, it's Duke." The opening of the door reveals three very happy-seeming people. Judd looks a little haggard. Pax is leaned back against the couch—eyes closed, apparently listening very closely to the music. Elizabeth is bouncing around, dancing, singing along with Butterfield.

He notices for the first time that she's not wearing a bra, and that she is very well put together. Funny that he had missed that in the presence of Claire; but he won't miss it again. She takes his hand and leads him into the kitchen, showing him the new bottle of red wine that Pax has brought, and with gestures indicates that he should pour himself a glass—the music too loud to talk really. In the sink he finds the jelly glass he had used earlier and pours some of the red wine. Turns to face these people. And though he needs to talk, he sits instead … And waits.

For a few minutes the music seems interminable and atonal; but as he allows himself to hear it, he finds the harmonies and the interplay of the various musicians soothing, even uplifting. When at last the album ends, he and they come out of their respective reveries and notice each other again. Judd grinning sheepishly. Pax seems almost embarrassed. Elizabeth is all smiles and sensuality.

Duke holds back, a little uncertain since he wanted to talk to Judd about Pax's work with the voter registration project. He finally decides just to go ahead with the questions anyway, because he won't rest unless he knows. And so turning to

Pax in the flat silence that precipitates out after the music dies, he asks, "Will you tell me what you're doing over in Tuskegee?"

The question surprises Pax and he pauses, as if he needs a moment to decide how much, if anything, to reveal. He wonders if there's some other reason to remember Duke, other than the bridge tables. Taking a deep breath, he says, "Why do you want to know about it?" Not defensive exactly, but not really forthcoming either. There's a little edge in his manner. His eyes are wide open now and the visual contact between these two is at high intensity.

"Well," Duke again hesitates. "I just wanted to know whether there is going to be a big showing in the next elections. And the reason is … can we talk confidentially here for a minute?" A beatific innocence and poorly concealed anguish spread across Duke's features. Undoubtedly something is bothering him. He needs to spill, needs a confidant. To the others he's taking a big risk.

Judd and Pax trade glances. Nodding, Pax says, "Sure, Duke. What's bugging you, man?"

"See, I've been dating a girl from over there. Her daddy owns that big restaurant downtown. I heard him and his friends talking about those 'outside agitators' coming in and trying to register the n … uh … coloreds to vote, and that it's turning the whole town upside down. He says that he'll lose his business if the coloreds vote and elect coloreds to run things over there. They all sound pretty scared about this to me." The concern is clear in his face—sincere worry for those people. But his ideas about justice hang in the room like a ripe plum.

The three seconds that Pax takes to gather his thoughts seem to stretch on and on, filling everyone and everything with electric anticipation—humming like a high-tension power line.

Pax picks the plum … He asks, "Is there any rational reason that you can think of that if a black man is the mayor or councilman of a particular place that a white businessman in that place should have to worry?"

The effect is like a gunshot in a closed room. Stunned silence in the aftermath. The confusion plays across Duke's face like the flickering of a movie screen. He wants to respond immediately, but the answer is elusive. The pat responses don't seem to have much merit here. He doesn't stammer, but feels in his chest that that is the picture of him they are seeing. Finally he manages, "I don't know," knowing even as he says it that it will never be a sufficient response. Nobody says anything—not one word. The silence grows. The pressure on Duke is wholly internal, and the more powerful for it. He turns the idea over again and again in his head. After all, why should Mr. Wilkins lose his restaurant if a colored man is the mayor? Or a councilman? What could that have to do with it?

The butterflies circle and come to rest in his gut. He's feeling more sure of himself again now. And with a chuckle and some genuine confidence, he says, "No I guess there's no real reason for him to worry. Hmm. Wonder what that's all about anyway."

The reshuffling and settling of new synaptic pathways in Duke's brain are almost visibly traced across his face. His movement toward a new way of viewing his world has arrived in a flash of insight, torched off by a simple question. But it's settling over him like a comfortable, old shirt. One he might have been wearing for years rather than the few seconds that have passed since his "aha!" awareness.

This shift, this growth, is not lost on the others in the room. Judd is smiling. Pax is relaxed and wide open now. Elizabeth, ever the practical one, says, "I didn't know that you were dating someone. Does Claire know?"

He almost laughs aloud. Thinks it comical that these two things—this threat that isn't a threat and whether or not Claire knows about Lynn—could be thought of in the same context. These thoughts are chased out by the surprising realization that he doesn't want to answer that question.

But he does answer: "I can't imagine that Claire would really care if I'm dating someone; but, no, she probably doesn't know. Why? Do you think that it would matter to her?" He already knows or thinks that he knows the answer to this question. He felt it in her kiss just minutes before, could see it in her eyes; but better to hear it from another woman.

Elizabeth rolls her eyes and shakes her head, "Are all men really this dense, or is it just some role that you all seem to have to play? I thought that you were more than just a pretty face; but if you don't know the answer to that question, I must be wrong. My god, Duke, when you're in the room everyone else ceases to exist for her. And she's not even very subtle about it."

Duke thinks, *Great. Another ball in the air. One more thing to deal with. But this thing in Tuskegee—what's the right thing to do here? Hell, I don't need to do anything, do I?*

Pax leans forward looking expectantly, straight-line into his eyes. Judd sits back now with a knowing smile on his face—like he knows something that Duke doesn't know but should.

Unable to hold back any longer, Pax says, "See, Duke, that county and town where your friend's dad does business and they probably live, is eighty-five percent colored and there hasn't been an elected colored official since Reconstruction. Only one reason for that, man. Colored people are not *allowed* to vote and are even afraid to *try*. I don't know this particular man, but I know that whites threaten Negroes with real and raw violence over there all the time. There have been lynchings, shootings, and beatings for generations. And I'm sorry, Duke; but it's just not right. You disagree with that?"

Duke is looking down a slippery slope. Behind him lie the teachings and traditions of generations of his family and of all the people that he has known up to now. In this moment it is all being called to question; and before him the world is unpredictable—and scary. Although he has personally witnessed several scenes from the Civil Rights Struggle—seen sit-ins by coloreds and the reactions of whites; watched and heard marchers who proclaim that they want freedom, while side-line observers sneer and curse and make overt verbal threats—it still hasn't been *real* to him. Just something going on outside of him.

He drove into work in Birmingham on the Monday morning after the church bombing had killed those four little girls, and he had been shocked by the presence of armed National Guardsmen in the streets. And even then it hadn't seemed real.

He and his buddy, whose father owned the hotel in another southern town (his hometown), had stood at the railing of the mezzanine and watched the coloreds stream in and sit down in the restaurant. He watched as the hotel managers had closed the doors, turned on the heat in the middle of that muggy August day, and then had dismissed the serving staff. Everyone waited. And waited. After an hour, one man tried to go to the front desk to ask for service; but found the door from restaurant to lobby locked. At that moment, the manager announced over the intercom that the restaurant was closed until further notice, and that the door to the patio and the outside would remain open. After the second hour, with nothing happening, people started drifting away. Duke had thought that had been a humane way to handle things then ... Tonight he's not sure *what* he believes about it.

And now this. Having to confront the *righteousness* of this cause—not in abstract terms.

Involuntarily the idea manifests: *No, this is not philosophy. This is the inescapable day-by-day reality of how some people have to live. The right to vote? It's guaranteed in the constitution, isn't it? How can Pax say that thousands are being denied? How can that be really true?*

Though he's thinking these questions, in his heart he knows the truth ... That far more wrongs are committed than are even being addressed at this point. He has never walked this path before, and once he starts down the trail of asking these questions, there may not be a way to turn back.

There is inevitability and resignation in his demeanor that threaten the casual mood of this house. But in the throes of his intellectual upheaval, right wins out. He says simply, "Yeah. You're right; what's going on out there is just wrong. And no, I don't disagree with what you're saying."

An inaudible sigh passes through the room. Everyone knows what has just happened but no one needs to comment. Whatever tension had been there is there no longer. Judd moves again toward the stereo. Pax reaches for the deck of cards. Elizabeth—pert, saucy, sexy—sits up close to Duke. Her knee and thigh press in along the length of the upper leg of his jeans. Touches him with the lightest of fingertips along his neck. Says, "So what are you going to do about Claire?"

He blushes a little, shifting back to that reality, thinking about the fire that he has seen in Claire's eyes and the imagined heat of her passions. Admittedly, he feels a little intoxicated by the closeness of this, yet another sensual woman, so closely against him and right in front of her boyfriend. As he leans back against the couch Elizabeth follows, brushing her wonderful breast against his arm. "I'm not gonna do anything about Claire. Hell, Elizabeth, there's nothing *to* do. Tonight's the first time we've gone anywhere and done anything except play cards at the Union. I mean, she's very cool and I like her a lot; but I don't actually owe her a full accounting of my life do I?"

Coyly now Elizabeth asks, "Well, does this other girl know about Claire?" Knowing that she has trapped him with the truth, she doesn't really care one way or the other; but she does enjoy his discomfort—enjoys it in an easy, pleasing, teasing kind of way. His involvement with more than one woman is as sensual to her as her bra-lessness is to him. Two peas.

Riffling the cards against the tabletop, Pax interrupts this secretly shared moment by asking, "So you wanna go and help us with the voter registration this weekend? All we do is help people fill out paperwork. It's pretty simple and you'll meet some nice people there."

Duke is shocked at first; but with a grin recalls a saying that he has heard from his mother all of his life: "In for a penny, in for a pound" ... and decides that here is the opportunity to learn *what's really going on*. So he says, "Sure; why not. When and where?"

"We'll just meet at my place at 2 o'clock on Sunday afternoon. We try not to take more than one car. I don't think that we're in any danger, but no sense baiting people by rubbing this thing in their faces. Judd and Elizabeth know where I live; maybe the three of you could come together." Then without further warning, he walks to the door. Saluting he says, "And to all a good night." The screen door bangs against the frame.

Jefferson Airplane plays on the stereo. Judd yawns, saying, "Look I gotta get some sleep. Quiz at nine. See you at the Union around noon? G'night, Liz. G'night, Duke."

This leaves Duke and Elizabeth relatively alone in this part of the apartment. Of course the only walls inside the place seal off the bathroom from the main room. Elizabeth gathers up a pillow from the big sloppy bed and comes back to Duke's side. She plops the pillow into his lap, puts her head on the pillow, and curls up on the couch. All he can do is shake his head. He knows that this is completely innocent—at least for her. He feels, or imagines that he does, the heat of her face against his crotch. For him it's just like everything else from this night—completely new. When the album ends, he eases her head and the pillow down on the couch, slips out the front door, and then down the steep stairs to the familiarity of the T'Bird.

CHAPTER 2

▼

A quiet place where George Washington Carver revolutionized the lowly peanut, Tuskegee Institute is a historical black university in Macon County, Alabama—a stone's throw (about twenty-five miles) from Auburn University. Hardly a hotbed of radical political movements.

Five white kids from Auburn tool along the back road, a short cut, seeming out of place. The car is Pax's new, black Ford Galaxie—red rolled and pleated interior, unremarkable from the outside, but with another of those big V-8 engines that Duke is so fond of under the hood. Quiet excitement on the drive.

Duke had offered to cram everyone into the T'Bird; but Pax firmly redirected his intentions with, "No, Duke, it's just too visible." Meaning to Duke that they're stealing surreptitiously into this town, so he's a little put off. Thinks, *If we're walking into danger, why isn't anybody talking about it?*

He, Judd and Elizabeth had gone together to Pax's swanky digs to find Pax and, surprisingly, Claire waiting. White heat in the glances between Duke and Claire—all smiles and casualness on the face of things. Duke's thinking, *I wonder if she and Pax are together and if Pax knows that we've been out together ... Of course! He came in at Judd's and saw us there, and then heard Elizabeth and me talking about her ...* He wonders if Pax even cares. Feels a little pressured about it.

As Duke sits in the back seat with Elizabeth pressed in between him and Judd, Pax is talking up front to anyone who'll listen, but especially to Duke. "The guy we're meeting with today is Dr. Milton Mohammed. He teaches sociology and history at the Institute and has arranged for us to be at the Mt. Zion AME Church as 'consultants'—sort of. A lot of the colored citizens of Tuskegee can't read or write, and are afraid to go in alone to get registered to vote. It's pretty intimidating to walk into those places where only white people work and not to be able to do what needs to be done on your own.

"Before you ask, yes, forms filled out beforehand and brought in for registration are legal and have to be honored. That's thanks to Bobby Kennedy. So what we'll be doing today, and most of the time when we come here, is helping people to fill out the forms. They have to be absolutely accurate and thorough. White clerks look for reasons to deny registration to these people. We also have to be sure that each individual has some sort of recognized identification to show when they go to register—like a birth certificate, a driver's license, or whatever."

The Galaxie slithers quietly into the parking lot of what seems to be just your average, garden variety, small town church. Gravel gives way to green grass. The church sanctuary and another building, probably a Sunday school classroom building, stand near a parking area. The Institute campus can be seen a block away—older brick buildings with white or green painted trim work, immaculate grounds with fields of green grass and flowers everywhere. Some structures are clearly dormitories, others likely classrooms. A few students can be seen in the distance. A building that is obviously a chapel sits in the middle of the campus. A basketball game is in progress on an asphalt court. Just a lazy Sunday afternoon in the Southland.

Elizabeth follows Duke out of the car applying a "love-pinch" to his rear end, then grinning as he shows surprise. Looking across the car roof his eyes fall directly, deeply into Claire's and he feels an involuntary tightening in his throat, only to have the moment broken as Elizabeth pushes him with both hands saying, "Get out of the way, Duke. Jeez, it was only a love pinch. Don't take it so seriously."

Claire gives him a big laugh—like he's been caught with his hand in the cookie jar. He even blushes a little for the benefit of no one. Far too many things to think about here, now. He feels like a stranger, an interloper. There are no other white faces in sight and he doesn't want to appear judgmental in any way. He has some vague sense that Lynn is over there somewhere watching—silly, she and her family are away for the day, all the way down in Troy. This is just paranoia.

A lone black man is coming across the parking lot toward the group. Pax sees and recognizes him, extending his hand, smiling. The warmth between the two men is visible. Pax turns to the group with his hand at the arm of the other man, saying, "Guys, this is Dr. Mohammed. He's our host today. Doc, these are my friends from Auburn—Judd, Elizabeth, Claire and Duke."

Dr. Mohammed looks at each in turn, this beautiful, serene smile on his dark face. He nods a greeting to each, but says to Duke, "I think I've seen you before." Duke feels color come to his neck, his face. His voice won't work so he says nothing, just nods.

Mohammed continues, "You're a ball player aren't you?"

And Duke breaths again. "Well I used to play a little. But that was back home in Gadsden. How would you know me from way up there?"

Completely at ease Mohammed croons, "Well my brother lived in those projects next to the ball field where that semi—pro team used to play; and he and I would sit out there by the fence and watch the games. That was good cheap entertainment. Haven't been up that way since Clovis died." Pause. Then, another smile and, "Good to have you with us."

Sweeping an arm that encompasses everyone, even Pax, he says, "Welcome and thank you all for coming. We're a little early, so let's go inside and get comfortable. Pastor Maxwell says that there will be a lot of folks here this afternoon, but they probably don't run their lives on the same time schedule that you young people are accustomed to."

Inside this darkened open room in the basement of the church, everything is clean but shows vague disorder from this morning's services. The smell of disinfectant still lingers. Tables are set up along two walls with a few chairs at intervals on both sides of one set, but none at the others. More chairs are scattered around the room. An older piano is angled across one corner. A doorway leads down a darkened hallway with a couple of other doors off it that are visible. Light fixtures that hang from the ceiling are a little dim, yellowed with age. The walls are concrete block and have many layers of beige to off-white paint.

The air is cool, but not air-conditioned. The few windows in the wall near the door to the outside are painted as well. All in all a comfortable, even inviting, place. The door that they entered off the parking lot creaks open behind them— Duke and Elizabeth are startled, and Dr. Mohammed, who apparently misses nothing, looks at Duke and grins. Then turning his attention and all that warmth to these newly arrived ladies, he says, "Ah yes, Miz Jemison and her lovely daughters. Come on in. Do you need help with anything?"

Miz Jemison is one of those big, rotund, always-smiling, colored women whom Duke has known for most of his life. As he reflects on this, he is surprised to realize that the only contexts in which he has known such women are as nannies or maids in the homes of some of his friends. His stomach turns over in the ridiculous fear that somehow these others know his thoughts, and he is profoundly embarrassed. He is so lost in his own mind that he almost misses Dr.

Mohammed's request that he go with Tisha out to their car and help bring in, "… those wonderful goodies that Miz Jemison always brings." And so surfacing out of his thoughts just in time, he heads for the door in the company of a cute, young girl, whom he had yet to notice. That will change shortly.

As he reaches around the girl to open the door for her, he detects the scent of Ivory soap. She's a tiny little thing, short and thin, but perfectly formed—like a doll. Dark hair that's kinda frizzy, like the hair of colored girls is so often—tied into ponytails with yellow ribbons that match the trim on her white dress. The skirt flares out only a little and is three inches above her knee. Her skin, dark against the dress, seems like velvet.

She nods her thanks to Duke and strides purposefully to a ramshackle old Pontiac, opens the trunk, and says, "I can get it." As she reaches into the trunk, bending forward at the waist, the skirt rides up another three or four inches showing perfectly formed legs that swell upward. Fabric tightly covers her firm, round rear. Duke finds it impossible not to look, and certainly approves. He's never looked at a colored girl in this way before. In fact he's never actually been this close to a colored girl near his own age before.

As she hands him the two bundles of food that she has brought up out of the car's floor with her, she leans forward, just enough to show a little cleavage from full breasts that Duke, again, had not noticed. She gives him a big smile like she obviously could see that he was staring, and that maybe it was OK that he was looking. Duke blushes again, but still checks her out as she bends back into the car for the rest of the food.

She seems to take a long time getting everything this time. Duke's pretty sure that this is a little bit of a show for his benefit, and likes that idea. He almost has time to wonder if there's something else that he should do, when her pixie face reappears. "Can you close it? I can't reach it with my hands full." Duke's mind flashes a picture of how high that skirt would ride up if she tried. But he closes the trunk lid and turns back to catch up with the rapidly retreating Tisha.

"So are you a student?" Better to be trivial than silent.

"Yes."

"Uh—at the college or the high school?"

Stopping her like a wall. She turns, looking angry, cocks one hip provocatively, inhales enough to accentuate her chest slightly. Says, "Do I look like some chile to you?"

Duke is flabbergasted. He blushes, scrubbing at the gravel with his weejuns. Staring unabashedly into her eyes, he holds that fire and ice connection. Thinks,

She's something else. And then smiling, says, "I can honestly say that I've never seen a child that looked anything at all like you. By the way, my name is Duke."

That seems to bank Tisha's fire. She smiles, says nothing more. Arriving back at the church door she turns and kicks it lightly with the side of her foot. Dr. Mohammed himself opens the door while in mid-sentence of a conversation with Pax. Duke follows the sway of Tisha's hips as she crosses the room to place the food on one of the tables where there are no chairs.

Miz Jemison stands there ready to arrange things. She looks at Duke with open, warm eyes and says, "Thank you, young man. I'm sure that Tisha gave you the heaviest ones." Before Duke can respond, she has taken the packages and begun to open and spread them around. Fried chicken. Fresh biscuits. A chocolate cake. Fried okra—*what a delicacy.*

Just as he's starting to feel like he should be doing something else or be gone, Tisha looks at him over her mother's back and says, "Mama, this here's Duke. You know, the boy that helped me bring in the food? Mama, he blush so easy. And he turn really red."

Miz Jemison looks first at Duke, who is proving that Tisha is exactly correct by blushing again; then at her daughter. She stiffens noticeably. Her color deepens; she says, "Girl, I'm not gonna have you come into this church house and embarrass our guests, and Pastor Maxwell, and Dr. Mohammed, and me. You apologize to this young man and you do it right now."

"But, Mama I …"

"I said now." In a voice as cold and hard as an iceman's tongs.

As Tisha is reluctantly mumbling an apology, Dr. Mohammed saunters over, breaking the tension. He seems to see everything and do the right thing every time. Duke is glad to see him. Admits to him that he hasn't eaten today. He's grateful when the good doctor tells Tisha to gather up a piece of chicken and a piece of cake and to sit with Duke while he eats.

Others are beginning to arrive now. Some are carrying dishes of food, while others are empty-handed. Many are dressed in the clothing of rural poor—overalls and plain dresses. The town folks, maybe slightly over-dressed, are wearing three-piece suits and fashionable dresses. The noise level has risen while Duke and Tisha have danced their dance. As he sits against the wall waiting for Tisha to bring his food, he looks across the room and catches the eye of Elizabeth. She has a big taunting smile on her face, shaking her head in pure amusement, all but shouting out loud that she sees him with this colored girl. Duke, catching her meaning, shrugs excessively and sees Elizabeth burst out laughing. At her side, Judd turns from his own conversation and Duke watches her reassure him that it was nothing, that she'll tell him later. Duke looks at the floor, just in case Judd follows Elizabeth's gaze and sees too much.

Dark legs and white dress interrupt his vision and his thoughts. A brown and ivory-palmed hand offers the paper plate with a drumstick, a sliver of chocolate cake and a plastic fork. Thanking her, he takes the plate and leans back in the folding chair motioning for her to sit beside him. Between bites he tries to apologize for what happened with her mother. Tisha is sullen and short with her answers, and finally Duke screws up his courage and says, "You know, Dr. Mohammed said for you to be nice to me. What are you so mad about anyway?"

"First of all, he didn't say to be nice, he just said get the food and sit with you. Second, I get tired of my mama always being so solicitous of white people. You see what she did? She didn't even want to hear my side of the story. You was right jus' because you white. You see that?"

And, well yes he had seen that. He tells her he doesn't really blame her for being mad, wishes that he could have done something to intervene. Can she somehow forgive him for not really having done anything except to be there … And—oh—by the way, how red *do* I get when I blush?

So she smiles and goes on and on about the deep red of his face and how when colored boys blush you can hardly tell it because of their dark skin. Then as she looks so directly at him, even though he had had no intention of saying anything of the sort, he says in a gentle and provocative tone, "I was afraid that you were about to tell her why I blushed in the first place." He holds this heavy eye-to-eye contact. She tries to play that off with a "well why did you?" But he knows that she knows. And she knows that he knows that.

After several long moments as the temperature between these two rises and threatens to announce itself to the gathered assembly by bursting into flame, she says, almost in a whisper, "I don't know why, but I *wanted* you to look at me." A pretty, sassy girl.

As he once again looks up and across the room, he locks gazes with Claire. He feels a tightening in his throat. Caught. Then looking back to Tisha, he says calmly, "I think the way you look is gorgeous. *And* I think that we'd better be very careful. Probably nobody here would like it if they knew what we're saying right now."

She nods agreement, then relaxes into the back of her chair. Looking across the room at Claire, she says, "That your girlfriend? She been watching us like a hawk. In fact so's that other girl."

For all the stirring that goes on in his mind and in his belly, he can only manage to say a meek, "No." And neither of them is 100 percent sure that it's true.

By now the crowd in the room has swollen to fifty or more. A stirring around the door to the parking lot gets the attention of everyone. Dr. Mohammed opens the door, greets, and looks around for Pax, who is already on his way to meet him. Three new white faces, young and awkward-looking, peer big-eyed around Dr. Mohammed. Seeing Pax they smile with relief. Those five now huddle near the door, talking, shaking hands. More smiles all around.

Dr. Mohammed walks with Pax toward the center of the room, one hand at his elbow. All growing silent as the two of them look up and around, somehow commanding quiet without saying even one word. Duke catches Tisha by the hand and moves toward the new arrivals, skirting the bulge of bodies that surrounds Pax and Dr. Mohammed. He says, "I think I know one of those boys. C'mon over here with me."

Approaching the three men from their obscured side, Duke touches one of them lightly on the sleeve. The new person is startled and turns to face him. Duke smiles and says in a loud whisper, "Hey, I'm Duke. I think I've seen you at the University."

A flicker of recognition crosses the newcomer's olive complexioned face. "Man, we're really glad to see you here … And to have found the right place. Yeah, I know you, Duke, I was in the Union the other day when you peeped Judd's hand and pulled off that overtrick. Great stuff."

His voice belies the rest of his look—it is deep and resonates with some sort of accent, like he's from New Jersey or somewhere—a totally unfamiliar sound. *The truth* is written in his every manner. He *is* glad to see them. He *is* glad that he and his friends are in the right place. He *does* remember Duke from the bridge tables and he *did* enjoy it.

Almost faster than it took Duke to catalogue all that, the young man says, "I'm Ron Bauman." He extends his hand to be shaken by Duke, then turns slightly to the other two newcomers. "This is Leo Kaplan and Jay Kahn." Handshakes all around. Before Duke can introduce Tisha, Dr. Mohammed is speaking in raised tones for everyone please to quiet down and that it's time to get things started.

"Folks, we are gathered here this fine afternoon to take another step in the grand scheme of"—pause—"*Free*-dom."

"That's right," from a nearby lady.

"We're here this day not to do God's work"—another pause to silence from the group—"but to do man's work with God's blessing and His help." … Amens all around.

"Like all true and significant efforts, freedom won't come all at once. You can't get all of it at one time. You got to work every step, every day, every way."

"That's right, doctor," a different, strong, female voice.

"You got to do your part, knowing that God has already done his part."

"Yes suh," from a large-framed, very dark-skinned man just in front of Duke.

"And you got to believe that He's gonna provide whatever else you gonna need. That wherever freedom and justice seek, he will see *to it* that they shall *find*."

Some hands are clapping. People get caught up in the mounting excitement of this moment. Duke looking around with chills at his neck and shoulders. Tisha is rapt as she hears the message of hope from Dr. Mohammed. Murmurs of approval all around. Ron, Leo and Jay are mesmerized—staring at the doctor, at the crowd, at each other.

Duke thinks … *He's got 'em now. Whatever he wants he can have.*

"You know, folks, in a democracy, like we're supposed to live in here in the United States, if your voice is *not* heard in the process of making rules and laws, then" (turning with each emphatic word) "You … Are … Not … Free."

"Tha's right, Brother Milton," two men dressed as laborers, even on Sunday afternoon, say in unison. They could be brothers themselves.

"So today, we line ourselves up. We sign ourselves up. Then come Election Day"—pausing, turning in a sixty-degree arc, looking at all the faces at once, everyone feeling singled out—"we gonna line ourselves up again."

Thunderous applause and a chorus of voices, Amens and yeses and whistles. All the whites are also clapping and looking enraptured, nodding their heads. Smiles light the spirit of each one here.

"That day's gonna be harder than this one." Quiet now—near total silence. Duke almost bursting with the pure thrill of this aggregate of moments into *MOMENT*.

Unspoken fears of violence pervade the room. These white youths for the first time understand that by continuing in the direction that they are now headed, there is the chance—no the *great likelihood*—of physical harm. This stark realization flashes through Duke's brain and he nods his head in acceptance, his entire body following in a sort of bow.

His thoughts move quickly from that to a sudden jolt of insight. These people live with that same lack of security, that fear … always. They have never felt the true wholeness of freedom. Like a palm slapping his forehead, he knows—*This is what's really going on.*

Very little noise in this room now. The eyes of each slowly return from the sidetracks of their own private anxieties to this room, to this *moment*. Mohammed looks downcast, like he's contemplating the true meaning of life or something. All souls empathize with what must surely be enormous pain. And as he looks back up, a tiny smile becomes a larger one, becomes a sly grin. And he says, "Won't have no fried chicken from Miz Jemison; no yams from Miz White; no fruit salad from the reverend's wife …"

The whole crowd is laughing now, seeing each other again, seeking out the names as he calls them, connecting with each other again after that moment of contemplating their fears. No, they are not alone. All these others, their neighbors, their extended families, their friends, even these white people are with them. That'll make it easier. They don't have to face the bogeyman alone.

Mohammed raises a hand and turns in that familiar arc, as the crowd quietens. He says, "You know the Lord sent us some more help today. These fine young people from the great Auburn University have come—actually we think they were sent—for no other reason than to help us do something that we've never done before. Scattered around on those tables across the room from the food are forms that are the 'Tickets to the Polling Booth'. They have to be filled out by every person who is registered to vote, and you are allowed to vote only after you're registered. We've mostly never even seen these forms. The white folks kept them locked up and if they didn't refuse them to us, they at least kept them a secret from us."

"Right on," from several quadrants. No small amount of anger in those words. Duke feels the rise in resentment grow all throughout the room, even in him, although he wonders if he is half-viewed as the enemy.

"But we got 'em now. Next we have to fill 'em out and get it exactly right. That's what these young folks, white and black, are going to help us do today. Let me introduce these young people to you. First, this is Mr. Pax O'Reilly."

Murmurs and "How-dos."

"He's the founder of the Auburn Human Rights Forum at Auburn University, and I'll let him introduce the white kids to you. Pax."

Spattering of applause. Pax with hand raised, grinning, seeming embarrassed, turns in the now-prescribed sixty-degree arc and says, "Thanks, folks, we're just honored to be here and to have been welcomed so warmly by you. We wouldn't have missed Miz Jemison's fried chicken for anything."

Some general laughter. One man saying, "Well at least they know what good food is." More laughter.

"I'll just tell you the first names of everyone, and let you get the rest later if you want to and there's time. If you guys would just hold up your hand as I call your name. OK. That's Judd with the long hair. Next to him is Elizabeth. That's Claire over there near the iced tea ... Well, if you've been over near the food you've seen Duke. I'm pretty sure that Dr. Mohammed stuck poor Tisha with him so there'd be something left for the rest of us." Duke raises not his hand but the remains of the chicken leg off the plate that Tisha is still holding, to the giggles and guffaws of the group.

Pax continues, "These three dilettantes—er—latecomers are Ron, Leo, and Jacob. Thanks again for having us." He seems relieved; but knows that he did it just right—enough showmanship to be accepted but not so much as to vie for attention with Mohammed. Perfect. Pax slides out of the spotlight and Mohammed just so smoothly slides back in. Never missing a beat. Perfect choreography. It's like they are dancing up there.

Mohammed smiling, clasping his hands at chest level in front of his pinstripe suit says, "We are also honored to have two of our own here to help out. Everybody knows Cho-La Brown." Mohammed gestures toward a tall, skinny, dark-skinned man, who also looks like a kid. Cho-La takes one step forward into the spot where all the congregants are looking. Snaps his fingers loudly over his head and points in a circle that is held tightly near to his body by the crowd around him. His head is like a light bulb. Big, almost bulging, dark eyes. Work pants end in huge tennis shoes. A work shirt with his daddy's name on it—wearing it proud-like. The people nearest him touch and otherwise acknowledge him as their own—proud *of* him.

New warmth passes through the room. Then Mohammed again, "And, of course, the lovely Tisha Jemison. Tish, everybody's had a chance at the food now. You can cut Duke's leash. And Duke, I know you're still hungry so go on back over there and help yourself and take those dilettantes—is that what Pax called 'em? Anyhow, take those latecomers with you. We want you well fed for the coming hours of work ahead of us."

Duke moves the new arrivals along the back side of the crowd toward the tables of food while Mohammed is saying, "Those of you that have time problems and need to get out of here early, come see me or Miz Maxwell. We'll get to everybody as long as you'll stay to do the work. It's not fast, and it's not easy; but we'll get through it. Be patient with each other and when these young folks come back and are seated behind the tables we'll begin. One person at the time at a table unless you have a problem that prevents you from doing the interview by yourself. Might as well start getting used to doing things for yourself."

Turning toward the young people he adds, "When you boys get yourselves a plate please meet with me and Pax and the rest through the hallway, first room on the left. That's the choir room. Thank you all. I think Chandra Gentle is planning a music program for everybody who will sing."

The crowd disburses into small groups, talking with each other. Some approach the young people thanking, encouraging, touching. Little, and not so little, colored ladies fix plates for the newcomers from tables that are now completely covered with dishes—far more, Duke notices, than when Tisha had slapped a single chicken leg and a sliver of cake on his plate. He gladly accepts a full one from Miz Jemison herself. He waits for Tisha, Ron and the others and together they move toward the hallway.

CHAPTER 3

▼

Walking down this darkened hallway now, Duke realizes that Tisha's hand is in the crook of his elbow—not an uncomfortable sensation. Ron, Leo and Jay, following along behind, exchange exclamations about the food and their surprise at the number of people that have shown up today. Tisha opens the door to the choir room where Pax and Dr. Mohammed are seated, elbows on knees, deep in conversation. Mohammed looks up at the young people entering the room. Mrs. Maxwell follows them carrying a notebook and copies of the forms. Cho-La Brown, with his own plate of food, steps in behind her.

Chairs are scattered in confusion around the room. A new console piano faces out from the far corner. Sheet music lies about in seats and on the piano top. Mohammed makes a sweeping gesture. "Gather around. We'll talk while you finish eating. This will be the only real training that any of you will get, and not much of it at that. Miz Maxwell, if you'll give everyone a copy of the registration form, we'll look at it together."

*　　　*　　　*　　　*

Looking around at all these bright, young, intelligent faces, Mohammed's heart is warmed. They know him as the professor from the Institute; but his true calling is with this group—right now. He is an ordained cleric who has come to believe that his impact will be far greater in his current role than as that of a minister at the church level. He has been at the school for fourteen years as a faculty member, having graduated from there with his Bachelor of Arts in history and music. His theological training is both formal and informal—a master's of divinity from Moorhead College; and then working on call as an associate pastor in the surrounding area for the first five years after coming back to Tuskegee from Atlanta.

The teaching job was brought to his attention by denominational leaders and established him with an income that allowed him to live well by local standards, and to travel to Atlanta—three hours by car—to continue his education. The denomination funded the doctoral program, but only if he studied history and sociology. That's what was needed, and he, Milton Leroy Spinks, had proven that he was smart enough and that he would work hard enough. It was during this period of his life that he had decided with his mother's approval to change his last name to Mohammed, casting off his "slave name", to which he felt no affinity.

This educational endeavor put him in the inner circle of Dr. Martin Luther King and his associate, Andrew Young. Intuitively, he knew that their non-violent approach to social change was the only way that it could actually happen. Other groups were espousing a violent, "race war" mentality, a notion Milton thought to be absurd on face value—how could 12 percent of the population hope to *take* power from the 88 percent by force? He saw these others as hotheads, as a threat to the success of the mission ahead, and as an entity that his group could in no way afford to join *or* to criticize publicly.

In a conversation with his mentors, Andy and Martin, one night at Moorhead, Martin had explained to him that, "Any public differences among colored groups will be seized upon by the whites and bantered about as 'tribalism'. They will use their media influence to fan those flames and the direction of the movement will be shifted from social change to that of a power struggle within the ranks of the colored community. So we have to believe what we believe and let them believe what they believe. When asked about their policies or methods, we feign ignorance and say, 'You'll need to ask them about that. We just don't know and wouldn't presume to guess.'"

Milton's own history propels him toward the work of expanding the base of options in life that are available to people of color in the South at this time. His mother worked as a domestic in the home of a wealthy white family, right here in Tuskegee. The man of the house had always treated Milton with kindness—teasing him, touching with gentle hands, giving him small bits of money—and for the first twelve years of his life Milton felt returning kindness toward the man.

Milton's father was a drinking man. He worked as he could as a farm laborer but spent almost all that money on alcohol, gambling, and—it was rumored—other women. He was a rough-talking, sometimes physically violent man. Milton and his two older brothers had both physical and emotional scars from this man whom they loved, whom they feared, and whom they sometimes hated.

The time came, as it did so often in these kinds of situations between black men and the white employers of their wives, when Milton's father in a drunken rage had first accused his wife of … "spreadin' yo' legs fuh that white man." She had, of course, denied it. He had struck her and struck her repeatedly, until Milton and the other sons had dragged him off her and wrestled him out the door.

It was said that the old man had next gone to the home of his wife's employer, this after dark in an all-white neighborhood. He had banged on the door and ranted, raved and threatened the life of a prominent white man. He accused the white man of forcing his wife into sexual congress by threatening her job. Neighbors had called the sheriff and the portly lawman and two deputies had come and dragged him off to jail. The sheriff said that they had held him for two hours, "…'til he sobered up some …" and then turned him loose.

They didn't know where he went or how. Nevertheless, two days later his body was found out near the quarry when the buzzards started circling. He had been beaten to death. No one ever knew who actually did the deed—whether it was the sheriff or the Klan, or if that was the same thing anyway. Milton had mixed feelings about this whole affair—on the one hand it was a relief to be free of the constant dread of having the old man come in drunk and take his rage out on wife or child. On the other hand, he loved his father in his own way and knew that killing a man just for saying the wrong thing was much worse than what his father had done.

He was still wrestling with the moral dynamics of this when he heard his mother and her sister talking in the kitchen late one night, when they were sure that he was asleep. Momma was crying and saying that Pop's death was her fault and Aunt Jenny was saying that she shouldn't be blaming herself. Then through her tears and with her heart breaking she said the words that Milton would never, could never forget. "I was just doin' it for a little extra money. It didn't mean anything. I don't know how he could have found out."

His father's suspicions had been correct. In fact his mother had had a sexual relationship with her employer. It happened because there wasn't enough money, and his pop's own behavior had contributed to the whole thing, and that … He couldn't hear or think any more. It was just too much for his twelve-year-old mind to comprehend.

However, the one thing that kept coming back was that the white man had used the power of his mother's job to take advantage of a situation to his own profit. A guilty conscience had probably made him give her a little extra money;

but the real price had been that, even if no one believed the accusations, Pop had to be silenced. Otherwise, the man's friends and neighbors would be tempted to think the worst. Even the slightest tinge of doubt could not be allowed. Neither the man nor the white community could afford to allow this sort of scandal.

To his small credit, the man did see to it that Momma got into another job, in yet another white home, and life went on; but not the same as before. In a matter of seconds, Milton Leroy Spinks had been changed forever, had been given a direction that would guide his life.

✳ ✳ ✳ ✳

"The Form is what we're here about today," Mohammed is saying now. "This will look simple to you folks. And in a way it *is* simple; but unfortunately simple questions have a way of breeding very complicated, sometimes impossible answers. Ron, I believe that in '64 when you came over to join us, it was after the unsuccessful registration period was over, right?" Ron nods with his mouth half-filled with cake, swallows and says, "Yeah, Doc, we just came over and provided transportation to the polls."

"I thought so. I hope that you've traded cars." A half-smile betrays the serious intent of the statement. "Tell young Duke here what your reception was like when you showed up at the polling places with a car full of colored folks who were hell bent on changing the world."

Ron, shaking his head, leans forward, forearms on his knees. Looking squarely at Duke he says, "There were people beating on the top and sides of the car. They called me 'Nigger Lover.' They threatened my life and the lives of anyone who got out of the car. They made a big show of writing down my license plate number. The sheriff came and checked my driver's license five or six times. If Washington hadn't called Governor Wallace and made him call the sheriff and the state troopers in the area, there'd have been some harm done that day. As it was there was just a lot of talk and bluster; but I know that I was very scared and so were the other people that were here to drive. In fact, I'm the only one here this time from that old group—well except for Pax, of course. I've tried to warn these new guys as best I could, but they're committed to going through with this."

Mohammed acknowledges him with a nod, "I know you were scared, son; we were all scared. And we'll be scared again, too, but being scared or because something's hard doesn't mean that you shouldn't try to do the right things in life. I'm proud of you and we're all grateful."

Shifting his attention back to the larger group, Mohammed continues, "The work that we have before us right here today is paperwork. It wouldn't seem like paperwork ought to be seen as such a big threat to the white community; but you know that it's the very device that has been used for so long to keep us from having a voice in anything related to governing.

"I'm sure you know the history. First the rule was that you had to own property, and of course, we didn't have many property owners among us. Then there were the literacy tests and, of course, most of our people didn't get to go to school because they had to work in order to contribute to the survival of the family. We've had poll taxes that we couldn't pay and zoning problems that we couldn't even understand, much less overcome. Now what stands between colored Americans—or I should say colored *southern* Americans—and the voting booth is just these simple forms.

"But then we get to the hard part. If you'll look with me at the form, you'll notice that it first calls for the applicant's 'Full Name'. Seems simple enough; but some of these folks don't know if they even have a middle name. For many there will be no 'official' birth record, because they were born at home. So there is no officially recorded proof of their very existence, much less what their name is and how it is spelled. That brings up the first in a series of hard-to-solve problems. We have found that there are two non-traditional sources that we can use to verify births, names and spellings that the courts have upheld as being legitimate. The first is the church's membership register; the second is the family Bible.

"So even on the first line of this *simple* form, we run into trouble. Maybe you already know this; but in case you don't, colored mommas in the South have been creatively changing the conventional ways of spelling the names of their children, or combining names in new ways for decades in order not to be seen as still in subjugation to whites. That's right, all those outrageous looking names that you have seen and wondered about represent nothing more than black women wanting for their children to be seen not as derivative from white America; but as uniquely Negro Americans.

"It's best if you can get the person in front of you to bring with them next time whatever document that you or they can think of to *prove* that they exist in some official capacity; and from that document take the spelling. Don't try to guess about it.

"Yes, you did hear me say, 'to bring with them next time', because it is unlikely that we will completely finish very many of today's applications. The exceptions will be those who live downtown or in the projects. They'll have access to official documents and their addresses will be easily definable. Pax and Miz

Maxwell have been through this before and will have ideas about the other obvious pitfalls that you'll likely encounter, and even some ways to look at possible solutions."

"Don't give up on anyone. Everybody who wants to vote ought to be allowed to do so; we'll beat the bushes if we have to to find a way to get this done for *every* person here. I expect that over half of the folks out there today will have to come back next week, or whenever, with documentation; but that's alright because they'll have to take that with them when they go to the registration offices anyway—might as well get everything in order now. Pax, if you and Miz Maxwell will take over now, I'll go back out front and start trying to get some kind of order into who will need to go first and then try to get things set up."

Somehow he manages to look at everyone at once as he rises toward the door. To Duke he seems tired and under strain. As the door to the hallway opens, music from the meeting room drifts down and slips into the little room—something slow and soulful, the rich voices of men blending with the softness of soprano and alto. It's just a brief flash of sound that hits Duke like some unseen wave. He is swept away momentarily into his own history—the school choir that he had sung in in high school and in which his supposed girlfriend, Ellen, sang and sometimes played piano. Lord, he hasn't thought of Ellen in days, hasn't been home in weeks, hasn't even called her. She's in college at a small school near home. He doesn't even want to think about this.

So he forces it out of his mind and tries to refocus on what Miz Maxwell is saying. She has the floor and is telling the group about things that they might run into, saying that even addresses are suspect, because some of the places where colored people have to live don't have street names at all. She explains that many folks get their mail through General Delivery, which is not a valid address for voter registration purposes. She adds that many Negroes use the address of the house that is nearest to where they live—and if the people that actually have that address know and approve, it will be fine.

She says, "Many people can't sign their name and must 'make their mark' and this mark must be witnessed and consistent. If someone doesn't *have* a mark, one must be created and taught. Most people do not have Social Security cards or numbers. These people must be listed so that getting cards can be accomplished in the future. It is the most widely accepted form of identification and will be useful for things that may come up later.

"There is widespread fear in the colored community of being visible and in line for punishment by the white community for things that may or may not have happened. Some people want to be able to vote, but don't want to be identifiable. They'll have to choose; but we will try to influence them. When you encounter this, call Dr. Mohammed or me. Don't try to get into it yourself. And by the way, you must write down something in the way of a name, so if you don't know what to write, call me or Dr. Mohammed."

Watching Pax, as these two talk back and forth, is like watching the conductor at a symphony performance. He introduces each topic, but then steps aside as Miz Maxwell delivers the meat of the information. He is ever attentive, adding a tidbit here and there, and at the same time willingly plays second fiddle. Duke and Judd exchange glances several times, as though they are thinking with one brain. This ten-minute segment is so well orchestrated that it must have been done many times before.

Duke continues to suspect that there's a lot more to Pax than meets the eye. Through his mind formless ideas flash: *He's so smooth with this and so thorough. He has to be one of those "outside agitators" that everyone in the South is so upset about.* Then, *He's from Boston, right? That's sure as hell Kennedy country. How did his uncle get to Auburn in the first place? No. Slow down. So he's from Massachusetts, does that mean it's wrong for him to be doing what he's doing? Is it wrong for me to be doing what I'm about to be doing? No, I'm local and I'll, by god, do what I think is right. I'm not all that scared of what others say. I wonder if he feels safe. I wonder if he has ever shot a gun, or if he would if things got too tough to talk his way out of. He may need me in ways that he's never even thought of. What about these women? Do they really know what the possibilities are? Is it right to lead them into this kind of potentially violent situation?* So many questions that don't have answers at this point.

The training session is breaking up. Everyone moves into the hallway and back to the meeting room. Music in the central room is light-hearted now. Someone is playing piano that sounds almost like ragtime. Singers freelance with experimental words. A few hands clap. Laughter. There's warmth here that won't be pushed aside. People are committed to getting done what needs to be done. All that rage that is written about in the pages of the newspapers isn't here—just determination and good spirit.

Cho-la Brown comes bopping and sliding into the room, hands and arms flying in rhythm with the music. Tisha bumps Duke's hip with her hip—right on time. Duke slides away but moves back for—not the next beat, but the one after that. Dancing in church. He's never seen that before. But it seems … well … just natural. Not unseemly. Joyful in fact. Celebratory. This is a happy place. Duke allows himself to be guided by Tisha to a seat near her behind the long table against the far wall. He feels steady as he awaits the next scene in this never-before-read script.

That steady feeling comes to an abrupt halt as the first person approaches the chair across from him. As he stares in awe, a gigantic, dark-skinned man in overalls and a checkered shirt chooses his place. This man might be six-feet eight inches tall and weigh almost 400 pounds. He is round everywhere. Hair grows in a fringe around the edges of his head—bald on top. Wrinkles seem to march up from his brow to the top of his scalp. He stands and waits. Looks with what Duke takes to be a scowl. Waits.

Duke is a little nervous at the prospect of initiating the conversation; but finally, almost in desperation says, "Yes sir, please sit down."

A big smile changes the complexion of the situation, but not that of the man. A couple of missing teeth, but the rest are dazzlingly white against the dark features. "Yes, suh. Thanky, suh."

Duke is a little taken aback at being addressed as "sir" by this obviously older man; but decides to wait on reacting. Pulls out one of the forms and prepares to get started. "Yes, sir. What's your name, please?"

"Yes, suh. My name Luther, suh. Luther Washington."

Duke softly taps the pencil that he's holding on the tabletop. He looks up from the form into these dark, deep eyes. The man is almost trembling. Attentive. He seems very anxious to please, breathing rapid/shallow. Duke is touched to his core as he realizes that this man is instinctively cautious toward him, fearful even. At the same time, Duke feels ashamed that his white skin is sufficient cause to evoke this sort of reaction. He shakes his head. Nevertheless, he continues to hold the eye contact with Luther. Empathy, oozing heavily, flows like lava from his eyes to the man across the table from him. After a few seconds pause he says, "Luther let's get something straight here. I'm just a college kid over here to help out. You don't need to keep calling me 'Sir'. In fact, it makes me uncomfortable. My name is actually Ashley DeWayne Windsor, but everybody calls me Duke. So that's what I'd like for you to call me, too. And relax, my friend, I'm just another guy."

"Yes, suh." They look at each other in silence as Duke waits for him to realize that he just did it again. He does and smiles as he corrects, "I mean awright, Duke." And he actually does seem to relax a little. Sinks back into the chair a bit. Duke wonders if the rickety wooden chair is going to support Luther's weight for the entire interview. Glancing to his left, Duke sees Mohammed looking at him, smiling, nodding.

Duke finds himself reluctant to start with heavy questions; but decides that he needs to know where things stand right from the beginning. So he regrips the pencil, adjusts the form and asks, "OK, Luther, can you read or write?" Almost dreading to look up at him, Duke is surprised to hear him say, "I can write my name. Can't read or write nuthin' else; but I can write my name." This is said clearly with pride, and Duke treats it with respect.

"Alright. Good, Luther, that makes it a lot easier. Now do you work? Or do you have a Social Security card?"

"I works down at the feed sto'. An' Mr. Pennington, he pay me cash money. Don't know 'bout no Social Security card, tho'. I can drive. Got me a driving license. Mr. Pennington helped me git it so's I can deliver things fuh him." Again pride shows through at having accomplished this thing that most of the whites that Duke knows consider to be automatic at age sixteen.

"That's great, Luther. We're gonna get you in the voting booth, no sweat."

Luther beams at Duke. He looks around at others in the room and beams at them also. The others respond to his enthusiasm. Smiles shine on Duke and he feels warmth in his belly that is at once pleasant and somehow sad.

Inspired, he says to Luther, "Let me see your license." And from this document he copies full name, address, date of birth. Fills out almost the entire form with information from the driver's license. Then asks Luther where he was born. Luther explains that he was born at home. And that "home" is on "the hill."

Duke thinks that he knows what that means; but asks if that is in the city limits. It's Luther's turn to look surprised now. He gives Duke a shining smile and says, "Sho' is Mistuh Duke, smack dab in the middle of th' quartuhs. All my brothers and sisters was born there, too." Curiosity piqued, Duke asks how many brothers and sisters and is shocked to hear that Luther is the second child, oldest son, of fifteen children that Miz Washington brought into the world.

Unsolicited, Luther tells him of the family's three fathers, that he has never known his own father, that only seven of the children still survive—three were stillborn, four were lost to illnesses and one other to a car wreck. This is far more information than Duke needed or wanted to have. Again he finds himself empathizing with this man who seems to want or need no empathy, who accepts his lot in life and is grateful to be alive and to have the opportunity to be registering to vote.

Asking Luther to wait for a moment, Duke gets up, seeks out Miz Maxwell, checks that the form is complete and accurate. He shows her the driver's license, and is told to have Luther to see her as he leaves. Returning to Luther he says, with hand extended, "Congratulations, Luther. By this time next month you'll be a registered voter in the city of Tuskegee, Alabama. Don't forget to go and vote now."

With a look that borders somewhere between the serious and the incredulous Luther says, "Don't hafta worry 'bout that Mistuh Duke, I'll be there when they opens up the doors. First one to go in, that'll be Luther Washington." Shaking his hand, he pulls Duke toward him to clasp a huge hand on Duke's shoulder. Both men are almost tearful with the joy of it all.

As Luther makes his way to Miz Maxwell, a small, birdlike woman comes and sits on the same chair and looks inquiringly at Duke, who bursts into his best toothy grin. Says, "Afternoon, ma'am. I'm Duke. Can you tell me your full name, please?" This interview will prove to be both easier and harder. Easier in that Duke is no longer hesitant to be himself; harder in that the information is so much more difficult to retrieve—Rose Ella is sure that her name is *two* names, not Rosella because that's what her momma told her. No driver's license, Social Security card, or birth certificate. She is also a "born at home" and never went to school. She knows that the family Bible has her name and date of birth in it, though.

She and Duke struggle through filling in as much as they can be reasonably certain about and then call Miz Maxwell over, but she is by now so overwhelmed that she asks Tisha to help. Tisha sits down by Duke and gets Rose Ella to agree to go home right now and get that family Bible and bring it back here.

Tisha thinks to ask, "And is there anyone else from your family here with you?" Sure enough there are two sisters and three brothers here; and all of them are in that bible, too. Gathering up these siblings and working with them while Luther drives Rose Ella home for the Bible, there is a major scoop brewing in getting six people done in about the time it would have taken to do one or two.

Mohammed comes and compliments Duke on this, but Duke is quick to say that it was Tisha who asked the right questions. Tisha is embarrassed at the attention from Mohammed; and Duke gleefully points out to her that now *she's* the one who's blushing and that he *can* see the difference.

Secretly, after Mohammed has left, Duke whispers that he's sorry that Mohammed automatically assumed that he (Duke) should get the credit. Tisha rolls her eyes; but thanks him for setting the record straight. "Thass th' only way they gonna learn that we just as smart as anybody else. You'd think that *he'd* know, wouldn't you?"

In what seems like only minutes the crowd that was there to get registration started has thinned out. There are folks left at a few tables still finishing up, but no one to occupy the chair in front of Duke. He's shocked to learn that it's almost midnight. Where did the time go? He looks around for something to do and sees Miz Jemison gathering up food and dishes. He approaches her and asks if there's anything that he can do to help. She directs his attention to Tisha who is gathering up a load of things and says, "You can help Tisha if you want to; but you've done enough for one night, son."

Walking toward Tisha, he can hardly suppress the smile that comes from way down deep. She's smiling, too. Taking the two largest packages from the stack, he indicates that they should go together to the car. He motions for her to lead the way so he can watch the back and forth swish of her as she crosses the meeting room and out the door.

It's deep dark outside now. No lights in this parking area. Night vision comes into play by the time they reach the old Pontiac. The air is warm and heavy with humidity and expectation. She speaks first. "People really liked talkin' to you. Everybody said how nice you are. You got a gentle way about you."

Of course, that starts him blushing all over again. "Am I lighting up the darkness with my blushing?"

She giggles, opens the trunk that was left unlocked, turns and astonishes him by speaking a heart-felt truth, "I think you know that you definitely lightin' up my night, and it's not by blushin'."

She reaches to take the two packages from him, pulling him closer. Then she turns and bends to place them in the trunk, pressing against him rear to front in a delicious, intentional, sensual movement. Turning back, she faces him, though they are barely able to see each other in the almost total darkness. They float in the delight of each other. The connection between them is like a fuse that's burning. Sparkle, smoke, and sizzle.

He knows that he's supposed to lean down to kiss her. He's almost trembling with wanting to do that; but the door to the church starts to creak open. They turn from the car in the darkness and walk back into that other reality, both knowing that this thing between them isn't over and that it won't go away by itself.

Judd, Elizabeth and Miz Jemison stroll out the church door laughing at something that's known to them and of no interest to either Duke or Tisha. They are carrying more dishes and packages and they pass in the night. Elizabeth gives him that look that says "Gotcha," but he just smiles and asks if they need help. They decline, and he and Tisha go back inside.

Alone at the food tables, he says in a stage whisper, "Saved by the bell, little sister."

With her back to him she replies, "Didn't need no savin'." Turning she adds, "And didn't want none either."

With a hum in his head, he senses more than sees Pax and Dr. Mohammed approaching. Mohammed says, "You two worked really well together tonight. I didn't know that I was starting a team when I put you together; but it worked out real nice. What you did with Rose Ella Curry and her family was a good piece of work, saved a lot of time. Good job, both of you."

Pax nods affirmation. Ron, Leo, Jay, Cho-La, Claire and all the rest gather near the tables and the sense is that the evening is over, but somehow no one wants to pull the plug on it just yet. So it's small talk and nervous laughter. Finally, Claire says that she has an eight o'clock class and everyone starts moving toward the door. Handshakes and good wishes and "be careful" all around. Thank you from these gentle folk. The white kids cram themselves back into respective automobiles and drive off into the night. Everyone has changed forever. Some are even aware of it.

*   *   *   *

U.S. Highway 29 is a two-lane, gravel-patched, black top road that curves around, climbs over, then slides back down hills and gentler rises between Tuskegee and Auburn. Ditches and pine woods and barbed wire fences that make it narrow in places and sometimes a challenge border it. But not this night. It's late, so there's no traffic. There's a fat moon and Duke says, "Last night was a full moon, know what they call the moon tonight?" And when no one answers he says, "Back home they call it a possum huntin' moon."

The big, black Galaxie rumbling across the landscape under the bigger, blacker galaxies. Windows down, warm breezes flow all through the car. Elizabeth's head is on Judd's shoulder. The radio is playing something sweet and soulful by Percy Sledge. Claire sways in time. Pax talks quietly about how well everyone did and how much it was appreciated.

Elizabeth can't resist the opportunity to mention how much Tisha seems to appreciate *anything* that Duke might do. He just lets it fly on past like more night air through the windows. It's all too mellow to argue or fuss about right now. Finally, he says that he feels really peaceful and that he's glad that he came to do this. Agreements all around.

Ahead a dirt track crosses the main highway. Headlights approach that intersection slowly from the field. No sweat. But they just keep easing on toward the roadway. The Galaxie's almost on them now and they're still coming. Pax easing back on the accelerator. Moving into the far lane. Claire stops her swaying, comes rigid, saying calmly, "Look out, Pax."

Elizabeth springs erect. Duke grabs her arm to hold her back. Pax acknowledges, "Yeah I see him. Hang on people." The lights are still coming—into the near lane now. Gonna crash if they don't stop. Duke braces his knees against the seat behind Pax and holds Elizabeth tighter.

It's an old pick-up truck with people in the back. It slowly turns into the near lane, leaving a little room in the far lane. The Galaxie's driver's side tires are on the roadway verge now. Gravel clatters onto the undercarriage, sounding impossibly loud. The car seems to be floating. The rear tires break loose a little and slide. Duke braces up good and tight and feels the rage rising in him—and the fear. He's thinking, *Stay tight, don't panic, ease on through this.* He looks out the side window as they pass alongside the truck and sees the men cocking shotguns. He's incredulous, shouts to Pax, "Punch it, Pax, they've got guns. C'mon hit it. Go. Go. Go."

They all feel the surge as the warning registers with Pax and he slams the accelerator to the floor. The big V-8 responds immediately, lurching forward and ahead into the relative safety of the open road. From behind comes the booming sound of shotgun blasts. Duke thinks, *Unbelievable. These bastards are shooting at us.* Then, *No wait. What th' hell?* Looking out the back window and sees that the muzzle flashes are going *up* not toward them.

As they pull away, the truck doesn't seem inclined or able to pursue. Pax is still winding it out. Finally Duke says, "OK, Pax, we're clear. Slow down. No sense killing ourselves unnecessarily."

"You sure?" Pax's voice is tight with fear. But he does begin to ease off the pedal, the car's speed coming back to a safer level. The radio incongruously still spins a slow and sweet melody. No one notices. "You sure, Duke?"

"I'm sure." He pauses for a minute. As his heart rate comes back to normal, he collects his thoughts. A couple of miles or so down the road Duke asks the others, "So, what do y'all think? Was that an attack? Was it a warning? Or was it a bunch of drunk, redneck possum hunters?" There is no immediate response.

He supposes that everyone assumes that they were being attacked for the voter registration work and hadn't thought that there might be a different explanation. He waits and lets it all sink in some more before saying, "Well, I can't know for sure; but I'm leaning toward the latter. I mean, if they had wanted to kill us they sure as hell had us dead to rights when we passed, and they *were* armed."

Elizabeth is fighting hysteria. In a voice that trembles she says, "Duke, you imbecile, they *shot* at us. Of course it was an attack."

He's still holding her and she hasn't even noticed yet. He strokes her upper arm soothingly and says, "Take it easy. They didn't shoot *at* us."

She turns wild-eyed, "But you said they had guns. I heard the shots." Saliva is drooling down her chin. She swipes it with an unconscious hand. Duke continues stroking her arm.

"That's all true. When I saw the guns I had to assume the worst, so I yelled to Pax to go. But after we passed they fired *into the air*. I watched them, Liz. We're safe. I'm bettin' that they didn't see us, that they've been out drinkin', calling themselves huntin' and just screwed up. They're probably as scared as we are right now, realizing how close we all came to dying. And I'm bettin' they're more sober now than they were five minutes ago. Adrenaline will do that, ya know. They probably all pissed their pants."

Touching Pax on the shoulder, he says, "You OK, Pax?"

"Yeah. I guess so. You did good. Thanks, Duke."

"How about you, Judd? Claire?"

Judd, so cool, says, "I can't believe that I had to wake up for a bunch of drunk-assed rednecks. But yeah, I'm fine."

Claire on the other hand is trembling. She snarls, "Those bastards. I can't believe that was just some accident. They knew what they were doing. Let's report this to the police, Pax. This is *not* just a freak accident. You're full of shit, Duke. How can you not believe that they were trying to kill us? It was a set-up to look like an accident; and they almost ran us off the road." Duke can't tell if she's in shock or really enraged. If it's rage, then she's one very tough cookie.

He tosses that one back and forth in his head. After a few seconds he says, "Well, you may be right, Claire, but I don't think that it's a good idea to report it to the police. I mean, what are they gonna do? We have no tag number. All we know is that it was a truck—not what make, model, year, color—nothing. And if we tell the cops why we think that someone might want to harm us, then we've just tipped our hand about the whole voter registration deal."

Pax joins in from the driver's seat, calmed down now, "He's right, Claire. It's not worth it. Let's let it be for a while and think about it. Everybody stay cool. Let's just get home and think about it and talk more about it tomorrow."

By now they are almost at the city limits of Auburn. The Galaxie eases into the drive at the parking lot at Pax's apartment and everyone goes their respective way—Claire to her dorm in her own car. Judd and Elizabeth, who is relaxing some now, pile into the front seat of the T'Bird. Elizabeth balances on the console and Duke drives them home in silence, acutely aware of where his elbow is forced to rest. Declining to go upstairs with them, he turns the T'Bird around and heads back to his own place.

CHAPTER 4

▼

Turning into the alley that leads to College Street, Duke pulls the T'Bird to the side and kills the engine. He needs to be alone for a minute to think. In the quiet of the late night he ponders the gravity of his situation. The changes of the past few days are dizzying. He wonders if his old friends can possibly tolerate his taking the position of helping coloreds to gain the vote and decides that probably they won't rather than can't. In another slant to this issue he asks himself whether such people should really be worthy of his friendship. The thought leaves him with a hollow feeling in his stomach.

With an internal grin he considers the excitement of the new women he has recently encountered. *All these women. Do I make a play for Claire? I mean it would be just for fun—so I'd want to stay straight with her about that. And Tisha—now there's a wild one—really cute and obviously not someone who could think that anything would be serious. Wait—is that true? Better think about that some more.* With a sense of dread and a twinge of guilt he thinks about Ellen back home in Gadsden. *I've got to call her tonight—no, tomorrow night. I need to get up there to see her. After all, we're supposed to be serious. I know she thinks we're serious.*

Next, he replays the ride home and the gunfire incident, wondering if he really wants to risk his life to help coloreds get the vote. *I can't believe that we were being attacked earlier. I've hunted all my life and if I'd wanted to cause harm tonight, there would be some messed up white boys out on 29. So, that was either an accident or a warning. If it was a warning, I'll get the straight of it later on and from the horse's mouth. I know all those players. And they know me. If I'm going to do this, then the .38 goes back under the seat. Would they actually shoot me? If so I won't go alone—and they'd know that, too.* He's thinking here of George and the other old boys in the Auburn Gun and Skeet Club of which he is a member and a past champion—he knows he's capable and so do they. His job, schoolwork, and money flit across his mind and he deems them all under reasonable control.

Finally, he thinks about his two new male friends. *I wonder if that "getting drunk" thing between Judd and Pax is really marijuana. It's a curiosity that I wouldn't mind finding out about. Have to be careful here. Can't give any ammunition to the other side; they just might use it against me or the project. Have Judd and Pax thought about this? I'll just ask them. That ought to be entertaining. Well, if we're gonna do these kinds of things together, we'd better be able to talk about any-damn-thing.*

Satisfied that all things pertinent are re-arranged in his head, he starts the engine, loving that purr. Revs up. Lights on. Eases down the alley and turns right, out onto a mostly deserted College Street. He drives slowly down to Mag and turns left. Past Biggin Hall—the architecture and design building—with lights still blazing on the second and third floors. Those crazies work all night most nights. Past Ramsay—dark as a crypt. The ancient infirmary slides by on his left. The men's dorms are next then the DTD house on the corner. The vast expanse of the dreaded drill field, where he had his first college failure in ROTC is near his apartment.

Fifty yards later is a small street on the right—Ann Street. It's easy to miss if you don't know it's there. He turns right toward the dumpy little shack he calls home. Thinks, *Hello. New Stingray out front. What th' heck. Who could that be?* He feels some apprehension at this—some of those good ol' boys come from families with money. *Well, no time to be timid, I guess.*

Wheeling left into his makeshift driveway, one car deep off the street, next to this rickety building that he rents. Stops. The door to the StingRay opens and Lynn appears like some specter. She's a tall woman—a former homecoming queen and majorette at Tuskegee High School. She has dark hair and a pretty face that's dark and glowering at this particular moment. Her body is spectacular, but coiled pretty tight right now. It doesn't take Sigmund Freud to see the anger steaming out of her. Slamming the door, she pulls herself up even straighter. "Duke, where the hell have you been? I've looked everywhere for you. I've been here for hours. I went to the library. I talked to Jonathan. Where have you been?"

This is clearly *not* a time for candor. In spite of confession being good for the soul and all that, it just doesn't register in the face of this. So, smooth as silk he says, "I've been playing bridge. You said that you would be in Troy until late, so I decided to go and play with Judd and Elizabeth. Whose car?"

Effortlessly and with complete control and calm, he leaves no room to be unduly castigated. Just matter-of-factly shifts the emphasis of this conversation to something outside the two of them. To this cool looking car—sleek and shiny sitting there in the moonlight. He opens the door and the interior light shows black and white leather bucket seats. The white paint sets off the stainless rims and wide tires. Lots of money in this one.

Lynn says, "It's my birthday present from my daddy. My birthday is on Saturday, you know." She pauses, not really ready to let go of the anger quite yet. "So you were out playing cards with your new hippie friends, huh? I don't see what you get out of that stupid game or out of those goofy looking creeps, either. I mean they're just weirdoes. They dress funny and they smell worse."

He refuses to rise to the bait with her. She's just blowing off steam anyway. Not used to waiting for anything—poor little rich girl. He eventually says, "Nah, they're OK. The smell is just garlic. They're as clean as we are. I admit that they eat strange stuff; but they're OK. And they're both smart as hell. Wanna take me for a ride?" He needs to get off this subject, too.

"Where are we gonna ride to at one o'clock in the morning?"

"Well, you could buy my breakfast at the Kopper Kettle if you want to." He's finding that the adrenaline rush from earlier is leaving him hungry, although he ate more at the church than usual.

He's not sure that he can avoid ending up in bed with Lynn; but really wants to try. That brings a smile inside—not wanting to go to bed with Lynn. That's gotta be against some law or something, but his energy level is low, low, low and he isn't sure that he could muster up the interest. This is a first. After years of trying everything imaginable to get *any* girl into bed, here is this gorgeous woman, and *he's* not interested. Thinks, *Maybe she won't be interested.*

Then, *Yeah, right.*

She agrees to buy breakfast. Duke, doing the gentlemanly thing, opens the driver's side door and holds it for her. She looks him, smiles, and she flashes him while getting in behind the wheel.

Duke closes her door and goes to the other side. He slopes down into the contoured seat—lots of legroom in there. She keys the engine, and goes around the block, back out to Magnolia Ave. The Stingray turns left and heads back toward downtown. Windows down, no music, the massive engine just sings along effortlessly. Duke can feel the tremendous unused power almost begging to be unleashed. Leaning across her to look at the odometer, he sees that the car has less than 400 miles on it. Says, "Damn, Lynn, this thing is brand new."

She just smiles that smile that rich girls have when they get to show off how much their daddies love them. "Daddy had it all picked out and sitting at Aunt Karen's house in Troy. When we drove up, I thought it was hers and didn't even pay any attention to it. After a while he asked me if I liked the car and, of course, I said, 'Yes'. Then he threw me the keys and said, 'Well, here's th' keys. Happy Birthday, baby.' I just about died. I couldn't believe it." Duke can't believe it either. He's never heard of such an extravagant birthday gift. Hell, she can't even drive the damn thing properly. But, no doubt about it, the car is a thing of beauty and Lynn is wearing it like a new necklace. Well, that's OK, too.

They drive through the main intersection again at College. One block further on the left is to the Kopper Kettle, an Auburn landmark. It's an all night diner that specializes in breakfast and caters to the late night, maybe less than 100 percent sober, crowd. As usual it's crowded, though not full like it would be on a Friday or Saturday night. The StingRay slides smoothly into this parking place across the street from the entrance, bumping slightly against the curb. Doors open and the two of them lever themselves up and out. A few faces appear at the window of the Kettle to check out this new car. Lynn is unable to stop her smile of pride in ownership. Duke understands. He gets that feeling with the T'Bird. They cross the traffic-less street. Somehow a city street at night feels special—just because it's empty.

Duke holds the door and Lynn slinks past him into the blast of high intensity light inside. His gaze circles the room and lands on a figure seated at the bar. It's George Blankenship, a Gun and Skeet Club friend. George looks up and sees Duke and Lynn, slowly recognizing the two as people he knows. He lifts a hand in greeting. Lynn follows Duke's gaze and says hello to George. He gets up to join them at the booth they are approaching. He signals the waitress to bring his order there when it's ready. He's looking a little wasted—disheveled jeans, dark cotton, long-sleeved shirt, old baseball cap on his head, red-rimmed eyes, odor of bad bourbon. He sings out, "Hey, y'all. Out kinda late aren't ya?"

Duke explains that they're test-driving Lynn's birthday present, inclining his head toward the door. George rises unsteadily and looks out the window and fastens his gaze on the Stingray. "Damn, Lynn, you got a tough life, you know it? Hell, I ain't ever had even *one* new car, and that's already two for you and this is, what, your twenty-first birthday?" The obvious effects of the bourbon accentuate his already thick drawl.

Lynn is fairly bursting at the attention. "Well it will be come Saturday. 'Til then I'm still not strictly legal. Daddy got it for me. Isn't it just the coolest thing you ever saw?" Duke notices that although her make-up is perfect, her hair is a little out of place due to the wind through the open windows in the Stingray, and wonders how she'll come to terms with that aspect of owning a car that begs to be driven fast and with the windows down or the top off.

It amuses Duke to watch George leering at her unabashedly. George is one of those types who could never expect to be seen socially with Lynn or anyone like her. He's smart enough, but has a history of being just inside the law—most of the time. He has an edge of violence about him and a complete lack of social grace—a rough and tumble guy who would as soon solve his problems with his fists as any other way, in fact might prefer it that way. Although he envies Duke his acceptance by Lynn, he also likes him for the times he has proven himself to be "one of the boys", both as an athlete and as a sportsman in the field. He doesn't fear Duke; but knows that the reverse is also true.

For her part, Lynn doesn't even know why she feels superior to George, but just somehow knows that he's from a different, lower-ordered world. She gives no thought to the fact that he is lusting after her—couldn't even imagine that. *Him? and me? Don't be ridiculous.* She asks semi-seriously, "So, how've you been, George?"

He's got a sort of drunken, country-boy grin on his face as he looks at the two of them. Says, "Just glad to be alive right now. Goddamn Rafe 'bout got us all killed tonight." This raises the ante for Duke, who makes an immediate connection, but will be patient and let this play out on its own.

Lynn laughs and says, "I'm not surprised by that. You're gonna learn the hard way, I guess, 'bout Rafe. What'd he do this time?" She looks at Duke as if the two of them are sharing some private view at how the "other half" lives. A big, deep, gut-felt smile of condescension crosses her features.

Duke thinks that this is *not* a pretty thing to see and resents somehow that Lynn actually believes that because of her family, George is beneath her. The Wilkins family is "old money" while the Blankenships are newly affluent. This registers in some deeper recess of his mind as worth remembering, that somehow this fact will play a much larger role in how he thinks about Lynn in the future— not so much now; but later.

Duke looks back at George to see how he's reading all this; but one glance shows him that Lynn could say just about anything to him right now and it would be OK. The alcohol and George's infatuation with this icon of his high school days would account for that. Whatever, he's still got that dumb grin on his face and finally shakes his head and says, "That drunk sumbitch pulled right out in front of a speedin' car out on 29 a while ago. If the other guy hadn't been watching pretty damn close it'd'a killed us all. I got so damn mad that I threatened to shoot him. In fact I did shoot, I was so pissed."

This is Duke's cue. "Whoa, George, you shot Rafe's car? Damn, you must've been really ticked."

"Naw. Naw. Naw. We was out huntin' on my daddy's place out there on 29. You know where it's at, Duke; we hunted birds out there in the fall. Anyhow we'd been drinkin' some and finally decided that we weren't gonna get anything and were gonna call it a night. So we go out that dirt road to come back to th' house. We was on daddy's old farm truck and Rafe was driving. I was in the back with Charles Ellis. We were gonna spotlight a deer, but didn't see any. We get to approachin' 29 and I saw a car coming, like from Tuskegee and figured that Rafe surely saw it too; hell it was big as goddam life and lit up like a fuckin' Christmas tree." George is shaking his head and arranging his food as he talks. Lynn looks at Duke and pulls a face that says, "disgusting".

George missed her communication and continues the story as he begins eating his breakfast of eggs and grits. "But Rafe just kep' chugging along. Didn't slow down much at all. I'm bangin' on th' damn roof of th' truck. Charles Ellis is yelling his fool head off, like that was gonna do some good. And freakin' Rafe just pulled right out on the road in front of that guy. Luckily, the guy must've seen us 'cause he moved over into the other lane, went half off the damn road, threw fuckin' gravel and grass everywhere, fishtailed a little, got around us finally, and roared off down the highway lickety-goddam-split. He didn't stop, or blow his horn or anything, just shot off outta there like a bat outta hell. Rafe finally pulled off the highway after me and Charles Ellis shot up into the air. I made him get in the back with Charles Ellis and drove us back to the farmhouse and got our cars. Should've left th' bastard out on th' highway. He ain't never goin' huntin' with me at night again." He nods in Lynn's direction. "Excuse my language, Lynn."

For all the anger implied in the tale, George is still smiling and shaking his head like it's some kind of comedy. Actually from this perspective, Duke has to admit that it sounds pretty funny—even to him. So he contributes a laugh. Inside he's seething that "Rafe the Redneck" has been allowed to threaten his life for the sake of a drunken hunting expedition.

He also knows that this sort of thing goes on all the time in his world. He's done it himself more times than he wants to admit to. But he's careful and Rafe, well Rafe isn't real smart to begin with and the fact that George trusted him to drive after drinking is equally not too bright. Then again, Duke can even reluctantly understand it—George wanting to be in the back so he can maybe get a shot at a deer. And even though it's out of season it *is* private property and it's not like they were just going to kill for the fun of killing. They would have dressed out the kill and it would have ended up on the table or in somebody's freezer.

With all these conflicting emotions Duke just laughs and says, "I wouldn't trust Rafe to be able to get me home from my own driveway; but hey, you made it out OK. Wonder what happened to the other guy?"

George snorts, "I don't know. I just hope he didn't come into town and call the sheriff. My old man will beat my ass if he finds out Rafe was drivin' th' truck and almost caused a wreck. I'm glad he didn't stop and come back shootin'. I mean it's not like we could've done much good with a bunch of damn shotguns." Inside Duke is sighing big sighs of relief. George has no idea who was in that car or what kind of car it was. He almost wants to laugh out loud, but is able to contain it.

Duke's and Lynn's food has been ordered, delivered and consumed around the telling of this tale. The clock has continued its march in its endless circles. It's now almost two a.m. and Duke is feeling the effects of a long and eventful day. Lynn pays the waitress for his food and for George's as well. They all get up to leave. Two cops pass them going in as they are coming out of the Kettle. George winces in anticipation; but nothing happens. In fact one says, "Hey George, Lynn. How y'all?"

Outside George crawls into his Impala SuperSport. A blast of noise slaps Duke and Lynn as they cross the street to the StingRay. George eases back into the traffic lane—revving, roaring, popping. He engages first gear, revs again, pops the clutch and floors the accelerator. The squeal of burning rubber and the accompanying blast from the glass-pack mufflers is deafening. Two black marks appear on the street as the SuperSport flies down Magnolia and power skids into College St., turns left, and heads out of town. The acrid stench of burning rubber floats on the smoky air. Duke grins at Lynn and says, "Maybe it was a good thing Rafe *was* driving." Lynn just rolls her eyes and opens the door to the Stingray. Duke holds it for her as she drops into the seat—flash. Knowing smile.

After the noise of the SuperSport, the sound of the Stingray is like a baby's lullaby—soft and sweet to the attuned ear. Floating along under power, they retrace their path to Duke's place and go inside. The front door is unlocked and she chides him for the hundredth time for leaving it so. He is unresponsive for the hundredth time. He switches on the light, walks to the small stereo in the corner, and spins a Johnny Mathis album that he knows that she likes. As he turns to her, she advances knowingly toward him and in the instant before they touch, he decides not to fight the urge—neither hers nor his. It's easy enough to be aroused by this gorgeous woman. But his ardor is less than 100 percent and, of course, she notices.

In the aftermath of mutually semi-satisfactory sex, they lie together and talk about things. He half-heartedly apologizes for being pre-occupied by money problems and worries about grades. She is subdued and maybe a little suspicious. Hurt. Thinking that maybe she did something wrong or that he doesn't really love her as she does him. He skillfully skirts the "love" issue and downplays that she has done anything to upset him, taking the blame for his "moodiness".

She decides to sleep over rather than trying to sneak back into the dorm and when she awakens at 7:15 he's gone with a note left on the table:

> "Lynn: You were sleeping so peacefully that I didn't have the heart to wake you. Class at 8. Gotta go by my job before then I'll be at the Union at noon, at the bridge tables.
> See you then or later.
> KISSES,
> El Duque."

Disappointed, she crumples the note into a ball and flings it across the room. Thinks, *Something's going on with him. I wonder why he's so distant. Maybe it's about my being gone all day yesterday. Maybe he really doesn't care about me. Damn. I just wish I could know for sure* … Hot tears rush down her cheeks. She lets them come and feels righteously justified in her misery.

Finally she dries her eyes and decides to get to the dorm, shower, dress and get to the nine o'clock history class that she hates so much and in which she is barely passing. Retrieves the crumpled note and tosses it into the garbage can. Writes her own note:

> "Duke, Call me. L-"

Short. Explicit. The ball is in *your* court.

Gathering her keys and clothing, she locks the front door, thinking that it would serve him right if he has no key. She smiles as she imagines him climbing through his own window, and then feels a little guilty at the thought. By the time she arrives at her dorm, she realizes that her new car isn't registered with the university, so after showering and changing, she skips history once again to go by the campus police office and get legal. She'll get her friend Sandy to get Duke's ex-roommate, Jonathan, to talk to Duke.

*   *   *   *

Meanwhile, the T'Bird sits in the second row of the parking lot at the Cabana Apartments. For the last fifteen or twenty minutes Duke has been watching the dew evaporate off the rear of the Galaxie, one row forward and two slots to his right. Thinks, *Pax needs to know that last night wasn't an attack or even a warning. I really wanted to get out of the house before Lynn woke up, too. She's gorgeous and all that, but what a snobbish little bitch! Nice in th' sack, but, man, the rest of the package ...*

He even felt sorry for old George, who had no idea that she was snubbing him. *I know things are bad when I have to feel sorry for a guy like George. Hell, he tried to get me to join the John Birch Society.* He recalls having gone to a meeting with George. He saw the Birchers as seriously angry guys. They want to put the "other guys" out of business on campus by looking for even tiny infractions so they can get their charters revoked. They didn't mention the Forum by name, and Duke didn't know anything about it then anyway, so it wouldn't have meant anything to him. It had seemed kinda silly to him and he told George that. They had a laugh about it, but George still goes to the meetings. He wonders now if this something else that Pax should know about. Looking up he sees him.

Pax in a light blue, buttoned down, short-sleeved shirt and khakis. His receding black hair is longish and brushed across his forehead and the emerging widow's peak. His round face always seems about to smirk. There's a gentleness about him that might encourage thoughts that he would be weak and fearful. But under pressure last night, on a country road in the deep, dark middle of nowhere, he was scared, but he didn't choke. In fact he did what needed to be done, and did it almost perfectly. He's got his head down now and from his serious expression could be solving the world's problems. Finally sees the T'Bird and angles toward it.

Raising a hand, he says, "Morning, Duke; you're up pretty early considering when we came in last night. Or were you like me and were so pumped up about the car out on 29 that you couldn't sleep?" Duke wonders how he spent *his* time and energy after he got home. Pax is certainly attractive enough to be a hit with women; but somehow he doesn't seem to put much priority to the matter.

Duke replies with a secretive smile, "Something like that, I guess. Look, do you have any time? There are some things we need to sort out. In fact, why don't you ride in to campus with me and I'll bring you back anytime you want ... after noon anyhow."

Pax pauses and looks up, thinking. The day's scheduled events roll across his mind's view-screen. He nods and says, "OK. Just a second. Let me get a couple of books out of my car. He steps to the Galaxie, pops the trunk, rummages around in it, re-emerges with books and notebooks, and slams the big black trunk lid with a satisfying "Whump". Grins his way to the passenger's side of the T'Bird, and climbs in.

Duke thinks, *I wonder how he's gonna react to this particular brand of confrontation. There aren't many folks in this world who can handle a blunt conversation about "How things really are". Everybody's so accustomed to holding up the masks so people see only the easy, the pretty, the unquestioned "goodness" of who we are. People don't want to grapple with difficulties and unpleasantness. Most either get coldly frightened, or hotly angry, or just choke up altogether. Every now and again, I meet someone who just sucks that up and gets very straight and honest. These are the people in my life that I can trust.*

Duke's tight features presage the beginning of this imperative discussion. He opens it with, "So, how're you feeling about last night. I mean, what do you think was really going on out on the highway?" He waits for a reaction looking sidelong at Pax. He engages the transmission and smoothes out toward the driveway.

Pax shifts left and their eyes make brief contact as Duke stops at the drive's entrance to the roadway. He turns right toward Glenn Ave., and goes slowly for the twenty yards to the main intersection. Pax is still considering, so Duke says, "There's a cap in the glove compartment, if you want it." Pax looks blank. "It's a convertible, Pax, the wind's gonna mess up your pretty hair."

"Oh yeah, I didn't think of that." He rambles around in the glove compartment and comes up with a Gadsden Pilot's baseball cap. Showing the logo to Duke, he asks if this is the team that Mohammed knew of. He puts it tentatively on his head. And Duke says, "Yes, it was."

Duke turns left onto Glenn and lets the hammer down for 100 yards. Pax falls back against the seat heavily. "Anyhow, I'm still not sure what to think about it, Duke. Until you said otherwise, I just assumed that it was an act of retribution."

"Retribution for what and by whom?"

"Well, retribution *for* meddling in the politics of the status quo in Macon County, Alabama. And by—well I don't really know. Worst-case scenario, the Klan. Or maybe just a disaffected country boy. Hell, I don't know." Pax is alternately nodding and shaking his head as the T'Bird eats up the distance too quickly between the Cabanas and the campus. He stares into space trying to conjure up other possibilities.

Duke slows down to about twenty-five mph. "Well I think that I can help you with some of that. I ended up at the Kettle late last night and George Blankenship was in there, too. You know him?" Looks to his right and sees the affirming nod. He also notices that Pax has gone rigid and a little pale at the mention of George's name. "Well, George was in that truck. Rafe Bowman was driving. Charles Ellis Johnson was in the back with George, and they had been drinking and 'hunting'." Duke steers with his knees as he makes finger quotes around the last word. "George was so pissed at Rafe that he wanted to shoot him or leave him stranded out on the highway. They were scared shitless and have no idea who they almost hit. They don't even know what kind of car it was. George and Charles Ellis fired their shotguns into the air in frustration and trying to get Rafe's attention to stop the truck. So that piece you can cross off the list of things to worry about."

As they turn left onto College Street, Pax says, "You hungry? Let's stop at the Grille and get something to eat." Duke agrees and looks for parking as they go up the hill toward the town's main intersection. He sees a couple of empty spots across the street and U-turns neatly into one of them. To Pax's amused expression he says, "Windsor Special." And shuts down the motor.

Inside the dim interior, Pax orders a full breakfast while Duke goes for coffee and a doughnut. Pax then asks, "So how do you know George Blankenship?"

Duke is startled that the tables are at least momentarily turned and that Pax brings the confrontational tone to *him*. But he recovers quickly enough and responds that he and George are both in the Gun and Skeet Club, and that they have hunted together a couple of times. And, "Why do you ask, anyway?"

"Because we're pretty sure that his daddy is high up in the Klan in Macon County. And that could mean a lot of things—like maybe he told you the truth and maybe he just told you something to cover the trail."

This news *is* news to Duke, but not earth shattering. He didn't *know* about the Klan, but isn't stunned by it. He's more surprised that he hadn't thought about that possibility himself. Thinks, *So Pax may need me in ways he hasn't thought of, eh?*

After pausing long enough to consider if this new fact changes his mind about the possibility of a threat, he looks up, locks eyes with Pax and says, "I'm pretty sure that the information that I got last night was the straight of it. He was a little drunk still, and we were talking in the presence of a mutual friend. He wasn't holding anything back. Yeah, I'm sure of that."

Their food arrives and it gives each a little time to consider things, until the cute little brunette finishes flirting with them and leaves. Making eye contact, Pax says, "I hope you're right, Duke. It's funny, but I'm leaning toward trusting you and your judgment awfully fast here. No offense, man, but I've only known you for a little over a couple of weeks and already we're talking damn heavy stuff. And it's likely that things are gonna get a lot heavier now." At this, he lowers his eyes and busies himself with arranging his food.

"Pax, this is great. I was wondering earlier if *you* could handle this kind of straight talk. We need to be able talk about the things that we're involved in and who each of us really is. It's clear to me right this minute that you can handle it. So my first question is if you are one those people that the local media calls an 'outside agitator'. Were you sent here to disrupt the status quo of Alabama?"

Pax pauses briefly then says, "Well, let me try to be very honest about this. I probably am an agitator from outside. I mean, the things that I stand for certainly agitate the hell out of most of white Alabama. And, clearly, I came here from 'the outside'. But, no, I wasn't sent by anyone except my Uncle Jimmy. And he probably hoped that sending me here would cool me out a little. Actually, the older generation of whites in Boston isn't that much different from those in Alabama. Oh, they talk about how terrible southerners are, but their schools are mostly segregated, too. Very few Bostonian whites have black friends. I used to get in trouble all the time with my father and my uncle, because I pointed this out to them and their friends." He fiddles with his food and looks wistfully at the plate, clearly remembering something. Duke waits.

"Anyway, they decided together that if I was going to talk about these things, I needed to come here and at least know what I was talking *about*. My father is a manager in Uncle Jimmy's electronics company. Uncle Jimmy got his degree right here in Auburn twenty-five or thirty years ago and *his* father financed his new company that makes electrical components—circuit boards and capacitors and stuff.

"Before I came back to school after my freshman year, I went to visit relatives in San Francisco. While I was there, a black guy from New York was stirring things up on the UC—Berkeley campus. His name was Stokley Carmichael. Ever heard of him?" He looks up at Duke to find him intently watching and listening. The doughnut is completely forgotten, the coffee is going cold, untouched in front of him. Sees the negative shake of Duke's head and continues, "He heads up an organization called the Student Non-violent Coordinating Committee. It's abbreviated as SNCC and pronounced 'Snick'.

"This group is involved in all kinds of efforts aimed at helping blacks across the country to gain the opportunity to compete fairly for education, and therefore jobs, and therefore an equal share of the available money in this culture." He pauses to let all this sink in and to eat some of his own food before it, too, gets cold and unappetizing. "I got involved with those folks and that's really where I'm coming from. There's no specific agenda, but the voter registration idea seemed like a realistic place for me to stand up for what I think is right. I went over to Tuskegee, met Dr. Mohammed, and just got involved. That's it, the whole deal."

Duke leans back against the slick vinyl of the booth. He looks around at the scattered tables and rickety chairs. Sports memorabilia hangs on the walls—pictures of athletes and Coach Jordan; even an old one of John Heissman who coached here forever ago, a jersey from an All-American football player. A school flag is draped on one wall, pennants scattered in other spaces. He reflects on how much he loves this place, this town, this university; and how much turmoil will ensue as the changes Pax is hinting at come to pass.

The brunette sees his wandering gaze and interprets it as needing service. She approaches and asks if everything is OK. Duke asks her to take his cup, pour out the cold coffee and bring him some hot in its place. She gushes that she'll be glad to, and is he sure that he even likes coffee? "No but I love to watch you walk back and forth between here and the counter." This breaks the tension enough for Pax and Duke to share a smile, Duke having given her the little attention that she wanted.

"You worry me, Duke. Sometimes I wonder if you even have any idea what you're doing with women. Then again sometimes I watch you and it's like you're a craftsman working in the medium you have in front of you." There is mirth in his face and he just leaves that comment hanging there. Bait for whatever fish may be floating by in these waters. The response he gets isn't what he expected.

"Yeah well, you know. Some get nailed, but some get hammered. That's th' way it goes with us craftsmen." Said with a grin and a wink. Both laugh out loud at this. "In fact, I've wondered why *you* aren't involved more with women. You ain't funny or anything are you?" Not giving him time to answer he rambles on, "You're a nice looking guy and I can see that women like you; but you don't seem interested You got a woman stashed somewhere?"

At the end of his laugh Pax manages, "One at a time there, buddy. First, no, I'm not 'funny' as you put it. But that's probably a whole other area that our culture is gonna have to re-think sooner or later. And, secondly, yes, I do have a woman stashed somewhere, namely at Vanderbilt. That's where I met Claire. You know, her boyfriend is about to graduate from there. 'Course he'll probably go on to med school there, too."

Duke's thinking, *That's probably more information than I actually wanted. It's better to know where all the cards are if you're actually gonna play the hand. Should've known that someone like Pax would have a girl somewhere. Not really surprised that Claire's involved with someone. Yeah, Vandy fits—definitely smart folks at that institution and money, too. It's expensive. Must be nice. Claire doesn't look like money, but she acts like money. Not snobbish like Lynn, but not hungry either. That's the real advantage of having money; you don't have to hustle all the time just to get to wherever it is you're trying to go.*

Pax is speaking again and it's like he is reading Duke's mind. "Claire's a big girl and you two can do whatever you want to; but I need to talk to you for a minute about Tisha."

Duke's head snaps up. Maybe a little fire in his eyes.

Undaunted, Pax goes on, "She's a real beauty, and anyone with half an eye could see the chemistry between the two of you. But, Duke, getting involved with her would be a really bad thing." This is delivered with not even a trace of judgment or humor. In Pax's mind it's a fact.

Duke's defenses coil in his mind. He thinks … *Hey! I'm all for honesty here, but is this really any of your business? I wouldn't do anything stupid, but I'll decide about this myself. Tisha and I weren't so obvious that I deserve a lecture.* Then he calms down.

"I'll listen." He moves his elbows to make room for the new and steaming coffee, but keeps his gaze locked onto Pax's. There's a little defiance in his voice. He says a distracted "thanks" in the direction of the waitress, who leaves disappointed.

Pax leans forward on his own elbows and looks at Duke's face like a topographer reading a map. "Well, it's probably pretty obvious, Duke. Most colored people feel the same way about things as most white people. Most aren't ready for inter-racial relationships." He holds up a hand to ward off an answer.

"You have to think about how the community would react. And about the reputation of the woman." His hand stays between them. "Wait. Next, what would the effect be on the project? And finally, what might be the repercussions to your white ass?" Palms up and extended toward Duke, he says with an annoying, almost-supercilious grin, "Now."

At first, Duke just gapes at being schooled so thoroughly and so calmly. The ideas swirl in his mind like a slow motion tornado. When at last he speaks, it is to say, "Damn, ask for a glass of water and get the fuckin' Gulf of Mexico." But he doesn't argue. He already understood most of this, and his resistance ebbs like an early morning tide. The real deal here is that someone else has put the issue in front of him. He wouldn't have allowed things to escalate too far with Tisha, but might have enjoyed the excitement of the tension for a while longer. His real lesson this early morning has more to do with his distaste for being told what he should do by someone else. Resolving his truculence he says, "You're right, of course. Point taken."

As Pax's attention returns to his food, Duke recovers and says, "I remembered something else about George Blankenship that you probably ought to know. He belongs to, or at least used to belong to, the John Birch Society here on campus. Their specialty is finding small discrepancies between an organization's University charter and the actual carrying on of business, and then using that information to try to have the charter revoked by the University. That might have implications for the Forum."

Pax doesn't even look up at this. He just grunts with his mouth full, swallows and says, "Yeah, we know about them. We've got it covered."

"OK, good." Leaning forward Duke lowers his voice. "Next, are you and Judd smoking marijuana?"

This gets Pax's attention. He looks up and makes full eye contact, saying nothing for a few seconds. Then, "Why would you ask that?" But Duke doesn't answer. Waits instead. "Is it because we looked stoned or something when you came over to Judd's the other night?" Still waiting. An infectious grin plays across Duke's face, pulling Pax into his confidence enough to say, "Yeah. OK, we've tried it. Why?"

"Well, two reasons really. First, is it possible that it might pose a risk to the voter registration project if you get caught or if the wrong person figures it out? And secondly, I think that I'd like to try it sometime." Somehow Duke feels a release of pressure that he hadn't known was there, after he's finished with this pronouncement.

Pax, too, relaxes and the tension leaves his face. He leans back in the booth and asks, "Did someone tell you about this? Or did you really 'figure it out', as you put it. If so, how?"

Duke squirms a little with this. He doesn't want to give away the hints that Claire gave, so he says, "No one told me. I figured it out from the several hints that you and Judd dropped in conversations that maybe most people wouldn't have even heard. You both had mentioned 'getting drunk' in ways that didn't match up with alcohol and that was just the only conclusion I could come up with."

Pax is feeling back in control now. He laughs and says, "Duke, you scare the hell out of me. I certainly don't think that I'm transparent; but then I didn't really think that you were that smart either. I guess you are, though. So we'll see about the three of us getting together soon and you can try it out, see what you think of it. For what it's worth, I'm pretty sure that we could walk across campus smoking a joint and nobody would even know what it is. For now, though, I've got to get to class, if you're ready."

They get up and leave together, leaving enough money on the table for the food and a nice tip for the brunette. At the door, Duke turns to the waitress and winks. They drive onto campus and Pax gets out for his class at Ross Hall. Duke finds a parking place, tilts the seatbacks forward, and makes it to the last half of his class.

CHAPTER 5

▼

Leaving the air conditioning of Dunstan Hall at straight up noon, Duke is blasted by the 100-degree heat. The sun beats down like some giant fist. Humidity so high that it's like swimming as much as walking. Judd catches up from behind, and Duke explains the previous night's revelations as well as Pax's misgivings about the credibility of the source. As they talk, they gravitate toward the student union and the waiting bridge tables. Judd is relieved that last night's drama is less threatening than imagined. Trust and camaraderie wash over the two as they find a kind of exhilaration in the knowledge that they are safe. At least for the present.

In the Union, Pax is seated across from Ron Bauman, riffling a well-worn deck of cards. "Alright. I was hoping that you two would show up soon. I was just telling Ron about our excitement last night, and about Duke's explanation of it. Come on and play." Chairs scuff as the newcomers take seats. "There's a tournament in Atlanta in a few weeks and Ron and I are gonna play in it, so we need to practice some together."

He shuffles the cards together expertly. Bangs them on the table. Shuffles them again and offers them to Duke for a cut. He just taps them, and the deal is on. Three hands later Judd suggests that maybe Pax and Ron should just sponsor him and Duke in Atlanta, as they have made two contracts on their own and set the others on the third. Duke is less certain that the play has been as good as the score would presume, and asks Pax what he thinks. Pax is enthusiastic in saying, "About average on your two contracts, but setting ours was very good. You're a natural for this game, Duke. You should give some thought to trying some local tournaments. I think you can play."

Ron asks, "Duke, do you know Terry Collins? He plays some over at the house and is one of the best local players I've seen. He really seems to know where all the cards are all the time. And I think that he's looking for a partner." The deal has passed to Duke and as he shuffles he considers the idea of tournament play. It's almost funny to think about, given Claire's outburst just a couple of weeks ago. It would be a serious challenge and he'd like to give it a shot. "I don't know him; but I'd be interested. Where's he from, anyway?"

"I'm not sure. He came over to play with one of the brothers who's from Montgomery, but I don't think he's from there." Ron pauses then adds, "Look, we're having a 'duplicate' party tomorrow night at the house. Why don't you come over and play in it? If it's possible, I'll get the two of you together. If not, then you and I can play. You know where the house is, right?" Duke notes the sincerity in Ron's face, and remembers that he has already decided that he trusts Ron from their previous exchange in Tuskegee. So he agrees to show up a little before 7:30 the next night at the A E Pi fraternity house on Thatch Ave. After an hour of cards, Pax asks Duke to take him home. Soon the two say their goodbyes and walk to the T'Bird, a block away.

Pushing the seats back to an upright position, they climb into the car. Pax wonders aloud if someone has been tampering with the car since the seats are leaned forward. Duke assures him that he did it himself so the seats aren't too hot to sit on. "If you own a convertible you have to know to do these things. It's like the hat in the glove box. There are also scarves in there for any female who might want to ride without blowing her hairdo away." They cruise back toward Pax's apartment. Along the way they pass the Sani-Freeze—a little ice cream shop that serves hot dogs and burgers as well. Duke whips across a lane of traffic and parks out front.

"Buy you a dog and a shake?" he asks. Pax declines with a faint look of disgust.

When he returns with his food, Pax says, "You know, Duke, they don't call that place the Sani-*Flush* for nothing. I can't believe that it's clean enough to risk eating the food."

Duke is nonplused in the face of such sacrilege. Chalks it up to Pax's being an outlander from up north, although he saw some pretty grungy looking eateries when he was in Pennsylvania playing ball a few years back. No matter. "You're culturally retarded." Restarts the engine and they resume their trip to the Cabanas. In the parking lot Pax invites him up to his apartment to eat his lunch. Curious about how these places look inside, he accepts.

Pax fumbles with the key, eventually gets the door open, and ushers Duke into the living room area. After his own dingy digs, Duke is semi-dazzled: Thick carpets. Low ceilings. Modern furniture—sparse but tasteful. Large prints on the walls. A dining area with a glass-topped table adjoins the living area. A doorway and a bar open onto a real kitchen. The hallway on the right leads to three doors—two bedrooms and a bath. To his left a sliding glass door at the end of the living room opens to a small balcony. Air conditioning has the place comfortable without being too cold. And the place is spotless. Duke says, "I'm scared to sit down. I might get something out of order."

Pax laughs, saying he's not really so orderly but that the maid came in this morning. In the kitchen he puts tuna salad on lettuce leaves on a plate. Duke looks through the opening from the bar, hoping he's not seeming to be too much of a bumpkin. He's uncomfortable with this much luxury and just watches as Pax comes back into the dining area. Puts his food on the table and goes over to a cabinet, which holds a large and expensive-looking stereo system. He puts on some music that is unfamiliar to Duke and tells him it's jazz. Well, Duke has heard of jazz, but this is the first he has actually heard.

Finally, Duke says, "You know, all through my classes this morning I kept replaying our conversation from the ride in. There's something I want you to clear up for me." Pax nods with his mouth full, so Duke goes on.

"When you were talking about George's daddy?" Pax nods an acknowledgment. "Well, you said, '*We* think that he's in the Klan', right?"

He nods again, but this time Duke thinks, *He's stalling for time. He knows what's coming next. Anyone could see it.* Anyway, he goes ahead and makes explicit what's hanging in the air there saying, "Who's '*We*'?"

Pax holds up one finger and takes a swallow of his milk. "I get a lot of information from the NAACP and the SCLC. You know those groups?"

Duke can only nod. His heart is in his shoes. This sounds like it's going to be his worst nightmare. Pax doesn't even notice his distress. "Mohammed is connected to both and he tells me about their thinking. Not everything. Probably not even the half of it, not even ten percent, but enough for me to know how to protect myself. He is very concerned about the safety of those of us who are helping him. Anyway, he told me the names of a few of the people who are suspected of running the Klan's operations in Macon County and Thad Blankenship was one of them."

Duke isn't sure that he wants to know, but asks anyway, "How about Robert Earl Wilkins? Is he on your short list?"

Before Pax answers, a cloud passes over his face and Duke knows he won't like what's coming. In addition to the cloud, his posture goes rigid. "Damn it, Duke. Don't tell me that you know him, too." Duke nods and Pax slowly shakes his head. Some kind of negation of Duke knows not what. "Maybe you'd better tell me about how you know *this* one."

The apartment and its finery have disappeared from their consciousness. At this moment there are only the two of them in the whole world. Duke now knows things about people that he hadn't suspected. He speaks through the growing nausea, "He's the man who owns the *Magnolias on the Square* restaurant in downtown Tuskegee. I've been seeing his daughter—sort of—for several weeks now. She spent the night at my apartment last night. She was with me when I talked to George at the Kettle early this morning. This is too damn classic."

Neither says anything for several minutes, letting the weight of this settle in. Duke chokes down the rest of his hotdog and sits quietly with the remainder of the soothing milkshake. Pax slouches down in his chair, his feet extended and crossed at the ankles. He's staring at the ceiling, putting it together for himself. Finally he says, "Let's not try to figure all this out right now. If you don't mind, I'd like to talk to Mohammed about who you know and whether it makes any difference in anything. Is that okay with you?"

Duke instinctively doesn't like giving up control of what's happening to him. He's being asked to give control over to Pax and even, to some extent, to Dr. Mohammed, whom he knows even less well. Before deciding, he wants to sort through all of it and to try to determine what the limits need to be or what the consequences might entail. Shaking his head he responds, "I need to give this a little time. I have to go to work until nine. Let me take that much time and we'll talk again afterwards. How does that sound? I could come by here after that if you're gonna be here."

Nodding Pax says, "Sounds fine, Duke. You're right to be careful about this stuff. I'll be here. I have a paper to write for next Monday and I had planned to start it tonight anyway. Here's the phone number. Call when you're leaving work."

Taking the slip of paper, Duke starts to clear his debris from the table only to be stopped by Pax's insistence that he'll take care of it. He heads distractedly to the door, turns to say thanks and to wave adieu, then disappears, closing the door softly behind him.

The jazz playing on the stereo seems too loud in the wake of Duke's exit. Pax switches it off and wanders across the living area, lost in thought. Now he's left here alone with the tensions that have been created in the past hour. From the balcony door he watches Duke as he slouches toward the T'Bird. He looks neither left nor right nor back. Pax thinks, *Knowing all those people and learning where they really stand has to be tough. Of course he's a pretty tough guy himself. He was sure cool under pressure last night.*

Pax is aware that all these entanglements can easily erupt into violence and that if it happens, Duke is in line to get blasted. He marvels that Duke seems no different, from the outside, having this knowledge than he did before he knew. The slightest tickle of an idea creeps into Pax's mind. *Although he knows a lot of people walking on the wrong side of the street in these matters, if he's as straight as I think he is, he could be a very valuable asset.*

He turns back from the window and refocuses on the tasks at hand. *Okay, my paper. Claire is coming at four to eat an early dinner. Have to call Uncle Jimmy tonight and my dad, too—time to report in. I have time for a nap, but I couldn't sleep now. Thanks, Duke. Wonder what the folks in California would make of this situation. What the heck, they've got problems of their own. Matter of fact, so do I. Let me get on with this paper, "The Economics of Regionalism in the Pre-War South".*

Pulling out a zippered case from the cabinet, he arranges papers, notes, and books on the table. His view of things "Southern" and especially his understanding of the Civil War have changed considerably since he came here three years ago, and even more so since he started the three-part "History of the South" class with Dr. McMillan. So to some extent his uncle's strategy in sending him here is paying off. His ability to refocus his attention to the task at hand is impressive, given the powerful emotions attached to recent events and revelations. As he bores in on the cotton trade between the states, tariffs, and trade between the Southern states and England, he loses himself. Then, his phone jangles. Almost distractedly, he answers and is shocked into attentiveness by the voice of his uncle.

"How's my favorite nephew?"

"Well, Uncle Jimmy, since I'm your *only* nephew, I suppose that means me. I'm doing just fine. In fact, I was just thinking of you a few minutes ago. I was gonna call you and Dad both tonight. I'm writing a paper that should make you proud."

"That's a scary thought, Pax. I know you think that I sent you down there to change your mind about your views of the South; but actually, I just wanted for you to know both sides of things." He is, as usual, upbeat and there is a laugh behind his words that Pax has always loved. "So what's this paper about? Are you making the case that the Emancipation Proclamation was, in fact, unconstitutional?"

"Well, I haven't converted to that extent yet; but I am beginning to understand why Southerners are always harping on the idea that the Civil War wasn't all about slavery. I had no idea about the politics of the economy during that era. I'm beginning to grasp that Southerners believed that they were being backed into a corner economically, that they resented the interstate tariffs, and felt powerless to determine their own economic future. From a northern perspective that still may have seemed related to slavery, but Southerners didn't see it that way. They saw one region of the country dictating to another." He delivers this with a certain flourish, then pauses, waiting for a response.

His uncle does not disappoint. "I'm impressed that you are able to ferret that out for yourself; but I'm not fooled, Pax. I heard from your sister that you got involved with that Stokley Carmichael character out there in California a couple of summers ago. I've asked around and some think that there is a connection between his group and Rap Brown who's talking about creating a *militant* group. That spells trouble any way you look at it. I'm not prying into your affairs, son, but I do want you to be very careful. I know those southern boys down there and they'll play rough with that sort of thing. Were you involved in the desegregation flap? I ask only because it sounds like the workings of an O'Reilly mind and it seems to have gone smoothly."

Pax thinks, *What's he getting at? I can't tell if he's angry or if he's proud. Best to tell the truth, I suppose.* He answers, "Yeah. I admit that I had a small part in it. But mostly it was the work of a colored minister and his congregation. Why do you ask?"

Uncle Jimmy says with firmness but not condescension, "Let me repeat myself. I know how those southern men are likely to react to someone from Massachusetts trying to create changes. I'm just telling you to be careful. That's all. Just pay attention to what you're doing and who you're doing it with. Understand?"

"Yessir, I understand."

"Good. Now, how are you doing personally? How are your grades? Got enough money? How's your love life?"

Pax feels a surge of warmth. He knows that his uncle loves him unconditionally. The bond is even more special since Uncle Jimmy has no son of his own. Pax has always felt a kind of pressure to please him, and knows that he has a lot of status with him. Certainly he feels more accepted by his uncle than by his father. He answers, "Everything is fine, Uncle Jimmy. I have plenty of everything. My grades are almost perfect. As to my love life, I've been seeing a girl from Charleston who is in school at Vanderbilt. I can't tell how serious it is, but it's good enough that we're having fun. And, by the way, just so I don't forget to say it, thanks for everything. You're th' best."

In mock self-deprecation Jimmy responds, "Yeah, you're welcome. You aren't getting anything that you didn't earn. By the way, you'll be interested to learn that there is a move here in Boston to bus black children into predominantly white school districts and the local citizens are raising hell. I guess you were right about racism transcending geography. Look I need to go. Remember what I said and be careful. I love you, boy."

"I love you, too, Uncle Jimmy. Bye."

Pax finally catches himself staring at the wall and still holding on to the now dead phone.

He thinks, *This all coming at the very moment when I'm wondering about Duke's loyalty is spooky. The warnings are so timely. I don't want to put too much emphasis on coincidence here; but I sure don't want to ignore things that may be trying to get my attention. Damn. Who do I know that might have a read on Duke? Or who do I know that might know someone else that might know more about him? No. Let me wait 'til after we talk tonight. Jeez. I've gotta work on this paper.*

✳   ✳   ✳   ✳

As the T'Bird glides onto the university campus, Duke is thinking, *What a mess I've got myself into. Suddenly, I'm pitted against people I know and care about and there are ripples from just doing what I believe is right ... Sometimes I wonder if I even know* what *I believe. It almost seems like anytime I hear a new idea, that idea becomes* The Truth—*until the next new idea comes along anyway. I know that I'm changing and that's OK. But I need to be careful not to reject old ideas just because there are new ways to see things. New ideas are seductive just because they're new. That doesn't mean that they're any better than the old ones.*

In his turmoil he realizes that all he can do is think it through as well as possible, and then do his best. If George's and Lynn's daddies are actually active in the Klan, he probably needs to avoid them if possible. When the weak are overpowered for no better reason than that it can be done, then he believes he has a duty to stand up.

He is so caught up in his thoughts that he almost drives to the apartment instead of going to work. Turns back and heads to the library. Finds parking place right out front. Right on time. Leans the seats down. No need to put the top up—not a cloud in sight. Up these concrete stairs to the front entrance. Glass and metal front wall. Glass and metal doors. Then, blessed air conditioning. Checks in with Mrs. Posey before going downstairs to the music desk. Her office is empty so he looks in the stacks here on this wing.

Whoa. Hello. Who's this? Dark haired beauty in a short skirt. Glasses stuck up in her hair. Lovely oval face. Dark complexion. Dark eyes. Intense concentration on … on what? Can't tell from here. Is she a student? New worker? Ah well. Where's Mrs. Posey when I need her?

As if summoned by his thoughts a small bird-like woman of indeterminate age appears at his side. Her brown-going-gray hair points in all directions. Her eyeglasses are a permanent fixture. In ordinary conversation, she is southern sweet and very intelligent. Not much taller than Duke's solar plexus, in work mode she's more like a Marine drill sergeant. She rules the library as a benevolent dictator. Duke is one of her favorites; but only because she knows that he would jump through the wall for her if she asked.

"Hey, Miz Posey. I was just looking for you. Just wanted to check in before I go downstairs. Do I need to do anything to help you?"

"Good afternoon to you too, Duke. And yes, I do want you to do something." Her low-pitched voice warbles. She takes a step toward this new woman, who looks up, glancing inquisitively at each of them as they approach. She smiles and Duke's heart flutters. He's swimming. "Duke, this is *Mrs.* Ann Lassiter. I want you to help her. She's reorganizing the card catalogue. When you're finished, go on downstairs and continue cleaning the records and go on with your normal workday." Not waiting for an acknowledgment, she wheels and walks back toward the front desk. Duke doesn't miss her emphasis on the "Mrs." *Wonder what she's thinking?*

Before he can even get into his best routine, this Ann Lassiter says, "Thanks, but I don't really need any help with this. You can go on and do whatever you need to do downstairs." Not unfriendly, actually. More like she's surprised or even embarrassed that someone would think that she would need help with such a simple task. Maybe a little dismissive. So he chimes in, "I can at least hand down the top drawers for you, if you'd like." She nods and says, "Sure, if you want."

He can't quite place her accent; but for sure she's not from around here. As he's pulling the top row of drawers from across the cabinet, he asks where she's from and she says New York, but offers nothing else in the way of conversation. Unable to stall any more, he waves and says, "Nice to meet you. If you want me to put those back up for you when you're finished, call me down at the music desk." Walking toward the stairwell, he looks back to see her stretched forward. The short skirt rides up and pulls tight. He ogles

By the time he gets downstairs and into the task of wiping down the vinyl records from "G" through "M", his mind has drifted back to the confusion and uncertainty surrounding him and his friends—all his friends.

I don't want to believe it, but I think I probably can't keep both sets. Sooner or later, the clash of values is going to make me choose between old friends and new.

He tries to look at the things he gets from each group. With the old set he does "fun" things with, while the new friends require things that are "meaningful". He plays bridge with these new folks, but doubts if any one of them has ever seen a skeet "bird" flying across a field, or felt the satisfying kick on the shoulder from a shotgun, or walked all day behind working bird dogs. None of them knows the first-time thrill and surprise of a covey rise of quail. They are thinkers and planners. But in social matters they are activists.

The old friends represent his doing the things that he has done all his life, without the likelihood of change. And that can be very comfortable. They will never require him to think, but will rely on his ability to do, reflexively, what is expected. They will want him to play shortstop on their baseball teams or point guard on their church-league basketball team. Or to stay up all night drinking and "coon hunting." Or to make up a foursome at the golf course. These are action-oriented men—outdoorsmen and athletes. And in social matters they are reactionary, conservative. He thinks it possible that both groups are one-dimensional.

This is the change that is taking place in him. He is developing a mindset that requires thinking, not just reacting. This dualism has always been present in his life. Even in high school, he played sports, but was a good student. But in this new phase of his life he won't have time to do both. So he'll have to choose one or the other, and that choice point is coming up pretty soon.

After mulling over the options he reaches some decisions about how he will proceed.

Later on tonight I'm gonna tell Pax to go ahead and speak to Mohammed. After that, I'll just see what happens. Well, that part is settled.

I know that there is a certain amount of danger in moving into these new directions. On the other hand, I feel no sense of danger in thinking about siding with old friends in this clash of values. What the hell does that say about me?

I need to put the rest of this on the back burner for now. I have studying to do and I get paid while I study. Can't beat that. Didn't hear from Mrs. Ann Lassiter. Guess she figures that she can get along without me. Damn, here come the music appreciation classes. Work fifteen minutes, then I can study for a while.

C H A P T E R 6

▼

Winding through the campus streets. Top down. The soft summer breeze blows through the convertible. Streetlights make islands of "other reality" in the evening air that seems to hold him suspended in a gentle grip. Floating. The world is at peace. The slow swirl of controversy involving Duke and his friends is only a piece of the larger landscape. The T'Bird, its rumbling engine, and the sweetness of the night are reality enough for now. Pax has been called and forewarned that he's going to have a visitor—no need to rush. Just poke along here by the girls' dorms. Catch a little scenery on the way. Young girls in shorts stroll and talk in groups along the sidewalks and onto the Quad area. Heads turn as he eases slowly by. He gives a one-fingered wave and wonders what they see. Notices that Claire's car isn't here.

Passing Lynn's dorm, he feels a little guilty. The Stingray sits forlornly in the parking lot. He has spoken with Ellen from the library and promised to go home this weekend—and, yes, he'll come through and pick her up. They should get some quality hours out of these few days. She's happy but stressed and says that they'll talk about it later, she has to study.

He expects that Lynn is less than pleased with him for leaving her alone at the apartment this morning; but he hasn't been home to see her note, so he has no way of knowing just how pissed his not calling has made her. No matter. That is a small problem compared to others he'll soon to have to face.

He passes through town now. Little traffic. Campus on the left and storefronts on the right. Driving slowly, he passes police cars at the main intersection. They are parked facing opposite directions, talking through open windows. Thinks … *Ah—Glad I was driving slow, and didn't go blowin' through town like I usually do.*

In the parking lot at Cabanas he finds Claire's car parked up in the front row and thinks, *Nice surprise. Never the wrong time to see her. Is there something going on with Pax and her? Maybe it matters and maybe it doesn't. I'll just ask him and go from there. She's such a beauty; it would almost be ungentlemanly of me not to try something.*

As he climbs the two-part stairwell to the second floor, he meets her at the landing in the center and stops to talk. "Look, Claire, I'm only gonna be here for a few minutes. You don't have to leave." She gives him one of those looks that says she really doesn't need his permission to stay or to go. So he shifts gears and adds, "And when we're finished, I think I'm going to the Casino for a beer. Wanna meet me there?" Her smile and agreement are instantaneous. She touches his arm. He leans and brushes her cheek with lips that singe her. Reluctant steps take them in opposite directions for now.

Inside the apartment, he gets down to cases with Pax. "I've decided that it's O.K. for you to talk with Dr. Mohammed. In fact, it may help me to get my own head straight about all this."

He listens as Pax explains his fears about their relationship and says simply that he understands, that he has had similar doubts about both Pax and Mohammed. Sharing sheepish smiles they recognize that they are really beginning to trust each other. Finally Duke can put it off no longer and asks, "Look, is there something going on between you and Claire? If so I don't want to cause problems for you, or her, or me."

"It's not a problem, Duke. In fact, she and I were just talking about the same thing earlier. She wouldn't want to jeopardize anything with the voter registration project by having a personal relationship with another member of the team. Not a problem, though." He's got this big shit-eatin' grin on his face and eventually says, "Lucky boy."

"What about the boyfriend at Vandy?" And Pax just shrugs. Same grin. The message being that whatever he and Claire do is between them. Now Duke's got the same grin, thinking, *Lucky boy is right.*

Duke really has to sit on his enthusiasm as he drives back through town not to floor the accelerator. The cops are still at the corner talking. He goes slowly back through campus, making sure that the Stingray is where it was earlier. *Yes … still there.* Back to College St. and turning south, out of town. The Casino is off to the left under a couple of old oak trees. It sits low to the ground—beige paint with two green stripes around the top under the flat roof. Looks cool, and is cool.

Claire's car sits under one tree, near the side entrance. No one uses the front. He crunches across the parking area, his heart pumping at an incredible rate.

Feels it banging against his rib cage. He slips in through this door to the smoky, dark interior.

She sits alone at a table with a long neck beer in front of her. Scooted forward to the front one-third of her chair. The short skirt reveals a lot of thigh. Her reddish dark hair almost hides her face; but she turns to look at him as he comes into the gloom. Her eyes are accustomed to the dark, so she can see better than he can at first. Thinks, *I shouldn't even be here, but for some reason I don't want to resist him. What is it about him? He's cute; but lots of guys are cute. He's ... I don't know. There's just something different about him. And heaven help me, I want him. And he knows it. I think that I'm about to be had. Or he is.* A devilish smile spreads across her pale features.

Ordering a beer at the bar, Duke has no idea what she's thinking. As he turns, though, her smile ignites and excites him. This is one of those rare situations—win/win. There can be something good for everybody, and no reason that anyone should get hurt.

Carrying his beer to the table, he becomes aware of Percy Sledge on the juke-box crooning "When a Man Loves a Woman." He sits and puts his chin on one hand and leans across the table. She responds in like manner and face-to-face he says, "I bet I can guess who played *that* song." She smiles and the whole room glows. He's never felt such radiance and doesn't know if the light comes from inside her or from inside himself. Soon they'll discover that together they generate a *lot* of electricity.

"OK, smartass, what's next then?"

"Oh, something soulful or rocking. Knowing you, it could be almost anything. And that's meant as a compliment." They look deeply into each other's eyes. "You're just gorgeous, Claire. I'm really glad that you came out here; and a little surprised, too." He reaches across the slight space between them and gently touches her hand with one finger, tracing the curvature of her little finger, down the backside of her hand to the wrist, then back again to the next finger.

"Don't tell me that the ever-confident Duke Windsor has so much humility that he thinks it possible that any woman could resist him." She pauses and then says with a start, "Duke ... Windsor ... Duke *of* Windsor. That can't be an accident. Tell me about this." She's laughing now, knowing that she's on to something. She sees that he's blushing a little and enjoys the power that conveys.

"Oh yeah. Nobody in this group knows about that. Well, you're right, it's no accident. When I first came to Auburn, I didn't have any idea how I would pay for a college education. I had a small scholarship that would allow me to do one quarter, so I came on anyway and thought that maybe I could figure it out from there. I searched around and eventually found that I could qualify for the Co-Operative Education Program, if I could make my grades. I did and they hired me to work at the main offices of Alabama Power in Birmingham.

"It was kinda embarrassing to go there, because I was only seventeen years old. My father had to go with me and sign all the paperwork *for* me, 'cause I was too young to sign for myself. Anyhow, when I went to work, I was commuting from Gadsden and had to get up at five to drive the seventy-five miles to Birmingham and be there by eight. I had no idea about traffic and how long that it might take me to get there, so the first morning I got in at about seven.

"I went into the office area where I had been assigned and sat at my new desk. I was looking around at papers, maps, and things when I heard a noise behind me. I turned and in the back corner in the darkest part of the big, open bay area was an older man. He was mostly bald and combed the few strands of white hair that remained over the top of his head. He saw me looking in his direction and asked in a gravelly, low pitched voice, 'You the new co-op?'

"A little intimidated I said, 'Yessir', and walked toward his desk. The name sign on the desk read 'Alfred Rosen'. I'll never forget his appearance; it was so strange to me. His skin had a yellowish tinge and his head seemed too large for his body.

"His glasses were oversized and thick and he wheezed more than breathed. A gold-toned spittoon sat at his left on the floor and in the corner of the back and side walls, and a sweet but foul odor hung in the air around him. I learned later that he had emphysema. I also learned that as a young man he had been a brilliant engineer at the company.

He looked me over and rasped, 'What's your name, son?'

"'Windsor, sir. Ashley Windsor.' I admit that I was in awe of him.

"'Windsor, eh? Haw. Haw. Haw. Duke of Windsor. That's your name for me from now on. Welcome aboard, Duke.'

"I didn't know exactly how to take it, but sure enough he called me 'Duke' for the whole time that I worked there. After a while, all the other people in the office started calling me 'Duke', and it just stuck."

During the telling of this story he has wound the fingers of one hand ever more deeply into hers. They're interlocked now. Palms pressed together. Perspiration flowing. She has been ultra-attentive, smiling at times, but mostly gazing into his eyes, looking at the shape of his face, his expressions. Her urge is to reach out with the other hand and touch him. His dark hair and dark eyes pull her in like a magnet and she is a little dizzy with his image in her head.

Recovering from her wandering thoughts she says, "Well the name fits. You look like a 'Duke'. I don't mean like royalty, just that Duke fits you somehow."

She thinks, *God I feel so dumb. He probably thinks that I sound like some teenage high school girl. My chest feels like it's gonna burst. This is some kind of energy that he's putting off. I feel like I'm suspended in his medium and if I stop looking at him, I'll crash to the floor. It sure is hot in here.*

On the other side of the table the energy level has also risen. Duke feels the intensity of her eyes in his. Some kind of understanding is taking place in his mind that has not reached consciousness yet. Mostly he is aware of his own sense of being afloat in *her* medium. And also like her, he is afraid that if they break eye contact the exhilaration will be lost.

Eventually, though, as Percy finishes his song and is replaced by the Mamas and the Papas, he remembers that they have beers sitting in front of them that are going warm and will soon be undrinkable. He reaches for his bottle with his off hand and slowly slip-slides his other, now damp, hand out of hers. Holds it in front of him. Eyes still locked into hers. Blows lightly into his palm. "Is it just me or is it hot in here?"

The coolness of his breath in his palm is unbelievably sensual. He reaches again for her hand. Takes her fingertips under his thumb with his index finger under her knuckles, stretching her hand backwards slightly. Blows gently into her palm and can almost see the muscles in her thighs as they flex, displayed like a movie screen in her eyes.

He thinks, *Yeah. This is right. How do I approach going to the apartment? Be careful here. Don't wanna assume too much too soon and make her feel cheap. Slow and easy.*

As he muses about how to approach the big move, she says, "If you'll finish that beer, we can get out of here."

That puts a different spin on things for him—*An aggressive female, and right here in Auburn, Alabama. Who'd've guessed? It's nice to be pursued.* So he turns up his beer and chugs it down as she laughs out loud, clapping her hands.

They go back out the door and into the velvet night. With his one hand on her shoulder they move together toward their cars. He asks, "You wanna follow me to my place or do you wanna take your car back to your dorm and ride together?"

"I'll follow. I don't want you to have to go back out, and I don't like being dependent on anybody else for transportation."

Claire's thinking, *He's nodding, but I caught that momentary flinch. Look at this; he's actually opening my car door for me. Southern men. I swear they're all imprisoned by their own sense of what's expected of them. Ah well, it's quaint, and it's even kinda nice to be taken care of sometimes.*

Easing back out into the roadway she wonders if he drives this slowly when he's alone. They cross campus, then turn into this small street she's never noticed before.

Standing behind him at the door she thinks, *I guess this is it. Pretty small. He's trying the door and it's locked. That makes sense. Searching through his pockets. Now this is funny.*

Duke can hardly believe it. *The freakin' door is locked? Oh yeah. Lynn. Do I have a key? Surely I do somewhere. Maybe in the car?*

"Hang on a minute, Claire, while I see if my key is in the car. May have to go in th' window." *Embarrassing. Damn. No key in th' glove compartment. OK, in the window it is.*

"Sorry about this. I am gonna have to go in the window. I guess my key is in the house." Taking off the screen that flanks the front door, a bookcase blocks his entry. Sliding one end carefully to the side, he's able to get one leg in and one foot onto the floor. Then, pushing off with his back foot levers him into the bookcase, which falls with a resounding thud and clatter onto the living room floor. *Christ. Crap all over the room. Let me get the door open and worry about it later.*

Opening the old wooden front door, he finds her standing and smiling smugly at him. "Smooth," she teases. "Let me help you pick up." Together they assemble the collected mass of books, magazines, papers and computer cards. Holding up a small sliver of paper, she smirks and says, "You might want to look at this piece." And holds up a note reading:

Duke:
Call me.
L-.

She thinks, *He's shocked. Like I care if another girl has been in his apartment. I'd probably be more concerned if there hadn't been. I'm betting that not many people get to see him like* this. *Maybe I can ease his mind a little.*

"Hey, don't worry. It's not a big deal to me."

Six different emotions run through him in rapid succession. Wonder. Shock. Anger. Embarrassment. Relief. Acceptance. *Of course she doesn't care about the note. Hell, she's got a boyfriend in Nashville.* He gives her a sheepish smile. Shrugs.

"Yeah. I guess not. I know you've got a boyfriend. I just hadn't seen the note. How about some music and something to drink?"

"Sure. Where's the bathroom?"

He nods toward the bedroom and says, "Through there." And hopes there's not a huge mess. Stacks three albums on the record player, grabs ice and a glass and fills it with juice from the fridge. He hears her returning from the bathroom.

Turns to speak to her and she is inches away, reaching for him, her hands to his shoulders, face tilted upward. She has a starved look—complete hunger. When he kisses her lightly, he hears the faintest moan that reminds him of a prayer—insisting that he answer. As their tongues dance in the shared space of their mouths, their feet slow dance toward the bedroom only a few feet away.

He pauses long enough to set the glass on the bedside table. His hands are moving across her body like a sculptor. Her head moves back and forth, her hair tossing against the sides of his face, which only stokes the fires. He senses their mutual need for relief, as their bodies press together, lock, grind.

He finds the button/zipper combo at the side of the tiny skirt and works practiced magic on them. Feels the fabric go slack and helps it fall to the floor. She feels the roughness of his jeans against her suddenly naked thighs. His erection presses against her as she stands on tiptoe to avail herself more fully to him and of him. She purrs quietly as the physical pieces of this dance create white noise in their ears, deafening them to the music.

She pushes up his shirt so she can touch his bare chest, and he reaches behind with one hand to pull the T-shirt over his head. Tosses it with nonchalance across the room. She giggles and puts both hands on his chest—massages, slides her hands around him and pulls toward him, pressing more firmly against him. Meanwhile his right hand has worked its way under her blouse and his fingers fidget with her bra. The elastic bands yield and she sighs. And he sighs. They sit together on the edge of the bed. At the edge of ecstasy.

She reaches to the buttons of the blouse, but his hand pushes hers away, enjoying the fascination of undressing her. They hold each other enthralled with magnetic eye contact. The buttons come free and her breasts spill out behind the now-slack bra. Pushing the fabric over her shoulders, she shudders, arms falling to her side. She's yielding and loves the feelings of letting go, trusting him. Shrugs the last remnants of the blouse to the bed. He gently, teasingly pulls at the bra and it slowly slides away from the treasures beneath. She shivers and goose flesh covers her upper body.

His kiss starts at her mouth and slips down her cheek and to her neck. She shivers again as he continues downward to her chest and ever so tantalizingly, slowly moving toward her breast. Her breathing is shallow-fast. She's almost certain that she's going to pass out. He's completely immersed in it all. Then, like a tall tree under the spell of a lumberjack, they topple in slow motion to the bed. Duke whispering, "Timmmm-berrr."

He is totally concentrated on her and she is lost in sensation. His tongue traces a luscious lap around her nipple as she strains mentally to pull him in, to have his touch bring fire there. His breath blows warmly across the dampness—hot and cold at the same time. Her mind reels. *How's he do that? Oh god—I think I'm gonna burst.* The heat of his mouth engulfs her. *I'm weightless here.*

His hand slides down her side—a forest fire racing down a hillside. Her belly ripples as he tickles his way across her waist. She thinks, *Hurry ... No, I want ... this to last ... I want it ... I want.*

His fingers slip under the top of her panties. His mouth moves again, crossing the pinnacle of her distended nipple, his tongue gliding down the side of this small mountain—a skier in a heat wave. Into the valley and again up the other side. Her breasts are full, soft, yielding.

His fingers inch underneath her panties. Feels the rough texture of her. She rises there like a volcano—all hot and damp with lava-like moisture. Threatens to explode if he touches her ... There ... Brushes lightly, making her squirm a little ... Squirming a little himself ... She's breathing heavily and is very close ... Sliding his fingers another millimeter to feel the bud that's at her center. Another millimeter deeper. Her hips rise off the bed and she sings his name like a hymn.

Duke inches his face back up next to hers so he can that he can look into her eyes. Her breathing is more measured now. The tension broken but not dissipated. He asks, "You alright? Wanna tell me about the tears?"

But she didn't know that she was crying. "It's just about tension release. No, I'm not distressed. Let's get out of the rest of these clothes."

Their voices are strained. Excitement still running at warp speed. Shoes and clothes are thrown haphazardly to the end of the bed.

As he lowers himself beside her, he asks, "Is there anything you want? Lights on or off? Fast or slow? More music?"

Guttural laugh as she reaches for him. "Too many choices. Just kiss me again and we'll figure it out."

His voice is thick as he whispers, "God I love to touch you." His hand opens and cups her breast, squeezes so sweetly. "Just perfect, Claire."

Duke's mind is awash in the experience of her. *What an elegant body. Tiny waist. Wonderful breasts. Glorious blue eyes. Skin like cashmere—soft and smooth. She's relaxed now with the urgency passed. Her face as she toppled over the edge. Her brow wrinkled. Her mouth open as she gasped for air. Her muscles tensed. Then, whispering my name as she moaned so softly.*

Their eyes focus only on each other as her hand moves down his chest. Her fingers spread, her nails create tingling furrows across his diaphragm causing involuntary ripples of stomach muscles. The same fingers dance at his waist, then slide further. Her eyes dilate. He gasps. At this moment nothing exists for them but this shared world of sensation. The sap is rising in him and he says gutturally, "Slow down."

"Come inside me," she whispers.

Moving from beside her to on top is like water ballet. He pushes up with one hand and she slides underneath. As he lowers himself, her legs part and he snuggles down gently into ancient, sacred ground. She guides him and the union is consummated. He glides smoothly into the deepest region of her and stops there. Pubic bones crush together. Then they are lost to each other, experiencing total suspension in self-absorbed pleasure. Blood rushes in their heads.

After moments or ages of inactivity they almost simultaneously feel the need for movement and begin that rocking, to and fro motion that barely withdraws him from her and then slips him back inside. This friction becomes the epicenter of a growing swell of need.

"I'm close," he warns. "Do you want to slow down?"

She gasps, "No. I'm close, too. Come with me."

She pulls him in deeper, feels his body convulse and then is lost again to her own rush of pleasure—wave after wave of sensation. She is only dimly aware of his straining as he spasms and drives against her. Unknowingly, she tries is to engulf him. "Oh god, yes."

He doesn't need encouragement to go with this. It's like being swept along on a rip tide. He gives up control and primal forces take over. Her legs spread slightly further and he pushes forward a little more deeply, engulfed in the wet warmth of her. The pressure of orgasm builds and has to explode. His arm around her waist pulls her more tightly against him as he bursts into her. Vibrant energy reaches out from his core to touch her. "Yes, there, Claire."

As breathing comes back into the normal range, the two stir and stretch. Duke once again pushes himself up on his left arm and she automatically slips out from under. He scoots himself up toward the headboard, turning to his back, and elevates his head slightly. Pants, "Whew. I don't think that I ever want to leave this bed. Let's just stay here forever."

Rolling over she puts her upper body across his midsection, arms folded on his chest and looks at him. "That was wonderful. I really needed for you to be gentle, Duke. Thanks … But I don't know about forever." Elfin grin.

Cocking his head to one side and grinning wickedly he says, "*Was* wonderful? Are we finished? I thought that we were just kinda taking a break. Want some of this orange juice?" And the grin spreads.

She's a little hesitant to respond, wondering if he's kidding. "You serious?"

Handing the glass down to her, he comes very close to her face with his own. "Well, I was, but if you're not interested that's fine."

She drinks, sits up on crossed legs, and leans across him to put the glass back on the table. This movement presents her right side from armpit to waist. And leaning down he kisses lightly along her rib cage down to her waist, then slips back again as she comes alert, straightening. "I mean, it's up to you."

So she dives into him, kissing him deeply. Her body slides against his, her breasts smash across his chest. Instantly they are at each other with a fury that is consuming. This time there is no holding back. No niceties. No total regard for the other person. This time they slam together, lock, and move in tangled circles, flying around the bed and against the wall, trying positions they had never known before. Finally, he gains leverage with his foot against the headboard and drives into her as she pulls him down and meets him move for move. Sweat pours from them and the power of their efforts propels them toward another climax—this one marked by grunts and demands of each other. When they collapse against each other, drenched and panting, Duke manages between gasps, "You mean gentle like that?"

And they crack up laughing.

Lying together in the afterglow, she has curled into the crook of his shoulder. This sort of peacefulness only comes from sexual exhaustion. No pretense exists between them. Neither feels expectation from or toward the other. He strokes her cheek unknowingly and she snuggles more deeply into his body-curve. Her hand bumps across the ripples of his abdomen and she says, "You turned out to be a surprise. You look like such a skinny thing out in public and then you turn out to look like this. How'd you get big?"

He snorts. "In my world I'm not big at all. I was just a jock, so I had to work out. I'm always surprised when someone says that. Even embarrasses me a little." His hand moves down her cheek and onto her chest. With one finger he traces the outline of her breast as he talks.

She says, "You always seem to be so self-assured. Nobody suspects that you ever feel embarrassed. I know it's not fair, but people feel some kind of security when they're with you. I feel it myself and I can sense it in Pax and Judd, too."

His response is reticent, "Yeah, I sense that sometimes with some people. Not everybody, though. Hadn't thought about it with you or Pax or Judd. I can't help wondering what that's all about for people. I don't think of myself as being … I don't even know how to say it … I can't be strong for *other* people. Hell, I have enough trouble managing it for myself." His hand has found its way back down her abdomen. Feels the damp tangle of her. His erection is growing again and he wonders absently how she'll react.

"But that's just it. People can see that you *do* manage strength for yourself and they think that if they just hang around long enough, it'll somehow rub off on them, and they'll have it, too. Or maybe they think that just being around you, if something happens, you'll take care of it and they won't have to. I don't know. Like I said, I know it's not fair to put that expectation on you …" She tickles his growing shaft and softly takes him into her hand. "My goodness. What's happening here?"

Pulling her with one hand and pushing against her weight with his other arm, he maneuvers her on top of him. If she's surprised or unwilling, she doesn't show it. With pushes and wriggles and a numerous giggles, they manage to insert him inside her. She gulps. Placing both his hands on her shoulders, he slowly pushes her upright into a sitting position. "Your turn to be on top and do the work."

Sliding back and shifting her weight a little, she finds a way to gain the fullest measure of their shared space.

"I've never done it this way before. I don't know what to do."—even as she begins to rock her hips back and forth, feeling the slightest push-pull of him. Eyes twinkling merrily, she says, "We're gonna be sore tomorrow."

"Yeah. Is that OK?"

"Better than that."

CHAPTER 7

▼

After classes and before going to work, Duke goes by Lynn's dorm and asks if she's in. The housing assistant, another student working for the University, dashes up the stairs and back down to report that Lynn isn't in her room and that her roommates are also gone. "Aren't you that guy she's been seeing?" To his nod she smirks and adds, "She's been plenty mad at you."

"Yeah, I'm sure. I've been awful busy and in fact have to go to work right now. Will you tell her that I came by? Or leave her a message that I'm at work?"

Walking across the quad, the scenery takes his breath—girls of every shape and height. Blondes, brunettes, even the occasional redhead. Young girls in short shorts. Lots of tanned flesh. All smiles and giggles and perfume. He sees Claire heading toward him. Angling across the diagonal walkway, he intercepts her. She asks why he isn't at the bridge games. He explains that he has to work this afternoon so he can play in the duplicate tourney tonight at the A E Pi fraternity house. She looks tired and sleepy. With his best smile he asks, "Bad night?"

"No. Actually, it was a very good night, but it was a late night. So I'm going in for a nap, and then studying. How about you, how was your night?"

"Fantastic. And you were right. I'm pretty sore today. Not that I'm complaining." Facing each other in the sun this way fills the space between them with a golden glow. They seem to be walled off from the rest of the world, secure in some kind of bubble—warmth, crystalline alertness, and mutual awareness of each other. Neither wants to break the spell, but both pull away at the same instant, Duke stammering that he has to go to work. As he moves to leave, she touches his arm and asks, "Why are you over here anyway?"

He hesitates, then says, "Uh.… well, to tell the truth, I came by to see Lynn, the girl from Tuskegee. I was supposed to have called yesterday." Blushing a little now, but with an arched eyebrow he adds, "Somehow I got distracted and forgot. I really do have to go, but this is a very awkward way to leave you."

"What? Oh no you don't. Look. This is fine. What we did was have fun. Let's not get goofy about things now, O.K.?" Her smile is rich and real. Her eye contact is full and accepting.

There is no trace of jealousy in her—how wonderfully refreshing. Duke's hackles lay back. Anxiety melts away. Looks at her upturned nose. The red highlights of her hair sparkle in the sunshine. Appreciation surges in him. "Yeah. It was fun. Good, let's not get goofy. Did you really say 'goofy'?"

Chuckles as they drift apart and go their own ways.

Duke's jogging now along these narrow sidewalks. He looks up to be prepared for any oncoming foot traffic. Doesn't wanna run anybody over. Down this covered walkway that joins one building with the next. The university won't let these cute coeds get soaked in the afternoon summer rains that are common in the Southland. Up this steep hill opposite "the Berry", as everyone calls the library. Crosses Mell Street. Up all these cement steps—one, two, Christ, three sets. He's panting, light sweat on his arms and forehead.

Opening the first set of glass doors he is immediately slammed with cold, conditioned air. He continues through the second set to a still colder lobby and into the offices at the rear of the main desk. Stops and talks to Mrs. Posey to explain that he needs to work afternoons for a few days. She waves him out, too busy to discuss it and not really caring anyway. He looks into the card catalogue room to see *Mrs.* Lassiter. Blows her a big kiss on a whim is rewarded with her first genuine smile to him. He leaps down the stairs three at a time into the orderliness of his workstation. Checks the listening rooms and finds not one soul there. Sigh of relief. He can work on those papers now. He breaks out notebooks and notes, slaps on his "academic hat" and begins to write.

✳   ✳   ✳   ✳

The Alpha Epsilon Pi fraternity house is a two-story brick house in a former residential neighborhood that is slowly being taken over by student housing. Even the loft has been converted to extra sleeping space. A graveled parking area stretches along the left-hand side as you face the house. Cement walks lead from the parking area and the front sidewalk to the stoop entrance. Lights blaze in all the windows tonight and the sound of music can be heard all the way to the street. At first Duke knocks on the front door, but when no one comes, he decides to enter and ask around for Ron.

The entrance to the living room is much like that of any other house. On his right, framed, double glass doors lead into a long room that appears to have been two rooms once. On the left are a dining room an a kitchen. Pass-throughs connect the kitchen with the dining and living rooms. Furnishings are new and clean. Directly across the room from him a hallway leads back into an area of individual rooms. Fraternity plaques and photographs adorn the walls. Every room he can see has thick carpet. As he closes the heavy door behind him, a voice calls out to him, "Duke. I'm glad that you made it. Terry is coming and wants to play with you." He shakes Ron's extended hand. "Wanna see the rest of the house?"

Taking the tour, he notices that the house is either newly renovated or at least recently painted. Everything is fresh and clean, not like the other fraternity houses he has visited. By the time they get back to the big room on the first floor, people are beginning to arrive.

Ron leads him over to a slight young man with dirty blond hair and introduces them to each other. "Terry Collins, this is Duke Windsor. I hope that you guys enjoy playing with each other and that you'll take it easy on the rest of us." With that Ron disappears to talk with others.

Terry's drawl is high pitched and nasal. "Why don't we go sit at a table and talk until this thing gets started." He leads the way to one of the half dozen or so card tables that are set up in the large room. "What system do you play?"

Duke just stares at him as if he were speaking some foreign language. "I'm not sure what you mean by 'system'. I've only been playing for a few weeks and just play the same way that people at the Union play."

Looking more closely at Terry now, Duke sees the inexpensive clothing and the deferential posture. He reminds Duke of many of the poorer people that he has known in his life, some in the public schools that he attended, others in his own family. Country folks. His too long hair has waves and curls. He uses too much oil to keep it in place, and far too much cheap cologne. His complexion has a yellowish cast and he is too thin. But at this cursory physical level, the resemblance to country folks ends. Terry is quiet and very articulate.

"Oh, I see. What you're used to is called 'Standard American'. It's the most common system of bidding used in playing. Have you ever seen 'duplicate' played before?"

Duke shakes his head and Terry explains. "Everyone plays the same hands. How that works is by a system of pre-dealt hands that pass from group to group.

The cards are separated into discreet groups and held in 'boards'. You don't play your cards into the center of the table, but keep them in front of you and turn them either perpendicular—for tricks won, or horizontal—for tricks lost. After each table plays the hands, they replace the cards into slots in the board. The bids and scores are recorded. At the end of the night, they calculate how each team has done on each board, then accumulate all the scores and a winner is determined.

As he's explaining all this, others are beginning to take seats at other tables. Soon Ron and his partner Jay join Duke and Terry. The two men in charge of the tournament pass out the pre-dealt boards, four for each table, and the evening begins.

The three and one-half hours that follow are a blur for Duke. Almost from the beginning he understands that his new partner knows far more about the game than he knows. In fact, Terry seems to have some kind of sixth sense about what cards each person holds. Some of the things he does make sense and others appear to be magical. The contracts are consistently higher than Duke would have thought possible to make. And Terry consistently pulls off miracles. On those few occasions when Duke has to play the hand he is very nervous, unsure of himself. He fails at two consecutive attempts and apologizes. Terry laughs and says, "No, actually that will end up being a good score." This is confusing, but after hearing it twice, Duke decides that he's in over his head and that it's better to try to make this a learning experience than to get too much ego involved.

While getting a cup of coffee from the table at the front of the room, Duke runs into Pax. They agree to meet at Judd's place around midnight to talk.

At the end of the evening, Duke again apologizes to Terry as they wait for the results to be tallied. Terry says, "Well, I think that we did pretty well. We'll know in a few minutes, but I'm pretty sure. We may have even won this thing."

Their second-place finish is a surprise to Duke and a little disappointing to Terry. Leaving amid the congratulations of Ron and others, they decide to go to the Kettle to drink coffee and discuss the evening. Terry accepts a ride in the T'Bird explaining that he owns no vehicle himself. "Did Ron tell me that you've been playing about three weeks?" Terry asks in the car.

Over the rumble of the motor, Duke responds that he's only *played* for three weeks, but that he has been watching and trying to figure things out for months. Pulling into the parking space directly in front of the Kettle, he notices George Blankenship's SuperSport a few spaces away. Though distracted, he hears Terry say, "You're really catching on. You played your hands really well—especially on defense. I remember the first time I played duplicate. I was so scared that I continually made mistakes. I could even see what I had done after I'd done it, but couldn't see it beforehand. I was pretty embarrassed."

Chuckling Duke replies, "Yeah. That pretty well explains how I felt tonight. It just seemed like I couldn't quite understand the hands until after they were played; and sometimes even then I didn't see why you made the bids or played the hand. I was very impressed. Not to change the subject, but are you from around here?"

"Yeah, pretty close. Actually from between here and Tuskegee. How about you?"

"North Alabama."

They're approaching the front door to the Kettle when George walks out. "Hey, Terry. Duke. How're y'all doin'?"

They nod, passing. "Just fine, George," Terry replies.

After they have settled at a table, Duke asks, "How do you know George?"

Terry explains that his family rents some land from George's father and that he has known George pretty much all his life. With a little prying around from Duke it emerges that the arrangement between Terry's father and George's amounts to sharecropping, only under the guise of "renting". It is clear that Terry is not favorably impressed with George, though he isn't openly hostile. It's an old story really—the peasant's son cannot openly criticize the son of the lord of the manor.

For half an hour they talk about the evening's game. Terry remembers virtually every hand. With some coaching, Duke is able to recall some of the hands and Terry explains the various strategies that he used and how he made certain deductions or assumptions. A new and growing appreciation for the game begins to take shape in Duke's mind. His respect for Terry increases accordingly. Finally at five minutes after midnight he says, "Look, I've gotta go somewhere. Can I drop you off or anything?"

To Terry's polite refusal, he waves goodbye and mounts up for the drive to Judd's. No traffic. Another soft summer night in the Southland. Up these stairs now. The door open and the screen door unlocked. Sticks in his head and announces himself. Judd and Pax are huddled over the round wire spool that serves as a coffee table in the room.

"Come on in. Hey, close that door behind you, Duke." This from Judd who is doing something with a record album cover. Duke complies and joins the two at the table. Judd is making a cigarette and Duke realizes that this must be marijuana. Judd checks him out, up and down, and says, "So, the new bridge master deigns to visit with us mere peons." All three laugh, but Duke tries to play it off, claiming that Terry did all the work and could have probably won if he hadn't been in the way so often.

Pax holds up a restraining hand. "Duke, shut up. If you can't learn how to win without embarrassment, you might as well quit playing. You're gonna keep winning. Ron's got you pegged. You can play the game, and you'll get better as you play more." Duke is really embarrassed now.

Semi-sarcastically Pax says, "Hey, it's just not that big a deal. So you can play bridge well. Does this make you a better person? No. Does it diminish the people around you? No. Will it feed starving children in China? No. It's just something that you happen to do well. No reason to feel proud, or embarrassed, or anything else. It's just *one thing* … So. How'd you like playing with Terry?"

Duke is relieved to change the subject. "Terry knows his shit. We just spent half an hour at the Kettle and he flat overwhelmed me with new ways to see and interpret the game. I'm serious; he's really smart about it."

"That's not all he's smart about," says Pax. "He's been in several of my history classes and he has almost a photographic memory. One thing's for sure. If the instructor grades on the curve, Terry's gonna fuck it up for everybody else. I haven't played against him, but I can see how he would be good. Congratulations anyway. Getting a 'second' on your first time out is an accomplishment, even if you were just along for the ride."

Judd holds up a thinly rolled cigarette and says, "Pax said that you might want to try this. Ever seen it before?" Duke shakes his head and Judd adds, "Just do what we do and try to hold the smoke down as long as you can."

And with that he lights up, tokes up, and passes it around. The three finish off the "joint", as Pax calls it, down to a half-inch nub, and then sit back. Duke becomes aware that music is playing somewhere and realizes that it was playing all along and he hadn't noticed.

He notices, in fact, that all his senses are sharper. He smiles to think that he notices even that he notices. His vision is crystal clear. Hearing is acute to the extent that he thinks that he hears the needle of the turntable against the vinyl of the record. The smell is like burning rope or grass—not exactly familiar; but not completely alien either. His head feels frozen. Movement seems to take longer and to be more tiring. Everything happens in slow motion.

And the music … If he pays close attention, he can hear each and every note, clearly and distinctly, as well as the whole piece of the song. This is fantastic. The furniture and other objects in the room seem somehow to be more intensely real to him. As he is taking stock of all these new sensations he becomes aware that he hears laughter. Turning his attention to his forgotten friends, he sees then hears that they are laughing and talking.

"Sorry. What were you saying?" This question to Judd, who wears a smile that can only be described as beatific.

"Actually, I don't need to ask, I guess. I was just asking if you could feel anything from the grass. But it's pretty obvious that you do." There's no mocking or teasing in this, no effort to put him down or make fun of him—just a statement. Pax nods his agreement.

Duke responds, "Well, yeah. This is really nice. It seems like everything is clearer, but that it's also in slow motion. Does everybody have that same reaction?"

Pax says, "Oh it's like everything else, different people have different views of it. Some people don't like it at all. But tell me, what was it that Terry was telling you about bridge that you found so new and surprising?"

"Holy cow. That seems like a million years ago now. Let's see if I can remember. Oh yeah. First of all, I didn't understand that sometimes it's worth more to go set on a contract than to let the others bid and make one of their own. I could see it sometimes, but still don't have a really clear understanding of it. He talked about 'vulnerability' in ways that I hadn't thought of before.

"He got me to understand quickly that I need to pay as much attention to the opponents bidding as I do to our own. He talked about something called an 'end play' that I don't get yet. Damn. There was a lot. He knows a lot of stuff."

He pauses and then plunges on. "He mentioned learning some 'conventions' and I halfway understood that. Something like a code; but one that both you and the opponents would understand. I wonder how that could be worth much, if everybody knows what it means."

Pax's head snaps back. "Whoa. So he's already talking about end plays? Jesus, nothing like throwing your ass into th' deep end. That's a tough skill to master there."

Contentedly Duke continues, "And guess what else? He knows George Blankenship. In fact, he's known him most of his life. His daddy rents land from George's daddy. Small damn world, huh?" This last freezes Pax in mid-grin. He looks confused, then looks down, and shakes his head. Duke feels a rush of guilt or some other undefined defensiveness. "Did I say something wrong?"

Pax shakes his head. Says, "Just so many coincidences. Your knowing all those people in Tuskegee, then George being an *associate* of yours. Now your teaming up with Terry and his having a connection to George *and* his daddy ... I'm just a little staggered by all of it together, but I'll get over it. By the way I called

Mohammed today and he'd like for you to come over with me tomorrow night and talk some with him. Can you make it?"

Duke has a hollow feeling in his belly hearing this. It seems like he's not trusted, almost like he's on trial or something. Wonders if the grass is making him extra paranoid. Has heard a lot of jokes about the connection between the two things—marijuana and paranoia. Well, he did tell Pax to talk to Mohammed.

After a pause, he answers, "Yeah. I think that I can arrange to get over there. Should we go together?"

Pax is more relaxed as he answers. "Yeah. Let's take my car. Wanna come over around six or so?" Duke nods his assent and Pax adds, "You OK? You look a little pale."

"I guess so. Look, Pax, I'm feeling kinda defensive about this whole thing now. It's like you guys don't trust me or something. What's going on with all this?"

Pax expresses exaggerated patience, nodding and thrusting his hands outward, palms up. "Yeah, I'm sure that you feel that way. I don't blame you, but I assure you that I'm beyond the sense of mistrust that we talked about the other day. I think that after we meet with Doc, you'll feel better about things. By the way, didn't see you *or* Miss Claire at the Union today. Too tired to get your ass outta bed?" This with a knowing grin that has warmth and teasing in it.

Duke glances at Judd who looks puzzled, but who realizes suddenly the implication of this and almost comes up out of his chair. "Aw no. You bastard. I can't believe that a scrawny fucker like you gets the big score with Claire. I gotta hear about this. C'mon give."

Duke blushes—and is little angry with himself for it. Wishes that he could be so urbane that he could comfortably talk about such matters casually, but it isn't in him. Instead, he says, "Aw, we went out for a beer and now Pax wants to make a big event of it. I'll tell you what, even if something *does* happen between us, it'll stay between us. You won't hear about it from me. I don't go for that 'kiss and tell' crap. People get hurt with that kind of stuff."

Now the blush passes to Pax. "You're right, Duke. I'm sorry I brought it up. I won't do that again. Anyhow, where were you this afternoon?" He's leaning back now and the intensity of the previous few minutes has dissipated.

"I had to work. And if I'm going with you to Tuskegee tomorrow night, I'll need to work tomorrow afternoon too. Will we be working at the church again? And if we are, are you going too, Judd?" Shifts his gaze to Judd, who is slumped in his chair.

Pax indicates that the plan is to work at the church until midnight. He, too, looks to Judd for an answer. Judd nods his agreement and they settle on meeting at Pax's place at six. Duke will pick Judd up and they'll go together. As they are arranging the rendezvous, Elizabeth appears at the door. With mock sincerity she says, "Door closed." Sniffs the air. "I know what you've been doin'. Did you finish it or did you save some for me?"

Judd says, "There's a roach if you wanna clip it."

Duke stares uncomprehending, 'til Judd explains that the tiny bit of the joint that's left is called a "roach" and that if you use an alligator clip or something similar, you can use up the entire amount of the drug. "This shit's expensive. Makes no sense to waste even a little bit. Besides, that's enough to get her off a little."

Duke watches fascinated as Elizabeth clips, lights and smokes the final bit. Almost immediately she becomes effusive. And as she laughs and jokes and cranks up the music, the tone of the room becomes light-hearted. Everything seems funnier than it really is, the music better than it really is. Ideas give the impression of being more profound than they really are. Duke decides that the drug simply amplifies things. He sees this as a pleasant and, so far, harmless activity.

Lazing back on the sofa, eyes closed, he allows the music to take him away. Images float rapid-fire across the visual screen of his mind. Imagination on fast-forward. Mind pictures, ideas, fragments all cascade without being summoned. Some things are serious others are silly. Some seem to be momentarily profound—but all are fleeting. He can't keep up with all the sensations and ultimately has to give in to the urge just to observe and hope that at a later time he can recall some of what roars past in his consciousness.

After a while, he begins to feel uncomfortable, an urgent need to get home and get some sleep. Rousing himself upright, he prepares to leave. The others protest that it is too early, but he feels compelled to leave. The good-byes are somehow more meaningful this night. And he makes himself take extra precautions descending the narrow stairs to the parking area.

Duke fumbles through his pockets to find keys. He decides to put the top up and begins unfastening the snaps that hold the cover. This takes so much energy and concentration that he changes his mind and refastens the snaps, gets them wrong, and starts over. In the midst of the changes he starts laughing and can't stop.

He hears the screen door open from the upstairs and looks around to see his three friends sitting on the steps watching him. He feels flustered until he finally gets it right. As he opens the driver's side door, he hears applause from up above, turns toward the sound, bows in their general direction. Says, "And for my next feat …"

He sits in the car and starts the engine, then raises his hands in triumph. More applause. He engages "Reverse" and backs slowly, turning around to exit the parking area. Everyone waves as he leaves. Turning right into the alleyway, he heads for home.

On College St. there is no traffic. Traffic lights have been turned to blinking mode at the intersections. He goes left onto Mag and realizes that he is going much too fast and needs to slow down. Looking at the speedometer, he finds, astonishingly, that he is traveling at 25 mph. Involuntarily, he laughs aloud and forces himself to speed up to at least 35 so as not to appear suspicious.

Thinks, *Ah, so this is why paranoia and grass are linked. It's hard to tell whether you actions are normal under this influence, and so people think that they're behaving in some strange way, and they get scared. It feels like people are watching me; but there's no one around to* be *watching. It's because I don't trust myself to be doing things right. Ha. That's how it works.*

Looking down he notices that his speed has now slowed to 20 mph. He laughs again and makes the effort to maintain the speed limit.

As he pulls into the single parking space beside his apartment, he notices the taillights of the Stingray going around the corner at the end of the block—leaving. *Whew. Just missed her.* He wouldn't want to try to make sense with her right now. Gets out of the T'Bird and walks to the door. A note is attached to the screen with a hairpin:

> *Duke:*
> *You could have at least called. I give up.*
> *You know where to find me.*
> *Lynn*

His reaction is located somewhere between guilt and hilarity—leaning toward hilarity.

CHAPTER 8

▼

As they pull into the parking lot at the Cabanas the next evening, Duke asks, "Judd, will you help me put the top up right quick? It feels like rain to me and I don't wanna risk getting my interior soaked again." When Judd accuses him of playing meteorologist, Duke grins and says, "I should have known that a city boy like you wouldn't know how to prepare for a rainstorm. You *do* have enough sense to go inside if you actually *feel* rain don'tcha?" And together they go through the routine of unfastening, pulling out the ragtop and frame, stretching this to the top of the windshield and clamping everything down.

"See, that was so easy that even *you* could do it, thanks for the help." Judd waves him off, not wanting to say anything that might provoke another teasing remark. Together they climb the stairs to Pax's apartment, but he meets them coming out, so they turn and all go down to the Galaxie together.

The Galaxie rolls along through the gathering dusk of this summer evening. Their talk is mostly of school, grades, and the papers that Duke has just written while at work at the library. He accepts their ribbing for having done his work early and then explains that he's going home for the weekend and that he won't be able to work there, mostly because of his girlfriend.

"Another woman? Christ, Duke. How many women are you stringing along here?" This from Pax and delivered in the same kidding tone as from before. "I mean there's this woman from Tuskegee, whom we have not met yet by the way, then there's Claire, then your obvious infatuation with Tisha. Now you're telling us that there's another one in Gadsden? How many is enough?"

"Enough? There's no enough when it comes to women. Besides, I'm not committed to anyone and everybody knows about everybody else. What's the problem? Do you see a problem, Judd? Or are we just in the presence of a morally superior human being here?" This is delivered from the back seat where Duke has chosen to sit. He can catch the nuances of their body language from here and might have missed the bantering overtone had he been up front.

In his smooth, almost seductive voice, Judd refuses to engage the matter. He disclaims any opinion about anyone else's decisions regarding relationships, but does compliment Duke for "at least telling everyone about everyone else."

"OK," says Duke. "Almost everyone." Pauses, then, "Well, some do." Another pause. "Alright, alright. At least Claire knows about everyone else. 'Course, we aren't really doin' much. I mean, we came to your place together once and went out for a beer once. That's about it. I guess maybe nobody else really knows anything about anybody else." Another pause. "You know, I hadn't seen this as a problem before. Are you seriously saying that there's something wrong with what I'm doing, Pax?"

Pax speaks to the rearview mirror. "I don't know about 'right and wrong'. But I'll tell you what *I* think. First, I couldn't take the pressure. I'd worry that one would find out and get angry, or something. I don't deal with that sort of thing all that well. I'm very uncomfortable in those situations. I get flustered and feel foolish.

"Secondly, I think when you show even the slightest, most innocent attention to some women, suddenly they think that you're sharing an exclusive relationship. And when they find out otherwise, well you're just the world's biggest jerk. Then there are more things to deal with. The pain that they go through as a result of their erroneous beliefs—pain for which you must share *some* responsibility. Then, there's the anger that spills over. Now we're back to my being uncomfortable with that. So, right or wrong? Hell, I don't know. I just know that I wouldn't put myself in the position of having to deal with it. It's like my uncle Jimmy says: 'Life is about position. And each person is in charge of his own position.'"

There is a prolonged silence as all three men think about what Pax has said. Judd finally breaks the ice by offering, "Well, your uncle's homily may have a hole or two in it. It is impossible to live in society and not be *influenced* by the other members. Also, you may not always be able to decide or even predict what's gonna happen to you."

In the back seat Duke ponders these matters, and slowly his own ideas come into focus. He explains, "I think you're each only partially right. We all *are* responsible for whatever position we find ourselves in; but there are forces at work in the culture that exert powerful influences on us. The thing to remember, though, is that they are only *influences.*

"Every conceivable point of view is out there vying for our attention and affirmation. Some of these ideas are in direct opposition. They can't all be right … Or wrong for that matter. Ultimately, I can't be responsible for anyone other than myself. The other side of this responsibility coin is that I can't blame other people or circumstances for my foibles either. Does this make any sense to anyone?"

Silence. The countryside flashes by as Pax has unknowingly increased his speed. "That's pretty idealistic, Duke. If you really believe all that, why are you trying to help out with the voter registration thing? In fact, why would anyone ever try to help out anyone else for *any* reason?"

With more heat than he knows is in him Duke replies, "Beyond the 'average person', whatever that is, you've got a point. Is it reasonable to expect the downtrodden, the ignorant, or the mentally incompetent to accept the kind of responsibility that we're talking about here? Probably not. I think we have to be careful about how and when we *do* reach out to others, though. If we get our hand slapped away, we shouldn't blame the other person for our own lapse in judgment."

They're pulling into the city limits of Tuskegee now. The trip has flown by. The men are all still grappling with these large ideas. Pax offers, "So, are you saying that you should only help someone who asks for help?"

The church looms two blocks away and Pax slows the Galaxie to give a little time for Duke's response. Instead Judd says, "No … It sounds like he's saying that you can offer help, but that you shouldn't feel slighted if it is refused; in fact, you might owe someone an apology. Right, Duke?"

One block away now, they're creeping along at 10 mph. "Kinda. That and a little more. You can make it known that you're available and maybe then it's likely that you won't step on someone else's pride by assuming too much. Maybe you can be a little more assured that you're trying to do the right thing in that circumstance. But sometimes there are people in situations who don't even know that they are being taken advantage of. They lack the information, and sometimes the intelligence, to understand it. These people you have to try to help even without their invitation. If they refuse, you can only try to educate them. You can't force help down anyone's throat" They're parked near the church as this last is said. The door opens and Mohammed peers out. Recognizing the car, he steps out and motions them forward.

"You boys arguing about something?" Mohammed asks this as if he could read their minds or their posture. When Pax explains that they were discussing the relationship between personal responsibility and helping others, he asks, "Are you beginning to question whether you should be coming here?"

Duke smiles at that and says, "I wish that was the point of this particular debate. It started with Pax trying to get me to be as moral as he is about women. Then we discovered that we see the whole responsibility thing differently. Unfortunately, I'm not sure that I'm up to his standards."

All four men laugh at this, and since the topic isn't relevant to the business at hand, They drop it. The three college men follow Dr. Mohammed into the church and down the hallway. A small crowd has already begun to gather in the larger meeting room. People speak and nod as the four of them make their way through. Duke catches the eye and the open smile of Tisha, and gives a brief flicker of a wave.

On the right-hand side of the hallway, across from the choir room, Mohammed stops and opens the door to a medium sized office. An old roll-top desk in a light oak finish sits with its top up. Papers lie scattered in disarray on top of neat stacks of leaflets, old bulletins, and what seems to be correspondence. Some of the stacks contain documents on various letterheads. Lined and unlined pages filled with typed and handwritten messages and lists are in the mix. Four wooden armchairs stand against two of the walls—two and two. Mohammed's diplomas and certificates hang on the walls. Pictures of known and unknown people decorate the desk and bookcase. This is clearly Mohammed's office.

"I thought that Reverend Maxwell was the minister here." Duke and his uncommon lack of tact. No malice in his statement, just innocent wonder.

Motioning the men to seats Mohammed explains that Rev. Maxwell's office is in the church-owned manse, where he lives with his wife, and that the church graciously rents him this space so that he has a place to work and to have as a base for his activities. Mohammed sits in his big swiveling, rocking, leather desk chair and swings himself around to face the others. He rocks forward, elbows to his knees.

"Duke, you know that Pax and I have been talking some about all these players you know from the Tuskegee area. I believe that you know Robert Earle Wilkins." Duke nods affirmative. "And George Blankenship and his father Thad?" Again the nod. "And now someone else who has a different kind of relationship with the Blankenships—Swift Collins's boy?" Yet again the nod. "Well, are these people to whom you feel some kind of allegiance? Or are they just acquaintances?"

Duke unconsciously strokes his chin with thumb and index finger. "I have known George for a year or two. I'm in the Auburn Gun and Skeet Club and so's he. We've talked some and hunted a couple of times. His daddy came on one of those hunts with us, but I wouldn't say that I really know him, other than to recognize him and speak.

"I've been in Mr. Wilkins's house a few times. I've been out with his daughter some and have met Mrs. Wilkins. We ate Sunday lunch at their restaurant three or four weeks ago, so I probably know him a little better than I do Mr. Blankenship. He seems OK in a gruff sort of way. Pax told me that you think that he is a ranking member of the Klan. I admit that my estimation of him took a tumble after that. Also from Pax, I get that George's daddy is a Klansman. That surprises me less. They are both—the Blankenships I mean—sort of rough and tumble types. I don't know that I feel any *allegiance* to any of them. 'Course I feel something; but I'm not sure exactly what it is—a kind of familiarity, I guess. I only met Terry Collins yesterday."

Mohammed says, "Do you know that I can't go into Robert Earle's restaurant to eat lunch without risking a cursing, a beating or worse? Not to mention they wouldn't serve me. Half the colored men in Macon County and Bullock, the next one over, have worked for Thad Blankenship at one time or another. My daddy worked some for his daddy many years ago. In fact, my momma worked in their house for a long time.

"He doesn't even realize how bad of a man he is. He thinks that because he hires and pays coloreds to work for him that we should think he likes us. Well, he pays poorly and treats all colored men like they don't have a lick of sense. He treats our women even worse. No. Thad doesn't *like* us. He just wants to *exploit* us. He'll gladly use us to build his barns and fences and rock walls or do any other kind of skilled or unskilled work that he can get done cheaper by hiring us; but he'd stop eating at Robert Earle's restaurant if we were allowed to eat in the same room.

"But worse than any of that, these two men aren't just Klansmen; they run the whole shebang. They make the decisions about what gets done. They are two of the wealthier men in the county, and I guess that they think that it's their divine right and duty to do these things."

At this, Mohammed sighs and sits back in his chair. He's perspiring he's so caught up in the explanation. There is pain and anger in his expression. What can't be seen is the depth of his passion about these men and the all too personal history.

Holding Duke in his gaze, he continues, "Duke, son, I'm not questioning your commitment to our project here. I know that you have thought through the risks to yourself that being here presents, but you may be able to help us better by doing different things."

Duke squints and says, "I don't understand, Doc. What else could I do?"

Mohammed answers, "If these men know and trust you, they may let you know about things that they plan to do that could potentially spoil our efforts. Or you might find out things that could even be dangerous to us. If you do hear those kinds of things, and would be willing to pass that information along to me through Pax, it would be a lot more help than coming here to fill out forms.

"I don't want you to think that we don't appreciate your coming here and helping; but this work can be done by anyone with an education. The position that you're in can't be come by in any way by any of us." He's leaning forward again. Duke can physically feel the sincerity emanating from him. His words do not plead but his eyes do.

Duke's impulse is to say no immediately, but he stops himself. "Doc, I need to think about this some. I mean, what you're asking me to do is to be a spy against people who trust me. My immediate reaction is to feel repelled by even the thought, but I don't want to rush to judgment on this. How about if we just go ahead and work tonight and I'll think about it over the weekend while I'm in Gadsden. I'll let you know something no later than next Monday afternoon. Is that good enough?"

Mohammed's dark features are somber as he nods saying, "That'll be just fine, son. Something else. If you decide to do this, you'll need to stay away from here. It's a matter of time before it is known that voter registration is being done through this church. If you're seen here, that'll make you untrustworthy in their eyes.

"Again, I don't want for you to think that we don't want you here. We really like you. Everyone who met you last Sunday thought the world of you. But this other mission is so much more important and so specialized that, for me, it takes precedence over what's done here in the church. You think it over and whatever you decide to do, we'll honor and support. If you decide to agree, nobody outside this room will know anything about your role in things—just the four of us. Pax more or less recruited Judd as a back up for him in case he is out of pocket and you need another way to get information to me. Well, let's go out and find something to eat; unless there are any other questions or comments."

"Did you say eat?" Duke jokes. Even though his mind is full of these ideas and propositions, Duke quick-steps back out into the larger meeting room. Tisha is waiting for him near the entrance from the hallway and together they go to the tables of food across the room. She's looking up at him like he's the prodigal lover. Sharing laughter, they seem completely at ease with each other.

Mohammed looks at Pax and says, "Some things never change. Tisha isn't gonna make this decision any easier for him."

Judd, who has been forgotten behind them says, "I wouldn't worry too much about that. Duke will make the decision on his own. He'll just have to think it all the way through. I'm glad that I'm gettin' to know him."

Mohammed chuckles and adds, "You oughtta see the boy play ball. Got a cannon for an arm. I'm surprised that he isn't playing at the university."

Judd says, "I think that I heard him telling someone that he 'walked on' but that there weren't any more scholarships. He's having to work his way through school and couldn't give up the time away from work to play without a scholarship. Big disappointment for him."

"Well there's the solution for what to tell Tisha when she asks why he's not coming back to work at the church." Mohammed has a satisfied grin on his face. "That was the only thing that I was worried about with this—how to explain his absence without making him look bad. Good. Glad that's settled. Well, let's eat and get started. I see that Cho-La Brown and Miz Maxwell are finished and are setting up at the tables."

Across the room Miz Jemison welcomes Duke with a plate featuring her fried chicken and okra. She's all smiles and tenderness. The invisible undercurrent for her is that she can see her daughter's affection for this nice young man and knows it can't be. She wants to warn Tisha, but refrains from it, not wanting to open up a new front in the skirmish line that, like most young adults, Tisha has engaged with her parents. She has decided that she'll just pray about it, although she knows that praying probably won't actually change Tisha. She is just as certain that she'll at least find some solace for herself there.

Tisha and Duke gravitate toward Cho-La and Miz Maxwell. They exchange greetings and Miz Maxwell goes on to tell Duke how things are working out so far. A few of the people who were here last Sunday have already finished their paperwork and hope to try to get verification of their eligibility to vote soon.

The crowd swells behind them. Duke wonders aloud if there will be enough help to get everything done and everyone registered. Miz Maxwell says, "You know Duke, I've been studying about that myself. I think that Dr. Mohammed is going to ask for some more help from other sources. You have to be registered by October 1st in order to qualify to vote in the coming year's election. I don't know. We'll just have to see."

Cho-La says that he's trying to get more support from students at the Institute. Many are afraid to be associated with "the movement". For others, their parents have forbidden them to take part. Still others are apathetic. But he believes that there will soon be more participation from that group. For now he's just glad that Pax and his friends are willing to help out.

Naturally, all this is rolling around in Duke's head like thunder in a canyon. For all of his "let's just work tonight and I'll think about over the weekend", he's more or less obsessed with the two sides of this dilemma. Certainly, anyone with an education *can* help fill out the forms. And the other work of gleaning information from rival camps is important not only to the success of the project, but vital to the safety of all concerned. On the other hand, if some of those who *can* do the work don't step up and *do* it, the project will fail anyway.

The scrub work has to be done. Not to mention his sense of friendship with these people. Not to mention the satisfaction of seeing each step completed. Not to mention the free food. Not to mention Tisha, wrapped around his arm and snuggled in so sweetly. A place in his heart aches to know that though she's never been his, he's lost her anyway. He knows also that it is correct and proper that it work out this way. Sometimes "right" just isn't very satisfying.

✳   ✳   ✳   ✳

One after another they come to the table and sit. Their stories are all different, yet so painfully the same as well. Duke's enthusiasm is blunted with the emerging knowledge that this will possibly be his last evening to serve in this capacity. At odd moments he can't help wondering if his nostalgia for the work before him is not really fueled by a latent fear of doing the work ahead. He mentally wrestles with the competing ideas of person-to-person service versus contributing at a higher, more vital level. And yet in the immediacy of this moment, one after another they come and sit before him. His heart is leaden. But his smile remains genuine. His caring for each individual who sits and shares the painful minutiae of a life smothered by the accidental blanket of race and color remains acute. He is struck by the fierce grip that poverty has on these people. And by the inhumanity of those who would insure, perhaps without volition, that the grip is not loosened.

At odd moments, images of raw violence rise up in his imagination. Anonymous men with blank faces threaten. Vistas of Klan rallies, burning crosses, and sheeted figures, the smell of kerosene, the rumble of men following a passion that is driven by fear and hate come unbidden to him. And at times his reverie is made all too frank, as he replaces the anonymity of the faces with the images of people whom he knows. Emotions fluctuate between anger and revulsion and anxiety. What if …

Mercifully the evening's work ends for Duke at a few minutes before midnight. Miz Jemison has almost finished consolidating the food that is left into a few dishes and has stacked the others together. Duke offers to help with moving them out to her car and they walk together into the warm night air. "I hope that whatever's bothering you works out for you, Duke."

"That obvious, huh?"

"Well, I know that you looked like you were sleepwalkin' tonight. And you look sad. I jus' hope it works out." There is no condescension or accusation in her voice or her demeanor. As he stands back up from having arranged the dishes in the trunk's floor, she places a hand on his arm and looks at him in the darkness with eyes that penetrate the gloom.

His heart is heavy and that heaviness threatens to overwhelm. Again she speaks. "If the burdens get too heavy, don't be afraid to ask the Lord for help. I ain't never seen him carryin' my burden for me; but they's been a heap o' times when the load got toted and I didn't know how." The softness of her touch on his arm is like a balm. The sincerity of her words lifts him up.

He smiles to realize that *her* prayers are being answered for *him*. *She* has lifted *his* burden. "Thank you Miz Jemison. That's by far the sweetest thing that anyone's said to me all day."

As they head back toward the church, they meet Tisha, who delights in teasing them. "Mama, what are you doin' out here in the dark with this white man?" A good laugh from the depths is another balm. Tisha slides in between them and hooks a hand into each of their arms. "I hope she hasn't been out here tellin' you 'bout all my secrets."

Miz Jemison explodes with mock ferocity, "LaTisha Maria Jemison, you know I don't tell nobody's secrets, 'cept maybe my own … Well, if I really had any, I might."

Duke feels warm and safe nestled in between these two women. The acceptance from them is a comfort. The moment is, once again, something that he wants to hold on to. Yet he knows that he can't stop the flow of life. Can't be in any one place other than in that moment, and then later in memory; but memory lacks the sweetness. It lacks the "reach out and touch" meaningfulness of reality—a poor substitute at best. With sweet sadness he imagines that memories may be all that he can carry forward with him. And that will just have to be good enough.

Just inside the door Pax, Judd and Mohammed stand in conversation. They look up and approach. Pax is saying that they need to get on the road back to Auburn. Tisha asks Duke if he'll be coming back on Sunday and he explains that he will be out of town. She is visibly crestfallen, but says, "I'll see you whenever I see you, I guess."

Longing in her face. Her mother drapes an arm over her shoulder as the three college men move out toward the Galaxie. Doors slam. The engine roars. Gravel crunches, then gets tossed back as they disappear into the night. Three black figures stand in the darkness until the car turns the corner. They are silent—each thinking private thoughts.

✳   ✳   ✳   ✳

Highway 29 is becoming more and more familiar as the trip is repeated. As soon as the Galaxie clears the city limits sign, Judd intones in that mellifluous voice of his, "I don't know if anybody's interested, but I brought a joint."

They kinda look at each other and grin. Pax says, "Sure. Why not? Fire it up." Almost instantaneously the smell of burning grass fills the car. Judd can be heard to inhale deeply and stop. The joint appears in front of Duke's eyes and he takes his turn and passes it along to Pax.

Round and round she goes.

The music gets louder all by itself. The windows are down to blast away the smell. The men don't talk at first—thinking, experiencing, listening to their own soundtrack. At a small service station at the last intersection before the highway plunges into darkness, Pax pulls over. The place has been closed for hours, but has drink machines outside. They forage their pockets and the car for change and come up with enough for a drink for each. Turning left on this narrow poorly paved road they meander seemingly aimlessly into the countryside. Pax explains that he thinks the road eventually connects with Wire Road and enters Auburn from the south side a little further west of town.

For no obvious reason Judd asks, "So what about accidents?" Laughter. Hoots. "No. I'm serious. Remember we were talking about life being about position and about individual responsibility? Well, what about accidents? Don't tell me that neither of you believes that accidents happen."

More laughter and Pax says, "Well, yeah there are some accidents; but I don't have to be involved in them." Chuck Berry is rocking on the radio. The night is pitch black around them. No houses. No farm lights. Mercury vapor lamps don't exist out here. Weeds and bushes grow right up to the verge of the narrow road.

"Oh I see, people just *choose* to be in accidents or there wouldn't be any, right?" Judd again. These words come out around the giggles that are taking control of his speech. "Tell you what. Let's choose *not* to be involved in one tonight. OK? No, wait. If we choose, then it's no longer an accident. Masochistic, maybe; but no longer an accident. So I say, let's not choose to be in a wreck. How's that?"

Pax becomes afflicted with a similar fit of hilarity. "I'm pretty sure that I already made that choice. See the whole idea here is that we have to evaluate situations and then make decisions that will not put us in harm's way. And that's really the best that we can do. So when I chose to take this back road back to town, I wanted to avoid as much traffic as possible, in case I'm not driving as well. So I'm narrowing down the potential for a wreck. Fewer other drivers to deal with means less of a chance for a collision. What d'you think, Duke?"

Without hesitation Duke replies from the back seat, "I think that all three of us are nuts according to that logic. Think about it. We are all putting ourselves in the path of danger just by being where we were tonight. If we're supposed to be considering life's situations and then trying to avoid danger, then why are we helping to do voter registration of coloreds in Tuskegee, Alabama? I'll buy that I have to be responsible for my decisions, but I can't buy that there aren't any accidents. Even a weirdo like Pax can't really believe that. He's just fooling around."

Pax interrupts, "Whoa. There you almost said it yourself. You're willing to accept that you must be responsible for your decisions, yet for some reason you can't take that one more tiny step and accept that those choices are what determines whether you are present at the scene of what you insist on calling an 'accident'. Let me give you an example.

"The first year I was in Auburn, my nephew came from California to visit me for a few days. My brother-in-law works for an airline and got him a free ticket to fly home to San Francisco. The catch was that the ticket was for a 2:00 a.m. flight out of Atlanta. This was in early February. So we left Auburn at about 9:00 p.m. to account for the time change crossing into Eastern Standard Time and I drove him to Hartsfield in Atlanta. On the way, we ran into a snow shower. We had fairly heavy snow for about five minutes and then it stopped and the road was clear the rest of the way. I delivered him to the gate and went back out to my car.

"I was driving an almost new Corvair at the time. I had a joint in the glove compartment and smoked part of it on the road. I was buzzing along at 65 mph or so when I topped a little hill and immediately ahead of me the roadbed was covered in snow. I just took my foot off the accelerator with the idea that I'd slowly get my speed down to a safe level. Rounding a curve I saw a tractor-trailer jackknifed across the entire road. When I hit the brake, I could hear the tires sliding along on the ice. My speed held at the same rate. I looked right and left. A ditch on one side and total darkness on the other. Nowhere to go. So I decided that I had to choose a place to hit the truck. Didn't wanna hit the fuel tank. Didn't wanna hit the tires and axle. So I moved the car over to hit him just to the rear of the last axle of the tractor. Just before impact, I laid over in the seat and was thrown into the dash … Now. Accident or not?"

Judd exclaims, "Never mind that now. What happened? Were you hurt?"

"Well, it was one of those slow motion moments like Duke was talking about the other night. I really did think of all those things before impact. I really did lie down in the seat, and with my feet on the clutch and the brake no less. The car was totaled—almost took the top completely off. But all I got was a cut about an inch long and a big lump on my head. I probably lost consciousness for a few seconds. The next thing I really knew was that the car was stopped and the engine was still running. I sat up and saw the truck driver climbing down from the cab. I rolled the window down and told him that I was OK and he said that he was talking to his dispatcher on his CB radio and would get the cops and an ambulance. I heard him tell his dispatcher that 'some asshole just plowed into the truck but *the truck* is O.K.'. And, 'oh yeah, he's says he's OK too.'"

Duke puts in at this point, "So what you're asking us is if you were in an unfortunate accident or if you're just a dumbass, right? Well this ought to be easy enough to figure out. I don't know about you, Judd, but I didn't really need this story to know the answer to *that* question."

Duke continues amid laughter all around. "But seriously, though, I can only give you about 60 percent on that one. You're right, of course, you should have known that the ice and snow were there and behaved accordingly. You shouldn't have been smoking while driving. But the truck was there independent of your control, so you didn't choose that part. So 40 percent accident and 60 percent dumbass."

Judd pipes in, "Right. Right. But that's only in that kind of situation. That time you had some foreknowledge. What if this had happened on the way *to* Atlanta instead of on the way back? See, my whole argument is that you can't always predict what's gonna happen. And to the extent that you can't, to that extent it's a fuckin' accident."

Duke says, "I agree. In this situation, you'd be more at fault than at some other times. But I see Pax's point, too, I think. We have to accept that the decisions that we make will inevitably land us *somewhere* and whatever happens as a result is our own fault to *some* degree. But only to *some* degree. I'm not ready to eliminate the word 'accident' from the dictionary just yet. By the way, is this story the reason that you're driving a Galaxie now?"

Pax answers, "You're right on the money, Duke. That's the sum total of what I'm trying, first, to say and, second, to live up to. I have to take responsibility for what happens to me. The answer to your question, though, is that the trucking company was so glad that I didn't sue for a huge amount that they settled for the value of my car and six times my medical expenses—check this out—which had been covered under my dad's insurance policy. My lawyer, who is also my cousin, said that that's a standard settlement. So I could afford the Galaxie and was glad to get into a big car instead of the tiny little Corvair."

As this conversation has rambled on, Duke from his seat in the rear has noticed that their speed has held to a steady 50 mph. He's thinking that some-how Pax has trained himself to pay attention to this when under the influence of the drug. He reasons that if Pax can do it, so can he.

The relatively slow pace, the complete lack of houses or any buildings for that matter, and the enclosed sensation created by the bushes growing so close to the sides of the roadway combine to create a feeling of security. And the very thought of security is enough to trigger in Duke the enormity of the decision that faces him between now and Monday afternoon. He wonders where *his* decision will land *him*.

He thinks about how his mom would react if he told her that he had decided to put his head into the lion's mouth. Quite sure that she'd say something like, "Son, you do know that they bite, don't you?" Not, "don't do this" or "you can't do that". No, she wouldn't try to force him to do things her way; but she'd sure God try to be sure that he sees the same things that she sees.

He smiles to himself as he thinks these thoughts, having warm feelings about his mom. He admires her spunk and her being opinionated, though they often disagree in principle. His debt to her and to his father is enormous. They have encouraged him to get a college education, and have told him honestly that they can't do it for him—financially or otherwise. He sees the stubborn strength of both of them and knows that he is like them, and that quality will serve him well.

Pax speaks to the rearview mirror. "Hey. Duke. What are you smiling about back there?"

"Actually, I was thinking about what Mohammed asked me to do; but then I got off track and started thinking about my mom and dad. I guess that I ought to give some thought to whether or not my decision will have a negative effect on them. It's possible, I guess. But probably only if I get caught and something really bad happens.

"I've been around people like George and his daddy all of my life and I know what they're capable of. I'm not going to go into this thing blindly. My mom might, in fact, do it; but she'd hate to know that *I'm* doing it. She'd be terrified for me even if she gave no thought to her own safety in the same sort of circumstance. She might even be angry since we probably don't see eye to eye on this.

"My dad on the other hand would join neither side and would believe that he had taken the moral high road. He would think I'm foolish for even considering trying to influence the outcome of the history that these parties are bound to be making. His idea would be that it has nothing to do with him and so he wouldn't be involved. I see his point, sort of, but I think he's wrong—this has everything to do with everybody.

"I also think that this Martin Luther King character makes a really arresting point when he says that in the end the coloreds won't remember the voices of their enemies nearly as much as the silence of their friends. It's clear that Negroes as a group have been mistreated in the larger culture. To me, this kind of analysis pretty much demands that everyone stand for *something*. I see that more clearly right now than I have at any time in my life. The implications are scary to think about.

"And, you know, this isn't all that far from the same kind of mentality that we were talking about a while ago, except that this is the other definition of 'responsibility'. Now we're talking about 'duty', and even that's a choice. Seems like no matter where I try to run to, I can't escape the fact of *myself*. It's like Mohammed said the other night, I guess. Just because a thing is scary and difficult, doesn't mean we shouldn't do it. Woo. That joint has really put us all in a philosophical mood."

An intersection looms ahead and after the right turn is made, Duke recognizes that they are on Donahue Drive, not Wire Road after all. He hadn't even know that this route existed. Auburn is largely asleep once again as the Galaxie meanders its way across town. As they pass the Kettle, Duke notices that George's SuperSport is parked out front. But he can see no one inside and the moment passes unremarked upon, as first the building and then downtown disappear from his sight and his thoughts.

Pax invites them in for a beer at his apartment, but they beg off and get into the T'Bird just as the rain starts to fall. The two are almost silent as they retrace their route back to town and Judd's apartment. At the intersection of Gay and Mag, the Stingray sits waiting for the light to change. Duke pulls up alongside and rolls down his window. Says, "Let me take Judd home and I'll be right back. Meet ya at the Kettle in five minutes."

He waves and accelerates to take a route around to the apartment, then turns to Judd and announces, "That was Miss Tuskegee in the flesh."

"From what I saw she's gorgeous. What's her name again?"

"Lynn Wilkins. If I'm gonna stay in that crowd, I'd best mend my fences with her. Man, what a job. To do it right I'll have to keep up a relationship with *her*. Well it's tough; but somebody has to do it. How come you and Pax get all the easy stuff?" He dodges the playful punch thrown at his shoulder, makes the loop dropping Judd, and returns to the very front parking space at the Kettle.

Before he can open his door, Lynn appears at the passenger's side. She opens the door and quickly slips into the seat. She tosses her head side to side and a spattering of water flies around. Raining outside. Raining inside. She's wearing jeans and a pastel shirt that she has tied together at the bottom, exposing two inches of midriff. Sexy. Very alluring. The dark red lipstick stands out boldly against her deep tan. Her big brown eyes look like they might leak, pleading even before she opens her mouth.

She's gushing, almost out of control, apologizing for unknown sins. Panic edges into her voice as she explains that she didn't know until today that he had tried to call several times. She explains that the outburst of anger in her notes was all about her fear of losing him. That she feels so ashamed of herself for not believing in him more. That she knows he's been very busy, and has tests. That exams are coming up in a couple of weeks meaning he has to study and write papers. Tears trace black rivulets down her cheeks as the mascara melts under the intensity. Anguish spreads across her face as she sobs heavily. Like the rain, her pain brings humidity into the interior of the car.

He reaches out a hand to her face and cups her cheek, her make-up slippery in his palm. She tries to smile through the tears but is only marginally successful. His heart reaches out to her, but he's not enjoying her display. Guilt creeps up his spine like a caterpillar.

Finally, he insists of her, "Stop. You didn't do anything wrong. It's just been one of those things. My life is probably a little more complicated than yours. I'm sorry we didn't connect after Sunday night. I did try to get in touch a couple of times, but I was so busy that sometimes when I could have called, I didn't think of it. I'm sorry you're in pain, but don't blame yourself."

She's drying up now—gets and uses a tissue from her purse. More composed, she explains that she has a quiz tomorrow morning in the history class that she's missed more than she's attended, and so she must go back and finish studying. Promising to come by the library tomorrow night, she tugs at the bottom of the shirt stretching the thin fabric tight across her chest. Duke notices and is tempted. It's hard for him not to want to touch her. But the urge passes and they say goodnight with chaste kisses and fondness. She jiggles as she runs back to the Stingray. Duke thinks that although he likes her well enough, he's really going to hurt her in the long run. He battles another twinge of guilt propelled by the certain knowledge that he *needs* to maintain close contact with her, but that he's going to help Mohammed by double-crossing his white friends in Tuskegee.

Cold as a fish. He's surprised to find this capability in himself.

CHAPTER 9

▼

Friday afternoon, top down and he's rollin'. Sun pours down as the T'Bird growls along highway 431, heading north. Home. His people—family and friends. Safety. It would be nice to get another perspective on all this stuff. Maybe he'll visit the man who bailed him out of so many jams in high school, the one adult he has always been able to talk to, his mentor, Daniel. No, he can't tell even Daniel about all the twists in the path that he's walking these days. Daniel is on the other side of most of these issues. No help there.

He's missing Lynn's birthday to come home for a "family emergency". *Ah what the hell. Let the wind blow this away for a little while at least.* He sits up a little higher and feels the force of air at 75 mph on the top of his head. Gliding through these small towns—checking out the babes and the cars. He signals with one finger at the local cops. Life is on hold. He can't see the end of all this yet, but knows there will be an end and he's determined to experience every single minute as it passes.

Duke is trying to allow the confusion in his life to reconcile itself. He feels like a paper boat afloat on a white water river. Thinks, *How did I get in this current. How could I "put in" and not realize that I was doing it? Or when I did realize it, why choose to go on with it? Silly idealistic boy in a man's game.*

Second thoughts. Second guessing. Second place. Second sight—it's going be ugly; but it's going be alright. Duke and Fats Domino rockin' through the countryside.

He makes the shortcut around Anniston, avoiding the traffic nightmare that is Quintard Ave., heading still further north toward Jacksonville State. He's feeling a little apprehensive at seeing Ellen in the wake of all that's happened in the past few days. It has been several weeks since he saw her last, but he has a clear image of her in his mind—honey blond hair, tall—5"8" or more. Brown eyes as deep as the pool under Noccalula Falls. Skin that holds her tan like it's galvanized. Soft and sweet personality. There's no malice anywhere to be found in this woman. Now the fires of the university experience are tempering her native intelligence. The campus lies straight ahead.

Magical transformation—Duke becomes Ashley, reassuming an identity that he left behind when he decided to go to Auburn in the first place. He makes that transition as smoothly as butter melting on his mother's cornbread. He makes the loop at the girls' dorm quad. This school seems so small after the cluttered and busy campus at Auburn—no lack of pretty girls though. Heads turn in the direction of the T'Bird. A male friend from high school stands with an unknown girl and waves as Duke nee Ashley parks on the circle and searches for Ellen in the crowd at the front door of her dorm. He waves back, distracted, then he sees her ahead with a small suitcase in one hand. Head down, she cradles two books in her arm. She seems so much smaller than he had remembered.

Looking up, her eyes search out and find his and another transformation occurs. The anguish in her heart from a moment ago lifts. She has moved from alone and fearful, dejected and gloomy to enthused and hopeful in a matter of seconds. Whatever was wrong is now right. Her trust in him to be the answer to her problems is total and without reservation.

He takes the books from her arm, lifting her physical burden as he has unknowingly lifted her psychological one. She drops the suitcase and puts both arms around him. There's an undercurrent of urgency in this. She looks up only slightly to say, "I've missed you. You look great."

Her touch, feel, and smell wash over him in the most intimate and familiar of sensations. His psyche oozes out to touch the core of this his long-time partner and soul mate. First love is a powerful thing. What he finds in her is puzzling. He senses that something is amiss, but can't quite figure it out. When he asks if she is ready to go, she unhesitatingly nods in the affirmative.

He carries the suitcase and the books to the rear of the T'Bird and pops the trunk open. After storing everything in with his few things, he follows her to the passenger's door and opens it for her. God bless the inventor of the mini-skirt. He asks, "Want me to put the top up?"

When she says no, he beams and reminds her where the hats and scarves are. She finds another baseball cap and squeezes her poofed up hair into it, looking like a tall pixie now. Filled with energy, Duke leaps over the door and into the driver's seat in a smooth bound—just showing off, just showing her that he's glad to see her. "So how are ya, babe?"

Hesitant. "I'm okay, I guess. Lots of stress, Ashley. I don't know how you keep up with school and work. Just school is getting to me. I'd really like to quit; but I know that you and daddy would be so disappointed. It's just hard right now."

"I have friends that go through this every quarter, Elle. You're probably doin' better than you think. I know how it is to feel behind all the time, but it all seems to work out in the end. You brought books. Are you gonna have to study over the weekend?"

She hesitates, feeling a little guilty, then responds, "I've got major tests on Monday and Tuesday. I haven't even read the chapters in the Western Civ class. I'll probably be OK in the Spanish class—thank god for that. So, yeah, I'll probably have to study some. Is that alright?"

She doesn't sound as dependent about this as Lynn might sound. But even at that he wishes that she wouldn't ask his permission to do her own work. Wishes that she would understand that he knows she has to do whatever is necessary to get the grades done. *Everything* else is secondary. Get the education. You can get everything else within reason as a result of having the education—lessons from his mom.

Back to highway 431 they pass the turn to the area where his father grew up. Two white houses sit across a plowed and already harvested field. A defunct railroad track passes silently between the houses and the fields.

A vague memory flits across his consciousness of the train that used to run through this place. Sometimes at night he could hear it coming for ten minutes before and as many after it passed by in the darkness. He remembers going out with his cousin one cloudy, pitch dark night and standing only a few feet from the tracks as the freight blew past. The wind generated by the train's force almost knocked them over. And somehow it was a thrill beyond imagination.

She interrupts his reminiscence saying, "There's something else, too, Ashley. I've got a big personal problem. I may be pregnant." Tears accompany this announcement. She looks so pitiful that for a few minutes he doesn't even allow his own reaction to surface. He reaches his right hand across to grasp her left. And she squeezes, needing to feel a *lot* of security right now.

Relieved, she thinks, *I'm so glad I've finally told him. It's been so hard carrying that all by myself. He'll know what to do.*

Duke is jolted. His eyes are focused but the brain spins. Shock. He knows he needs a clear mind and time to work through things. Hesitating, giving himself that time. Eventually he says, "That's a scary thought. We'll need to take our time and think about this. Lots of options to consider. Why do you think you're pregnant? Are you late?"

"Yes. I'm about two weeks overdue; and you know me, you can set your watch by my period. My breasts have been tender and tingly, too." After a pause she adds, "What do you mean 'lots of options'?"

"Well, all I can think of right now is to get married and raise the child or have an abortion; but there are probably other things that I haven't thought of. I'm not too keen on the idea of putting a child up for adoption unless you have to; and we wouldn't *have* to do that. What have you thought about?"

She bolts upright. In his periphery he notices that her eyes are scalding across him. She holds her breath against the rage. When she speaks the anger boils out, "Well I certainly haven't thought about abortion. I can't even believe that you'd say it. That's absolutely out of the question. I had thought about marriage; but I didn't want to mention it first. At least you're thinking that way, too."

The incredulity at his mentioning abortion lingers in her. She thinks, *I can't believe this. How could a good Christian boy like him think such a thing? What's happening to him? He can't be serious about something like that. Neither of us would even know how to go about it anyway.*

For the first time in their relationship, she has doubts. Unable to restrain it any longer, she asks, "Ashley, you were just kidding about the abortion thing, right? I mean, you wouldn't really consider it, would you?"

He blows an exhalation—blowing his anger/fear/frustration/confusion away. A long silence follows before he attempts to answer. Finally he says, "Honestly, I just don't know. I'm not saying that's what I would want to do, but the thought occurred to me. Look, we aren't even sure that we have to make a decision about this yet, so I sure don't want to get into some long, hard argument about it. We'll deal with it when we know what's there to deal with. We're smart people and we can find a reasonable solution if we need to."

She's mollified. He's mortified. Anger and confusion burn in Ashley's mind right now.

They've reached the outskirts of town and turn right toward the bowling alley and then past it. Turning left again out toward the river, they reach her parents' home on the corner lot of this new sub-division. Trees border the little stream that cuts through. A small white bridge crosses the narrow waterway and provides access to the front door. It strikes him that he never uses the driveway to the garage, that maybe he sees himself as a guest.

The T'Bird rolls to a stop in the shady yard. He pops the trunk and retrieves her bag and books. They stroll to the house and enter. Her mother greets Ashley and sends Ellen to the laundry room to start her dirty clothes washing. No hugs. No kisses. Ashley declines an invitation to dinner, saying that he needs to be with his own parents tonight. He promises to return after supper, around seven-thirty. Kisses Ellen on the lips and her mother on her hand, jogs to the T'Bird and heads toward the other side of town.

Back on the four-lane now, he stops at a red light and glances to his right. He is, of course, in the fast lane. He sees Marcus's GTO and hears the revving of his engine—an invitation to race. The light cycles to green and they blast off the line toward the next traffic light 600 yards away. Marcus edges ever so slightly ahead until they both break off to approach the red light. Marcus shouts over the noise of his cammed-out, Pontiac, "Damn Ashley, what th' hell you got in that thing anyhow? Ain't no T'Bird supposed to keep up with this hoss."

"Isky cam with two four-barrels. If it was a straight stick, I think I could take you. But it ain't." Slipping easily back into the slang patterns of home. "So how've ya been?"

"Good. Ellen home this week?" Ashley nods an affirmative. "See ya at th' Stag after midnight then."

As the light releases them, they go separate ways. Ashley winds his way up near the foot of the mountain to his parents and the familiarity of home. He pulls into the big lot that used to be eight lots. The garden is yielding its last gifts of tomatoes and string beans, okra and peppers. The spent stalks from the corn crop stand at a burned out attention in straight lines.

He sees his mom through the window at the kitchen and knows that she's cooking his favorites: fried chicken, mashed potatoes, green peas, gravy, corn on the cob, rolls, salad. Suddenly he's aware of being very hungry. He carries his laundry bag to the back door and enters. Stopping at the washing machine, he throws in everything at once. His mom says from the next room, "I'll do that, son. Just leave it. Your dad's in the shower anyway."

To him there's nothing like the smell of his mother's kitchen. It represents all that's good and right in the world. There is a peace there that nowhere else can ever provide. She stands with her back to him, doing something in the sink. Pauline Byrd Windsor—Polly as a girl, but Pauline now. She turns her head and smiles a welcome, "It's about time you came home. We've missed you."

He takes the dish that she's washing from her and puts it on the counter. He spins her slowly around to hug her, and she mock fights him, "I'll get you all wet." But he doesn't care about the water, and really neither does she.

"So how's my very best girl?"

Holding her is like holding a bundle of twigs. She's just so tiny—mostly skin and bones, maybe a hundred pounds, maybe 5'4". But make no mistake; the small exterior masks a dynamo inside. From here comes his own energy level. The speed at which they live and do things is almost identical, as well as the tendency to be opinionated and even to act on things. They don't really agree on much; but the differences are unimportant and don't often get between them.

Her philosophy stands them both well: *You'll just have to believe it however you believe it and I'll believe it like I do.* It's such a simple way to avoid conflict; living out the obvious—We can't change other people's beliefs unless they are willing to be changed. But he only thinks he understands this.

As mealtime approaches, his father joins them, all clean and smelling good. They exchange greetings. Ashley senses the caring and the hesitancy in him. They've had some glorious arguments. Randall D. Windsor has very rigid limits. Inside those limits anything goes; but if you cross the line you could find yourself in a fistfight.

Ashley has seen this side of Randy a few times, has noted the calm calculation of what is too much to forgive, and then the decisive move to action when that limit is reached. The worst aspect of this was not the violence. Rather it was that the limits were understood by Randy, but not always made explicit. That left Ashley not always being able to predict what might happen, and therefore he could not completely trust. He had hoped that as his college education proceeded, his father would back off his need to be the final authority on everything. It hasn't happened yet though.

The single burning issue between them has for years been the separation of the culture by race, without regard for individuals. There are many other less volatile differences as well, including religion, music, and whether Ashley should go to Auburn rather than the University of Alabama. From his father comes the stubborn streak that will save him, if it doesn't kill him first.

An incident from Ashley's childhood marked the beginning of their conflict. The basketball goal for the neighborhood was in a flat spot in the family's back yard. It stands there still, forgotten and netless. But in those days there would be a game most evenings. On one sunny summer afternoon he and his friends were starting a game and had only five players. They were going through that harangue about which two could play evenly with the other three when a colored boy rode by on his bicycle. Without thinking even once about it, Ashley hailed him and asked if he wanted to play. An hour or so later when Randy arrived home from work and saw the game in progress, he called out that everyone had to go home, that Ashley had chores to do.

When the yard had cleared, Ashley felt the force of his father's wrath. "Ashley, what was that nigger boy doin' in my yard? You know better than that. What's he doin' here?"

"Well we were playing ball and didn't have enough to make even teams, so when he rode by, I just asked him to play with us. Why? What's wrong with that?"

Randy was trembling, not wanting to give over to the full vent of his anger. "Doggone it, son, you know you can't have niggers playin' around here with other white boys. I expect I'll be hearin' from some parents about this. White people just don't associate with them. Don't you ever let that happen again. You understand me, boy?"

Here a clear line was drawn. Ashley had seen this trembling before. He had been the object a few times when that trembling had signaled that Randall had lost all control and given over to rage. He had once been held up off the ground and struck with the razor strap until his mother had intervened to stop it. So he was wary at that moment, and knew the path out of harms way, "Yes sir."

Still trembling, Randy had stomped back into the house to the newspaper.

That old story has about played its last with them by now. Back then Randy had towered over his son, standing 5'10" and weighing 230. His size had prompted his friends to call him "Train". Now Ashley stands 6'2", though he weighs only 165. Fear no longer stands between them. It has taken a lot of adjusting to come to this conclusion: his father is a product of his time. Randy has never actually *known* a colored man other than to tell him what his job for the day at the plant would be. He still believes that the masks worn in the work place represent the true men.

What Randy believes might never change, but how he would act was going to be transformed. Ashley had tried to warn him. They drove together to Auburn that day in 1963 when George Wallace stood in the schoolhouse door and convinced a majority of Alabama whites that he would prevail if only they, the voters, would just keep putting him back into office. Ashley had warned him that "th Guvnah", as he was known throughout the state, didn't have the power to defy the president of the United States and the Supreme Court. He had tried to spare him the agony of being beaten down for the wrong reasons. Had suggested that the th' Guvnah was just putting on a show.

But the explosive Windsor temper had shouted him down. Th' Guvnah would, by God, show those Washington boys that they couldn't come down here and tell us how to run our own business. But before the drive was finished, the colored students had been taken around to the back entrance of the registrar's office and enrolled as students at the University of Alabama. Ashley felt no jubilation about this, but he was certainly less perturbed by it than Randy had been. In fact, that day marked the beginning of huge changes in Randall D. Windsor.

Ashley's ease with the moment was likely a factor of having less history with segregation than his father. He recalled that in one of their arguments, Randy had said that if things kept going the way they were that Ashley would have a hard time getting a good job because *they* would have all of them. Ashley laughed and responded that he was pretty sure that he could compete. This attitude frustrated Randy. How could his son not see the risk? On the other side Ashley wondered that his father could feel threatened by people whom he considered to be inferior to him. Just didn't make sense; but it was one of those issues that was way across the line, that they couldn't safely discuss.

*   *   *   *

As tonight's meal progresses, the conversation passes through family issues, college, and sports. Eventually, Randy asks, "So what do you hear about all the sit-ins and the voter registration stuff going on. Ya'll havin' any of that kind of trouble down at Auburn?"

Ashley dreads heading down this familiar road. He imagines that the two of them will end up shouting at each other, and is disgusted that he won't back down any more easily than his father. Looks up from his plate and says, "No. We're not having any trouble that I know of. How about here?"

"Not much. But they're sure raisin' sand over in Selma. I wish you could make me understand why they would want to go to our schools. Seems like they'd be more comfortable with their own kind than having to be rejected by the white kids. You know that the white kids won't have anything to do with them. It just doesn't make sense to me." At this he sits back in his chair and looks at his son.

Strangely enough Ashley feels no aura of taunting. He's tempted to think that maybe he really *does* want to understand. He figures that he is being set up, but decides to take the plunge. After all this is home. There is safety here. Says, "I might be able to *show* you, if you're really serious."

Randy astonishes him by saying, "OK."

So taking Randy's Crown Vic and with Ashley driving, they make their way to the two local white high schools. At Gadsden High a building project has recently been completed adding a new chemistry and physics wing, elegant architecture and grounds, lots of glass and brick in the new building. At Emma Samson High School the new building is a band and choral complex. Again, new brick and glass with landscaping make for a beautiful and prosperous-appearing sight. Ashley says, "Man, they're really putting some money into these places. Looks great, doesn't it?" Randy looks sidewise at his son, sort of already figuring out what's coming next.

At the foot of the mountain and back toward downtown lies the colored community, wrapped around the base of the hills like a dirty blanket. Rundown houses and littered streets mark the territory. Ramshackle old cars that look as if they haven't moved in years line the curbs. The residents of the area glance up to see them, then immediately look down or away, afraid to make eye contact, not knowing what these white men might want in their part of town.

There in the center of all this mess stands George Washington Carver High School. Grounds are littered with paper and empty bottles. While the brick appears substantial, the paint around the doors and windows is peeling. Some windowpanes are missing and the empty spaces are filled with wood or even paper taped in place. No new architecture here. No landscaping whatsoever. The whole place reeks of depression and failure.

Slowing down to circle the block where the school stands, Ashley says, "Well, dad, where would you rather I spent my days trying to get prepared for making my way in life?"

"My Lord, look at this place. They've torn it completely up. Son, they just don't take care of things." Randy's repulsion is very real, but his spontaneous rationalization is that somehow the neighbors are responsible for the condition of the school.

"Yeah. I figured that you'd say that. Just try to hear this without proving me wrong. The neighbors near Gadsden High and Emma Samson don't go there and clean up the place, paint it, or repair broken windows and such—the city school system does that. The white citizens don't pay all the taxes in this town, everybody does. But you can see that 'separate but equal' isn't playing out here. This ain't equal. This is garbage. I wouldn't want to go to class either, if this was what I had to put up with. And if you were told that I would *have* to go here, you'd be mad as hell and would try to do something about it just like King and his band of merry mischief-makers are doing. I know you and you'd be right out there with them. In fact you'd probably be worse."

A sober moment indeed. The father cannot repudiate the facts before his eyes, can no longer consider repudiating the son. A delicate time for Ashley, who at this moment is actually more Duke than Ashley. Fortunately, he says nothing and allows the visual truths to make the point. For once Randy Windsor offers no bluster. He sits, instead, in confused silence.

As they make their way back home, Randy eventually breaks the silence, saying, "I always knew that you would do this. I've watched you since you were just a kid, always pulling for *them*, backing the underdog. And I knew that sooner or later you'd have me out over it. I'll have to get this into some kind of perspective. It may take a while, but I see your point."

Ashley feels conciliatory and says, "Hold on, Dad. This isn't my point. I just saw it before you did. I'm not even sure what I'm supposed to do with it myself. This is a crazy time with controversial issues all over the place. Everybody's rights are being called into question here. How far is too far? How do you get what you need without tearing the whole social fabric? We've all got a lot to figure out and I'm afraid this stuff is just beginning." He pauses and considers, then says, "Thanks for going with me and for listening."

The energy between them feels completely different now. Neither would hazard a guess as to how long it might last, but for now they sense an equanimity that is totally new. They arrive at home to find Pauline on the front porch swing with the latest in her endless parade of books. She looks relieved that they're both alive and is surprised to see the amiability between them. Joining them at the back door she announces, "There's pie and coffee if y'all are ready."

Since the family's habit is to eat at five o'clock, it's still only six-thirty. There's plenty of time afterwards to shower, shave, dress and be on his way to Ellen's house with a quarter hour to spare. One of these days maybe he'll get to tell his dad about the five deals that he made to get the T'Bird for less than $300 of his own money. But not today—gotta go. Waves to his dad. Kisses his mom, who tells him to invite Ellen for Sunday lunch. Then he's out the door to meet this perfect evening. Back across town, he times the lights on the four-lane and makes every one. He arrives at Ellen's house in time to say goodbye to her parents who are headed to a show in Birmingham, 70 miles away.

CHAPTER 10

▼

From the hallway Ellen beckons. She wears shorts and a bra and holds her shirt in her hand, completely unself-conscious. She kisses him with warmth and says that they can just stay home and watch TV if he wants to, but since she hasn't eaten they decide to go out for a burger and then come back to the house. She pulls on the sleeveless, checked shirt that still shows lots of tanned skin. In Duke's eyes she is stunning.

Heading into town he says, "You seem in better spirits. What happened?"

"I don't know. I've been doing this for days now, down one minute and up the next. I guess I just feel safe, now that I'm home. Daddy always makes me feel completely taken care of.

"I have to admit that I'm still kind of in shock about that whole abortion comment, though. It was really strange to hear that kind of thing from you. But you're right, we don't have to make that kind of decision until we know for sure that I'm pregnant."

All this is delivered in a calm self-assured voice. She's wearing a light blue scarf over her hair. Thinks it smart to have several different colored scarves in the T'Bird to match different sets of clothes. She feels a kind of kinship with this car. Lots of guys won't let their girls mess with their toys.

The tour around town is short. They don't see even one person from their high school group—everyone has left, gotten married and is home with their new family, or is working. Ellen decides that she's not hungry after all and they trek back to her house with Cokes and snacks. Once at the house they sit for a while on the swing in the back yard and allow the last bits of daylight to extinguish before their eyes, leaving a darkness that is nearly total.

There is no ambient light here in this hidden glen, created by her father for his own private moments. Flowering shrubs and ornamental evergreens create the seclusion. They talk about the possibility of Ellen's going to a doctor in Jacksonville and Ashley agrees to pay for it. She'll go not next week but the following week. Next week she has the last quizzes before finals also.

Now that there is at least a plan in place, they relax and talk about their days at school. She's taking nineteen hours and it's too heavy a load. She has term papers in three of the classes, and quizzes and final exams in four. Her look of exasperation tells him more than her words.

Ashley listens, shaking his head. When she's finally finished he says, "Damn, babe, that's more work than I'm having to do. I'm only taking three classes, but have my job, and I can study there—usually two or three hours each day. It's quiet and well-lighted and I can't go to sleep or be bothered by a roommate. So I stay current, even ahead most of the time. I can see why you're so stressed."

He has moved to the far side of the swing and pulled her feet into his lap. He removes her shoes and drops them on the ground nearby. He begins to massage her toes in a slow and gentle circular movement, tugging at each just enough to stretch—not enough to hurt. Then he squeezes and pulls the fleshy toe-pad between his thumb and forefinger.

He turns to face her, arranging his right leg up the back of the swing. Crossing his left foot across the seat, he pulls her feet further into his crotch, and works on the footpads. He massages slowly and gently, talking to her all along. He tells her that she needs to be organized and to forego at least some of her socializing ... conserve her time ... focus her mind and her energy ... not let other people decide how she'll spend her evenings ... pay attention and make herself relax. His voice is soothing, almost hypnotic.

His hands move further down her feet, crossing the arch with very little pressure to avoid causing cramps. He finds her heels and applies the same circular motion to them, and can feel the tension flowing out of her. Her lower back settles some and she presses one foot against his groin. He feels himself thickening and expanding at the touch of her foot. His fingers move up the back of each foot, along the Achilles tendons and further to her smooth and well-defined calves.

He has fallen silent and she whispers, "Ooh. That feels so good. I've never walked so much in my life. My legs get so tired. I need you there to do this every night."

Encouraged, he leans into his work and runs exploring hands along the outsides of her glorious, long legs. Slips a leg to each side and leans further toward her. Their lips find each other and cling in a soft kiss. This is the work of practiced lovemaking. They know and seek out the favored and most sensitive places. Pleasure is traded back and forth. In a voice gone lust-husky she murmurs, "Let's go inside."

But he convinces her to stay here in the outdoors. On these cushions from the swing. In this lush grass. Under these friendly, early evening stars. This daring decision heightens the desires that drive them. Naked in starshine. Coupled on terra firma. Simultaneous orgasms that they think may wobble the earth on its axis.

In the aftermath they snuggle and laugh. Time stops and barriers disappear. The layers of separation peel away one by one, leaving not even a residue between them. They have merged for the moment into their own mutual identity, still functioning as individuals, but also sharing a synergistic existence quite apart from their individual experiences. This is one of those life-moments that will go forward with each of them as part of their personal and shared lore. All too soon other physical needs bring them to move inside—to food and creature comforts.

Near midnight the phone lurches them alert from the semi-conscious stare that late-night TV has produced. She unwraps herself from his embrace and goes into the adjacent kitchen. She returns smiling. "Daddy says for you to go home now. They're staying in Birmingham and he wants for you to lock me in as you leave. I guess that he thinks if you stay all night we might do something that we're not supposed to do."

They share a laugh at this; but begin the lengthy task of his leaving. She will study during the day tomorrow, and he'll wash his car and visit with Daniel. On Sunday they'll have lunch with his parents before heading back out to school. He'll call her in the afternoon tomorrow and make plans for the evening.

Together they say, "Goodnight. I love you."

*   *   *   *

Riding through a sleepy southern town in the summer nighttime with the top down is an unparalleled joy. Slow, fast. No matter. It's the awe of being enveloped by the warm air. The streets are empty. Stores and shops wear their evening apparel. It's the feeling of being part of the world and yet apart from it, too. It's being surrounded by the soft, city lights of the evening—at once brilliant and subdued.

Riding with the top down calls self-confidence into question. If there's fear in your heart, you'll feel exposed, vulnerable, and uncomfortable. But if you are centered by self-assurance, this experience can become the epitome of freedom. You're floating, flying along on invisible wings. Somehow all the bumps disappear, and if you know the town, you know where to find the action.

The Stag—one of those late night places where single southern guys go after they take their dates home—sits on a midtown side street. Nondescript. It's a combination pool hall and gambling establishment. A huge blackboard covers virtually one entire wall. On this wall is painted the daily mural of the "sports book"—scores and "the line" from all the games being played in whatever sport is in season. Right now baseball season is running full blast, so all the Friday games appear, posted in chalk. Another section lists tomorrow's games, along with the probable starting pitchers. Shorty, the rack man for the pool hall section, constantly moves from table to table—racking balls for specific games, collecting money, joking, and making change. He's hustling … And so is Marcus.

Ashley enters the smoky room through the familiar, creaking, spring-loaded front door. It crashes closed behind him, as if the interior should be kept a secret from the outside world. As if no one in town knows what's really going on there. The windows are painted over in green.

Eight tables in three rows (three, two and three) define the large room—plenty of room for them and for players to move around comfortably. Each table has a light suspended above it. A cabinet-like affair stands between the two tables set in the center of the room. From here money is collected and paid out. One can buy betting slips or redeem them. A cash register sits in a built-in alcove of the cabinet. Slots for various types of transactions are cut into the bulk of it. Perched on the tall stool at the register is Pete, the owner and chief mover of this place.

A chair-height bench rings the entire room against the walls. Cigarette butts lay squashed flat on the floor. Arrayed along the walls, racks hold a phenomenal number and variety of cue sticks stored upright—"house sticks". Interspersed between the rows of cues are wooden stands holding cones of talc, used to dry the perspiration from the players's hands.

At this particular time only three of the tables are being used. Puddles of bright light frame those tables. About fifteen people sit or stand in the gloom of the fringes of the room. Cigarette smoke permeates the air. Prime time isn't for another hour or so. The "money game" occupies the customary table between the cash register and the blackboard. Center stage. Tonight the game is Nine Ball and Marcus is shooting against a man whom Ashley doesn't recognize. Ten dollars a game. A small crowd encircles the game, watching and occasionally commenting on a particularly good shot or bad break.

Marcus is winning. He notices Ashley and announces to the room, "The new dual four-barreled, Isky cammed-out T'Bird driver has arrived." Heads turn and he goes on to reveal that Ashley's new T'Bird almost outran his GTO earlier today and that everybody should avoid racing him. Laughter and good-natured teasing come from the Chevy men gathered around.

The McCormick brothers, Robert and Preston, motion him over to their corner and offer the Mason jar that's thinly disguised, sitting in a brown paper bag on the bench between them. Ashley buys a grape soda from Pete and drinks off a third and replaces the loss with white whiskey from the jar. The first taste sears his mouth and throat and burns its way to his stomach. He can feel it all the way down. Within minutes he is once again one of th' boys here in his hometown. He plays a few games, wins and loses and participates in the rituals of his culture of origin. A lot of off-color and racist joking passes around him and he notices that although he is accepted as part of this group, he no longer shares the bulk of their views and values. An odd kind of realization.

An older man sits alone near the money game. Tall and portly. When he speaks to Ashley, it takes a moment to recognize R. D. "Tommy" Thomas. The same Tommy Thomas who led the local high school football team to its last state championship, fourteen years ago. He's a little soft now, but still big. Pats the bench beside him for Ashley to join him. Asks how college is treating him. Reminds Ashley that he, too, had gone to Auburn—but to play football. Then he reminisces about the blown-out knee and the loss of his scholarship. No anger, just nostalgia.

The desegregation issue comes up and Ashley reminds him that there was no problem at Auburn. Tommy then surprises with his statement that Wallace's stance at the University of Alabama was a ridiculous sham. "I don't know why I'm saying this to you, Ashley. I sure wouldn't say it to anybody else in this room right now, 'cept maybe ole Pete over there. You know what he said to me two or three years ago when all those lunch counter sit-ins were happening? He said as long as the fella' next to him didn't try to get in his plate with him, he didn't give a damn what color he was. I thought that was great. I guess he made me think about things like that in a different way for the first time. I heard Marcus say that you're driving a new T'Bird. Is it outside?"

"Yeah; but it's a '58, not a new one. I don't think I'd want a new one. Wanna go take a look?" So they go out into the humid early morning. The T'Bird sits at the curb like a big cat waiting to leap at its prey. Tommy is properly impressed and Ashley offers a ride. Tommy retrieves something from his car, a big Packard Clipper, and climbs in beside Ashley. Says that there's a real sight to be seen out

"Th' Drive", if he's interested. So Ashley heads out of town on Rainbow Drive toward the southwest.

Tommy holds up a thin cigarette and asks, "You care if I smoke this?" Ashley's surprise is total. He's known people in this town all of his life and has never heard anyone make even a reference to marijuana, and now suddenly a joint appears before him. So he says sure and Tommy fires it up. Inhales. Passes it to Ashley, who stops after the second pass. Won't let himself get out of control in this car. The radio plays a Birmingham all-night station. Quiet, soulful R&B accompanies the ride for several miles. Eventually Ashley remembers and asks, "So what's this 'sight' you were talking about?"

"You know they're building that new dam on th' Coosa River out close to Ragland. Well they're clearing land out there now and—hey, I don't want to spoil it for you. We're two minutes away. Just trust me on this one. I was out here late last night coming home from a job in Birmingham. I promise, it'll be worth the time.

After a pause Tommy continues, "You seemed kinda uncomfortable back at th' Stag. It's hard to be gone for a while and then to come back and feel like you belong, huh?" Tommy flicks the remnants of the joint into the night.

Ashley searches through his recollection of the past hour and says, "At first I felt just fine. After a while, though, I could see that most of those guys are the same now as they were when I left here four years ago. I think I've changed a good bit and I'm changing more all the time. I guess I look the same to them; but they have no idea who I *am* at this point. Feels kinda weird. What made you notice?"

In a sincere voice Tommy answers, "I don't really know. Maybe because I went to Auburn too. When I came back here I was surprised that the same things were still happening that were happening when I went off. It was like I didn't have anything in common with these people any more. Still feels that way to me. Maybe I figured that Auburn would do that to you too. Hold on. Slow down and take that next left."

Left onto this dirt road. Ruts and rocks. Ashley slows to a crawl to avoid throwing loose stones against his paint. An open field gives way to a copse of hardwoods. Up this hill, through the trees, and at the crest the T'Bird glides soundlessly to a halt. Ashley is breathless. As far as he can see there are fires and embers of spent fires. The land has been clear-cut and the unusable wood piled at intervals. Some of the piles are hundreds of feet long and much higher that his head. A light wind carries the smoke away from them and the scene is like something from Dante. Stunning. Powerful in its otherworldly beauty. Volcanic reds and oranges overlay the black earth and glow against the sky.

Ashley reaches over and shuts off the radio. Doesn't want anything to interfere with experiencing this unusual sight. Cuts the engine and the lights. Steps out of the car and sits hipshot against the front of the T'Bird. "You know, Tommy, at first I was moved to say that we've discovered Hell; but the longer I stand here the more this feels like some kind of omen to me. This whole race thing is just about to explode in totally new and more dangerous directions. Things are about to get hot. That's gonna be the next conflagration. And I sure as hell hope that I don't get my little ass singed in the process. They're doing voter registration in Macon County and that strikes pretty close to home."

Tommy considers for a moment and says, "You're right. The blood's already flowing over it. They killed that colored guy over in Mississippi and another yesterday in Selma. You'd best stay away from all that shit or you might get more than singed. You know, your boy Marcus back there is the loudest Klan man around these parts nowadays."

Ashley is shocked. "You're kidding." Tommy shakes his head. "He's my age fer Chrissakes. What the hell is he doing? Coloreds are no threat to him ... What are they all so scared of? This stuff really pisses me off."

Reaching to the inside pocket of his sports coat, Tommy produces a flat flask. Raises it in Ashley's direction. "Robershaw's white—still the best hooch in the county. I know what you mean. It gets to me too. Just be careful who you talk to about how you feel. It could get you hurt."

Tommy takes a pull from the flask and passes it to Ashley with the warning to take it easy. Good advice as it turns out. Ashley coughing and spluttering. Fire inside matching the fires outside. And with a laugh, praises the Lord for allowing the invention of good moonshine whiskey.

*   *   *   *

Sunday afternoon and Pauline's pot roast is settling nicely underneath the last gasps of the coconut meringue pie. Stacks of the remnants of the weekend's big meals are wrapped and packed for Ashley to take back with him. There's sadness in her hug as she lets go her only son once again. But she's resigned that it's in his best interest to go and grow. Even if it puts him beyond hers and Randy's reach and influence.

She also hugs Ellen and secretly hopes that they will stay together. She loves and admires this beautiful young woman. Knows that she isn't close to her own mother, and enjoys being able to teach her how to do things. She stands with Randy as Ashley turns the T'Bird around in the yard and with a wave drives out of her life once more. She doesn't cry, but tears well up. In his rearview mirror Ashley sees the two of them standing arm in arm waving him away. Their gestures this weekend have touched him.

Crossing the Coosa on their way out of town, he remarks that soon the dam project will begin in earnest, and wonders what changes it will bring to the landscape. Ellen mentions that her father has been extremely involved in the project. She goes on to explain that the surveying was contracted out to his company and that he is planning a resort along the northern edge of the lake.

They retrace their journey from two days previous. The radio hums along. Ashley has given her the fifty dollars that his mom pressed into his hand this morning before she went to church. So the doctor's visit is paid for. Each is somewhat preoccupied with upcoming tests and having to part again. Silence reigns, laced with dread, as they get closer to the turn back to Jax State. Suddenly, Ashley jerks forward. "Listen." Turns up the volume on the radio to hear:

"To repeat, two students from Auburn University and several members of the congregation of the Mount Zion AME Church were severely beaten in a confrontation at the church in Tuskegee, Alabama this afternoon. The confrontation occurred when three carloads of whites arrived at the grounds of the colored church and demanded that the voter registration efforts taking place be stopped.

"When no moves were made to comply, the men retrieved ax handles and other weapons from the trunks of their cars and began beating people and dispersing the small crowd gathered there. The names of the Auburn students have not been released as yet. They were taken to a hospital in Lee County where they remain. Church members were being treated at the Infirmary on the campus of Tuskegee Institute. There is no information on the identity of the attackers. We will bring you more information on these events as it becomes available."

Ashley/Duke's face drains of color and his fists pound the steering wheel.. "Oh my God, Elle. Those are my friends. Dammit. I can't believe those bastards went there in broad daylight. I know that those coloreds didn't even put up a fight. They're nonviolent. Oh man, I wonder who all is hurt and how bad it is." He trembles. Rage wells up in him.

He pulls the T'Bird to the side of the road and sits staring at the radio as if he can somehow understand more or be transported to the scene by staring at it. Ellen interrupts his anxiety saying, "Ashley, how do you know so much about this stuff? How do you know that those were people that you know? You need to tell me about this."

In a voice tempered with worry he says, "I know because I've been working in that church with those people. I'd have been there today probably if I hadn't come home. Damn. I could have helped. Most of those people don't have any idea of how to protect themselves. Others think that protecting themselves violates their principles. And they weren't doing anything wrong. Elle, this is terrible. Look we need to get on to Jacksonville so I can get down there."

Horrified she blurts out, "No you won't. You're not going down there into that mess, Ashley. Why in the world would you be doing voter registration with the nigras anyway? That's none of your business and it's against the law anyway. I won't have you being involved in that. I just won't. What if I *am* pregnant and you get killed or something trying to help a bunch of ignorant nigras do something that they don't even know how to do. Then what would I be supposed to do? No, Ashley. You need to stay away from all that."

Fire jumps to his eyes. "What on earth are you talking about? Would you have me sit around and do nothing while my friends are being beaten?"

With an equal amount of anger she replies, "It serves them right. They have no business being there in the first place. There's enough trouble with the nigras without a bunch of white agitators coming in there and stirring things up worse." There is no tenderness between them now. Lines are drawn in the sand. The limits asserted, their differences loom like a cold war gone hot.

She adds with conviction, "If you go back down there and into that, I'm gonna really be mad. It's not your fight and you're on the wrong side anyway. My daddy would die if he knew that you'd been registering them to vote. Ashley, what's happened to you? You used to be so sensible."

Trying to calm himself he explains, "Look, Elle, there're a couple of things that you need to pay attention to. First, these are human beings and Americans that we're talking about. As such they have exactly the same rights that you do or I do or anybody else does. I don't know how you can go to church with your daddy and then come out saying that *they* aren't deserving of the few things that they're asking for. And, secondly, and hear me on this one, it's *gonna* happen whether the white community likes it or not. Read the Constitution, Elle. It doesn't say that only white people are entitled to the vote and equal protection before the law. It's right and it's *gonna* happen. Not only that but there's a lot more coming until everybody has an equal opportunity to live a good life."

Ellen stares and thinks … *What has happened to him? The man I love has suddenly become "the enemy". He's still the same person, only with totally different ideas. How could this be happening? I've known him almost forever. He's the sweetest and kindest man I know. How could he just turn on his own kind? It doesn't make sense.*

What am I supposed to do now? If I'm pregnant, how can I trust him? Oh, I think I'm gonna be sick. Her world is upside down. Her future, which had seemed so clear hours ago, is, at this moment, a blank.

Ashley again finds the cold streak in himself. His vision turns to a focused stare. Thoughts are running hot and threaten to steam. But he's found that place again and knows that he won't let things boil over. Now is a time for quiet, calm reasoning. He thinks … *Maybe if she just has a little time to think about all this, she'll see it and understand it. I didn't get it myself until a few weeks ago. Maybe we can find a common ground here somewhere. Or maybe we can't. I may not be able to fix things right now, but I could sure break them beyond repair if I just explode on her. She's gotta be scared to death. This is terrible timing. If she's pregnant, thing's are gonna get really ugly. God, I feel sorry for her. But at the same time, I can't be somebody I'm not just to please her. She'll have to love the real me or not.*

After he eases back onto the highway, he spots the sign for Crystal Springs and turns left to go to Jax State. They've been silent since their outbursts after the radio broadcast. The music has continued to play softly in the roar of the surrounding wind. Both are feeling miserable. As the campus looms in the windshield, he feels compelled to say, "Look, babe, we'll work this out. We have to take it one step at a time. But we're gonna be OK. Let's get through the next two weeks and then we'll figure out what needs to be looked at and what doesn't. Alright?"

Her reaction is less than accepting. She is hurt and scared and angry. In fact, at first she doesn't respond at all. Her silence is intended to be inflammatory, but he outlasts her. Waits. And waits. Finally, she says, "I can't believe that you are so selfish. All you can think about right now is this stupid *cause* that you're in love with. What about *me*? What about *us*? All I know right now is that I'm confused and mad. Just take me on to the dorm. I'll figure out what I really want later."

She won't even look at him. Knows that if she does, she'll just cave in and do whatever he says, and this is too important not to think about for herself.

For different reasons and from different directions their thoughts coalesce. On his side of the car Ashley thinks that she needs to think things through for herself for a change. This thought is somehow liberating. He's freeing himself from the bondage of another southern male fantasy—that somehow men are supposed to think for their women. He doesn't want to have to *convince* her of anything. He doesn't want her to be with him if she doesn't want it for herself. It isn't enough for him to want it. *She* must want it also or it's empty. He's not even sure how much *he* wants it now.

One level of stress in his stomach releases, when she goes into her dorm. Another flares brightly as he turns his thought to his friends.

*   *   *   *

Back on the highway and into the mountains. Slamming through the curves and blasting down straight-aways. Speed creeps up and up until he's approaching 100 mph and notices for the first time that he's stretching the T'Bird out. He slows a little for a few minutes. But as his mind fastens again on reaching his friends, whichever ones are injured, the red-glowing needle that's measuring his speed once again creeps toward triple digits.

He sees nothing but the 1,000 yards of roadbed that lie immediately ahead. Concentration is total now. No thoughts at all about Ellen and that impending tragedy. *Not now, dammit.* The need to reach his friends supersedes all else. Imagines broken bones and bruises, tubes and masks. Dreads seeing them but knows he must. Can't see that his fear involves how he might have to react. A slow boiling rage grips his abdomen. Two words whisper over and over in his mind—"Get there."

The miles and the minutes temper his emotions a little. Slowly he finds the resolve building in him that he will indeed accept Mohammed's mission. As he approaches the intersection where 431 meets the Auburn-Opelika Road, tension has brought a vague ache to his neck and shoulders. Then, he turns left for the short run down the block to the hospital entrance. He sees a parking space in the first row, right out front. Across the macadam parking lot and into the emergency entrance. A crowd milling in the small lobby surprises and annoys him. He needs to get to one of the nurses.

He notices a young woman in scrubs and with her mask dangling. She stands in a hallway in front of closed doors. He approaches and smiles, asking if she's working the ER. She says that she is. He asks if his cousin, Pax O'Reilly, has been brought in. "My name is Duke Windsor and I'm the only family in this part of the country. If he's here somebody needs to know. There are things that will need to be done." She waves him in through the doors and follows.

Inside she says, "Do you know what happened to him?" Searches his face with eyes that are filled with apprehension.

"No. Not really. I assume that he was beaten up pretty badly; but I don't actually know to what extent. Why?"

They're standing just inside those closed doors. She leans back against them and deflates before his eyes. "I guess that's what happened. Apparently he was working with that bunch of coloreds in Tuskegee and a group of white men came in on them and beat up a lot of them. He's in bad shape, Mr. Windsor. There is a punctured lung that collapsed and a lot of internal bleeding. He's got cuts and bruises, cracked ribs and a broken left arm, too; but it's the bleeding that is life threatening.

"The doctors have repaired the lung and are running continuous tests to try to isolate the bleeding. Nothing so far on that. The arm is set and cast. The cuts are stitched and he has received two units of whole blood. He's in ICU now. If you want, I'll take you up there. I'll warn you right now; there are reporters up in the waiting room and they're asking questions of everybody. And, Mr. Windsor, he looks real bad. Just be prepared."

Up the elevator to the third floor, then out again into a hallway. Three men approach as the nurse takes his arm and hustles him through more closed doors and toward the nurse's station. The men are shouting, "Nurse. Excuse me, ma'am. Can you tell us.… ."

She takes Duke to an area behind the station desk and tells the charge nurse that he is a family member of Mr. O'Reilly. The floor nurse advises that Pax is probably asleep, but that she will take him in to look if he wants. As he turns to thank the ER nurse, he sees that she is back in the hallway now fending off the reporters.

Pax lies in the first of these glass-walled rooms. His face is swollen and battered. Stitched cuts on his face are unbandaged. His head is shaved on one side to accommodate repairs to a sizable cut. Dried blood appears in several places on his face, head, and arms. His left arm, swathed in a fresh cast lies outside the blanket. The right arm sports an IV, feeding a clear liquid into him. Bruises are already turning blue on both shoulders and upper arms. Another, larger tube extends out the side of the bed, undoubtedly a catheter. Traces of blood appear in the yellow liquid. A monitor array sits at the head of the bed with gauges and graphs. Electrical wires attach this, too, to Pax. Duke shivers in the cold. He stares at Pax, pale and unconscious. He touches his right arm above the IV site and finds his skin very cold to the touch. Rage and revulsion well up as he stands looking at his friend.

In a daze Duke turns to leave and finds the floor nurse standing close by. An older woman, she looks on wistfully. Graying hair, cut short. She is dressed to exacting standards. Neat and trim. Glasses hang on a silver chain around her neck. Her nametag reads: L. Whitmore. She asks, "Are you all right, son?" And he just manages to shake his head. She asks if he would like a cup of coffee. He nods in a daze. They return to her desk and she pours him a small cup of very black coffee. She asks, "Have you notified the rest of the family?"

That's enough to snap him out of his stupor. He tells her that he'll need to get Pax's keys so that he can get to his address book to call everybody who ought to know. As she's retrieving Pax's personal belongings from an envelope under the desk, Duke asks, "Miz Whitmore, is he gonna be okay? What should I tell Uncle Jimmy or his momma?" Saying this he realizes that he has never heard Pax speak of his mother and wonders about that. He's glad that he remembered to ask the question, but is afraid of the answer.

Lena Whitmore leans forward and touches his arm gently with her hand and says, "Officially, I'm supposed to say that we can't tell yet. And, of course, we can't really tell yet; but unofficially, after fifteen years of experience with these things, I think that he's going to make it. He's got some hard days ahead of him, but I think that he'll do fine. He's young and seems to be in good health." She hands Duke the envelope and he takes out the keys. Spontaneously, he reaches out and hugs her and says thanks for her help. He promises to return in the morning.

Duke scurries down the back stairs. Feeling better now that he has some assurance that Pax is going to survive. Also, now he has a mission and something to accomplish. Congratulates himself at thinking to take the stairs to get outside, thereby avoiding the reporters. Back into the early evening now, he takes a focused path toward the T'Bird. Hears, "Sir, excuse me. Can I talk to you for a minute? Hey, wait up. Look, I saw you go into the ICU earlier and I'm wondering if you can tell me how that young man is that got beat up."

Duke turns to see a short, thin, redheaded man whom he had seen earlier in the hallway on the third floor. The man looks to be about thirty or so and is carrying a small notebook and a pencil. Duke waves him away and says, "I got nothing to say, man."

Of course the little man persists. Asking question after question. Duke's walking faster and faster toward the T'Bird but before he can reach the safety of his car the reporter reaches out and grabs him by the sleeve. Duke spinning around and momentarily losing control of all the emotion that has been cruising around in his system for days now. Grabs the man's shirtfront with his left hand and slaps him hard, pulls him close in to his face, "Did you hear what I said?" No response. Panic in his eyes. Duke pushes him back a little and asks again. "Did you hear what I said?"

The redhead finds a quavering voice. "Y-yes. Say, take it easy. I'm just trying to find out what's going on, for the paper."

"Look, I've got nothing to say about any of that. Don't ever grab me like that again. You oughtta know better than to pull something like that anyhow. Now move out of my way. I've got things to do." Opens the door to the T'Bird and gets in. Fires the engine and backs out of the parking space.

The little redhead is persistent if nothing else. "Can I at least get your name?"

Peeling rubber out the driveway, Duke sees him writing something in his pad and realizes that it's his license plate number. Curses under his breath and thinks that maybe he should have hit him in the stomach instead of slapping him. Too late now. He may be foiled in his new part in the Tuskegee scheme before he even gets started. Can't worry about that now though. He needs to notify Pax's family and figure out what to do about his car.

CHAPTER 11

▼

Speeding along the four-lane, Duke realizes that he's trying to run away from pursuit that isn't pursuing. He has been fixed on the destination and focused so that nothing else interfered. But now he slows down. As he turns into the parking area at the Cabanas, it occurs to him that there were *two* Auburn students hurt in Tuskegee. In his relief at finding Pax, he completely forgot the other student. He'll call Miz Whitmore later and find out if he needs to do something for some-one else.

Up these stairs to fumble with the keys and become frustrated at not being able to get any of them to work. Stops. Slows down. Looks at the tangle of eight keys and wonders, *Why eight?* Separates out the obvious car keys—four of them. Then begins a systematic attempt with the other four. The second opens the front door and he enters. All is quiet. A little spooky to be in here knowing that Pax lies unconscious in the hospital.

Checking out the books on the kitchen counter near the phone, he finds a small, brown, leather-bound volume that is the right size and shape for an address book. Opens it and pauses to try and figure out what name to look for. Turns to O'Reilly and dials the number next to the entry for "Dad". Eight rings and no answer. He's feeling frustrated and anxious now. Calls the number listed for "Uncle Jimmy" and a deep bass voice answers at the second ring. Relieved, Duke asks, "Is this Mr. Jimmy O'Reilly?"

"Yes. Who's calling please?" Very smooth voice. Soothing.

Duke forces himself to speak slowly and logically: "Mr. O'Reilly, my name is Duke Windsor and I'm a friend of your nephew Pax. Has anyone been in touch with you or any of the family about him today?"

A pause on the line indicates that the man on the other end is assessing the situation. "No. Is something wrong? Is Pax OK?"

"Well, sir, he's gonna be—at least I think he is; but there's been a … uh … an incident down here and he's hurt pretty bad. He's in the hospital at Lee County." Duke searches his limited experience bank for the right words to convey bad news and finds that the file on this is empty.

His pause, however, allows Mr. O'Reilly the time to assume the initiative. "Duke, Pax has mentioned your name to me. Listen, now. I want you to get me the number of the hospital. While your looking through the book, tell me what happened."

Duke reaches for the local phone book and says, "I'm not exactly sure what happened, Mr. O'Reilly. I know that he was with some other students in Tuskegee at the AME church. They were helping with voter registration. Apparently a group of whites came in on them and beat up a bunch of people in an effort to stop what was being done, and Pax was one of them. I was out of town and just heard about it on the radio. So when I got back here, I went to the hospital and told them that I am his cousin so they would let me in to see him. Wait, here's the number: 555-3323. Before you hang up, let me tell you that he's not awake right now. He's in ICU on the third floor. The charge nurse is named Miz Whitmore. And, Mr. O'Reilly, he's beat up pretty bad."

"When you say 'pretty bad', what do you mean? Do you know the extent of his injuries?" A hint of anxiety in his voice now.

Duke isn't equipped to say these things in a diplomatic way, so he just shoots from the hip, "I just know what the ER nurse told me. She said that there was a punctured and collapsed lung, cracked ribs, a broken arm, cuts and bruises and internal bleeding. I saw him and he's all hooked up to monitors and IVs; but the charge nurse, Miz Whitmore, said that unofficially she thinks he'll get through it. I tried to call his father, but there was no answer. Will you call him?"

Uncle Jimmy's voice is like honey now. "Yes, I'll take care of that. Don't worry about it any more. You've done well, son. I appreciate your calling. Let me check the nurse's name and the hospital number."

They get the details firmly established and Uncle Jimmy says, "You be careful, Duke. We'll be down there as soon as possible."

Duke calls the hospital next and asks for ICU. Miz Whitmore answers and he asks if she knows anything about another student who might have come in at the same time as Pax. She gives him the name of the ER nurse and connects him to that extension.

"ER. This is Angel." Voice like an angel. Duke remembers the petite blonde who ran interference for him with the press and got him in to see Pax so quickly.

He is properly grateful and turns on the Windsor charm full force. "Hi, Angel. I didn't know your name until Miz Whitmore told me just a few minutes ago. This is Duke Windsor. You helped me get up to my cousin a little while ago. You were certainly *my* angel. I'm very appreciative."

"Oh yes, I remember. You're certainly welcome. I just wanted you to be able to get in there without having to be pestered by those horrible people. How was he when you saw him?"

"Well, to tell the truth, he's not so good; but I think that he has a good chance of making it. You know, I got so concerned about him and getting in touch with the rest of the family that I forgot to ask you about the other student that came in with him. Can you tell me who it was?"

Her delay tells him that she's weighing out the confidentiality issues. Finally she says, "All I can really tell you is that he was treated and released. He had bruises and one rather large cut that was sutured and bandaged. That's all I know. My team didn't work on him. We were much too busy with your cousin. I think his name might have been Jacob, but I can't tell you that."

Duke is relieved. "Great. I know him, too, and that sets my mind at ease. I'm glad he's OK. I'll check on him later. Again, I want you to know that I really appreciate your help today. I'd like to buy you a cup of coffee sometime."

He can almost feel the glow of her smile across the phone lines. "How could anyone *not* want to have coffee with the Duke of Windsor?"

Even from two miles away he blushes, not certain if she's teasing or being sarcastic. "I'll be coming over to see Pax some during the next few days; can I come down and see you?"

No hesitation, "Why don't you call me from the nurse's station?"

"Great. I'll do that. Thanks again and I'll see you soon."

Looking further into the address book, he stops at "M" and finds Dr. Mohammed's number in Tuskegee. Dials and waits for an answer. After five rings he hears Mohammed's resonant voice and just the sound of it spreads a smile across his face.

He asks who was hurt besides Pax and Jay, and Mohammed says that five colored men had minor injuries as they stood between the attackers and the women until they were safe. A few cuts. Lots of bruises. Much in the way of injured pride. But Pax had by far been singled out as a white person helping in the colored cause. Duke explains the extent of Pax's injuries and that the nurse seemed to think that he would make it. There is relief in his voice as Mohammed also warns Duke to be careful.

"Doc, I've decided that I want to help out in the way that we discussed last Wednesday. I'm not sure how good I'll be at this, but I'll try my best. I've also been wondering about Pax's car. Is it still over there and should I try to do something about it?"

In measured tones Mohammed says, "Yes, the car is still here, but you don't need to come over here and be seen around the car or the church or me or anybody else. You're gonna have to start thinking in a completely different way, Duke. You can't afford to slip up and be associated with us. Understand?"

His words are not condescending. He clearly has Duke's best interests in mind with this. Nonetheless the ideas sting and are hard to digest. Not being associated with the others seems to Duke to be taking a cowardly approach. He knows better, but can't help the feelings.

Sensing his reluctance, Mohammed adds, "You know, Duke, if they find out that you're playing both sides, you'll get much worse that Pax did. You got to be real careful, son. Talk to Judd if you hear anything. You'll be in my prayers. I've told others that you are having to work full time and can't be with us any more, but that your heart is still good. Everybody understands. Just don't take unnecessary risks."

Looking again in the phone book, Duke finds and calls the number for the AEPi fraternity house. After a few minutes, Ron Bauman is found. Duke asks about Jacob and is told that his physical wounds are superficial, but that he refuses to return to Tuskegee. Duke sees this as a moral victory for the other side. He then asks Ron if he can figure out some way to get Pax's car back from Tuskegee. He suggests that he call Mohammed, and gives him the number.

His next call is to Lynn at her parents' home in Tuskegee. She answers the phone on the second ring and excitedly tells him about the accessories for her car that she received unexpectedly as more birthday gifts yesterday. "I'm so glad that you called. Are you back in Auburn?" And when he says that he is, she immediately decides to return. She'll leave for his place in an hour or so. "G'bye. I love you." Excited and anticipating.

Duke sits in a trance. He had a sense of dread and impending danger as he stood looking at Pax. Somehow Mohammed's words underscore the degree of the anxiety. Wonders how well he'll handle a real violent confrontation. Doubts he will be able to stand still for a beating. That leads him to ponder whether his beliefs and those of the people he's involved with are truly congruent. Decides, *Clearly not, but close enough.*

Leaving the apartment he is somehow exhausted. Thinks, *Maybe I should go by Judd's and see that they're O.K. I feel like I could sleep for a week.*

Points the T'Bird in that general direction and like a sleepwalker finds the garage apartment where Judd and Elizabeth live. Up these stairs again. Music seeping through the screen door. Something classical for a change. Knocks and opens the door. Judd sits at the couch, poring over a book. Elizabeth is on the bed with papers arrayed around her like a geisha surrounded by her fans. "Hey guys. Is everybody here okay?"

They each look up at him puzzled. "Did y'all go to Tuskegee today?" They shake their heads in unison negatively. "Lucky you. I guess that you heard what happened."

Blank stares. So he gives them a rundown of the events, as he understands them. Both become animated and want to do something, but, of course, there's nothing to do now. Just wait. He also explains the dilemma about Pax's car and that he called Ron Bauman about it. Judd says that he'll get up with Ron tomorrow after his exam and see if he can help with that. Duke reminds him that he can't tell Ron why he (Duke) can't help.

Satisfied that everything that can be done has been done, Duke takes his leave and goes home. On his door is a note from Claire that she wants to talk to him, and would he please call her or look her up tomorrow. He is glad that he got here before Lynn arrived. Strips to his shorts. Writes a note to Lynn: "Come on in and wake me up." Then with a sigh he gratefully falls onto his bed and is asleep before he's completely stretched out.

Coming out of this deep sleep, Duke sees that it's dark now. Some flickering luminescence from the kitchen. *What th' hell could that be? What's that rustling noise? Ah her shadow. She does that slow striptease, not knowing that I'm awake and watching. Her lack of awareness makes it even more erotic. Not that she needs any help. Man, the slope of her belly in this half-light—ripples and smoothness. Her breasts are perfect orbs as she leans forward. Peach-colored pears. My mouth is watering. But I'll wait and let her finish whatever it is that she's got planned. More parts of me are aware of her than my eyes and brain. What a great way to wake up.*

Her long dark hair spills down obscuring her face for an instant. Then he can see that she brought a candle and that's why the light is so soft and golden. As she turns he closes his eyes and hopes she doesn't notice that he was watching. Feels her moving toward him on tiptoe. Her hair touching his face an instant before her lips touch him. She smiles mid-kiss, and he feels her joy. Slides the covering sheet off him and her body slips against his. Kisses growing in magnitude and intensity.

Crawling over me and guiding me inside her with fingers that are just cold enough to notice. Shiver and surge. Leaning back with slow and languid movements of her hips and lower body. Slip sliding. God she's wet. And incredibly beautiful right now. My hands on her shoulders push her gently into a sitting position. Maximum penetration now and I can see the glory that is her lush body. Dark, insistent nipples. Intense pleasure distorting her face as she gives way to physical need.

She moves only slightly backwards, but changes completely the angle and coefficient of friction. He strokes her sides, gradually tracing the curves to her breasts, and feels her pace increase. Her breathing ragged now.

If she goes off, I'll be carried along like so much dust before the wind. We're teetering at the precipice. Falling through these clouds of cotton. Riding the wind. Orgasm rolling across us and transporting us beyond the bed, the street, the city, the earth. Where is this place that we all visit?

As she collapses again to his chest he turns her to the side and rolls on top. Their sweat serves as reminder that they're still connected. Her legs fall further apart and he sinks down into her. Just stops. Raises his head and shoulders, weight on his elbows. Looks into her face as she returns to the bed from whatever far off place that she had visited in the grip of rapture.

She opens her eyes and says, "Surprise."

His affection is total. With a shared look of happiness he replies, "Gee and I thought it was *your* birthday. I love it when I get the presents for someone else's birthday."

Her reply is ingenuous, "Oh no, Duke. That was my present to *myself.*" As he presses down deeper into her he feels himself becoming aroused again and whispers, "Well, here's *my* present to *you.*"

Afterwards they share a shower and go to dinner. Opting for *Prather's* out on the Auburn-Opelika Highway, they settle into a booth and order. After his coffee and ice water and her sweetened iced tea come, they wait for their meals to be served. He casually mentions, "Lots of excitement over your way this afternoon. Any idea what happened?"

"You mean with the nigras?" Pauses and after he nods affirmative, goes on, "Well daddy went over there and apparently a bunch of outsiders were over there stirring them up and talking them into registering to vote. A bunch of his friends got real mad about all that and tried to run the outsiders off and they must've started something. You know how those Yankees are. Probably smart-mouthing and such. And some of the men just got mad and started fighting with them. Some of the nigras got into it too and it got to be a mess. How'd you hear about it?"

"It was on the radio in Gadsden. Must've been right after it happened. They said that some Auburn students were hurt. You know anything about that?" No real inflection in his voice. Sounds like normal curiosity. Feels totally comfortable drawing the information from her. A sponge on a spill. And she spills.

"I don't really understand why those people come down here and stir things up like they're doing. The nigras haven't wanted to vote enough to pay the poll tax for all this time. I don't see why suddenly they're saying that they shouldn't *have* to pay it. Everybody else does. They should have to, too.

"Most of the men around town think that if they get the vote, they'll elect all nigras and the town will just be ruined. You know how they live. They don't take care of things, and they'll just let the town go to hell in a hand basket. But the people who've built the town up in the first place aren't gonna let that happen." Her face glows with the intensity of a zealot. She is certain that her perception, or rather the perception that she's been programmed to believe is her own, is irrefutably correct. There is no room for any alternative interpretation.

Squelching his reflexive wish to educate her, he says instead, "So you don't know about whether some of those involved were Auburn students?"

"Oh I think that I did hear that that guy from up north who started the Human Rights Forum was there, but I didn't hear whether he got in on the actual fight. I doubt it. They usually just stir things up and don't do anything really, don't they? Other than that I don't know of anybody. Why?"

"Well, I was just wondering. I play bridge with those guys from AEPi fraternity and a lot of them are from somewhere else. I wondered if I know any of the ones who were over there. Just strikes close to home is all." He leans back raising his elbows as their food arrives.

Angrily she snaps at him, "You just *think* it's close to home for you. My family stands to lose their whole way of life and to hear those TV people talk you'd think that *we're* doing something wrong. My daddy won't even listen to the TV news anymore. I don't know what it's gonna take to stop this, but I hope it happens soon."

Duke's thinking: *This is harder than I thought it would be. I thought that I was being pretty neutral and she's defensive, as if I had challenged her people's actions.*

Instead he says, "You're right. Lynn. I'm sure that it's a lot more real to you than to me. I didn't mean to make it seem unimportant by asking about those guys. Sorry. How *is* your dad dealing with all this? He must be scared or mad or both all the time." A little balm for that accidental wound. Let her talk more about herself and her family.

She doesn't need much encouragement. "Yeah, he's mad a lot; but he's sort of quiet most times. Momma says that she's scared that he might do something bad or stupid. I worry about both of them. After that stuff this afternoon, Momma said she's scared to go to town or the grocery store or anywhere. She's not sleeping much either. You know, Duke, if you stop and think about it, the whole town practically is colored. If it were to get really bad, whites wouldn't have a chance."

She's picking at her food and her face shows anxiety and concern. Duke isn't eating much either. He marvels that a mere few weeks ago he would have seen her reasoning and agreed with it. It's amazing that now that he has taken off the blinders and looked at the other side's point of view, her reasoning is completely *un*reasonable. She can't see that if the area is so prevalently colored that those people should have a voice in how affairs of the area are conducted. *How can she miss it? How did I miss it for all that time?*

Finishing the meal and getting a "to go" bag to take the leftovers, Duke pays with the little bit of cash that he has left in his pocket. They climb into the T'Bird and head back home. Outside the evening is like so many summer evenings in the Southland. Humidity brings the air up close to the skin. The sun's departure leaves a radiant warmth to the darkness. The moon and stars seem to have a haze around them—seem to be suspended in the liquid dome of sky. First-time visitors are uncomfortable in this environment, but natives luxuriate in the stability and security that they draw from it. And now, for most, that security is threatened.

Change looms like a tornado-watch and people are worried, not knowing what's on the other side. Perhaps there is an undertone of guilt-induced fear, fear of retribution for years, decades of mistreatment by their forefathers and, more recently, by themselves.

Duke understands that most white southerners are unaware of their racism. They perceive life and their surroundings as they were taught to see things. They rarely have an active *hate* for coloreds or anyone else. They simply think that they are living as things were meant to be. If it were supposed to be different, it would be, wouldn't it?

There's the problem. The change is coming, but it's not of their choosing, so they'll resist. And resisting to a southerner is a long-term kind of proposition. For many, the Civil War is still called the War of Northern Aggression. Some don't even acknowledge that that War was actually lost. Duke grins to himself to recall the words of an Alabama politician who stated, "… if Missouri is the 'Show Me State', then Alabama is the 'Make Me State'." This was half in jest, but only *half.*

Pulling into his place, Lynn has made it clear that she's afraid to come in because she has to study. If she goes inside, she would be tempted to stay; so instead she leaves in the Stingray. He decides to go to the library to study for his own quizzes. Rolls slowly across campus to find a parking spot almost next to the door.

Making his way to the stairwell inside, he is surprised to see Miz Lassiter seated behind the main desk. Wanders over in her direction. Says, "Hi. Didn't know that you were working evenings. How are ya?"

She looks up and graces him with another smile. That's two now. Lights him up from the inside. She says that her contract calls for her to work one weekend each month and to be responsible for the closing of the place at midnight for one week each month as well.

With a wave he says nonchalantly, "I'm gonna use a room in the music section, if one's open. Call me when it's time to shut down and I'll give you a hand." He spends the next three hours re-reading French literature and parts of the Spanish novel that will serve as the basis for that quiz.

At fifteen minutes before midnight he is interrupted by her soft and somewhat alien voice, "It's almost midnight, Duke. You don't have to do this, you know. I can handle it with the other students."

He grins and closes his two books and approaches her, as they prepare to extinguish the lights. "It's not a problem. I didn't work all weekend and you guys did, so I don't mind helping. What are we talking about here, fifteen minutes?" So they close it down together.

*   *   *   *

Meanwhile thirty miles away. Two pick-up trucks roll almost silently down the street toward the church where the afternoon's bloody confrontation took place. Six men clad in overalls quietly park the trucks, take out their tools, and set up their altar, their movements stealthy. The cross is simply two-by-six pine boards that have been nailed securely together. Burlap bags have been wrapped around the boards and tied into place with baling wire. As quietly as possible they dig a hole with post-hole diggers just deep enough to support the whole array for a few minutes. When the hole is deep enough, the rags are soaked with kerosene that soaks through the pine as well. Then they hoist the cross into a standing position beside the black car. They tamp earth in along the sides to hold it firmly upright.

Almost as an afterthought one of the workers splashes the remnants of his can of kerosene onto the car. Others seeing this, chuckle. Then the leader signals and they retreat to the trucks. From within they gather their ceremonial robes and dress themselves for the ritual. Each man's white robe fits exactly, having been worn many times in other rituals over the years. They don their conical white hats with the accompanying face shields. Then, attending to correctness, they approach the newly constructed altar.

The leader leads them in the secret words that are never repeated outside the brotherhood of the Klan. All feel a religious fervor in their participation. Their voices unite to praise the inviolability of their race. Spreading apart, they form a semicircle around the cross and the car. The leader pulls a torch from the truck bed and with a cigarette lighter drawn from his robe pocket, lights it. Another of the followers approaches and solemnly takes the torch from the leader and raises it high and faces each member of the assembled brothers.

With movements that are almost military he approaches the cross that towers some twelve feet into the dark nighttime sky. He rubs the torch onto the lowest of the bags and steps back as they catch fire. Flames creep up this secular cruciform. When he's certain that the fire in the altar will indeed self-sustain, he tosses the torch onto the hood of the black car sitting innocently nearby. With the remnant of kerosene it, too, begins that kind of slow burn that kerosene produces.

Flames now light up the semicircle and the men bow their heads until the leader proclaims, "We will preserve the sanctity and pre-eminence of the white race. We pledge ourselves to do all that is in our power to stop the unholy intrusion of the inferior masses into our places of honor. Let it be known that this brotherhood will destroy all efforts to establish the mongrel races as dominant in our society." His followers shout their agreement.

Across the way a porch light comes on and the men withdraw shotguns, which had been concealed under their robes. They fire into the air and the porch light extinguishes immediately. In their near-delirium they fail to understand that this cross at this church mocks the doctrines that their own churches proclaim to be *The Truth*.

No other lights show. No doors open. No people appear. The men linger there in their outlandish attire until the cross burns itself out, toppling across the hood of the Galaxie. The flames on the car have long since burned themselves out. There is some disappointment that the gas tank did not rupture. Nonetheless they retreat to their trucks and drive back out through the darkening streets. They have served notice. They have stood up for their race and their way of life.

The collective thought is: *Let the niggers beware.*

CHAPTER 12

▼

The clock radio does its job on Monday morning. The soft sounds of music and intermittent voices waft to the bedroom from the kitchen. Duke wakens slowly and not well. He feels disoriented and groggy and emotional. Realizes that he had been dreaming, but that the content has disappeared, leaving behind some vague uneasiness. His stomach churns as he turns off the radio and turns on the coffeepot. Then he hears the rain—not a downpour, but the steady sound of a soaking rain. He races to the front door, looks out at the T'Bird, and is grateful to see that he had put the top up last night after all. Then the event slowly reassembles itself in his mind and brings about his morning's true awakening.

*　　　*　　　*　　　*

He and Miz Lassiter ("call me Ann, please") made the rounds after everyone left the Berry. He checked the second and third floors, while she walked through the main floor and the basement. They meet at the front, set the alarms and lock the doors behind them. There's an intimacy in their leaving and locking a building that makes no sense to him, but that he feels. They make eye contact that is brief, but something resonates between them. Unspoken. Unbidden. Undefined. And unrushed.

Down the three sets of steps together, he doesn't see a car that would be hers. "Where are you parked?"—just assuming that she has a car there. When she explains that she will walk to her apartment, he is appalled. "Why doesn't your husband come to pick you up?" He realizes immediately that he has presumed too much. "Look, I'm sorry. That's none of my business. It just seems unusual to me that you'd have to walk home after midnight. I mean, it's safe and everything, but it's not something that I'm used to. Can I give you a ride?"

"It's OK, Duke. My husband and I aren't living together right now; but I'd appreciate it if you didn't mention it to anyone. Right now he and our daughter are in Kentucky with his parents. I'll be really glad when they get back—my daughter, at least. And I'd appreciate a ride very much. Is that your car there?"— pointing at the T'Bird sitting at the curb like an angel prepared for flight into some heavenly realm.

Duke beams. He's absolutely certain that this woman is completely out of his reach. The aura about her exudes knowledge and presence and class. That and a kindness in her demeanor stand out in his estimation of her. Competence, class and kindness—all that and classical beauty. Dark hair and sharp, well defined features. Maybe 5'2", Maybe 110 pounds. Dark complexioned, clear skin. Great legs. Ample chest. Fine boned. Hyper-alert, deep, brown eyes.

A very pretty woman who seems somehow mature beyond anywhere that Duke sees himself as having reached *and* she's married with a child. So Duke finds that he must simply *like* this woman. As a person. Maybe the very first attractive woman that he's ever known whom he has not objectified. At least not exclusively. Still, he *is* holding the door of the T'Bird for her and hoping for the incidental flash that doesn't happen.

"There are hats and scarves in the glove compartment if you'd like to protect your hair." But she declines and his respect for her climbs another notch. He even thinks how absurd it is that he places respect on the fact that she doesn't require headgear.

No, she doesn't think that it would be a good idea to go somewhere for coffee. Her place is in the opposite direction, so he wheels through the intersection and, making use of the extra room afforded by the confluence of two streets, he executes a sweeping U-turn and rumbles back down Mell St. toward the older buildings for married students, up on the hill.

Making conversation, he asks how she likes being in the South and she explains that for a while she had attended college in Greensboro, North Carolina. "That was the Women's College of the University of North Carolina. We called it 'W.C.'; but they started admitting men last year," she explains. "Then my high school sweetheart and I got serious and I left school to marry him. He's an architecture student here at Auburn. So being in the South isn't brand new. But I'll say this. It's certainly different from how I grew up on Long Island. For example, I don't think that I've ever actually been in a vehicle that did a U-turn like you did back there. Does everybody down here drive like you?"

He explains that that maneuver is called a Windsor Special, thank you very much, and is reserved for the sons of families of at least ten generations in the South.

"Ten generations. Are you serious? My parents came here from Austria and Germany, so I'm first generation. That must be nice to have such a deep connection to your home. I don't even know my parents' families of origin, what's left of it. Most of both families were wiped out in the war. I think that there was one cousin from my father's family who survived."

Duke is awestruck. He has never known such a creature. Most of his friends and acquaintances have similarly long bloodlines within their culture. "Actually I'm the fourteenth generation that we know about. My Aunt Jeanne is into that genealogy stuff. I'm interested, but it's not very high on my priority list."

"What is?"

"What is what?"

"High on your priority list. And while you're at it could we have a peek at this list?"

He knows that she's teasing a little and is flattered to think that maybe she's also a little bit interested. Thinks, *She's just so completely composed. Maybe that's what growing up in New York City does to you. You are at ease with new people and able to converse without strain.*

The way he's thinking here isn't characteristic of Duke. He's pretty composed himself, and he sure didn't grow up in New York City.

Arriving at her apartment, Duke gets out to open her door for her but she beats him to the draw, opening it herself. They laugh when she explains that until she came south it had not occurred to her that anyone would open her door for her. She finds that particular tradition a little quaint and sweet, then admits that it's hard to remember to wait.

He intuits her resistance to his walking to the door with her and, not wanting the moment to end says, "It feels like rain to me. Would you mind helping me putting the top up?"

She laughs out loud and serves notice that transparent devices will be summarily dealt with. "So is that a line that you use often? Or are you really Windsor Weather Man? Or could you not think of any other way to extend our time together?"

Duke's tone goes sly and he says, "You know, those good schools up in New York may have given you an elegant vocabulary, but you probably shouldn't be expected to know much about nature, I guess. A cup of coffee says that it rains by noon tomorrow. Whaddaya say?"

Without much in the way of hesitation she replies, "You're on. I like mine black. And I'm on duty at three tomorrow." They pull together on the frame and top. Fasten the clamps. Well, he tells her what to do but then has to show her and finally has to do it himself. She's not mechanical. And that's very feminine to him, and sensual somehow. He knows that he can stop noticing if she smiles now. She's smiling because she likes him.

"I like mine black, too and I'll be there when you get there. By the way, you're right. I did want to extend our time together. You're really different from anyone I've ever known. So I'll see you tomorrow. And don't forget your umbrella." With that he climbs into the T'Bird and, waving, drives home.

*   *   *   *

So now it's early morning and quizzes line up before him like a gauntlet he has to run. The coffee is ready and he sits with a cup in a straight wooden chair facing the screened front door, watching the gentle rain falling outside. He knows the material that he'll be tested on, and now it is a matter of getting psychologically prepared.

It seems fundamental to him that if you're relaxed in the face of testing, whatever you know will be more accessible to you. Of course if you haven't done the work and don't know the material, no amount of relaxation will help. Staring at the expanse but seeing nothing, his mind begins to come into focus. A sense of well-being pervades. Finds that he can shut things out or open himself to externals as he wishes. Knows that he can concentrate as needed. And so he retreats to the shower.

A convertible, at speed in the rain is going to leak. The newer the car the less leakage, but it's going to leak. With this foreknowledge Duke creeps across campus, trying to find a parking space close to the Union. He wants to go in for breakfast and to have the T'Bird nearby, when he's finished with his tests. On the circle in front of Ross Hall, next door to the Union, he finds not one but three open spaces left by a delivery truck's evacuation. He scoots quickly into the one closest to the door, grabs notebooks and baseball cap, opens his door and sprints to the dryness of the overhang at the upper level entrance.

Through a bank of doors and immediately down the stairs. The long and darkened hallway to the Union cafeteria is tile-covered. His sneakers squish as he makes his way to food. Pulls open the heavy metal and glass door and enters a world of sounds, smells, and light. The room is surprisingly filled with students similarly awaiting the beginning of this week of testing—some with dread, and others with the anticipation of getting it finished and going on to the next thing. Through the line, choosing scrambled eggs, sausage, toast and coffee. Paying for this repast, he looks up to choose a spot to sit.

Across the way he sees George Blankenship sitting alone with emptied plates before him and with a newspaper in front of his face. Makes his way there and unloads his tray and his books to the tabletop. George looks up, smiles and says, "Come in th' house, Duke. How you doin' this mawnin'?" And not waiting for a response goes on "Have you seen this bullshit in th' paper? They write this stuff like they know what's goin' on and they ain't even got a clue. They're sayin' there was a Klan rally at the nigger church last night in 'Skegee. Hell, ain't never been no Klan rally at no nigger church. These people are crazy, and the people who read this don't know the difference half th' time."

Looking up, Duke says, "I didn't hear anything about that. What happened? Has it got something to do with what happened at that church yesterday afternoon?" Arranging his plates and cup. He sits across from George and begins the process of eliciting information. He knows that is what he's doing, but the process just unfolds naturally without his having to work at it. People have always talked to him. Even when he doesn't want to hear it, they come anyway and lay their troubles on the table in front of him as if by doing so their burden is somehow lightened.

He sees the gleam in George's eyes and manages not to react when he says, "You talkin' 'bout runnin' them outsiders out of town and breakin' up th' nigger votin' meetin'?"

"Yeah that's about what it sounded like from what I heard on the radio up in Gadsden. I went home to tend to some family business and it was on the news up there at about three. What actually happened? Sounded like there were some Auburn people involved in it. Is that right?" He has cut his sausage into neat little squares and chopped the scrambled eggs into a fine heap, preparing his assault on the food.

Looks up occasionally to make eye contact with George. Thinks, *That'll keep him talking, while I eat. Man, the look in his eyes is downright scary. He's almost grinning and hasn't even gotten into the story yet. I'll play along. And I'm ashamed to admit that I know how to do that—smile and laugh as if inflicting pain on others is my idea of a fun afternoon. And most of all, I've gotta keep a straight face.*

And so the story tumbles from George like salt from the shaker. "Well, daddy and 'em heard that the church was being used to drum up volunteers to register to vote downtown. They had the actual paperwork filled out so that all the niggers would have to do would be show up with a witness, prove their identity and sign the forms in front of the clerk. That new law is gonna outlaw the poll tax and the literacy tests, so there ain't gonna be anything to stop them if they can get down there and fill out the paperwork and sign.

"So daddy and 'em figured that the easiest thing to do would be to go down there and put the fear of God into a few of 'em. And maybe even find the paperwork and tear it up. They really didn't expect to find outsiders there, and especially not Auburn people; but sure enough, they were there. Daddy was so mad that white people would be in there helpin' *them* out that he just went a little bit crazy. Him and ole man Collins beat that one boy from up north pretty bad; but they didn't want to kill him. They figured that if they just beat him up real good, that maybe it would discourage any of the others from comin' around."

By the end of this George is alight with glee. He believes that what has happened is not only justified, but something to cause veneration by the public at large. "One thing's for sure, if they come back around after this warning, they'd better give their hearts and souls to the Lord, 'cause their asses are gonna be ours."

Duke forces a laugh through his mouthful of food and says, "Oh, I 'spect they'll figure it out and stay away. Sounds like a pretty good whuppin'. Who was the guy? Do you know?" Fishing a little here. Wanting to see how much real information they might have. And if they have an intelligence network. Or do they find things out by happenstance, serendipitously. Having names and addresses is different from identifying Pax as "that guy that started the Human Rights Forum". But that's the only identity that George supplies, and that is a relief to Duke, though it may be a false positive.

George is going on, "Anyhow the point I was trying to make before is that last night a group went back down to the church and performed a little cross burnin' ritual for the benefit of the residents of Niggertown. These idiots in the 'paper don't know the difference between a ritual and a rally. You don't grace Niggertown with a rally, though you often have to perform a ritual down there just to keep 'em thinking right. It was funny as hell. I guess that that guy who was beat up had left his car down there, and it got hooked up with the cross somehow, and it burned too. A brand new Galaxie. That oughtta get his attention."

Duke is having a hard time with all this. His friend is in the hospital, his recovery uncertain, his car burned for no reason. And here George sits all smug and looking for praise, for knowing the details or for being a participant, Duke's not sure which.

Duke asks, "So who were the other white guys out there? And how come they didn't get hurt?"

More information. And George is no more difficult to pry it out of than Lynn had been. "Got no idea who they are, Duke. They didn't get hurt 'cause they ran like hell. They got in some car, nobody noticed what kind, and took off outta there headed south on 29, and everybody was too busy to follow. I wanted to go down there myself, but daddy wouldn't let me. He said that there was a rumor goin' around that there might be federal marshals around, and he doesn't want me to get in that kind of trouble."

Duke listens raptly, paying close attention to the words and to the man. He isn't sure just how dangerous George is, but plans to assess that as best he can. Good idea. His own survival may well depend on making the right call on that one.

Finishing the last remnants of his meal he says, "I gotta go take some tests, George. Try to stay out of trouble, OK? And good luck on your tests, too." Moves to disengage from this situation.

George raises his hand to signify goodbye but says, "I don't have any tests, Duke. I'm not in school this quarter. I just got up early and drove through 'Skegee to look at that car and decided to come over here for a cheap breakfast and a newspaper. Let's go bust some pigeons soon.?"

"Sounds good, man. I'll see ya around."

Duke's thinking, *I've gotta get outta here before I say or do something that'll cause more problems than it'll solve. I can't believe this asshole is thinking how righteous he and his family are when they're buying their pleasure at the cost of blood—other people's blood. "Bust some pigeons", huh? I oughtta get him out on the skeet range and bust his ass. I better settle down, get the work done, and then figure out how to cope with this rage.*

Walking back outside into the misty rain helps to diminish his anger. He makes his way through the alleyway that leads to Dunstan Hall, where he'll spend the rest of the morning writing in French and Spanish. The rest of the world has to go away for a little while, so that he can take care of business.

By the time the tests are finished and the notebooks are turned in to professors, the sun has made an appearance. The moisture from the rain is evaporating up from the streets, creating a kind of steam bath atmosphere. Having finished the academic requirements, Duke feels unburdened. Heads back toward the Union for a sandwich, an apple and a coke. Finds the bridge tables functioning, except there are only three tables playing with few spectators instead of the usual eight or ten. Ron Bauman sits at Judd's elbow, kibitzing.

Duke kicks a chair over near Ron and asks, "So, Ron, how's Jay?" He seats himself close enough that Ron's answer won't necessarily be heard beyond the range of the three of them. Ron explains that Jacob is so terrified by his experience that he won't leave the fraternity house. He seems to think that those men will be waiting out there somewhere for him and that he'll get the same treatment that Pax got. Without being too specific Duke tries to explain that he's sure that the men do *not* know Jacob's identity. Ron himself is a skeptical of this. He tells Duke that he and Judd have arranged to go to Tuskegee to pick up Pax's car and asks if Duke has the keys?

"Listen, Ron, I talked to a guy from over there this morning and he told me that there was a cross burning at the church last night and that the car got burned in the process. So I think that we have to just leave it alone and let Pax's uncle and dad deal with it when they get here. Maybe they can send a wrecker, or whatever they want to do. I'm not a hundred percent sure that it would be safe for you to go over there and mess with it.

"Right now the Tuskegee people don't even know that anyone other than Pax was hurt. And that's why I say that they don't know anybody else's name." They are only inches apart and each feels the intensity of the other. All are torn between wanting to help out their friend and the practicality of being safe.

Judd leans back into their sphere and asks, "So what's gonna happen with the project now?" Everybody shrugs. They'll have to wait for Mohammed to contact them or for Pax to get well and provide his usual leadership.

Ron says, "So have you heard what SNCC put out this morning? Carmichael announced from Washington that SNCC would be sending two busloads of Freedom Riders to Alabama next week. They're sending whites and blacks together and calling it 'Freedom Rides Again'. He says that they'll be going to Selma where there's some big protest rally being held in conjunction with the voter registration project there. You know that's where the turmoil started that resulted in the Voter's Rights Act that's just passed. Anyhow, he's asking the president to provide protection for the Freedom Riders and to insure that people who want to register to vote are allowed to do so. This is a big one, don't you think?"

There's a studied silence among the three. Duke asks when this announcement occurred and Ron tells him that in was less than an hour ago. He thinks about George and wonders how that gang of outlaws will react to this news. Shudders. Remembers the satisfaction in George's voice and face as he related the details of yesterday's violence in Tuskegee. Says, "This is going to be interesting. We need to wait a while before we do anything.

"I'll say one thing; those guys have got balls to announce that they're coming down here after what happened to the original Freedom Riders in '61. I'll never forget that fiasco. People dragged off the buses and beaten while cops stood by and watched. Buses burned. That happened next to my hometown. It was disgusting."

He silently remembers how shocked and ashamed he had been. Remembers that many of his friends were delighted that the "agitators" had been taught a lesson. He feels again the nausea that he had felt then. Feels the sting of incipient tears of rage and dreads having to go through all this again. Hopes that somehow the result can be different; but doesn't know how it could be. Another involuntary shudder. Jaw clenched, he gets up and leaves the group. It's too early to go to work so he goes instead to the hospital to check on Pax.

✳   ✳   ✳   ✳

Walking in the front door of Lee County General, he spots the red-headed reporter standing near the elevators. They glare at each other. Undaunted, Duke walks directly to the call button and pushes the UP arrow. Steps back and waits, hands clasped in front of him, gaze locked on the floor. They enter the car together and, silently, each waits for the other to choose a floor. Duke reaches across and punches the button for the third floor and leans against the wall, as the car ascends.

The reporter rocks him by announcing, "So you're Ashley Windsor, eh?" Duke stares at the floor and says nothing. The elevator jolts upward and hums. "Ya know, I could've pressed charges for that little incident yesterday, but decided not to." Waits. Still no response. "Pax's gonna be OK. His Uncle Jimmy and his daddy will be here in a little while."

Duke's wondering, *How does he know all this? Why's he telling me? So he's got a friend at the PD who looked up my tag for him. Big deal. If I just keep quiet, maybe he'll leave me alone. By now he knows that I won't take a whole lot of crap from him. I'm not even going to look at him … Damn, I'm sure glad Pax's people are coming. I hope I can stay here long enough to talk to them for a minute. I doubt that they know about the car yet. Hurry up, elevator.*

The car slows and just before it settles the reporter says, "I called Mr. O'Reilly myself. He told me that you're OK. Whenever you figure out that I'm safe, call me. Here's my card. My home number is on the back." He hands Duke a card, and as the doors open, each steps out and turns in opposite directions.

Opening the doors to ICU and approaching the desk, Duke is assailed by myriad thoughts. He's intrigued by the man's tenacity and his seeming lack of rancor regarding the cuffing that Duke meted out yesterday. Also, if he really did call Mr. O'Reilly, maybe Duke owes an apology. He'll wait and see on that one.

Miz Whitmore exits Pax's room and turns to find Duke looking questioningly at her. A smile wells up from deep inside her and bursts across her face. "He's better. The bleeding is just about stopped." Reaches out to touch his shoulder, sympathy in her eyes. "He's gonna make it, son. He's got some hard days ahead of him, but he'll be just fine. At least the physical part will be. You never know what going through something like that will do to a person's mind. How about you? Are you okay?"

For the second time in the last hour tears are so close to the surface that his face burns with shame. He's never heard the word "stress" except as it applies to metal. Has no idea that these tears are the good kind, no idea that there *is* a good kind. He thanks her and makes his way to a nearby chair and sits down. Miz Whitmore offers a cup of ice water, and pulls another chair next to him to sit with him. "His uncle called, and then later his father did too. They're probably on their way from Montgomery by now. They flew out of Boston early this morning. You ready to hear how it's been going or do you need a few minutes?"

Mercifully, the tears retreat and he signals that he wants to hear about Pax's progress. She says, "He woke up for the first time sometime in the night. The duty nurse wrote that he just asked where he was and if he was going to be OK and then went back to sleep. That was around two. When I got here at seven this morning, he was moving around a little in the bed. By the time breakfast was being served to the others, he was awake. He asked about whether his people knew about what had happened, and I told him that you had taken care of that, and that his uncle and father were coming later today. That seemed to comfort him and he went back to sleep. His vitals have been steadily improving and, as I said, the bleeding has almost stopped. He's got some pain, but his condition isn't critical anymore."

Relief washes over Duke. He asks, "Is he awake? Can I see him?"

"He's kinda in and out. But he'll want to see you. Let's go take a look."

They move together to the glass-walled room where Pax lies amongst the tubes. If anything, his appearance is worse today than yesterday. His face is swollen to roundness. Bruises and scrapes are blue and red and brown. Stitches pull against the swelling and threaten to break apart. His shoulders are blue and green from the blows. His hair is mostly missing at this point and more stitches show on his scalp than Duke had noticed yesterday. The remaining hair looks oily, and has clots of blood embedded.

Duke stands in a kind of reverence, looking down on his friend and thinking that he's so much tougher than he had originally appeared to be. Duke's thoughts go to Jacob and the psychological problems that his involvement seems to have caused. He wonders what the effect will be on Pax. Reaches over and touches him—as gently as a shadow falling on the wounds.

Pax's eyelids flutter open and ever so slowly he focuses on Duke. His voice is husky and weak. "Thanks for calling my folks. Is everybody else OK?"

Duke smiles and says, "Everybody's fine, Pax. You took the heat for a lot of people, old son. Everybody else got away with minor cuts and scrapes. Your dad and uncle oughtta be here in a little while. Do I need to get up with your instructors and let them know that you're in the hospital?"

Pax hasn't thought about that part yet. "If you'll just tell Miz Latham, the secretary at the department, that I'm in the hospital and that I'll call as soon as I'm able, she'll take care of it. Don't tell her what happened. I'll have to figure all that out later. But, yeah, thanks. That's a good idea."

"Can you think of anything else?" As Pax shakes his head slightly and winces with the effort, Duke says, "Look, you rest some. I'm gonna hang around for a while and if we can think of anything else that needs to be done, I'll do it this afternoon. I've gotta work from two 'til midnight. See ya before I leave." Backing out of the room he sees his friend's eyes close and imagines that he's relaxing into peaceful oblivion. Almost envies his not having to think about the turmoil. Seeing Pax's improvement has put his mind at rest.

Back at the desk Miz Whitmore has made and offers coffee. Duke asks what the process should look like from where they are right now. She says that if all goes well Pax could go home as early as Wednesday or Thursday. The broken ribs will likely to give him the most pain, and there's really not much to do about them. They will likely wrap and tape him but it will take two or three weeks before he will have much relief. Now that the bleeding has stopped, the only other real worry is whether there will be some residual problem from the concussion.

A noise from the waiting room gets Duke's attention. He peers around the curtains and out the small window in the unit doors. Two men talk earnestly with the reporter, and one shakes his hand and claps him on the back. The two older men then head toward the doors and Duke has to scramble to get out of the way in time. First in is a robust, gray haired man with alert blue eyes. Seems to take in everything at once. Dressed nicely but casually in a golf shirt and a sports jacket with gray slacks, he's about Duke's size at 6'2", 170 pounds. Walks directly to Duke and says, "You must be Duke. Or is it Ashley? Red told us that you were here. How's our boy?"

This is a guy you can like immediately. Or fear. Or despise. Intensity rolls off him like summer fog off a river surface. No doubt in anyone's mind who is now in charge. Shaking his hand, Duke says, "It's both actually. But I'm known around here as Duke. Are you the uncle or the father?"

Looking beyond him Duke sees a carbon copy of the man. Same size. Same gray hair. Only this one wears glasses and is more retiring. They exchange nods. The first Mr. O'Reilly says, "I'm the uncle. I'm Jimmy. This is my brother Andrew, Pax's father."

The three men continue to size each other up. Duke ventures, "He's better, Mr. O'Reilly. I was in a few minutes ago and he woke up for a little while. He's still pretty rocky, I guess, but he's better today than yesterday. I'm sure that Miz Whitmore will let you go back."

"Good. Might as well start calling us Jimmy and Andrew or 'Drew', as we call him at home, otherwise we'll all stay confused. We'll go in to see him now. Hang around if you can. And by the way, Red outside is OK. I know that you two got off to a bad start yesterday. We'll get it straight, though. Thanks again, son." Pats Duke on the shoulder and leads his brother toward Miz Whitmore.

As the three of them disappear into Pax's room Duke is left alone, realizing with dread that he needs to go out and speak to the reporter. Takes the card from his pocket and reads. Charles "Red" McKinney.

Duke has heard all his life that when you screw up, you should apologize as soon as possible. Crow tastes better warm than cold.

Backing through the doors and into the waiting area he sees Red standing near the windows, facing away from him. He feels the urge to walk quickly down the hall and avoid the embarrassment of this, but he knows he could never actually do that. Approaches Red and says, "Mr. McKinney?" Red turns and faces him squarely. "I'm not real good at this apologizing stuff, but I'm sorry about the misunderstanding yesterday. I was on unfamiliar ground and you kinda forced the issue on me. I reacted poorly, so I'm sorry. Maybe at some point I can explain to you. But for now, I'll just say I'm sorry."

Red looks sternly for a moment and then breaks into a wide and sincere grin. Extends his hand and says, "No hard feelings. I shouldn't have grabbed you. I must say that you didn't give a whole lot of warning. But Jimmy told me there are some good reasons that you reacted as you did, and his word is good enough for me. Maybe at some point we can help each other. We'll see about that. For now, let's call a truce and let it go at that, fair enough?"

Duke hasn't had a lot of practice at admitting that he screwed up so badly. He'd like to believe that that means that he hasn't screwed up all that much; but actually he just hasn't always been willing to see it. This one would have been hard to miss. And the apology wasn't so bad. There's something about this guy that he likes. Maybe it's that he just let him off the hook for behaving so badly. Or maybe it's the tenacity that he noticed yesterday. Duke grins as they shake, and manages, "Thanks, Mr. McKinney."

Predictably McKinney says, "Just call me Red. Everybody else does. We'll be all right in the long run. Let's walk down the hall and get something to drink."

Before they can get to the drink machines, the door to ICU opens and the O'Reilly brothers exit. They look relieved and slowed-down now that they have seen Pax for themselves. The four men congregate in the hallway and Duke explains that he has to work this afternoon and into the night. Jimmy says they want to go to Tuskegee and pick up Pax's car.

Duke says, "I hate to tell you, but I've heard that the car was burned last night. I don't know how badly or even if it's drivable." He explains the details, as he knows them.

Jimmy O'Reilly's face goes red and his jaw clenches. Drew looks disgustedly at the floor. Duke wonders how they'll handle this situation. He hands over the keys and offers to lead them to the apartment on his way to work. Downstairs, the brothers in their rental car, fall in behind the T'Bird. Red falls in behind them and the motorcade makes its way to the Cabanas. From the front seat of the T'Bird Duke points and says, "Take those steps to the second level. His place is the second door to the right. I'll talk to you guys tomorrow."

He wheels the T'Bird in a casual semi-circle. Turns out onto Glenn and heads back toward campus. He knows that he should feel enormous relief, but somehow the pressure hasn't lifted as much as he thought it might. Although others carry most of the load now, that's just Pax's part of the deal. He still has his own role to continue to play.

He can't help thinking about the "Freedom Rides Again" project. Wonders why they would announce it. For the publicity, of course. But at what cost? Approaching the library he spots George's SuperSport leaving campus and heading south. When he parks in the lot at the side of the building, he leans forward and feels under the seat for the .38 revolver that he put there this morning.

It's there. Loaded and secure.

CHAPTER 13

▼

After the events of the past few days, Duke feels tired but restless. He sits at the music desk in the basement of the library and hopes that no one will need to listen to anything for a while. His mind sifts through the details of all the scenes he's playing in. Thinks about Ellen and is a little shocked at her angry reactions to the idea of abortion and to his participation in the voter registration effort. Wonders and worries about the possibility of her being pregnant and knows in his heart that he is not ready to be a parent—and also that if that's the way it plays out that he'll give it his very best shot.

He smiles as he remembers Lynn's energy level as they made love at his apartment. He thinks that being close to her and, therefore, to her father might pay off. He's past the guilt now—mostly anyway. And she's so damn gorgeous. It's hard not to want to stay close to a woman like that.

As he tries to make sense of George and to figure out how to deal with him, he recalls that Claire had wanted for him to call her. He searches around under the desk for a phone book, but finds nothing there. Slips around the desk, races up the stairwell, and bursts into the lobby just as Ann Lassiter comes strolling in the front door. She waves and says that she'll see him later. Almost snubs him as she walks on by. He goes to the front desk and asks for the phone book and looks up the number for Claire's dorm. He's a little put off by Ann's demeanor.

Back down in the basement he calls the dorm, asks for Claire, and waits while someone gets her. When she picks up the phone, he finds himself smiling. Says, "Hi, Claire. This is Duke. You wanted me to call?"

"Oh, great. Thanks for calling. I just need to talk to you. What are you doing?" He explains that he has to work until midnight and she asks if she can come to the library. Of course! She'll come as soon as she changes.

She had called the hospital and knows about Pax's condition, but didn't know that his uncle and father are in town.

"I'm glad they're here. That was really scary, Duke. We all ran off to Leo's car so we could take Jay to the hospital. He was bleeding so badly that I thought he'd die before we could get him there. It was a real relief that nobody followed us, but we all felt guilty about leaving Pax."

He understands the guilt thing. He tells her that he feels guilty, too, for not being around to help, but that if the four of them hadn't run, four more people would have been hurt. He encourages her to look at it from that slant. "I'll try. See ya in a few minutes."

Claire arrives at the library wearing shorts and a sleeveless shirt. Her demeanor seems different to Duke. She looks small and fragile as she approaches the music desk, her arms crossed and hands rubbing her upper arms, fending off the chill. Her features are drawn and her eyes dart around, searching—for what?

They sit in the office behind the desk and he asks what the problem is. And she tells him—she's pregnant and there's not any doubt about it. She's already been to the doctor and she's about seven weeks along. She doesn't want to continue the pregnancy, but doesn't really know what to do. "I was going to ask Pax to help, but that seems unlikely now. I have money from my boyfriend in Nashville, but no idea how to find the 'service' in the backwoods of Alabama. Can you help me?"

Recovering from his shock Duke says, "I don't really know how to do it either, but I'll try to help you. I may need the same thing for my girlfriend, anyway."

That brings a smile and she looks so relieved that he smiles along with her. In fact they've put so much energy into holding onto their secrets that the tension-break allows them to understand that it's just another problem to solve—a big one, but still just another problem. Loosening up, he asks if she knew about the pregnancy before their encounter. Claire gives him her deepest, most guttural laugh and says, "Of course, you were my *revenge* fuck. And it *was* sweet." They laugh together, but Duke's not sure how he really feels about that idea. With profuse thanks Claire leaves to study.

After she leaves, Duke considers the things going on in his world. He thinks *... One more time someone leaves unburdened, and I'm stuck with another ball in the air. How will I ever figure this one out? Obviously, I'll have to have help, but who do I call on for something like this.* Running the list of people he knows through his mind, he can only come up with Daniel, his erstwhile mentor. And he's 130 miles away. *Guess that's not such a big deal. Certainly not an obstacle that can't be overcome. I was afraid to talk to him about the voter registration stuff. I wonder how he'll react to this one.*

While this turns over in his thoughts, Ann appears in the doorway to the stairwell. "Was that your girlfriend that was here before?"

"No, just a friend."

Ann touches his shoulder and responds, "Well, she looked like she needed a friend. Is she all right? Matter of fact, are you? You don't look so good yourself."

Raises his right hand as if to wave it all off, but then surprises himself by saying, "To tell you the truth, there's a lot going on right now. I'm gettin' bombarded from every conceivable angle. And a few that *weren't* conceivable until they landed in my lap. To say that the lady who just left is okay wouldn't be completely accurate. Can we keep a few things just between the two of us?"

Back in the area behind the main desk, they discuss, over the next hour, the issues of abortion, civil rights in general and the current voter registration crisis specifically. When he's convinced that she isn't judgmental, in fact that her views match, even exceed, his changing ideas, he begins to weave his current realities into the fabric of the explanation of his current dilemmas. She watches his expressions closely. She touches his hand when he struggles. Her voice is soft. She asks questions that make him focus his mind toward answers. She self-discloses some of the difficulties in her own life that are similar in emotional distress if not in fact. They sit in a bubble that no one else can pierce.

Looking at her watch, she realizes the time and disengages, saying, "If you need time to be away from work, just let me know and I'll get things covered." His gratitude is for far more than the offer of respite. He thanks her for listening and for her help. Says that he'll be able to work and that he needs the pay. Turning to leave, she says, "I have to go upstairs, but I'll be around if you need to talk more."

*   *   *   *

In the heat and humidity of the afternoon two men sweat and curse as they brush the cinders and wood fragments from the hood and top of the scorched automobile. The shock that greeted them as they drove up to the church's parking lot has dissipated, replaced by rage and incredulity. In the trunk of the rented car is the tow bar they rented to move the vehicle if it isn't drivable. The work gloves that they bought at the hardware store are already black with soot and slick with the residue of kerosene.

They have noted with relief that the tires did not burn and that the gas tank didn't rupture, creating the hope that it will be drivable under its own power. That would be much faster and easier than attaching all the rented devices and slowly pulling a disabled vehicle the twenty-five miles to the Ford dealer near Opelika. When enough debris is removed, they open the hood and see that the wiring seems to be intact and decide that they may as well try to start the engine. It turns over and catches on the first try. Jimmy kills the motor, slides back out, and tells his brother that he'll drive the car rather than towing it.

As they continue brushing away debris and carbon from the windows, another vehicle cruises to a stop in the street. A big man exits the vehicle and walks toward the brothers. They stop and look at him. The top button of his white shirt is open and his tie is loose, pulled down slightly. His trousers are baggy dress pants held in place underneath his belly by a black belt. He's wearing black leather-soled shoes and moves toward the men and the car.

He is glowering and purposive. "What d'ya'll think you're doin'? We're leavin' that car there as a message to any other nigger-lovin' sons-a-bitches that think that they can come in here and run our business for us."

Jimmy looks at his brother and shakes his head slowly. He's already angry, and now this overweight redneck thinks that he can tell him not to move his own vehicle. Still, he tries to stay moderate. "Actually, this is my car and my nephew was just driving it. So I'm gonna take it to the dealer over in Opelika and see what can be salvaged." He barely deigns to look directly at the man and continues his work without further comment.

"Maybe you didn't hear me just right. I said that we'uz leavin' that car right where it's at as a sign. So y'all might as well git back in your car and git on out of here while you still can." He's big, menacing, and accustomed to having people do what he says.

Jimmy stops his work and seems to go slack in the shoulders. He turns and faces the big man, sighing loud enough to be heard. Asks, "So does that mean that you were with that bunch of cowards that burned this car and beat up my nephew and those other people?"

This takes the big man aback but he recovers quickly enough. "What if I was? You got something to say about it? I'd just as soon give you a little taste of what they got."

Jimmy smiles and holds up his right hand. Moves a step toward the rental car. Says, "Hold on a minute." Another three steps. Looks over his shoulder at the bigger man and says as he opens the driver's side door, "Come over here and let me show you something."

He leans in and waits. As the man approaches, Jimmy suddenly wheels with the .38 caliber, Smith and Wesson Police Special. Cocks the pistol as he presses it into the soft folds of the other man's throat. His blue eyes are steady and hard. His lips are pulled back slightly as he struggles for control.

"You fat-assed son of a bitch. By all rights I oughtta blow what little you've got in the way of brains through the top of your thick skull. But you know what, Fatty? I'm not going to jail for a fat turd like you. Not unless you force the issue anyway. If I have to shoot you, I will. Gladly. But you don't really seem to be worth jail time."

Jimmy turns to his brother and says, "Drew, you go over to big boy's car there and see if he's got a CB radio in it."

The man with the glasses moves quickly to do his brother's bidding. His eyes are open wide, lots of white showing behind the lenses. He's wakened from his trance now and calls back to his twin, "Yeah, Jimmy, there's a radio in here. Take it easy now. We've still got to get out of here, you know."

Jimmy's almost laughing by now. "Yeah, I know. Pull the microphone out of the radio, wires and all. Yank 'em out." Turns his wolf-face to the fat man now. "Can't call your buddies now. Wonder how you'd do in a fair fight. What's your name, Fatboy?"

"Name's Robert Earle Wilkins and if you put that gun away, we'll sure as hell find out about how who does in a fight." He's sweating bullets, but he's more confident with this man talking about a fair fight. Hell, he outweighs him by almost a hundred pounds. *Skinny little Yankee bastard. Puttin' that gun away will be something that he'll regret.* Of this Robert Earle is certain.

"We just might get to that, Mr. Robert Earle Fatass Wilkins. Hold on a minute longer." Calls out, "Drew, take the keys out of the ignition and put 'em in your pocket. And look under the seat for his pistol. When you find it, empty the shells out into your hand and throw 'em out into that field across the street as far as you can." Now the blue eyes are dancing. He's watching Wilkins and cutting his eyes to Drew and the grin keeps spreading.

"You got any kids, Mr. Fatass Pigboy? What did you say? A daughter? Oh that's even better. Before the festivities commence here, I want for you to think for a minute how you'd be feeling if it were you who'd been at the hospital today seeing what had been done to your little girl by a gang. Not one person in a fair fight, but a *gang* beating and kicking her 'til she couldn't move, and then still going on with it.

"I want you to think about her having a broken arm and broken ribs, bruises, a punctured lung, and internal bleeding. Think about her facing death because somebody else doesn't like the way she thinks. You got that picture in your head yet, Mr. Fatass? 'Cause, see, me and the boy's daddy there just came from the hospital and saw for ourselves what a bunch of chicken-shit cowards like you can do to helpless kids and colored women and children."

"Drew. Come over here for a minute. Give me those keys. Alright, now go get in the rental car and go on to the dealership. Tell them all the particulars. I'll be there in … oh probably no more than fifteen minutes. Mr. Fatso here doesn't look like more than fifteen minutes worth of tough to me."

He pockets the keys as he moves away from Wilkins a few steps. Over his brother's protests, Jimmy maneuvers Drew to the rental and waits for him to start the engine. "Now when you pull out, get th' hell on out of here, Drew. Understand?" As Drew accelerates Jimmy throws the gun into the seat beside him and wheels on Wilkins.

"Well now, Mr. Fat Turd. Looks like it's just the two of us here in the middle of Niggertown. I'm guessing that you don't have a lot of friends around here right now. That about right?"

Circles left with that gleam in his eyes. Wolf grin. "You seem kind of hesitant, Fatty. All the air out of your balloon?" Lashes a stinging left hand to Wilkins's right cheek and eye. Blood oozes from the broken skin. "Let me tell you what's about to happen here, big boy. First I'm going to whip your ass. I'm going to mark you up so you can tell all your friends how the coloreds beat you up in an unfair fight. But you're going to find out what it feels like to be beaten … And you and I will both know it was a fair fight."

Wilkins rushes at Jimmy like a bull charging the matador. Jimmy slips to his left and as Wilkins exposes his entire right side going by, cracks a sharp left to his ear and temple. Wilkins goes down hard in the soot and ashes and debris. He's stunned and slow to recover. But Jimmy waits. "I don't believe in hitting a man while he's down, Fats. 'Course I wouldn't expect a piece of crap like you to understand anything like fair play, but I'll try to teach you as we go along here."

Wilkins rises slowly to his feet and glares at Jimmy. He tries a roundhouse right hand that Jimmy sees long before it gets near him, and jukes backwards. Then he moves right back in with two, three right-hand uppercuts to his Robert Earle's big, soft belly. Hears the satisfying sound of the air rushing out of him. With the wind completely out of him, Wilkins is defenseless.

"See, Fatass, right about now, you and your kind would be in control. You'd see that your opponent is helpless and you'd really pour it on. That's not my way, but I *do* want for you to know how helpless that feels."

With his open hand he slaps him hard, then slaps him again and again. Wilkins's look is somewhere between terror and rage. In desperation he lunges at Jimmy with hands raised, reaching. Another uppercut to the brisket leaves him without air and slumping against the burned Galaxie. "You know, you're not much fun in this game. I would've thought that a big tough man like you could at least put up some kind of fight. Are you getting the idea yet how it feels to be on the other side of a beating? And think about it, I'm just one, single, skinny guy against you. Not the four or five that you used on our boy."

Wilkins makes a surprising move and catches Jimmy a glancing blow with a haymaker right hand. Jimmy's dancing again now. "Alright. That's better. See, unlike you and your chickenshit buddies, I'd rather fight somebody who at least fights back." Darts a jab to the mouth. Wilkins tastes his own blood now. Another jab to the other cheek and eye. More blood. Wilkins is breathing hard while Jimmy dances.

The next flurry of punches to the body yield the satisfying crack of ribs separating or breaking. Wilkins is completely breathless by now. Stepping back, Jimmy peppers his face with more jabs and the blood flows freely from around both eyes and cheeks.

"Kind of out of breath there aren't you, Fats? Don't worry this won't last much longer. Oh yeah. I said I'd tell you what was gonna happen, didn't I? Right. First the ass whippin' … We've about got that done haven't we? Well after you're not able to know anything else for a while, I'm gonna hog-tie you. That's appropriate for a pig like you, don't you think? Yep. I'm gonna lay you out right there where the car's sitting now and hog tie your fat ass so you can't move.

"Then, I'm gonna get in that car that you and your friends burned up and I'm gonna leave you here helpless in the middle of Niggertown. Let's see, it's almost six o'clock and the sun ought to be going down here in an hour or so. I halfway hope that the residents, who are undoubtedly watching all this right now from the comfort of their living rooms, will come out here and finish you off. You've certainly earned that much. Agreed?"

"I'll kill you for this." This threat is muttered through grotesquely swollen lips. Wilkins's eyes are closing from their hammering.

Jimmy answers with another jab to the mouth. "What did you say, Chubby?" A feint with the left and a crossing right puts Wilkins on the ground again. To his credit he struggles back up and throws an ineffectual punch that Jimmy picks off.

"It's pretty hard to be real scary when you've spent all this time on the ground, boy. You've been wallowing around in that shit there enough now that you look like you could live in this neighborhood. I wish your little girl could see how her daddy looks now. I'm sure she'd be real proud."

Another jab. Wilkins's nose explodes crimson. He gurgles now as he breathes. Another jab. More blood.

"I'm about tired of this, Turd man. How about you? You doing alright over there?" A straight right hand to the point of Wilkins's chin finishes the deal. He stands for a moment. His eyes roll back and he topples to the ground. Jimmy opens the trunk of the car and takes out the chains that he had put there himself before Pax left Boston with the new car. He rolls Wilkins around and into position, then expertly hog-ties him, face down in the debris of the burned car and cross.

And leaves him there.

*　　*　　*　　*

At nine o'clock Duke goes upstairs and asks Ann if he can use the long-distance WATS line to call his friend in Gadsden. She gives him the code to use and he returns to his area in the basement to phone Daniel. They catch up for a few minutes and eventually Duke says, "Daniel, I've got a problem and I need some help with it. I have a friend down here who knows that she's pregnant and wants to have an abortion. She has money but no idea how to find that 'service', as she so daintily put it. You know people around. Think you can find out the where and how and how much for me? OK, I'll call you back on Thursday evening. And, Daniel, thanks a lot, my friend. No. No, it's nothing to do with me. Thanks again. Talk to ya on Thursday. G'night."

Almost as soon as he drops the phone into its cradle, it rings. Lynn in a blind panic says, "Duke, I've got to get home and I'm afraid to drive. Will you come and drive me? Please. Daddy's been beaten up by the nigras and I don't know how bad it is. Momma needs me there and … and … Oh, I just need you to help me, Duke."

He gets her number at the dorm and tells her to stay there right by the phone. Up the stairs again and finds Ann in the stacks shelving reference books. Briefly explains that he has an emergency and asks if he can leave. Thinking that she knows at least part of the problem, she agrees and he returns to the front desk, calls Lynn and says that he'll be there in less than five minutes.

She is waiting at the curb in front of the dorm quad when he drives up. She gets in and they're off. Out on the back road that he learned from Pax, he airs out the T'Bird. Lynn is crying softly and he decides that she's better off not talking about it. They arrive at her home to find several cars sitting along the street. Inside several men sit in the living room, including George Blankenship and his daddy. After Lynn goes to her parents' bedroom, Duke finds a seat near George and asks, "What happened? Does anybody know?"

Before George can respond, his daddy says, "Th' niggers beat him, tied him up and left him for dead. That's what happened. Somebody'll pay for this. You can bet your last damn cent on that." George looks at Duke and communicates that there's more to it than he can tell right now. So they lapse into silence. George's father, Thad, eventually breaks the silence saying, "They found him over by that nigger church, beat up, hog-tied and covered in blood, ashes and dirt. Nobody knows how he got there or why. His car was right there on the street with his radio disabled. Somebody called the sheriff this evening about eight. No telling how long he'd been there."

Thoughts spin in Duke's head, connecting this event with Jimmy and Drew. He wonders if the coloreds were involved at all. Eventually he thinks to ask, "So is Mr. Wilkins gonna be alright?" A man across the room whom Duke doesn't know says that he should be fine but sore from the beating.

Lynn comes out from the bedroom and sits next to Duke for a moment. She's stopped her crying now and is deeply angry. Lacing her fingers in his she says, "Daddy wanted for you to come back with me for a minute."

Inside the bedroom Mr. Wilkins is covered by a sheet and looks remarkably similar to how Pax had looked on Sunday. Through puffy lips he says, "Thank you, Duke, for bringing Lynn home. It's good to know that there's someone around that she can depend on. I think she'll stay here for a day or two and her momma will take her back to Auburn. I appreciate it, son." His voice is strained and weak. He appears to be in pain but has refused to go to the hospital in Opelika. Duke mumbles an acknowledgment and turns to leave. In the living room he bids farewell to the Blankenships and the others.

Lynn follows him to his car and kisses him chastely on the lips, thanking him for his trouble. As he leaves she is certain that this is her one true love. He's beginning to feel certain about a few things too, but none of them have to do with love. He manages to suppress his grin until he reaches the darkness of Highway 29.

＊   ＊   ＊   ＊

It's near midnight when he arrives back in Auburn, and for no real reason he drives by the library. Realizing that Ann will be closing up in a few minutes, he parks out front and goes up the stairs to the front lobby. A crowd of students is exiting the building, having been expelled from their studies by the staff. Student workers also leave and Duke sees Ann putting the finishing touches on closing up shop for another day. She smiles as she notices him waiting for her at the front desk. "Did you take care of the emergency?"

Duke wonders why he has come here, but is glad that he did. His heart thuds away in his chest in a way that seems odd to him. He feels his insides light up just seeing her and hearing her voice. Finding his voice he says, "Well, sort of, I guess. Say, don't you owe me a cup of coffee?" Through a genuine smile she agrees that she does. "Can we get coffee from somewhere and talk for a few minutes?" When she agrees again, he feels exhilarated.

Later with steaming Styrofoam cups they are nearing the far western end of Mag Ave, and she asks, "Where are we going? Is this some sort of abduction?" They share a laugh and he explains that once he drove out this way and found a site where someone had laid out either an apartment complex or the beginnings of subdivision, and then had abandoned the project. This left a large field, now overgrown with weeds and high grass. The dirt tracks that were to become streets are still discernible.

Easing into the maze-way, Duke finds his way to a hillock that is at once open to the night sky and secluded from the nearby roadways. When the engine shuts down, sweet silence falls over the car, the occupants and the area—from rumble, roar and rushing wind to the implosion of utter quiet. Together they get out and put down the top of the T'Bird, then sit again enjoying the coffee and the quiet. No light but the night sky's stars and the insignificant moon. He falls back against the seat and lets his head relax on the headrest.

His silence invites a question and Ann supplies it, "So, did you get the emergency taken care of?"

With this opening he spins his tale. "This is pretty wild and I guess it's what I needed to talk to you about. You know the voter registration stuff that I was telling you about? Things there are getting very complicated."

He's fairly bursting to rid himself of the pressure of all that he knows. "What happened tonight is that one of the men who beat up my buddy was himself beaten up today. They are saying that the coloreds caught him at the church and beat him up or beat him up somewhere else and brought him to the church and leaving him tied up in the churchyard. I'm having a hard time believing that. I just can't make it make sense. I can see them maybe beating him up, but why would they leave him at the church? Seems like that would point to incriminating themselves.

"Anyhow, the guy's daughter is also a friend of mine, and she wanted me to take her home when she found out about it. She was too nervous to drive herself—that was the emergency. When we got to Tuskegee, another of the men and his son, who is also somebody that I know, were at the house. I found myself having a hard time just keeping my mouth shut and not confronting the whole lot of them."

Her perfect oval face gleams in the sky-shine. She considers the matters put before her seriously. Her eyes are oversized orbs in black and white. When she breaks the silence, it is to question, not to judge or scorn. "Do I understand this correctly? Did you say that your *friend* was beaten up by the parents of your *other friends*?" He nods. "So are you wondering where your loyalties really lie?"

He hesitates before responding. Flashing through his mind are ideas like: *Am I really committed to this cause now? How can I think that I have friends in both these camps? How much of this can I afford to tell her?* And then finds resolution in affirming that he *had* friends both camps, but maybe no longer; and that he needs to tell someone, if for no other reason than that he needs to sort it all out for himself.

"Ann, I'm not sure how much of this you really want to hear. I don't think that any of it would necessarily put you in danger, but I suppose it's possible. Are you sure that you want to hear the whole story?" She wouldn't need to be Freud to know that he wants to tell her, but she respects his willingness to let her decide. And besides, this sounds like pretty juicy stuff, so she says for him to tell as much as he wants to tell.

Relieved, he begins by saying, "I'm sure where my loyalties are now. The people in Tuskegee are people I knew before I got involved in the voter registration thing. Once I began to understand the real issues, a lot of what I believed before has changed. I had no idea that I would end up in the position that I'm in, of possibly betraying my former friends in the service of *ideas*. The folks who are running the voter registration project have asked me to sort of spy on my former friends and, by extension, their associates. They think that maybe I can learn things that might help keep the project going, head off plans to block it in some way. Or that I might hear of much more dangerous things.

"I do have some feelings of guilt about doing this, but it seems like the greater good to me and so I'm gonna do it. I hope that nobody else gets hurt because of my role in things. I've had a hard time seeing people on *both* sides of this now who have been hurt badly. If my supplying information results in more people getting hurt … Well, that'll be hard for me."

They sip their coffee and think their own thoughts for a few moments before Ann offers, "It sounds like people are going to be hurt anyway and that your efforts might reduce the chances of the Negroes and your new white friends being the ones who are. You can't have it both ways, Duke, You either have to take a side and play it all the way out or you need to step back and out of the game altogether. Not that I know anything about all this, but it sure seems like something that you can't do part way.

She pauses and then continues, "I'm more concerned about the potential for your being hurt. I would think that if the Tuskegee whites find out what you're doing, you'd be in real trouble. They don't sound like understanding and forgiving types."

A long interval passes before Duke replies, "I must think about that less than anybody else. Several people have warned me to be careful, and every time it almost surprises me. I think I know that I have to be careful. Maybe I'm kidding myself; but I think that I *am* careful. I don't sit around and consider all the things that *could* happen. I just go along and do my best. Honestly, the hardest part is to keep everything straight and not to say the wrong thing to the wrong person."

"That sounds like a lonely place to be, Duke."

"Yeah. That's a good way to put it. I guess that's why we're here right now. I needed not to be alone with all this. I appreciate that you're willing to listen." From his upright, coffee-drinking posture he slinks down in the seat to a dreamer's pose. Stares into the depths of the sky and tells her all the details as he understands them. She occasionally asks for clarification, but doesn't interrupt the flow of things.

At a lull in his reminiscence he points upward and says, "Look. A shooting star."

She amazes him by laughing and saying, "Right. Like there *is* such a thing." She says that she has heard the expression before, but doubts the actual existence of such a thing. After he convinces her to get over feeling like she's on a snipe hunt and just to stare at the sky, they are both thrilled by her first sighting.

Soon they decide that they need to return to the campus and their separate lives.

As she starts again to walk away from the T'Bird, he whispers, "Goodnight. Thanks. See ya tomorrow, or rather later today."

CHAPTER 14

▼

By Thursday Duke's world has changed yet again. He has learned from Miz Latham at the History Department that Pax has been granted a temporary leave from school for medical reasons—not withdrawn from classes, but not attending either. He is in Boston for at least a couple of weeks and will return when he's ready and able. He's doing his class work without the benefit of instruction.

Duke and Ann have had fleeting moments together as she continues to work nights and he has had an afternoon schedule for a couple of days. But tonight he is back at the music desk for the seven-to-closing stint. At nine sharp he places his call to Daniel and waits for an answer to his request for help with Claire's problem. Daniel is evasive at first and eventually asks, "You sure this doesn't involve you, Ashley? I mean, I found out some stuff, but these are some sleazy folks to be dealing with."

With some vehemence Duke replies, "Hey, it's not about me, OK? I'm doing this for a friend and I may even help out more, I don't know. But it definitely isn't about me. So, whattcha got?"

Daniel continues, "Well, I found this woman who used to be a nurse in an OB/GYN office. She has done this sort of thing before and seems to know what she's talking about. But she'll only do it if you go to a specific motel out near Birmingham. She'll want the female to be accompanied. She charges $300 and will want it in cash before she does anything. She'll want the place to be darkened when she gets there and for the person accompanying to wait in the car—kind of a lookout, I guess. She'll bring whatever equipment and explain to the female what to do and how to take care of herself." All this was delivered matter-of-factly, as if he were reading it from a card.

Ashley reacts to the pause by saying, "Is that the whole deal? I mean, that doesn't sound all that complicated. Or unusual. What's your problem with this?"

Daniel's labored response is, "I'm not even sure, Ashley. First I thought that it was because of this woman. But, really, she seemed okay—beyond the fact that she knows how to do this and is willing to do it. And that she'll do it for money. That sort of begs the question of whether it is a valid *service* to engage in. But then again, I guess that someone is going to be doing it, so why not someone who has at least worked in the area. It's not really that either. I just feel sort of *dirty*, somehow. The whole idea is alien to anything I've ever considered."

Listening to Daniel, the Duke part of him is already re-shuffling the cranial deck. "You're not the only one to say that to me about this idea. It's alien to me too, but I think that I've made a kind of peace with it. My thinking is that this sort of decision has to come from the people who created the problem in the first place. If a child is born into a situation where there is any doubt about the commitment of the parents, its chances of having a really effective life are already compromised. And the further you get from that commitment by the parents; the worse the chances of the child are. Anyhow, I'm glad it's not my choice to make. I'll just try to stand by my friend and support her."

Duke can almost hear Daniel's head nodding as he latches on to this rationalization. He wants and needs a way to release himself from the guilt that he's been feeling and this will work for him. "*I'm* with *you*," he says, "I'm glad I didn't have to call this one either. Well listen, Ashley, you talk to your friend and call me back later tonight and we'll see about making the arrangements if that's what she wants to do." And with the pressure of this thing allayed, they catch up for a few minutes and agree that Duke can call back around midnight.

*   *   *   *

Upstairs he passes Ann's empty office and continues around to the stacks. As he rounds a corner she is on tip-toes reaching books onto a high shelf. Calf muscles pop from her lower legs. The short skirt rides up strong, shapely thighs. Her rump is caught in perfect profile. He's gawking. Things stir around in him. He salivates. An involuntary smile wells up from way down deep. And when she turns, sensing his presence, he's still gawking.

She faces him squarely, hands on her hips. Cocks her head sidewise and asks, "What are you doing?" The only response that he makes is to broaden his smile. "I'm serious Duke, what do you think you were doing?" Strong eye contact but no real fury behind her words. Strong words nonetheless. And she patiently waits, not giving an inch. She will be answered.

So he stammers as he admits, "Uh…. Well … I guess you'd say I was looking at your legs."

"And …?"

"And? Oh yeah, and your butt."

She laughs out loud. "And …?"

This time he has to turn the question over in his mind. Thinks that she really wants an evaluation. But instead he says, "Uh … and … well you caught me." This time they both laugh out loud. "Oh yeah," he amends, "and wow. You look great tonight. In fact you look great every night." It annoys him that he blushes furiously. "Sorry. Hope I'm not too far out of bounds"

Through her own blush she says, "So you're taking it back now?" And walks toward him. Stops a few paces away and crosses her arms. Looks so vulnerable standing there. Her gaze is frank but neither inviting nor resistant. She's waiting to see if he's gonna deal the cards or just keep shuffling.

Without even knowing that he's done so he shrinks down to be able to look into her face more clearly. Reaches across the space between them to touch her cheek. She doesn't move. They float in each other's eyes. "No, Miz Ann Lassiter, I'm certainly not taking it back. I just don't want to assume too much. I just wanna keep things straight and clear between us."

Her smile is genuine enough as she asks, "So other than satisfying your voyeuristic impulses, what did you want?" Her tone is sarcastic and implies that this is not the place for this conversation to go much further.

"Oh yeah. I was looking for you to be sure that it is alright for that girl, Claire, to come over for a few minutes. I may have an alternative for her to consider and she needs to make a decision about this stuff pretty soon. Is it OK with you if she comes over and we use your office for a little privacy?"

"That'll be fine. But Duke, I don't want to know any more about what's going on with this stuff. I've thought about the position I'm in and I just need to be careful. So, do what you need to do but you can't say that I know anything about it. Agreed?"

"Look. I sure don't want to put you in an awkward position with my crap. If you'd rather I talk to her somewhere else, that'll be fine."

Ann shaking her head, "No. You want to keep things straight and clear, and so do I. That's all. Now go away or I'll never get this re-shelving done." Duke spins around to leave and keeps spinning—a 360. Winks and says thanks. Keeps spinning—540. He heads back to the main desk and into the privacy of the office behind. He calls Claire and tells her that she needs to come over, that he has some information.

While he awaits Claire's arrival, he is surprised to find that he is feeling nervous. He attributes this to the abnormal sensitivity of the subject matter. Goes to the main desk and busies himself alphabetizing the cards from today's checkouts, anything to fill up the time. He is relieved when Claire comes in the front door. His breath catches in his throat as he looks at her. She radiates. The dark red hair setting off her pale complexion creates a dazzling contrast. Her smile is miles deep and she appears to be confident and in charge of herself as she approaches him. He smiles back and points to the office. They sit there together.

"Damn, Claire, you look spectacular. Sit down and let's talk."

"Oh Duke, you probably say that to all the fallen women in your life. Actually if your saying that you have information means what I think it means, then I'm so relieved and pleased that it probably shows. Talk to me."

"Well I was able to find a way to do this if it's still what you want to do." She nods her head and rolls her hand in a motion that indicates he should keep going. "Here's the deal ..." He spells it out to her. She absorbs the whole story, pauses and then frowns.

Just before the tears come she says, "Duke, I can't tell anybody else about this. Will you go with me and help me out with this?" Tears have pooled in the corners of her eyes but she refuses to allow them to spill. He is quick to tell her that he had already thought that it might come to this and had decided that he would go if needed. Her relief is total and the tears are now allowed to flow. "You know, I've never had a friend like you."

Duke plays the joker card, "Hey, it's the least I can do for my favorite fallen woman. We'll get through this. You have to understand, now. I don't have any idea about how this will be. I'm a *guy* fer Chrissakes. But I'll do my best and somehow we'll get through it. You okay for money?" Through the smile and the tears she says that the boyfriend sent $500 so they'll be fine.

"Duke, this may be too much to ask, but do you think that I could stay at your place tonight. I don't want to face being at the dorm with this information so fresh on my mind." And, of course, he tells her to go to the apartment and that he'll take care of the arrangements and be there between midnight and 1:00 am.

As she's walking away, he notices that the view is still good; but he feels a completely different emotion toward the woman. Recognizes that he is feeling protective and gentle toward her. The lust has drained away for the time being. He is aware that his own tears are not too far from the surface as well and wonders what th' hell that's all about. Lots of new ground these days. Sometimes he doesn't recognize even old, known places because the feelings are so different.

Everything tumbles around in his mind and eventually he is still left with having to continue doing his mundane daily routine—in the center of this whirlwind.

Near midnight he hears Ann's step as she comes down the stairs. He's sitting at the desk in the center of the downstairs lobby. No one else is in the place. The moment she turns the corner his demeanor changes from pensive to sudden ebullience. The contrast is startling to him.

He asks, "Time to close up? Can I help?" And they parcel out the few and familiar tasks involved in getting the library put to rest for the evening. As she is gathering her personal belongings and visiting the restroom, he calls Daniel and says that the *service* is on. He copies the details on an index card .

Walking together outside in the humid warmth he asks to take her home and she agrees. As they poke along Mell Street, she asks how the business with the girl, Claire, went. He explains that the "service" has been located and arranged for, and that he will be taking Claire to the rendezvous and staying with her. Tenderness modulates his voice and Ann is aware of the fragility of this moment and nurtures it with silence. Her respect for this man is growing and she's being very guarded with allowing her emotions too much free rein. After all, she's still married. And a mother.

A block or so before her apartment the street has no curbing and a giant oak tree sits fifteen yards into the verge and slightly downhill. Its massive limbs stretch out for many feet and create a deep pocket of shadow. Without asking or apologizing, he glides underneath the protective embrace of the tree, shuts down the engine and turns toward her. "I know this is gonna sound crazy to you; but I'm having a lot of feelings toward you that are really strong. I'm probably way out of line here, but I just want to say that I'm very attracted to you and don't know what to do about it or even if I should think about doing something about it. Does this make any kind of sense?"

For the first time in the few weeks that he's known her she doesn't have an immediate response. In fact she, too, is so accustomed to having an instant reply that she almost starts answering before realizing that she isn't sure what she wants to say. Electricity fills the air around them. Their senses are hyper-alert. Their hearts race. Thoughts can't keep pace with the blur of images, and scintillating traces of feeling/thought synergy, of intellectual/sexual energy. They are trapped in charged silence.

She reaches her hand across the infinity stretching between them. Strokes his neck and shoulder. Each knows that the other is choked up and neither knows why. Her voice is almost a whisper, "I can't really have much in the way of feelings right now. Relationship matters in my life are pretty screwed up. I know that I'm attracted to you, too. But I can't let myself get involved in something else until the marriage is resolved."

Her words calm the atmosphere, at least for the moment. Ice seems to have collected in both their chests. The electric sound in their ears changes from high pitched and popping to a lower, slower hum. He takes her hand in both of his and kisses the fingers gently but passionately. Hears her sharp intake of breath more than sees any difference in her face in the shadows. He says in a voice made husky by the intensity of this moment, "I know that you're right; but I'm having a very hard time not wanting to be with you more." Pulls her closer hesitantly. She doesn't resist and their lips meet so softly. Each trembles with the pure sweetness of the touch. Tiny crackles of lightning dance along the fault-line created by their lips. Both breathless. Slight suction involves sensation that fans the flames. The sound in their heads changes back to its former intensity level.

When they grudgingly release each other and semi-collapse in their respective seats, each is consumed with the mixed feelings of euphoria and dread. Interestingly, Duke embraces the euphoria and would like to reject the dread, while Ann feels almost overpowered by the dread and fears the euphoria. As they settle these conflicting emotions into their minds, Ann says so quietly that he could have ignored it and claimed not to have heard, "We need to go."

He can only reply, "I know."

From the parking space near her front door he watches her disappear toward the freestanding apartment—actually one end of a converted Army barracks that has been outfitted as married student housing. There's a dull ache in his belly. He's unsure whether he has really offended her or if she's as confused and conflicted as he. Regardless, he has to go home to Claire and be her friend. Again tears are just under the surface. *Where are they coming from and what do they mean?*

*   *   *   *

Inside her empty apartment Ann walks to an armchair and sits, needing a moment to sort through the conflicting feelings and thoughts that bombard her. In her practical mind she knows that she cannot afford to become involved with another man when she isn't even certain that her marriage is over. On the other hand she's almost certain that the marriage *is* over and it seems silly to withhold herself, awaiting changes in her husband that she is sure will never happen. She isn't sure even that she would want the relationship if the changes *did* occur.

The early days with her husband Alex had been happy. She left college to be a wife and mother and had believed that this was what she wanted. When she had to go to work in a job that demanded so little from her intellectually, she found herself wondering about that choice. If she had to work, she would rather be in a profession than a job. But Alex opposed her continuing her education. As time passed and his attitudes about her value became clearer to her, she realized that he needed to feel superior to her. He wouldn't discuss it with her. He worked also and threw himself into work and studies. Shut out, she felt alone. After another year, the happiness completely lost its luster. He wasn't capable of giving—only taking, and she couldn't live like that.

Today she also wonders about the sincerity of Duke's announcement of his feelings, finds it hard to believe that he could have serious feelings based on having known her for only two or three weeks. Imagines that he's more likely to be "in lust" rather than "in love". She smiles at that idea, feeling deliciously wicked at the accompanying thought that maybe that isn't such a bad thing either.

Another explanation comes unbidden. He has been under a tremendous amount of stress and has confided in her his dark and dangerous secrets. It is certainly possible that the release from the loneliness has created a false sense of closeness.

The thought depresses her. She can acknowledge that she doesn't want that to be the case, that she really wants him to want her. No. She really wants him to *care* about her. But she wants that to happen later—not now. Things aren't settled now.

✳   ✳   ✳   ✳

Duke has aimed the T'Bird toward the apartment and drives on automatic. Unlike Ann's, his mind has proven to be blank. But his emotive state is on fire. Images of her face float across his mind-screen. A physical longing lingers in the bottom of his emotional pool—sweet heaviness. He isn't suffering from ideas, but reveling in emotion.

The lights burn dimly through the open screen door and drawn curtains. Music plays softly from the stereo. As he peers through the door, Claire sits in the straight-backed chair in what serves as a kitchen. She reads and is aware only of the music from the college station. She has washed the dishes and emptied the overflowing garbage can. The table and counters are wiped clean and the papers that were scattered around the living room area now sit in neat piles. *What's this? Has she swept the place as well?*

Her tears from the library are nowhere to be seen. She turns as he opens the door. He feigns annoyance, "What happened to all my stuff? How will I ever find anything? How could you do this to me?"

Of course she's not buying it. She sniffs and says, "Would you mind taking off your shoes before you come in here? This place has obviously never been cleaned before, so don't get it dirty again, OK? And if the sight of this makes you a little weak in the knees, just sit down for a minute. It'll pass. This is how real, honest-to-god adults live."

So he flops in the rickety overstuffed chair near the stereo and looks wide-eyed at the splendor that once was his grubby digs. "Thanks. You didn't have to do this; but I appreciate it."

Her nose wrinkles as she grins across the room at him. "I just needed to do something mindless and it needed doing, so it all worked out. Besides, I do appreciate that you're letting me stay here tonight and I wanted to do something to earn my keep. Coffee's ready. Want some?"

With the coffee their conversation turns to the logistics of the "service". He tells her that everything will have to be confirmed tomorrow but that they will likely need to leave shortly after noon—a scant eleven hours away—and drive to the Birmingham area. He has the name of the motel that will serve as the meeting place. The procedure itself will take no more than a few minutes. She has already packed an overnight bag and is ready to go.

Moving into the bedroom, he retrieves his gym bag from under the bed and throws underwear, socks, shorts and two tee shirts into it. She's standing in the doorway and jokes that he is very thorough in his packing for the trip. In mock defensiveness he asserts, "Hey, in the morning, after I shave and brush my teeth and everything, I'll finish the packing."

She slithers the four steps or so that separate them. He's sitting on the edge of the bed, and she joins him there. "Do you have a big ol' tee-shirt that I can sleep in? I mean a clean one."

He leans behind her and pulls a shirt from a stack on the dresser at the end of the bed. When he sits up and hands over the shirt, she hands him an envelope and says, "This was in the mail box when I got here."

He takes it and looks it over. Ellen's handwriting. Thin envelope. Not much in it. Tears off the end and blows inside to open it up. Removes a single sheet of stationery, tri-folded. Inside is a fifty-dollar bill. A short note is scribbled on the paper:

"Ashley. I didn't need this after all. After my first test on Monday, I was walking back to my dorm and felt myself "start". So the doctor's visit won't be necessary. Also, I've been thinking about our disagreements about integration and abortion, and I don't think that I like the person that you've become. I want to start seeing other people. It's too hard, keeping up a love relationship while we're so far apart. You're a nice guy, Ashley; but I don't see how we can stay together if our values are so far apart. Have a happy life and maybe we'll see each other again sometime. Ellen."

To say that he's shocked would be to understate the matter greatly. The bottom of his stomach drops out. He has forgotten to breathe. He stares at absolutely nothing. The primary emotion is not sadness or anger, but disbelief. He's stunned. It has never occurred to him that Ellen or any other woman might choose not to be with him. Claire watches and when he remains silent she asks, "What is it? Are satisfied women from all over sending you money for services rendered?"

Clench-jawed, he hands the letter to her and sits staring as she reads it. He's beginning to feel angry. As he turns toward Claire she says, "This may not sound good to you right now, but you are better off being rid of her. And if she's referring to my having an abortion, it's really none of her damn business."

He shuts her off with a raised hand and explains that this is the girlfriend that he had mentioned to her. They had thought that they might be facing the same decision in the future and that was why they had discussed abortion.

Shaking his head, he goes to the kitchen for more coffee. When he shouts to offer her a refill of her own cup, she declines. Returning to the bedroom, he finds Claire pulling the "big ol' tee-shirt" over her head. She's wriggling and jiggling around in white panties and the shirt. He is surprised at the thrill he experiences at seeing her half naked body. And as her head pops through the top opening, he thinks that his heart will stop. But it doesn't. In fact, blood rushes and pulse pounds. But nothing sexual will happen here tonight. He's sure of that.

Through her unselfconscious smile she asks, "So are you better now? I mean I know that you're upset and all; but are you gonna make it?"

He puts the coffee mug on the dresser and begins undressing. "Yeah. I guess that you're right. It's probably best. I was—hell still am—shocked that she would do that. She has always seemed like the dependent type. I wouldn't have thought that she'd break it off with me. Now I have to wonder if she's already been seeing someone else all this time and that this is just an excuse to do what she wanted to do anyway."

"Duke, it doesn't matter anyway." By now he's down to shorts and reaches to turn off the overhead light. As her eyes adjust to the ambient light from the streetlights outside and she can see him vaguely, she purrs, "Well, her loss is the world's gain."

"You're so good for my ego" he sighs. Dropping to one knee on the bed he asks, "You want the inside or the outside?"

"I don't care. I just want you to hold me." He guides her to the inside and she nestles into the body curve that is becoming familiar and lets go her tension. Soon her breathing becomes regular and deep.

And before he knows it Duke, too, slips into an untroubled sleep. His last remembered thought is of the fifty dollars that his mom gave him.—he's glad that he didn't have to spend *her* money on *that* problem.

CHAPTER 15

▼

Birmingham is a noisy, dirty city. The chief industry, steel, leaves the air thick and often stifling from the many smokestacks that proliferate in the town. "Vulcan", the largest cast iron statue in the world, sits atop Red Mountain, the highest point in the city, and is visible for miles. This steel-hued representation of the Roman god of fire reminds the visitor that it takes heat to make steel. The furnaces, startlingly visible at night, pump out smoke and haze that regularly blanket parts of the city.

Traffic zooms along the four-lane highways until the shifts change at the mills at seven and three, then again at eight and five when the large business district opens and closes for the day. At these times the cars creep by at snail's pace and the genteel temperament of southerners is put to a severe test. The seven o'clock rush is overtaken by the eight o'clock business traffic and three o'clock rush bleeds into the five o'clock outpouring. For two, sometimes three hours, chaos reigns as people try to get to work in one direction in the morning or home, church, ball games, golf courses, or fishing holes in the other direction in the late afternoon.

Duke and Claire are fortunate enough to be coming *into* the miasma rather than going out at half past three this Friday afternoon. They encounter little traffic flow, even as they approach the downtown business district. With the top down and good directions to the motel, Duke threads his way along streets lined with tall buildings of brick and marble—banks, investment houses, and upscale businesses.

In the very recent past Martin Luther King had allowed teenagers to carry the weight of the protest movement in this town and along these streets. Locals have been surprised to find the press and other media so unsympathetic to the treatment of these young ones. This tactic offered the first hint of change in the lot of Southern Negroes. Still, very few colored faces inhabit the shopping areas frequented by whites—and those speak softly, making no eye contact with whites.

The Whitehall Motel sits on the left-hand side if the road as the T'Bird approaches from the south, having turned north onto Highway 11. This neighborhood in the city is middle to lower middle-class in its makeup. The businesses have seen better days. Everything could use a coat of paint. Though it appears to be headed that way, the area hasn't reached rundown status yet.

The address that was given is sufficiently far from the mainstream of the city proper that the verges of the highway lack curbing. At a nearby shopping center weeds grow tall at the edges of the parking areas. The Doughnut Shop advertises 24-hour service and several older cars sit there now. A restaurant offering barbecue serves as a landmark, and from his directions he knows he's close.

He drives past the motel the first time through, sees it and circles the block to approach it from another direction. Duke stops at the office and goes in to register in the pre-arranged names of Mr. and Mrs. Harold Roundtree. The process goes smoothly and soon they are inside Room 17, an end room, sitting diagonally across the swimming pool from the office. It is only 4:00 p.m. and the nurse won't get there until eight-thirty. They turn on the wheezing air conditioner and the TV. The atmosphere between them hangs heavy and anxiety-laden. Claire looks pale and frightened. For all of her bravado she's still just a few short years past having been somebody's little girl. Sitting tensely on the bed, Claire, the woman, struggles to keep that little girl from taking over the center stage in her life's present tense drama.

Reaching out for her hand Duke says, "Didn't you say that you needed to buy some things from a department store? We passed one about two miles back on the way in, so let's go get that taken care of and maybe find something to eat." She nods as he pulls her to her feet and quietly follows him out the door to the car. Her eyes seem oversized and blank. In Duke's imagination "FRAGILE: Handle With Care" is etched across her face.

As they drive back along the roadway Duke turns the volume down on the radio and asks, "How're you doing, Claire?" His hand to her thigh. Pat, pat. Reassurance or something. She practically pounces on it. Her tiny hands are too soft and too wet with the perspiration of fear. She squeezes his hand and pulls it into the space between her breasts. But she is squeezing so hard that the feeling evoked is *com*passion not passion. Duke is certain that no other living human has seen her this vulnerable, and treasures the trust she shows him.

In the parking lot at the side of the W. T. Grant department store Duke retrieves a notebook from the zippered case in the rear floor. Says, "Let's make a list before we go inside. I hate walking into a place and walking around a dozen times because I don't know what I'm looking for." She writes down an item or two and pauses. Concentration seems to elude her. Looking wide-eyed at him she blurts out, "Duke, am I doing the right thing?"

His response is measured. "I don't know, Claire. You seem to have thought it out pretty clearly; but I don't know much about the right and wrong of it. I guess sometimes you just have to do what you think you have to do. What would happen if you change your mind? You still can, you know." Duke feels a knot in his own stomach as he realizes how close he and Ellen came to having to decide this same issue.

Her eyes focus as she considers once again the likely consequences of carrying the fetus to maturity. Shakes her head with conviction and says, "No. This is the right thing but it's sure scarier than I had imagined." With a sigh she continues, "One thing I know now that I only thought I knew before—there's a lot of difference between the idea of something and the reality of it. Deciding was hard enough, but carrying out the decision is a whole other thing."

Duke mulls this over and responds, "At the risk of sounding too much like Doc Benson at Auburn, I guess that you never really decide until you actually *do* something. Until you act, it's just thinking and that's pretty much air, maybe even less than air ... Let's go get these things done. By the way, I think that you're being really brave about this."

A few minutes later they return to the T'Bird with a bag filled with feminine products, tissues, and towels. By now Claire has regained her composure and their conversation flows freely. She has spoken derisively about her thoughts of how others may evaluate her decision, recognizing the deed as unusual within this culture.

She is frank in her distaste that others would presume to judge her if they haven't faced the decision themselves. They agree that most women in the culture would more likely to decide this incredibly important thing based on what they believe others would want them to do. Her confidence has returned, expressed in her customary cocky attitude.

With time to kill, they drive around until they find the Five Points neighborhood and choose The Pancake House. Sitting at an outside table, they watch in wonder as the curious residents of the vicinity stroll past. Men with beards. A few young people with long and stringy hair. Long skirts and mini-skirts in multiple colors and textures. Jeans. Beads. Some people are barefoot and look a little dirty.

They hear exuberant, animated conversations. Laughter predominates. Although there is a lot of energy here, a calm seems to pervade and embrace. Young and old co-mingle.

Claire suggests that these people are trying to emulate what they believe to be happening in San Francisco with the so-called "Hippie Movement". Their discussion leads them to decide laughingly that they only have *ideas* about what that means since neither they nor the local residents have been to San Francisco and so according to earlier agreed-upon truths, they can't possibly *know* what "Hippie Movement" really means. They also agree that it would be interesting and exciting to find out.

During their conversation, Duke hesitantly offers that he is becoming infatuated with a new worker at the library. Claire laughs at him and says, "Don't worry Duke, it'll pass. It always seems to with you. You're a rolling stone if ever I've known one."

Catching her eye momentarily he says with more gravity than either expected, "I don't know, Claire, this feels really different to me. But there's a problem, see … She's married."

Claire can't contain her mirth. "Duke, you seem to be drawn to the impossible … No, I shouldn't say that. You don't seem to *believe in* the impossible. Let's say the 'unlikely'." Seeing his apparent pain at this statement she asks, "Are you serious, Duke?"

"I really don't know, Claire. I know that she's something special, though."

*   *   *   *

By eight o'clock they have found their way back to the motel. The anxieties that were left behind there await and attack. On the way inside they take the time to put the top up on the car. Darkness has fallen and Duke is pleased to see that the motel isn't brilliantly lighted. A few minutes before the appointed hour, he goes outside and sits in the T'Bird with the windows down. At eight-thirty on the minute a new Buick pulls in beside him and a dark-haired woman gets out. She wears a white lab coat over her dark colored dress. She says in a husky voice, "Are you Mr. Roundtree?" Duke nods and says, "That's right." She motions for him to join her inside.

Claire has changed into Duke's "big ol' T-shirt" and is sitting on the bed with one light burning. The woman smiles at her and sits in one of the two rickety chairs near the bathroom door. In the half-light she appears older and haggard. Shadows block a true view of her entire face. She wears thick make-up and lipstick. But when she speaks there is compassion in her voice and in her body language. "This will only take a few minutes to do, but I want to explain some things to both of you before we begin."

As she pauses and looks first at Claire and then at Duke, he finds the other chair and sits down. "There is always a little pain associated with these kinds of procedures. But the pain shouldn't be excruciating. If you get to hurting really bad, then something is probably wrong." She stops and looks at each of them until they nod and respond verbally that they understand.

She pulls her chair close to Claire and taking her hand says, "I know that you're scared, honey, but this should be alright. Just do what I tell you and take good care of yourself. Unless something unusual and unforeseen happens this will be over in a few days. I want to tell you exactly what we're gonna do so there aren't any surprises." She reaches into the pocket of her lab coat and withdraws a small zippered pouch. Opening it she removes a sealed package containing a thin piece of plastic or rubber tubing.

"This tubing is sterile. I'm gonna use a gel for lubrication and insert the tubing into the womb. See it has a rounded end so it shouldn't hurt at all. I will blow into the tube to get air into the cavity and then I'll withdraw the tube. That will induce what will seem like a heavy "period" for the next four or five days. That's the whole procedure. What comes next is the part that *you* will have to be responsible for. You with me so far?"

After Claire nods to the affirmative the woman turns to Duke and asks, "How about you? You still with me on this?"

Duke has heard of the womb but is a little uncertain as to exactly where it is. He nods and says, "I guess."

Although her nerves are taut, Claire giggles, figuring out that he's lost. In response he says, "Just tell me what to do and I'll do it."

Now the nurse snickers and says, "Well, honey, at least you've got him pretty well trained already. You'll probably be just fine."

Some of the tension lifts from the room and she continues, "Next I'll have to pack you with this sterile gauze material. This will need to stay in place for at least twenty-four hours. After that you can remove it. You're going to bleed a little more heavily than you do for your normal period, so you'll need to use pads, probably a lot of them. I see that you have a couple of boxes over there on the counter and you'll probably need a couple more just to be sure. Other than that you should experience a normal, though heavier, monthly period. You'll feel a little pressure until the bandage comes out tomorrow evening.

"That's really the whole procedure. You just have to be careful for a few days and keep yourself as clean as possible. That will be a little difficult. When you urinate, the bandage will want to come out, but you'll have to keep it in. The purpose of the bandage is to apply pressure to control bleeding. Remember it needs to stay in place for at least twenty-four hours. Don't get up any more than you have to until tomorrow night. No walking more than necessary for three days. No running or lifting for a week. Alright, do you have any questions?" She looks at Claire who shrugs and seems to be getting scared again.

Duke asks, "Is it OK for her to ride in the car? We were going back home tomorrow, if it's safe."

"It should be fine," she states hesitantly. "But it would be best if you could wait until, say, Sunday afternoon. Just use common sense and judge what you do based on how she's feeling. And this last and most important thing—if something bad does happen, get her to a hospital immediately. Too much pain or bleeding that can't be stopped can pose a threat to her. That means she could die if the bleeding can't be stopped. Understand?"

Solemnly, Duke nods and feels the grind of grown-up anxiety in his gut. Pledges silently to himself that he will not let anything happen to her. And now the woman is escorting him out the door to sit in the T'Bird and wonder how things are progressing in the room. He feels helpless and uncomfortable at the lack of control.

Soon the door opens a crack and the nurse motions him inside. Claire sits in a sort of daze and says nothing. Realizing that he is now expected to pay, Duke fishes the envelope out of his pocket and hands it over. Without even opening it the woman takes the money and walks to the door. Before leaving, she turns and says, "Remember, be careful. Take care of yourself. And if anything too unusual happens, go to the hospital. Good luck to both of you." And then she is gone.

The closing of the door after her seems to have sucked all the air and noise from the room. Duke sits alongside Claire on the bed and almost whispers, "How do you feel? Do you need anything? Do you hurt?" She just shakes her head and places her fingertips gently over his mouth. Together but far apart they sink back to the headboard of the bed—each thinking private thoughts. Her hand finds his and holds on with a clammy grip.

After a few minutes she says, "You know how sometimes when you go to the dentist and they stuff cotton in between your cheek and gum? Well that's about how it feels. It doesn't hurt exactly, but I just feel *full*. It's hard to explain. And I know that I'm holding on tight everywhere. I can't seem to relax."

He asks, "Is there anything that I can do to help? I mean, can I get you something to drink or anything?"

"No. I really want to go to the bathroom; but I'm scared to. I'd like to go to sleep and just avoid the whole thing. I just feel so out of control."

"Let's put on the TV," he suggests. "Maybe that'll distract you from thinking so much just about *that*." He stands and switches on the small box. A variety show is playing and he adjusts the volume down to a low level.

"You know," he says, "what's been started will have to run its course. You *can't* stop it, but you need to remember that you did make the choice to start it, so you're not *really* out of control. It's just something that you have to endure.

"And besides, this is just one part of your whole being. It may seem like everything right now; but it isn't. You may as well stay focused on the things that you *do* still control rather than mourning for that part that you gave up in order to get something else that you want."

Almost sarcastically she says, "You sound like my father. He's forever telling me that I can't have everything. Maybe this is the first time in my life that I actually understand the truth of that. I still think I'm doing the right thing for me right now in my life; but I could do without the pressure and the fear." She smiles a little at this and seems to let go a little. "You're being pretty rational about all this."

A kind of peace is settling over the two of them. He sits on the chair near her and says, "Well, I've been thinking about this stuff a lot lately, so I'm just repeating what I've been saying to myself. Besides, it's not all that hard to be rational when I'm over here and it's you going through the pain and discomfort." It's a relief to see her smile and relax a little more. "Tell ya what, I'm gonna go back down the street and get a couple of doughnuts and coffee. Do you want something?"

"I'm craving a fountain coke. Do you think that they will have one there?" She looks like an elf. Her eyes no longer have the dull glazed look that was there before. But as she moves to sit up, she winces with pain and falls back against the headboard.

Reflexively he reaches for her, but there is nothing to do. The glazed look returns. "Want me to stay?" She shakes her head and waves him out of the room.

When he returns fifteen minutes later, she is in the bathroom. Locking the outside door, he puts the four doughnuts on the counter and sets the fountain drink on the bedside table near the spot where she was sitting. On the TV a spectacled reporter is interviewing a thin black man. Duke's attention is arrested when he hears the name Stokley Carmichael. That's the guy Pax mentioned to him before.

The black man is saying in response to the reporter's questions, "We are planning to send at least two busloads of volunteers into the city of Selma, Alabama to attend the protest rally and to assist with the registration of black voters. The president has agreed to send U. S. marshals to monitor the situation and to insure that these people are not prohibited from voting any longer. The volunteers will represent men and women, blacks and whites, young and old from many different parts of the United States."

To another question he replies, "There are already black and white volunteers in the state of Alabama working for this just cause and we will bolster their efforts. We are grateful for the efforts of the president and his willingness to send marshals on our behalf. We expect to leave from the Greensboro, NC area in a few days and we should arrive in Alabama on Thursday or Friday. We are a non-violent group and do not anticipate problems." Duke thinks, *Yeah good luck on that one, man.*

The interview continues as Claire reappears from the bathroom. "Who is that guy?" she asks. Hearing that it is Stokley Carmichael, she laughs and says that it's funny how people who do big things often seem so small in physical appearance. She also wonders aloud if the appearance of another round of Freedom Riders in Alabama will touch off another round of violence from whites who are so against coloreds having an equal voice.

"I'll tell you what I think," Duke offers. "I think that white people are not going to voluntarily give away any power. They believe that easing the restrictions on voting to the coloreds will result, first, in elected colored officials. But ultimately what they believe is that it's just the first step toward interracial marriage and what they call the mongrelization of the races."

Her response is immediate and leaves no room for doubt as to her own thinking on the matter. "Jesus Hobart Christ on a bicycle, Duke. Don't tell me that you actually believe that crap. The races have been being mongrelized for centuries. Go down to Mexico or Central America and you'll find whole countries populated by mestizoes, or mixed blood peoples. The Spanish did a real number on the Inca and Maya races there. Or think even further back with the Celts and Normans. Or the Moors in southern Europe."

Duke raises his hands in mock surrender. "Easy, Claire. I didn't say that *I* think that way. I was saying that the predominant racist attitude in the South is driven by fears along those lines. I agree that the idea of a 'pure race' is probably pretty much a myth by this time in history; but what I think doesn't matter a lot to the folks around here."

As she calms down he adds, "In fact I'm not sure that this isn't just evolution at work."

Then changing gears he asks, "So how are you feeling? How was your trip to the bathroom?"

With a sigh she says, "So far, so good. She was right about the sense of pressure. It seems to be getting worse as I go along. But it isn't so bad right now. I'm about ready to try to sleep. How about you?"

He finishes his second doughnut and strips to shorts, douses the light, and joins her on the bed. She curls up inside the protective arc formed by his long frame once again and they both stare out into the darkness. As their breathing evens out she softly says "Thanks." He begins to stammer out a response and she whispers, "Don't say anything. Just accept that I appreciate your help and let it go at that."

"Yeah, alright."

They pass the night fitfully. She is up and down several times. The experience is surreal—like a dream—but neither sleeps well enough to have dreamt. Morning finally arrives, overcast and dreary. Duke goes out into the drizzle for food and returns to find Claire crying quietly. She angrily rejects his attempts to comfort her and he withdraws into his own funk.

At two in the afternoon, Claire says that she wants to go home. After a brief discussion he agrees, if she will stay at his place until Sunday night. Dodging rain showers, he packs their things into the T'Bird, checks out at the desk, and anxiously helps Claire to the car. He has stolen two pillows from the room and she makes herself as comfortable as possible. After consulting his map, Duke decides to take little traveled Highway 25 eastward to connect with 231 and then eventually 280 that leads back to Auburn.

Driving in the rain only adds to the tension that has accumulated in Duke's shoulders. Claire is silent and seems once again to be holding on for dear life. His few attempts at conversation are met with curt replies and he eventually stops trying. Highway 25 proves to be slow going and this too adds tension. Duke wishes that they were already back on familiar ground.

As they approach 231 Claire says, "Duke, I need to stop if you see a gas station or something. I'm gonna have to change this pad. I think I'm bleeding more heavily now." Her voice is level and without urgency, but Duke is nonetheless stirred to further action. He asks a little more of the T'Bird and begins a vigilant search for an appropriate stopping place. But nothing appears. No gas stations. No stores. Nothing.

Claire stirs and reaches behind to find a towel. She maneuvers this between her legs and looks at Duke with big eyes. The color has drained from her face. Finally at the junction of highways 231 and 280 there is a truck stop. She asks Duke to follow her to the ladies room and not to panic if she has bled through to her shorts. Duke's stomach is tight as he walks closely behind her to the restroom area. She has in fact begun to show blood at the rear of her shorts, but not too much.

In the hallway, the sounds of the restaurant echo off the concrete block walls. Music from the jukebox and the jumbled voices of several conversations converge into a sickening din. He leans against the door facing and feels the mugginess of the air. Condensation trickles down the glass. The light seems to be dim and there isn't enough oxygen. She's been in there a long time. *Jesus, what if …*

As his concern escalates to the level of fear, thankfully, the door to the ladies room opens and Claire stands there. A deer in the headlights. Pale. Her face glistens with perspiration. She's trembling. "We need to go, Duke."

They wobble to the T'Bird to make their way out onto the highway for the last leg of their journey home. She says, unconvincingly, that she'll be OK and Duke can only drive her homeward. But soon she says that maybe he'd better plan to take her on to the hospital after all. "All of the packed in gauze came out when I used the toilet. I'm bleeding pretty badly."

They agree on Lee County Hospital as the nearest trustworthy place to go and it is almost fifty miles away. Easing down on the accelerator their speed increases to 70, then 75. When the road opens up to a four-lane section, they go even faster. The rain has stopped but the roadbed remains wet. He tries to balance speed and control. His concentration is total and the clench in his jaw begins to ache. He refuses absolutely to allow himself to think of anything past driving the T'Bird as fast as he can safely drive it.

The dripping landscape is a blur as they tear through the countryside. At some point she begins talking. "Duke, unless you can't help it I don't want my daddy to be contacted. But if you have to I'm writing down his name and a phone number where you should be able to reach him. On Saturday sometimes, he isn't home. But try there anyway. The second name and number is for my mother. I *really* don't want her to be told *anything* about this unless I'm dying or something. If you reach my dad, tell him that I don't want him to say anything to my mother. And don't tell him why I'm in the hospital; I'll do all that when the time is right."

The road ahead narrows back to two lanes as they approach the turn to Auburn. Straight ahead six or eight miles away is the hospital and, gratefully, there has been no rain here, so the road is dry. His glance to Claire shows that the towel soaked red with blood. She says, "I'm really tired, Duke. I may be passing out, but I think that I'm still alright."

In his head he hears "... could bleed to death...." Fear rises up in him like bile. His jaw throbs, but from somewhere down deep he finds the determination to finish this task.

Light traffic on the highway now as the T'Bird closes in on the hospital. Duke blows the horn and then blows past all interference. Sees the Emergency entrance ahead. Slows to make the turn and slides to a stop at the doorway. Looks to his right and sees Claire with eyes closed and a smile on her face. He opens his door and sprints into the entryway of the emergency room. A woman dressed in white and looking strangely familiar looks up from the reception desk. Before she can speak, Duke blurts out, "I need help. I have a woman in my car and she's bleeding. A lot. Come on, help me."

The nurse wastes no time but jumps up from the desk and asks, "Is she conscious? Can she walk?" No panic here. Competence and calm. A professional. Duke answers, "No. I don't think that she's conscious and I'm sure that she can't walk."

The nurse turns and calls out, "Leroy, grab that gurney and come out here and help me. STAT." She turns to Duke and says, "Where's the car and what's the patient's name?"

"The car is as close as I could get it to the door and her name is Claire."

By this time a slight, older, colored man with a furrowed brow and gray at his temples has arrived at a trot pushing a stretcher on wheels. "Where to, Miss Angel?" She points to the door and the three of them move quickly in that direction. On the way to the car Duke realizes the reason that the nurse looks familiar. She has helped him before.

At the car Leroy has opened the passenger's side door and is checking for a pulse. The gurney sits nearby. As Angel approaches he says, "She alive Miss Angel. Got a good strong pulse, but she lost a lot of blood." There is concern in his face, but no panic.

Angel turns to Duke and says, "Go to the other side of the car and help us as we turn her and lift her out."

On his knees in the driver's seat Duke holds Claire's limp body as Leroy swings her feet and legs around. Then as Leroy and Angel pull her from underneath her legs he pushes her gently forward until they can grasp her and pick her up. When she is on the gurney, Angel turns to Duke and says, "You stay here and move your car. And then clean it up. When you're finished, come inside and we'll talk about who to notify. Don't even think about coming in now; you'll just be in the way."

As he stands there in the parking lot, they wheel her away. He feels empty and strange and all alone, like a part of him is being ripped away. He goes through the motions of moving the car to a proper parking space. Looking down he is shocked at the amount of blood pooled on the seat. Searching through the things in the back seat he finds a couple of towels and begins to soak up the blood. As he does, the stress catches up and tears begin. Soon he realizes that he is sobbing uncontrollably. Swipes at the tears with a corner of one of the towels. Wipes more blood from the seat.

Tears and blood—the anatomy of tragedy.

CHAPTER 16

▼

Each hour since she mailed the fifty-dollar bill and her note to Ashley has brought increased depression to Ellen Dunn. She has wandered aimlessly through the end-of-term tests, and as Friday arrives she realizes that she doesn't want to be here anymore. After breakfast she calls home collect and tells her mother that she's coming home. Her mother hears with a mother's ear and asks, "Are you alright? You don't sound good."

"Yes, Mom, I'm fine, but there are no classes on Monday and I just don't want to be here. Sara Beth is coming home, too, so I can ride with her."

After a pause, Mrs. Dunn responds, "It'll be fine, Ellen. We may go to Birmingham for dinner. If we do, I'll leave the keys to my car on the table with some money. There isn't much food in the house, so you'll have to find something for yourself. Bring some milk, too, for breakfast. We'll let you know if we're gonna stay overnight."

Ellen rolls her eyes. Thinks that if her father wants a home cooked meal he has to go to Granny's or cook it himself. "That sounds fine, mom. Y'all have a good time and I'll see you either tonight or tomorrow."

Having a goal in mind relieves some of the depression for the moment and she throws herself into a flurry of activity—goes to Sara Beth's room, secures her ride home and agrees on a time to meet, collects dirty laundry, packs, decides to take a couple of books in case she wants to study, and makes it to her morning classes.

✳   ✳   ✳   ✳

As Ellen and Sara Beth near the Dunn residence, Ellen spots her parents going in the opposite direction. She waves out the window at them but they have their windows up and the air conditioner and the radio going, so they don't see her. Sara Beth pulls into the drive and helps her unload.

With her laundry started Ellen, unpacks her suitcase and wanders into the kitchen. She takes a Coke from the fridge and sits at the kitchen table. She's trying to evaluate her decision to break it off with Ashley. They've been together five years, but the distance between Auburn and Jax State has really hampered the last three. *I'm still the same, but he's changed, and it's the change in him that I can't stand. His being willing to help coloreds to vote makes me so mad ... And abortion— I can't believe he said that he would consider it. It's just too much. How could I be around that? How would I ever know what to expect from him?*

Then her emotions kick in. *What do I do now? Everybody assumes that we would get married, so I'm "off limits" to all the boys I know. And I miss him. He always took care of things. Holy cow! First my daddy did everything for me, and then Ashley did. I don't know how to take care of myself. I'm in college because Daddy and Ashley wanted me to go and I hate it. Maybe I should just quit and get a job. Surely daddy could get me a job until I decide what I really want to be doing.*

Hearing the washing machine stop, she goes to the laundry room and changes the washed clothes to the dryer and starts another load. Back in the kitchen on the counter she sees the keys to her mother's car and a twenty-dollar bill with a note:

> *Elle,*
> *Go and get yourself something to eat. We'll probably come back*
> *tonight, 'cause I have work to do in the morning. Welcome home.*
> *Love, Daddy*

In a different hand scribbled below this message is her mother's reminder:

> *Go ahead and do your laundry and don't forget the milk.*

Typically there is no signature at the end, no hint of caring, just instructions. In the near silence she hears the splash and clatter of the washer and dryer and thinks about how the dorm is so much noisier, but also so much friendlier.

Later, driving her mother's Cadillac is like guiding a ship in the ocean—huge, slow, and cumbersome. She drives across town to a burger joint that was the favorite hangout of her crowd in high school. Parking at the side of the building she goes inside and orders a burger, fries and a Coke. She sits near the window overlooking the four-lane. Her movements are languid and she is distracted without being focused on any particular thought. She's lonely and doesn't even know it yet. Traffic drifts by, seen but not noticed, so that when Marcus Davidson's GTO rumbles into the parking lot, she sees it without recognizing the car or the driver.

Interrupting her preoccupied stare at the world, a tray appears on the table next to hers. Behind the tray is Marcus's bulk. Big grin. "So can I join you or is Ashley coming in right behind you?"

He's a big man—taller even than Ashley, and broader. Short brown hair combed to the side. He looks soft but Ellen knows he has a reputation as roughneck and maybe a little on the wild side. Jeans, boots and a shirt with the sleeves cut out. He's handsome in a rugged sort of way, though a little baby-faced.

"I don't think that Ashley's in town this week, but I'm not sure. We're broken up." Saying it out loud for the first time, she waits for his reaction and doesn't have to wait long.

Marcus looks up at her, shocked. "What happened? Jeez, I thought surely that you two would get married after college and all."

She can see the wheels turning in his mind. He's assessing his chances and she's flattered and to some degree relieved—she's still attractive to the male population. "I don't know, Marcus. He just seems to have changed so much that I didn't enjoy being with him anymore. And I didn't really want to be in college. I just went to satisfy him and my daddy. I don't think I'm going back."

She's trying out this line too. In the back of her mind she's already dreading raising this issue with her father.

Around a mouthful of French fries Marcus nods and says, "I know what you mean. My folks wanted me to go to the junior college, but I felt like it was a waste of time. My daddy got me a job at the waterworks and I'm doin' just fine. You don't have to go to college to have a good life." He hesitates before asking, "So what are you gonna do?"

Unsure of herself she says, "I'll probably try to get daddy to see if he can find me a job here somewhere until I figure it out. Maybe I'll just go to the business school downtown and be a secretary. I don't know. I'm not as sure what I *want* to do as much as I am what I *don't* want to do."

She can feel his eyes boring into her and is surprised to find herself responding to the attention. She had forgotten the thrill of having another man want her. She had relinquished her sexuality to the relationship. And now she can feel the excitement growing inside her. Thinks, *I wouldn't mind going out with him.*

Maybe he's a mind reader. He asks, "So what are you gonna do *tonight*? I mean do you want to go to a show or something?" He's feeling the tension too, and anticipates the likelihood of catching her on the rebound and nailing her.

While she's calculating she says, "I have to be at home tonight because my folks are in Birmingham. They're gonna call if they're staying over, so I'll need to be there in case they call."

Bells are ringing in his head. *Hot-damn—Jackpot!*

"So can I come over and hang out and watch TV or something? I could stop and get something to drink, and chips if you want."

Even though she knows that she wants him to come over, she pauses; this is new and carries its own brand of anxiety. *Would I know how to act? Would anybody else know if he just comes over? How far might he try to go?* But finally she gives in to the urge and says, "Sure. And Coke and chips would be nice." She's tingling inside with excitement. She hadn't thought that being apart from Ashley would be fun. Suddenly she feels released from months of pressure that she hadn't realized was there.

"Look, Marcus, there are a few things that I have to do. Why don't you come over at about eight-thirty." When he nods, she goes on, "I have to go by the grocery and get some things for my mother and some other things too. I'm gonna go now. I'll see you after while." Clearing her mess, she leaves with a smile and a wave.

*   *   *   *

At half past eight Marcus rings the doorbell at Ellen's house and she invites him in. After dropping the Cokes and chips in the kitchen, they go into the den and she turns on the TV. Their choices are a western, a game show and a variety show. "What do you want to watch," she asks.

"Whatever you want will be fine."

There's awkwardness between them. He's not sure what to expect or what is expected of him. She wonders if she has been too bold. As the TV rambles on unheard, he asks, "So what really happened between you and Ashley?"

"Marcus, you wouldn't believe the things that he's doing now." She hesitates having almost spilled out the whole business about the pregnancy fear and abortion, then goes on. "He told me that he has been working with the nigras in Tuskegee."

Marcus looks up, quizzically, from the couch. "What's that supposed to mean? Does he have a job over there or something?"

"No. He's been working with some group that's trying to help them get registered to vote. When all that business happened last week at that church, we heard it on the radio and he said that if he hadn't been home for the weekend, he would probably have been there himself. And he said that the people who were hurt were his friends. We had a big argument about it. It's probably the main reason that I decided that I didn't want to be with him any more."

Marcus shakes his head in disbelief. "You know, I saw him that weekend, too. He came in at the Stag after he left here that Saturday night. I didn't get to talk to him much, because that Tommy Thomas guy and him went for a ride in his new T'Bird. Man, who'd've thought that he would get involved in something like that? What'd he say about it?"

Her pulse races as she unburdens herself. "Let me think a minute. He said something about it not being fair that the nigras don't get to vote, because they have to pay taxes just like everybody else. He also said 'It's gonna happen anyway whether anybody likes it or not' or something like that. I don't remember all of it. I just want to put it and him behind me. I'm disappointed that I wasted so much time on somebody like him." She's leaning forward from the chair, her face glowing with intensity.

She adds, "You know, he practically never came home anymore. I should've known he was doing *something* down there. I just thought that with working and classes, he was too busy … Oh yeah! He told me that he's started playing bridge. I thought that was a game for old people, but he plays all the time. I can't figure out how he passes his courses. It's like I don't really even know him after all this time together."

Marcus feels the fires of betrayal beginning to burn inside him. *There's already so much trouble with the niggers that about the last thing I can put up with is a white man siding with them. That kind of person has no idea what the mixing of the races is gonna cause to happen. It's almost like people didn't learn anything from the Bible and that story about the Tower of Babel. Well, I know some folks down in Montgomery and some others in Columbus that will be glad to know who one of these turncoat bastards is. We'll see how they react to a local boy deciding that everybody else is wrong and he's right. That sonofabitch.*

Meanwhile, Ellen is still rambling on about what an disappointment Ashley is. Marcus hasn't heard anything for several sentences and tunes back in in time to hear her ask, "Don't you think that I did the right thing?"

He reassures her that she made the right decision and asks where the bathroom is. She directs him down the hall and goes to the kitchen to fix glasses for the Coke and to put chips in a bowl. While she is busy with her tasks, Marcus returns quietly behind her and, admiring the view, hugs her from the rear. She doesn't resist but her stomach rolls a little from the unfamiliar roughness of his touch.

She turns from the counter with a bowl in her hands so he has to let her go. Setting the bowl on the table, she says, "Let's just sit here in the kitchen."

Thwarted and disappointed, he agrees to sit there. Feels angry and frustrated. *This little bitch is playing with me. She's a tease. She lured me into coming over here with her "Ashley and I are broken up and my parents are out of town" routine and now she's not wanting to come across. We'll see about that. I know that Ashley had to have been tapping her, so she wants it; but she don't want me to know that she wants it. Maybe if I just insist, she won't have to feel bad about it.*

They make small talk for a few minutes and Ellen gets up to pour more Coke. When she turns from the counter this time, he is standing in front of her and very close. His huge arms engulf her and he pulls her face to his for a rough kiss. Ellen is panicky. She knows that she invited him here and that at the time she was feeling attracted to him, but now she's not feeling receptive to this. Her hands come up between them to his chest and she tries to push him away.

He whispers gruffly, "It's OK, Elle. I won't hurt you. I know that you want this, but don't want to seem trashy. Just let it be all my idea."

Guilt washes over her and she lessens the pressure on his chest. He, in turn, loosens his bear hug. She's looking at the floor and he's trying to make out with her. Mentally she has given up—she asked for this and has no right to turn him away now.

She feels his hands as they touch her roughly. He kneads at her breasts and what had been a source of joy and pleasure with Ashley, seems dirty and tasteless. Sensing her revulsion, Marcus pushes her away from him. "You snooty little bitch. You think you're too good for me? You too used to that wimp Ashley feeling up your titties? Well let's get a good look at them."

As he reaches to tear off her blouse, the doorbell rings at the carport, just a few feet away. She looks up at Marcus fearfully. He hesitates then nods her toward the door and she steps away from him. Opening the door she finds Mary Beth standing there.

Mary Beth's chipper voice has never sounded so good to her. "Hey, Elle. I hope that I'm not interrupting anything, but I think you may have picked up my Western Civ book by mistake. When I got home I couldn't find mine and I saw that you had one. If that's not mine, then I need to borrow it or to sit here sometime this weekend and read my assignment. We have a chapter quiz on Tuesday and I'm barely surviving in that class as it is." Looking past Ellen, she sees Marcus and waves, "Hi, Marcus. How are ya?"

Ellen sighs with relief. *Saved by the bell. Maybe she can help me get Marcus out of here.*

She says, "Come on in Mary Beth. Do you want some Coke and chips? We were just sitting in the kitchen, talking. Sit down. I'll get you a Coke. We can check on the book in a minute." She maneuvers Mary Beth past Marcus to the table and goes about the business of getting her a Coke.

Mary Beth sits down and asks, "So what are you doing with yourself, Marcus? I haven't seen you in—what—two years?"

Marcus nods thinking, *Well shit. That takes care of that. I'm done here for tonight.*

He says, "Oh my daddy got me a job with the Water Board and I'm just working. Me and Josh Curley have a house over on South Fourth Street. I play a little ball and bowl on Tuesday nights. We hunt in season, go to the local ballgames. That's about it. Pretty boring, I guess." Actually he *enjoys* his life, but somehow when he's talking to these college girls he feels like he ought to be doing something more.

Mary Beth says, "I think that's great. I know several guys that we graduated with who still don't work or anything. They're living off their parents. So, good for you. I imagine that those guys are gonna get drafted before long anyhow. They'll probably end up in Vietnam or something."

Marcus waves her off with his hand, and to her that looks like a gesture of shyness about being complimented. In fact, he's thinking, *Yeah I bet that you think my job at the waterworks is great. You're just like Ellen and the rest of the bitchy college girls in this town. You're too good for ol' Marcus.*

But he says: "Look y'all. It sounds like y'all've got studying to do, so I'm gonna get outta here. Good to see both of you. Ellen, maybe I'll call you later." With hunched shoulders he walks out the door and the women hear the rumble of the GTO as he leaves the house.

Inside Ellen semi-collapses and thanks Mary Beth for "saving my life". She goes on to explain that she thinks that Marcus might have raped her if the interruption hadn't occurred. Mary Beth looks skeptical but her eyes widen as Ellen tells the story and where things stood when the doorbell rang.

"Good heavens, Elle. I'd never have dreamed that Marcus could have grown so mean. He didn't seem like such a bad guy in high school. Tell me about why you and Ashley broke up."

"I'll tell you; but first, will you stay the night here? My folks may stay in Birmingham for the night and I don't want to be alone with Marcus in that kind of mood."

Mary Beth agrees, calls her mom and the two settle in to gossip and study. Ellen's previous thoughts of leaving college and working in town have vanished from her mind.

✳   ✳   ✳   ✳

The GTO blasts through the curves and down the straight-aways on its way to town. Marcus is in an almost blind rage. He's sure that Ellen is telling Mary Beth what a creep he is and that it was all his fault—probably leaving out the part about her flirting and the invitations.

They're all alike. The goddamn rich bitches and their pansy-assed boyfriends. She thinks she's a goddam princess or something. And Mr. Ashley Niggerlover Windsor … Well I'll by god see to it that he gets his. If the boys from down south don't light his ass up, then me and the local gang will. Me and Preston McCormick will drive to Montgomery tomorrow and talk to Rube. He'll either do something or know who to notify in Tuskegee to get something done. Surely there's Klan in Tuskegee. Hell, there's a damn nigger college down there; they'd have to have some way to keep 'em in line.

His ruminations occur while his jaws are clenched and his hands grip the steering wheel so tightly that his wrists ache. When he reaches the four-lane, he drops the GTO into second gear and peels rubber around the corner and down Meighan Boulevard. He winds the car through third and barks the tires changing to fourth. The speed gives vent to the rage that has been building since he left Ellen's house feeling humiliated. Pulling up in front of the Stag, he gets out and goes inside.

"Hey, has anybody seen Preston McCormick tonight?" he shouts into the room.

Several people look up but no one says anything. Pete yells from the back, "I think he's pumping gas at that new Phillips station over in West Gadsden."

Tommy Thomas is at his accustomed seat against the wall. He calls out, "Marcus. Come over here a minute. What are you so het up about? You're sweatin' like a racehorse. Sit down here a minute and take a pull off this." He passes his flask in Marcus's direction.

Marcus sits but is restive. He takes the offered flask and tips it up. The burn moves his attention from Ashley to his own throat and stomach. Grateful, he passes the flask back to Tommy and asks, "Didn't you talk to Ashley in here a couple of weeks ago?" Tommy nods. "Did he say anything about working for the niggers down at Auburn?"

Tommy is shocked. "No, he didn't say anything about it to me. Why?"

"'Cause Ellen Dunn told me that he told her that he was trying to help 'em get registered to vote. That'd be just like that pansy son of a bitch. He's always thought that he was better than ever'body else. I'm gonna get somebody to fix his ass."

Fear scratches at Tommy's mind. "Hold on a minute, Marcus. You say that Ellen told you this. Why would she say that? I mean that's her boyfriend. Why would she try to get him in trouble?" Tommy is trying to buy some time and de-fuse this situation. He knows that Marcus could really put Ashley in a very dangerous position.

"Naw. He ain't her boyfriend no more. She dumped his ass when he started talking all this nigger-loving shit. I was over at her house a little while ago and things was just about to get interestin' when that goddam Mary Beth Engle showed up and fucked everything up. She sure as hell said it and I believe her." He's beginning to get angry again. Sweat glistens on his forehead. His jaw works and the muscle at his temple pulses.

"Now wait, Marcus. All you know is that she *says* that she dumped him. He may've dumped her and she said all that stuff to make him look bad. Hell, you've known Ashley most of your life. You played ball with him and against him. You've drunk good white whiskey with him. He hasn't ever seemed to lean that way, has he? You don't want to go accusin' your friends based on what could be the word of a pissed off woman." Tommy takes a drink from the flask and passes it back to Marcus.

Taking the flask, Marcus seems to consider this alternative view of things. He takes another swallow and passes the flask back to Tommy. "Well, maybe you're right, but maybe she's telling the truth. If she is, then the folks down there ought to know about it. They could at least check into it and do something if it's true. I'll have to think some about this, I guess." The rage is mellowing as the glow grows in his belly.

*   *   *   *

On Sunday afternoon Marcus and Preston McCormick are riding along Highway 77 toward Talladega, where they will pick up the highway to Montgomery. Marcus is again telling Preston the accusations that Ellen has made about Ashley. Preston, like Tommy, is skeptical. He says, "I just don't believe it, Marcus. I lived next door to him for ten years and he's just like you and me. He ain't never done nothing like this and I feel like I'd've seen it in him. I've thought it over since you told me last night and I don't believe it. B'sides why should I believe a stuck-up bitch like Ellen Dunn? She ain't never had the time of day for me, or for you neither. Sounds to me like she's trying to make him look bad so's *she* don't look so bad."

Marcus is annoyed that Preston questions his judgment about this. After all he's the leader of the Etowah County area Klavern of the Ku Klux Klan. Preston should follow, not question. He thinks, *Why won't he accept this and just do what I tell him? Even if this turns out to be a wild goose chase, it's better to check it out than to do nothing and let it keep happening.*

Finally he says to Preston, "You didn't talk to her like I did. I think she was tellin' th' truth. And I think that I'd've got in her pants, too, if that damn Mary Beth hadn't showed up. She wanted it, all right I could see it in her eyes."

He pauses and thinks about how good she looked and about her inviting him to her house, knowing that her parents were out of town. Then he continues, "B'sides it won't hurt nothing to get Rube and his bunch to check things out. I never did trust that asshole Ashley anyhow. He always acted like he was better than the rest of us, to me."

The GTO turns right in Talladega onto Highway 21, then on into the mountains and toward Montgomery. The two men continue to discuss the problem, and Preston doesn't budge. Marcus eventually gets frustrated and yells, "Just shut the fuck up, Preston. Goddamn it you're supposed to be following your leader in these things, not arguing with every damn thing I say. Now just let it be and we'll go on and do what I've decided on." The rest of the drive passes in silence, both men are angry, neither convinced of the value of the other's point of view.

At last Montgomery comes into view—a sprawling, sweltering city. The large downtown area seems run-down and disregarded. The governmental buildings are well kept in real contrast to the rest of the district.

As they pass the State Capitol, Marcus says, "You ever been over there to the capitol? There's a bronze star on the floor there where Jeff Davis was sworn in as the president of the Confederacy. Biggest mistake of the war was moving the capital to Richmond. Let's stop by over there and pay our respects."

He wheels the GTO around in the area in front of the pristine, white, neo-classical building, parks near the entrance and the two men get out. They walk up the steps to the outside verandah and Marcus points out the star. With amazement in his voice he says, "This is hallowed ground, my friend. I can't believe that we didn't win that war."

Soon the two men realize that they've gotten off track and make their way back to the car. Marcus finds a phone booth and looks up the number and address of Ruben Townsend. When his call is answered at Townsend's home, Marcus says, "This is Marcus Davidson from Gadsden. D' you remember meeting me at the regional convocation?"

"Yeah I think I remember you. What can I do for you?" He is not convincing in his supposed recollection.

Marcus wants to be heard on this matter and plunges on with his requests, "Any way we could meet somewhere? I need to tell you about something that I think you'll want to know. I'd rather not talk about it over the phone."

When Marcus explains where they are located, Townsend gives him directions to a Waffle House nearby and says that he'll meet him there in 30 minutes. Marcus and Preston find the place easily and go inside to wait. A newspaper lies on the counter and Marcus picks it up. The headline story covers the interview that Stokley gave to reporters on the previous Friday night, promising to send another set of Freedom Riders into Alabama, this time to Selma.

As Marcus reads, the anger rises up in him again. He says to Preston, "Can you believe this shit? Seems like this son of a bitch would've learned that if he comes back down here, him and all his friends are gonna get their asses handed to them, just like the last time. I 'spect that somebody's gonna have to die before this smart-ass nigger gets the message. Well that's OK too. I'm thinking that we'll need to send a delegation from the Gadsden klavern to this one. What d'you think, Preston? Is that something that you'd like to go do for us? Maybe take a couple of the fellas and see if the Selma boys need any help?"

While Preston considers the question, Marcus spies Ruben Townsend getting out of his truck out front. "Here's Rube. Now we'll see if my idea is so far-fetched." Raises his hand toward the door to signal to the man entering.

Ruben Townsend is medium height and big. He stands under six feet and weighs in at 245 pounds. No fat. Big burly arms. Broad, slightly bowed shoulders. A fringe of graying hair runs around the sides and back of his slick, bald head. Dressed in blue poplin work pants and a fresh white shirt, he stalks to the table with a half-smile on his face.

Marcus rises to shake his extended hand. "Hey, Rube. This is one of my lieutenants from Gadsden, Preston McCormick. Sit down and join us. Want coffee or something?"

Rube catches the eye of the waitress, points to Marcus's coffee, and motions for her to bring him the same. Then he sits down and asks how their trip down was. They make small talk for a while before Rube notices the headline on the newspaper. "What d'you boys think about the niggers bringing in more Freedom Riders?"

Marcus laughs and says that he was just telling Preston that the Gadsden Klavern needs to send some reinforcements to Selma to help out. Rube nods and shows that he's impressed with that idea. "If you can get some boys to come, you let me know and we'll meet up somewhere near there. I know all the men over there, and they'll be proud to have as much help as they can get. You know that damned turncoat Lyndon Johnson is probably gonna send U.S. Marshals with 'em this time. If he activates the National Guard, some of our own men will be forced to stand against us … I mean they wouldn't actually *do* anything; but they'd have to stand on the other side, and that'd mean fewer of us. So, hell yes, send some men. Many as you can."

"I'll sure do that. In fact I think Preston here is gonna lead the group, so it's good that he was able to meet you today. That way you'll know to recognize each other. Look, the real reason that we came down here today is that I think a boy from our neck of th' woods has gone over to the other side and is working to help the niggers register to vote in Tuskegee. I thought that somebody down there ought to know about it." He sits back in the booth and waits for Rube to respond.

"You damn right somebody ought to know. I'm one somebody myself. Hell, we can hit Tuskegee with a rock from Montgomery County. Who is this son of a bitch and how do you know that he's working for the niggers?" Rube's face is flushed with anger and he leans forward in anticipation.

"His name is Ashley Windsor. I've known him all my life, and wouldn't't've never expected him to do something like this. But his ex-girlfriend told me that he said so himself. Said that if he hadn't't've been in Gadsden two weeks ago that he'd've been at that nigger church that got the 'visitation' from the Tuskegee bunch; 'least I reckon those boys were from Tuskegee."

Marcus revels in the telling of this, and the attention he gets from Rube. After all, Rube is a big man in the Klan. It's always good to be friends with the people at the top. "He's supposed to be a student over at Auburn. He's about 6'2" and prob'ly weighs about … I don't know …'bout 165 or 170, I guess. Brown hair. Never noticed what color his eyes are."

Rube has written this information in a small notebook that he replaces in his shirt pocket. He leans his elbows on the table and says, "We'll sure find out about this and if it's true, we'll take care of that too. I'm glad you boys came over."

Then speaking to Marcus he says, "If you can get some boys together, you need to call me tonight or tomorrow. The niggers are supposed to show up in Selma in a few days. We'll want to be ready for them. Give me your phone number. You've got mine. You call me and I'll call you back from a pay phone. I think that my phone is bugged. Th' feds ya know."

As the three men take their leave, Marcus feels vindicated in his judgment. In the GTO he says to Preston, "So d'you still think I was wrong to talk to Rube about Ashley?"

"Naw. I guess you were right … I reckon I'll head up whatever boys you can get to go to Selma, too. It's good to see that there's other people out there that believe like we do. I appreciate you bringing me along on this. I'll do whatever you think is right."

CHAPTER 17

▼

Duke approaches the door to the Emergency Room with dread. His emotions are back pretty much in check after the drive through the countryside. The tension no longer burns in his belly. But the fear that he was too late hangs there in his head. He opens the door with trepidation.

Inside, Angel Hattaway is exiting a curtained-off area. She motions him toward the admitting desk. "You need to help us out here. We need her name, and the name and address of her next of kin." That sounds ominous to Duke and the question in his eyes is answered before his mouth can speak it, as Nurse Hattaway says, "She'll probably be fine, but we don't know how old she is and if she's a minor we'll have to have parental consent to treat her. Looks like she's had a miscarriage, so she'll most likely need a D&C. She's conscious, but she's weak and has lost a lot of blood."

The term "miscarriage" sends waves of relief through Duke. One hurdle passed. He asks if he can go in to see her and the nurse reluctantly agrees. He approaches the bed quietly. Her eyes are closed and she appears to have lost five years—looks like a fifteen year old. Her vulnerability strikes Duke like a fist, and he feels guilty for his part in putting her in this position. As he stands silently beside her, she opens her eyes wearily and smiles. Wiggles her fingers so he will take her hand. She is cold to the touch.

He whispers, "They think it's a miscarriage." She nods. "I'll only give them your father's name and phone number." Slight squeeze from her fingers. She tries to muster the strength to say something, but can't quite manage it. He nods his head, "It's OK. You're welcome." A tear appears at the corner of her eye and he wipes it away. "You're gonna be fine. You rest now and I'll come back after while." With that she relaxes back into welcome sleep.

Back at the nursing station he looks over the piece of paper with the name Judge Julius T. Hollister written on it and he learns for the first time that her father is a federal judge. He says, "Her name is Claire Hollister and this is her father's name and phone number." As he gives the paper to the nurse he asks, "Do you think that I should call him?" Her assertion that the phone call falls in her area of responsibility brings another relief. He realizes that she has made the wrong assumption, but decides to wait until later to unravel it.

He listens as she places the call and marvels as she handles the delicate news in a professional and clinical manner, pronouncing the word "miscarriage" with no particular emphasis. A fact not a guess. She tell the judge that the D&C is necessary, that she should be fine but does need to have the procedure done now, that, no, it shouldn't wait until he drives here from north Alabama. Then she puts him on hold while she gets him to give the doctor verbal permission to proceed. She nods to Duke, as she returns to the curtained area and leads a white-clad man to the phone. He goes through a similar round of assurances with the judge.

When he hangs up the phone, the doctor swings into action. "Hattaway, start that IV while I call a surgeon. As soon as you've got that started, get her draped and get Leroy to help you wheel her down to the OR."

He turns with the phone, consults a list and calls in a surgeon, explains the nature of the need, and confirms that the surgeon will be at the hospital in fifteen minutes. He then calls the operating room, tells the staff there to prepare for an emergency D&C, and that Dr. Ralston is on his way. They are to prep the patient and await Ralston's arrival. Nurse Hattaway will bring her down, and will hand off necessary paperwork.

The precision of the team is very impressive, and Duke relaxes, believing that Claire will make it through this. As they wheel her out of the ER, Nurse Hattaway turns to Duke, gives him a "thumbs up", and says, "I'll be back in a few minutes."

Looking at his watch for the first time in hours, Duke wonders how seven o'clock could have arrived so quickly. He feels a little queasy and realizes that he hasn't eaten much today, so he is hungry. A second nurse appears at the desk in a fresh uniform. She filters through the various papers on the counter and looks around the waiting area. "Do you need some help, sir?"

"Uh, no thanks. I'm waiting for Nurse Hattaway to come back and tell me about a patient." As he says this, the interior door reopens and Hattaway nods in his direction. The two nurses confer for a moment and Angel approaches Duke.

Speaking quietly she says, "She's gonna be fine. If you'll wait a few minutes while I do rounds with Miz Kelly, you can buy me that cup of coffee you owe me." He nods and asks the way to the snack bar.

*   *   *   *

The hospital, which had seemed empty to him earlier, is filling up now with the evening crush of visitors. Duke finds a Coke and sits tiredly at a table. A familiar figure appears at the cash register and Duke squints to recognize George Blankenship. As George turns to leave, Duke waves to get his attention. George sidles over to the table and sits. "What's happening, George. What are you doing at the hospital? Your family all OK?"

George responds in his familiar drawl, "Naw. That ain't it. My family's all fine. Where the hell have you been? Lynn's been lookin' all over the place for you. It's her daddy that ain't so good. His spleen ruptured on Friday and they had to rush him up here to the hospital. Turns out that it swelled up after that beatin' he took and busted. He's had surgery, and it was nip and tuck there for a while, but he's gonna make it."

This news awakens Duke and he asks, sitting up, "Is Lynn here right now? I mean is she upstairs with her daddy or something?" He's running on adrenaline and dreads having to put on another act, to see and talk to the Wilkins family, especially Lynn.

George seems amused, "Naw. They left a few minutes ago. He's stable now and they aren't staying around the clock like they were. My daddy's up there right now. They were talking about doin' something to avenge Robert Earle's beatin'. I don't know, Duke. I found out that it wasn't th' niggers that beat him up at all. In fact it was the uncle and father of that O'Reilly boy that they caught at that church last week. But they're gonna use the beatin' as an excuse to put a little fear of retribution in the niggers. Maybe they'll give up on this stupid voter registration stuff. I don't care much for th' dishonesty myself—who needs it?"

Duke's interested now. "So how did you find out that it was those white guys that beat him up? And what do you think that they'll do for revenge?" They are speaking in intense but lowered voices. The snack bar is crowded with people now.

George leans even closer and whispers, "I heard Robert Earle tellin' my daddy about who did it. He found out who they were from the sheriff. They had gone to Jimbo to ask what he was doin' to arrest the people who beat up th' agitators and burned th' car." George snorts a laugh into his fist and goes on, "I ain't real sure what they're plannin' t' do, but I suspect that somebody's about to get hurt. They'll have to do something, 'cause Robert Earle laid out there in the street in Niggertown for like two hours before anybody did anything. He knows that all the niggers saw him out there and believes that now they think that they can take him on too, just like them white men did. This is some serious shit here."

Duke feigns conspiratorial agreement, "Yeah. I can see that. Wonder what they'll think up."

"I don't know, but if I was colored and lived anywhere near that church, I wouldn't come out of the house for a few days."

Duke hesitates and then says to George, "Last time I saw you, we talked about bustin' some birds. You wanna go shoot skeet tomorrow or Tuesday? I've got the key to the club's storage room and we can get the thrower and the birds from there."

George happily agrees to meet on Tuesday afternoon and as he takes his leave from the snack bar, Duke says, "If you see Lynn, tell her that I had to go to Birmingham this weekend and that I'll try to be in touch in the next day or two."

*   *   *   *

Duke is folding the information into the proper files in his mind when Angel Hattaway joins him at his table. Sensing his distraction she says, "She's gonna be fine, Duke. You might as well quit worrying about it now. I talked to her daddy just before I left the ER and told him you probably saved her life. He's real anxious to meet you. I guess that you're not too surprised to hear that, huh?"

Duke is amused and annoyed. Resets. *Oh yeah. Everybody's gonna think that she was carrying my baby and that I had to bring here in because of that. Jesus, I can't take the time to get one area straight before I have to put out some other fire. This is getting a little complicated. First things first.*

He looks at Angel and smiles. "I know that you think that she's my girlfriend and that she just lost my baby; but it's not like that. I'm just her friend and she got me to help her out. I barely knew anything about this, but she needed the help, so I tried. I guess her daddy thinks the same thing; but Claire will set him straight when she can. Is he headed down here?"

Angel leans back and has a "Sure, whatever you say" look on her face. "Yeah, he'll be here sometime this evening. Probably no earlier than nine-thirty. She should be out of surgery by then. Are you planning to wait here for him? You sure have a lot of friends who get in trouble, Duke."

Duke blushes a little and says, "Yeah. No kiddin'. But no, I'm not gonna stay here. I'm about to starve to death. All I've had to eat today is a couple of stale donuts. I'll come back later and see th' judge. Do you wanna go eat? We can just add that to the coffee that I already owe you."

Angel sits back up to the table and gazes at him levelly. "Tell ya what. I've been working since seven this morning and I'd like to get a shower and get out of my working clothes. If you can wait that long, follow me over to my house and then we'll go somewhere."

No hesitation. He follows her out to the parking lot, and then to the small house just off the Parkway. She parks, climbs the three steps to the porch, and unlocks the door. "C'mon in. I won't take but a minute."

Inside the little house Duke notices that everything is immaculate—clean and orderly. Angel guides him into the small kitchen, points to the fridge and says, "There's tea and ice water in the fridge, make yourself at home. I really want to get a shower."

She returns after a few minutes dressed in jeans and a halter-top. She is careful to lock the door as they leave. "Nice car, Duke. Can we put the top down?" Duke gives instructions and with Angel doing her share they lower and cover the top. The twilight air is fresh and clean from the earlier rains and the wind feels fine on their faces as they speed along the Parkway to the Dee-Lite Café, three miles away. No talk. No anxiety. Just peaceful.

Once they're seated and their food has been brought out, she asks, "So is she really not your girlfriend? Or were you just saying that?"

"She really *is* just a friend. Her real boyfriend is at Vanderbilt, obviously too far away to be called on. She almost waited too long to realize how serious things were." The lies are coming easily now. "It's a relief to know she's gonna be alright. I imagine that her daddy's not gonna be too happy about this. I reckon I'll find out afterwhile."

She waves her fork in the air and says, "You don't have to go back over there. In fact, if what you say is true, maybe you should let them work it out for themselves. Nobody there knows who brought her in but Claire herself. I didn't put your name in the records. I don't know … You decide."

Duke thinks about the *real* story behind this and recognizes that he doesn't know what Claire might have told th' judge. Realizes that he might accidentally do more harm than good. "Thanks for not putting my name in the records. It'd probably be best if I go back tomorrow. I'm sure Claire will handle things with her father. I'm gettin' deep in debt to you for favors. Thanks again."

"Sometimes we all need a helping hand. Think nothing of it. Pass it on. It'll come back. Besides, this way I didn't have to cook dinner and eat alone."

*   *   *   *

Two men confer in determined tones in the fluorescent glow of the hospital room's light. One, a corpulent man gone pale from the trauma of surgery and loss of blood, lies tilted up in the bed. IVs drip precious fluids into his arm. The other man is rangy and wiry, his face leathery from working in the sun. He wears dress pants and a sports shirt open at the neck. Anger floats freely in the atmosphere. Resolution lurks in their proposals. The one demands violence of the other. The second, though willing, seeks direction from the first. They explore and discard options one by one.

In frustration the tall man stands and declares, "Goddammit, Robert Earle, you want me to do something so th' niggers don't get th' idea that they can just beat up on a white man; but ever'thing I suggest you give me ten reasons why I can't do it. What do *you* say we ought to do?"

He gets no answer. "Then, I'll tell you what I *am* gonna do. I'm gonna take a couple of boys with me and I'm gonna blow ever' damn window out of that nigger church. If old preacher Maxwell comes out and says anything, we'll teach him a little proper respect. Then we'll wait 'til you get well and do anything else that you decide on. And that's just th' way it's gonna be. You might as well go on to sleep now. I'll let you know how it goes when you get home."

So saying, and before Wilkins can find fault with this plan, Thaddeus Blankenship walks rapidly from the room.

Robert Earle, then, lies alone with his thoughts, his rage and his shame. Thinking back on that day a week ago, he still can't believe that he allowed himself to be so thoroughly beaten up by a man half his size and more than ten years older. These facts are unknown to Blankenship, who believes that both the relatives of the O'Reilly boy bear responsibility for his friend's defeat. Still, no matter how hard Robert Earle tries to convince himself that the brothers teamed up to whip him, he knows the truth. So each plan advanced that would wreak vengeance on the coloreds falls short somehow. The shame and the rage, so closely married as to be indistinguishable to him, cause him to shake and sweat. And in the end he rings for the nurse and asks for more pain medication.

＊   ＊   ＊   ＊

In various enclaves across the state, in each of the state's sixty-seven counties, men of a single purpose gather and discuss the response needed to the impending invasion by Stokley Carmichael and his hordes of Freedom Riders. In every meeting, whether in homes or coffee shops or roadhouses, they reach the same conclusion: The niggers and their friends will not be tolerated in the state. They, the men of the Brotherhood, will band together with their brothers in Selma and destroy the threat. They will preserve the white race. The interlopers will be crushed, beaten, killed. Every klavern will send men to the aid of their brothers.

＊   ＊   ＊   ＊

At the Wilkins home in Tuskegee, Lynn hangs up the phone and stares into space. Mrs. Wilkins looks at her daughter and asks, "What's wrong, honey. Who was that on the phone?" Tilly Wilkins is thinking that she doesn't need any more problems to deal with just now. She has never liked her husband's involvement in this Klan business. Now he's recovering from a beating that threatened his life, and she doesn't want to have to deal with Lynn's childish difficulties.

"It was George. He said that Duke was at the hospital just now and that he told him to let me know that he had been in Birmingham this weekend. He didn't say why he was in Birmingham; and he didn't say why he was at the hospital. I wonder what that's all about. I've tried to call him at the library a half dozen times since Friday; but that Miz Lassiter just says that he's not working and that he's off this weekend. Something's going on, Momma."

"Lynn, you're gonna have to learn not to ask so many questions, or you'll never be able to have a relationship with a man. Men just do things and don't always tell their womenfolk why, or what it's all about. Duke seems like a very nice young man. I'm sure that no matter what he was doing, he'll let you know as much as you need to know. We're all tired and edgy, and shouldn't make too many decisions or judgments until we're more rested. I'm going on to bed and you should, too." With a sigh she walks heavily to her lonely bedroom to try to sleep without the security of her man's presence.

Distractedly Lynn replies, "Yes, Momma." But she thinks that something's going on and she'd better find out what. *Maybe I'll just get in my car and ride into Auburn. Maybe I can find Duke and see what's really happening. Oh dammit, my car's in Auburn. And I don't have a way to get there. This is so frustrating. I hate hav-*

ing to be the trusted daughter. Be here for everybody else. Help look out for Momma. Dependent. Taken advantage of … Dammit. With a sigh of her own she, too, walks heavily to her room and forces herself to bed.

✳   ✳   ✳   ✳

A couple of hours later George sits on the front porch of the family's farmhouse home. He is adrift in the night sounds of crickets and, more distantly, frogs at the pond—all combined with the clear moist air. He's been thinking about the events of the past several weeks and somehow for the first time in his life he isn't satisfied that all is as it should be. He had been in school when Auburn integrated and was more or less glad that there had been no violence. He didn't really know Pax O'Reilly, but he'd heard of him and figured that without him Auburn would have looked just as bad as the University of Alabama had when Wallace had stood in the door. Now Robert Earle and his daddy planned to hurt somebody and use a *lie* to justify it. Then a few minutes ago Ruben Townsend called from Montgomery. George knows *him* and this can't be good news.

He hears the approaching vehicle long before he can see the headlights across the fields. The sound of his daddy's truck is unmistakable, like the voice of a family member. He thinks maybe he won't tell his daddy that Ruben called … *I know I will. If I don't, it'll come out in the end and I'll have another confrontation with the old man. One of these days Daddy'll hit me and I'll strike back. And that'll be the end of the inheritance.*

He holds on to this anger like a precious secret. Without the security of knowing that the farm will be his someday, the world is a frightening place. *Where would I go? What could I hope to do? How would I live? Everything that I know and care about is bound up by these buildings and fenced fields.*

The headlights slow on the county road and turn right into the chert driveway. He can hear the hum of the engine and the splash the wheels make as they roll through the puddles left by the rain. As the truck approaches the house, the creaking of the springs and shocks again provide him with familiar sounds. Sees the glowing arc of the spent cigarette that Thad flicks out his window. Winces as the headlights sweep across him, the truck headed to its usual parking spot near the porch. He sits in dread as his daddy gets out of the truck and stomps into his presence.

"What are you doin' sittin' out here in th' dark? Has your mama done gone to bed? Is there anything to eat?" All spoken in a nasal growl. All rhetorical.

He doesn't even slow down as he walks past, even though George is answering, "Just sittin'. Yes sir, she went to bed a while ago. I think she left something on th' stove." But he's thinking, *If you want to know anything else, you'll, by god, hafta come out here and ask.*

Nonetheless he knows that he'll eventually get up and go inside to report the phone call from Montgomery. Knows that he'll feign interest and subservience again. Knows it's like the old man says, "You don't hafta like it, you just hafta do it."

In the kitchen Thad sits in the dim glow of the light from the stove. A glass of milk and a plate of cold food have done little to improve his mood. He's still smarting from the numerous put-downs Robert Earle inflicted on him at the hospital. *Can't figure out what's got into Robert Earle anyway. He ain't th' same since them fellas ganged up on him. Then Emma goes off to bed at nine o'clock, leaving supper cold and nobody to talk to. Well, hell, better to eat alone than to go hungry.* He hears the creak of the screen door opening and closing and then sees, with annoyance, his son coming in to disturb him.

"Daddy, Ruben Townsend called from Montgomery about an hour ago."

"What'd he want?"

"He didn't say."

"Did you ask?"

"He said that he'd talk to you about it later."

"Did you get his number?"

Pause. "No sir."

"Goddammit, George. How in th' hell am I supposed to call him if I ain't got th' damn number?" Silence. "Aw hell, forget about it. I swear, son, I don't know how in the hell you are *ever* gonna be able to get a goddam thing done. You don't think to do the simplest things. That ought to be absolutely obvious to anybody. You just don't get it sometimes, do you?"

Silence.

*   *   *   *

Sunday morning finds Judd and Elizabeth sleeping late. When the phone rings Judd gets up and goes to the living room area to answer. He hangs up and sits staring for a moment. Elizabeth notices his serious manner and, sitting up in bed, asks, "What's th' matter, babe? Who was that on the phone?"

Judd's blue eyes come back into focus and he turns to her. "That was Dr. Mohammed from Tuskegee. He called from a pay phone. He was asking if I had seen or heard anything from Duke. He's apparently scared that something's gonna happen over there because of the beating of that Wilkins fella. He ended up in the hospital on Friday bleeding internally. When I told him that I hadn't seen Duke in several days, he said that I should look him up and see if he's heard anything. So I was just thinking that I *haven't* seen Duke in several days and was wondering if everything's okay with *him*. Know what I mean?"

"Yeah, I understand what you're saying; but Duke's about the last person in the world that I'd worry about. If you're really concerned, though, we could drive over to his place and check on him. In fact let's get dressed and do that. While we're out you can buy my breakfast and we'll pick up a paper."

CHAPTER 18

▼

Elizabeth's raggedy old VW Beetle shudders and shakes across town. No sign of life at Duke's place. Coughing and sputtering, the car manages to make it back uptown to the *Grille*. While Judd finds a newspaper at the rack in front of Toomer's Drug Store, Elizabeth chooses a booth at the front window. They order, divide the newspaper, then read and chat while waiting.

Before their food arrives, Elizabeth looks out and sees the T'Bird sitting at the red light—top down, windows down. Her jump out of the seat startles Judd, who exclaims, "What is it? Hey, where are you going? Elizabeth …?"

He glances in the direction of her flight and sees her waving and yelling at … "Duke!! …," who laughs out loud, backs up and U-turns into the parking space next to the VW.

Judd smiles to see Elizabeth grab Duke and hug him like he's some long lost brother or something. He knows that she feels genuine affection for him. Shares that affection as well. Duke looks rested and recently showered and shaved.

Elizabeth wears a very short skirt that sculpts her perfect rear, and a tube top that covers at least some of her excellent chest. Her sandals accentuate the difference in their heights. She holds on to his arm like he might try to escape. She's laughing and teasing him about how he drives. And he's being comfortably aware of her breast rubbing against his arm as they walk, adding to the warmth that he otherwise feels for her. Duke sits down across from Judd in the seat that Elizabeth had occupied, so she scrunches in next to Judd.

"So where've you been Duke? We were just over at your house and missed you there. Need to talk to ya. How've ya been?" Judd is glad to see his friend and to know that he's safe. He won't tell him that he has been worried—wouldn't seem fitting somehow. Certainly wouldn't want to call into question his ability to take care of himself. But still the phone call nags at him. Thinks, *In good time …*

"Aw. I had to take a friend of mine to Birmingham. I'm just getting back from washing the car. I was really busy last week and haven't seen you guys. How have you been? What do we need to talk about?" He's thinking, *Oh no, another fire to put out. What now? Have I forgotten something? Then, man, Elizabeth looks better every time I see her. I mean—down to there and up to here and out to there. Hoo-boy.*

Judd interrupts his wandering thoughts. "Yeah we've been busy, too. Tests and all that. But what I needed to talk to you about is …" Pauses and looks around to ensure privacy. "Mohammed called me this morning. The folks over there are scared that something is going to happen because of that guy Wilkins getting beat up. He was wondering if you had heard anything about that. He seemed pretty concerned and asked me to get in touch with you, to find out if you know anything. That's why we went to your place earlier."

Duke leans into the table and speaks in a low but firm voice. "Let me bring you up-to-date on all that. I *did* hear something last night. First, that Wilkins guy is the father of the girl that I was, or rather am, dating over there. He actually was beaten up by Pax's uncle, not by coloreds and not by two or three white guys, just Pax's uncle. Of course he would never let that kind of story get out, so he told the community that he was beaten up by the coloreds. He has told his closest friends that those two white men ganged up on him and whipped him—and at gun-point. I met both the father and the uncle and I guarantee that the father didn't throw a punch.

"Anyhow, Wilkins ended up in the hospital with a ruptured spleen and some broken ribs. And sure enough, they are plotting some kind of revenge—but not on the guys who actually did it. I ran into George and he told me that they're going after some undisclosed target in the colored community. He said anybody living near the church oughtta just stay inside for the next few days."

The waitress arrives with food and Duke decides to order too. When she has safely retreated to the kitchen area, he continues. "I'm supposed to spend some time with George on Tuesday. Maybe I'll know more after that, but probably you oughtta tell Mohammed that much now. What do you think?"

While he peppers and cuts into his biscuit and gravy, Judd nods his agreement and says, "I'll go over to Pax's apartment and call from there. I've got keys. You're right, they oughtta know about this. I'll tell Doc that I'll call him back on Tuesday evening, too. Does that sound about right to you?"

Duke is relieved that Judd sees things the same way he does. "Yeah. That sounds good. You'll have to come to the Berry on Tuesday night, because I've got to get back to work. I've missed way too much time lately. In fact, I'm gonna try to work some tonight. When are you going to Pax's?"

Around a mouthful of food Judd replies, "Soon as we finish eating. Why don't you take Liz home and I'll take her car over there. No sense in exposing her to any possibility of danger, although I don't really think that there's any in this—right now anyway."

"You're probably right but we have to start thinking like that. You never know when these country boys will break loose. And these beatings have raised the stakes."

*　　　*　　　*　　　*

Their business concluded, Judd concentrates on his food and soon Duke's eggs and grits arrive also. When finished the friends pay their bill and go outside. Judd gets into the VW and starts the engine while Duke and Elizabeth still stand on the sidewalk. Duke waves and shouts, "Turn that damn thing off a minute."

He goes to the rear of the vehicle, opens the hatch, looks at the engine, turns something with his fingers and says, "OK. Go ahead." And, of course, the engine miraculously purrs as well as a four cylinder, 28 horsepower VW engine can purr.

Judd drives off and Elizabeth says, "You're such a smart-ass."

Laughing, Duke replies, "Why? 'Cause I know a little about engines, suddenly I'm a smart-ass? It was the butterfly valve … It's tough to score points with you, Liz. If you're ready, let's go; unless you have something else that you need to do."

"I don't. Let's go … Oh wait, I need to go back for our paper." Duke stands and watches her jiggle her way back into the restaurant.

*　　　*　　　*　　　*

Sunday evening services at the church have been canceled. Miz Maxwell herself called each and every person on the church's register and told them that the Reverend wasn't feeling well and that, no, there would *not* be a music service.

Eudora's saying, "Eldred, I don't like calling off services because we are *afraid.* It feels like they're winning when we do that. Or maybe, I should say that it feels like we're giving up. How do we really know that something's gonna happen? And do we stop our faith every time there's some kind of rumor that something *might* happen?"

Miz Eudora Maxwell has been at the right hand of her husband throughout his long ministry. She has taught school, and retired from her profession. She has helped to administer the finances of the family and of each church to which they've traveled. Together they've raised their three children in the church. They've saved enough money to supplement the scholarships that the denomination provided, so their kids are educated and working themselves in foreign missions in Africa. If she has an opinion, she speaks it. And she doesn't back down very often.

Patiently as ever, Pastor Maxwell responds, "'Dora, I've told you three times already that Brother Milton suggested that we cancel services tonight. I don't know why he said that. I don't know what information he might have, or where it might have come from. But I *do* know that his opinion is worth hearing and his advice is worth heeding. If nothing happens, we have lost nothing. The good Lord will understand why we are worshipping at home this evening. And if something *does* happen, well, we'll be grateful that our people are safe."

His calmness often infuriates her, but over the years she has learned that he usually makes good decisions. Like when he had bought up that remote piece of land and multiplied their money by ten when the federal highway department had bought a corridor for what will eventually be an interstate highway. And they still own the property surrounding the planned exit ramp. Or the time that he convinced the denominational leaders to investigate the possibility of investing in the stock market by contacting influential Negroes in New York City and Los Angeles, where people of color had access to that sort of public trading.

After a pause he goes on, "What I'd like to do, and I'd like you to join me, is to turn out the main lights in the house and sit in those chairs in the bedroom and read the Bible for a while and talk. You know that I'm always interested in your ideas."

Eudora shakes her head and would like to be angry still. But she can't suppress the smile at his weak attempt to deflect her. "I know that you don't honestly believe that throwing me that compliment is gonna change my mind about this. But I will go into the bedroom with you, even if it's only to read the Bible."

Her teasing grin signals him that the harsh words are over and that she agrees without having to capitulate. As she's turning out the lights in the living room, she shivers with an inexplicable knowledge that her husband is in mortal danger.

He's standing in the bedroom in his pants and undershirt when she comes through the door. She reaches for the Bible that sits on the bookshelf, and from outside they hear a booming sound. Eldred rushes across the room and roughly pulls Eudora to the floor. The booming is steady and continues. "What is it, Eldred?"

His voice is husky with fear. "Sounds like shotgun fire. You stay put. I'm gonna sneak into the living room and look out the windows."

The hint of danger from before echoes in her mind. "No, Eldred. Don't go out there. It's too dangerous. Just stay with me. I'm scared. Just stay here."

But he's pulling away and crawling on hands and knees to the living room. *Nothing hitting the house. I'll just see what's going on. No big deal. Check out the church and all. Won't make a silhouette. Slide myself up the wall here by this window and peek out through these sheer curtains.*

In the near total darkness he sees the vague images of several men standing around the church at various intervals. Each has a long barreled gun and is calmly shooting into the direction of the church. The flash from each blast lights up the immediate area of the gun and Reverend Maxwell recognizes at least two of the shooters.

At first the shooting seems random and makes no sense to Maxwell. But after a few seconds the truth dawns on him. In horror he thinks, *Oh my God. No. They're shooting out our beautiful stained glass windows. Oh please don't let them be doin' that. Oh, Jesus, please stop them from desecrating your sanctuary.*

Without realizing what he's doing, Maxwell opens the front door to the manse and begins running across the lawn, the street, the churchyard. He shouts, "Stop. Oh please, stop. Don't defile God's house. Why are you doing this?"

Unthinking, he reaches for the first shooter's arm. The man slashes at him with the barrel of his weapon, striking him along the side of his head and the top of his shoulder, knocking him to the ground. Again calmly, the shooter reloads and turns back to his work, continuing to deliver round after round into his assigned section of the church. A total of nineteen works of art are being systematically reduced to shards of colored glass.

Thad Blankenship stands at the front of the church taking care of the big circular window that sits in the center of the tower that holds the church's bell. He is also responsible for the two smaller windows on either side of the double doors. He places his shots carefully, avoiding the bell and not drawing further attention to this *necessary* work that he and his fellows are performing. He watches as Maxwell approaches the man next to him, Ricky Parsons, and sees Parsons knock him to the ground.

More hyena than wolf, Thad walks toward the stricken minister who, though stunned, is awake and struggling to regain his feet.

With the barrel of his gun he centers the minister. "Get on up, boy. We got talkin' t'do. Walk on over to that white truck and git in th' other side." Following Maxwell with his gun trained on the center of his back, Blankenship feels a surge of rage rising up in him. The urge to pull the trigger and vent this rage is almost overpowering. But then they reach the truck and Maxwell is on the other side and out of his line of fire. The rage, though quieted, lives on in his heart.

Maxwell closes the passenger's side door and Thad joins him in the truck's narrow front. Thad leans out the window and whistles. All the firing immediately ceases. The men—four more in all—meander toward the other two trucks and Thad says, "We'll meet up at the entrance to the Forest."

Everyone seems to know what that means and the engines all purr softly. They leave the street as quiet as it was fifteen minutes earlier. Quiet, that is, until the lone voice of Eudora Maxwell is heard wailing in the darkness, "No, Eldred, don't go with them. If you have to die, die here with me. Don't go."

As the trucks pull out, her plaintive begging changes. Suddenly *she* feels the rage. Focused rage. "I see who you are Thad Blankenship. You won't get away with this. You'd better not harm my husband. I'll hound you to my grave."

All this is heard clearly in the cab of the truck. Maxwell turns to Thad and says, "She won't do nothing, Mr. Thad. She just upset now and talkin' crazy. She won't say nothin'."

Thad glances sideways at Maxwell and says, "Shut up, preacher. There ain't no plan to do anything to you, so I don't care what your old lady says. We've just got to talk some and we'll do it on my terms and at my location. There's some things that you're gonna tell us, and then we'll let you go."

"What kind of things?"

"I said shut up. We'll get to this in good time. I want everybody to hear what you have to say."

"But I don't know.... ."

Thad backhands Maxwell hard to the face. "I said, shut up."

✳   ✳   ✳   ✳

Seven o'clock on Sunday evening is a quiet time at the university library. A few die-hard students study but have no need of the services of the music clerk, so Duke reads his assignments at the desk, unimpeded. Although he has missed only one day of classes, he feels pressured at not being on pace with the class schedule or ahead of it. Sitting with the Spanish/English dictionary at his elbow, he is so intent on the novel by Calderon de la Barca that he doesn't sense the presence of Ann Lassiter. When she has stood there for a full minute and he continues to read, she clears her throat. Startled, he turns and is about to ask if he can help.

The sight of her fills him with warmth. "Hi. How are you? What are you doing here? Surely you didn't get trapped into working again this weekend." He's gushing and knows it but doesn't seem able to stop.

"What a nice surprise. You look wonderful," he continues, noticing now that she's not in working attire. In fact she's wearing Bermuda shorts and a scoop neck peasant blouse.

"I don't much like admitting this," she says, "but I actually came over to see if you had made it back and had come to work. If you hadn't been here, I would have found a book to read or something. In fact, I'll probably check one out just to cover the embarrassing fact that I was missing you." An embarrassed blush creeps up her neck turning her golden complexion a deeper shade of tan. She leans against the desktop.

"You were missing *me?*" His turn to blush now. "This is the nicest thing that's happened to me in days. Come and talk. This is too good to believe." He wouldn't have dared think that she would miss him—much less admit it.

Going on and on in his head, he almost doesn't hear her say, "Why is that so hard to believe? I thought that we were getting close. Have I presumed too much, Duke?" She's spluttering and beginning to feel foolish.

"No, no Ann, stop. I really meant it. I'm very surprised—and very pleased that you came here. Maybe I'm being too careful or something, I don't know. I don't want to be presumptuous with you. Maybe I can't allow myself to even hope that someone like you could be attracted to someone like me." It all just tumbles out and the honesty of it is like a thunderclap—startling and followed by silence.

She shakes her head and finally says, "'Someone like me, someone like you'— I don't have any idea what you mean by that, Duke. I'm just an ordinary person and as far as I can tell, so are you. What is it that you're seeing that I don't see?"

His blush grows deeper as he replies, "I'm not even sure myself, I guess. Maybe it's because you come from New York and were educated there. Here in Alabama I've heard all my life that the education system is inferior. Maybe I'm afraid I'm not smart enough for you. Or maybe it's because it seems like you come from a family that has money and culture; and, well, my family has neither. It's just hard for me to expect much from you." He is both glad and ashamed to have said it all.

In her shock at his outpouring, Ann would like to run away to think about these things. Her feelings are mixed also, but for totally different reasons. Part of her struggle with the deterioration of her marriage is the financial well-being of her child. She has little regard for the impact on her own life, but as a mother she has to consider what's best for her daughter. "We'll have to talk about this somewhere else, Duke. But just so you know, my father was a blue-collar worker, so that's what I'm accustomed to. And I don't really know many people who are smarter than you are. You've read as much as I have and that's a heck of a lot. So put some of that to rest and we'll talk about the other later. How late are you working?"

Still a little embarrassed by his disclosure, he says, "'Til closing. Can I come by your place afterwards?"

"No. I don't think that would be wise. Drive in that direction and I'll meet you somewhere. Maybe near that tree where we stopped the other night."

He nods and, before he can say any more, she turns and walks out the door. Suddenly his world is empty again.

He finds it impossible to read the Spanish novel now.

✳   ✳   ✳   ✳

Three pickup trucks move purposefully along the narrow paved road inside the geographic confines of the Tuskegee National Forest. Thad Blankenship is in the lead and turns onto a dirt track that could be a road, or maybe just a path. A half-mile through the foliage, the track leads them to a clearing that has obviously been used as a campsite in the past. Heavy logs are arranged in a rough rectangle surrounding a fire pit, a circle of stones that have been smoked black over the years. The central area is swept clear of underbrush. Well-worn parking areas lie at odd angles in the trees. All six men disembark the vehicles. Thad says, "Collins, did you bring that jar with you?"

A grizzled man in his late forties answers, "Yeah. It's in my truck. I'll get it."

"Bring some of them paper cups out of my truck too. Preacher, you just sit down there on that tree stump. We'll be gettin' to this in just a minute." Swift Collins returns with a quart mason jar half filled with a clear liquid and part of a sleeve of paper cups. Thad pours a small measure in two cups and hands one to the preacher.

"You can understand that I don't drink no alcohol, Mr. Thad. I 'preciate the offer but it's not something that I've ever done."

Collins roars, "Goddam nigger preacher thinks he's too good to drink with honest white men?"

He menaces toward Maxwell but is restrained by Thad. "He didn't say that, Swift. He's too good to drink with anybody. Hell, he's a preacher. He's supposed to be better than most." Blankenship turns back to Maxwell, "We just want a little information, Preacher. One of our acquaintances from Montgomery tells us that you've had a fella named Ashley Windsor working with you in your voter registration business. Is that true?"

"Mr. Thad, I don't know the names of all them folks that have been over there. I don't remember no Ashley. They wuz a Ron and a Judd, I think; but I don't remember no Ashley." He's trembling as he sits on the tree stump. He has made up his mind that he will probably die here tonight in spite of Thad's reassurances in the truck. "Another one's name was Jacob—he was over there that Sunday and got beat up. And, oh yeah, there was a Duke and a Pax, too. But I don't recall no Ashley; and that seem like a name I'd remember."

Swift Collins lunges toward the man and strikes him a glancing blow on the cheek. The others laugh except Thad, who says, "Swift, I said that we just need information. If we need to beat it out of him, we'll do it; but, by god, we'll do it when I say do it and not before. I want to find out about this traitor if I can."

Collins voice is like glass ground under his boot. "You ain't in charge of me, Thad. I don't give a damn whether you want to protect 'im or not. His church is where them other jungle bunnies gather up and are sure as hell gonna take over our damn town if we don't do somethin' about it. You know what they say: 'Cut off th' head of th' snake and th' whole thing dies.'"

Thad is firm. "Not 'til I get th' information I want. You need to just cool your damn jets for a minute." Turns to Maxwell and says, "You see what I'm havin' to deal with here, Preacher. You need to go on an' tell me th' truth before things get sho' nuff outta hand. Who is this Ashley Windsor character and where do we find him?"

"Mr. Thad, I'm not a brave man. If I knew who you was talkin' 'bout an' it would save my life, I'd tell you. I just never heard of no Ashley Windsor, and that's th' truth." His voice is trembling and he's fighting hard for self-control.

He knows that he is in the presence of the enemy and doesn't want to show weakness in front of them. He hates that he has reverted to giving these men more respect than they have earned, that his educated speech has been abandoned in order to appear deferential. But he has fallen back on a strategy that he, his friends and forebears have employed for centuries.

Before Thad can reassure him, Collins shoves his way back into the picture and this time he has retrieved his shotgun from the front seat of his truck. "He ain't gonna tell you nuthin', Thad. He just as stubborn as th' rest of them black bastards. I'll take care of this problem once and for all." And so saying, he raises the shotgun and discharges it full in the face of Reverend Eldred Maxwell. The body is blown backwards off the stump and onto the ground nearby. The head has been blown away, landing with a thud in the bushes behind the stump. The torso is splayed grotesquely. Twitches and goes still. Blood spurts for a few seconds and then even that stops.

Silence reigns in the clearing. None of the men, not even Collins, is prepared to deal with the reality of the murder that they have witnessed. One of the men, Cracker White, turns and throws up in the fire pit. Ricky Parsons whispers, "Goddamn."

The third, Gene Hill, turns away to walk slowly toward the vehicles. Thad Blankenship fights with the emotions inside him—rage at being disobeyed, and yet a certain satisfaction that some other rage, in some other part of him is released. He is the first to speak. "Goddammit, Swift. You've done it now." Turns to the other men and shouts, "Hey, pay attention here. We're all in this together. Ain't no choice about that at all. Ever' man here is as guilty as any other, whether you pulled th' trigger or not. It's called bein' an accomplice and that means ever' last one of us. We've got to think for a minute and cover our asses here."

Hill stammers, "I … I … didn't sign on fer no murderin' business. I ain't no part of this. Swift, that's all on you as far as I'm concerned."

Ricky Parsons says, "You fuckin' wish, Gene. It don't make no difference what you 'signed on' for. We wuz all here and we'll stick together. We have the perfect alibi, if we stick together. We'll just say that we wuz at Cracker's house playin' poker."

"What about Eudora? Y'all heard what she said." Hill's voice is cracking with tension.

With heavy sarcasm Parsons replies, "Who they gonna believe? Five white men or one nigger woman? 'Sides, we know where th' sheriff will stand." Snorts a laugh. "Hell, Jimbo's gonna be pissed that we done this without him gettin' t' be here. Whaddya say, Cracker? Wuz we playin' poker at your house?"

Timothy "Cracker" White isn't married and lives in a rental house. Hill, divorced, lives in one room in a private residence. White reluctantly agrees to the plan and the men decide that they need to move the body, since this spot is one that they are associated with from hunting parties that they attend here with other acquaintances.

Cracker rolls the body in an old blanket from his truck's toolbox and three of them toss it into the bed of Collins's truck. They have decided on a spot nearby where they roll the body down a cliff side and into a gully over a hundred feet below the roadbed.

Later they gather at Cracker's house to play poker. Before the game starts they stand in silence as the blanket burns in a steel barrel in the back yard. As the flames flare up and then slowly die away, Cracker says wistfully, "Now I'll have to buy another blanket." The laughter that follows is strained, but is also the beginning of the collective amnesia that will infect these five men for many years to come.

*   *   *   *

Sheriff James "Jimbo" Turner stands at the front door of the Maxwell residence. He is a big man—not so much tall as heavy, with a protruding belly and big arms and legs. His face is corpulent and strained in the dim light of the Maxwell front porch. He's trying to be patient with Eudora Maxwell, but she wants more than he can possibly give her tonight. "Miz Maxwell, I'll do my very best to help find your husband and to get the report done on the damage done to the church, but most of that will have to wait until morning. I can't see in the church well enough to do a proper or useful investigation, and I wouldn't know where to begin looking for your husband. I can't believe that Thad Blankenship would come over here and kidnap him. I will most certainly go to Thad's house and see what he has to say about this, but this sounds too far-fetched to me right now."

Eudora is incredulous. "What do you mean 'far-fetched'? I saw the man force my husband into his truck at gunpoint. There's nothing far-fetched about it. I *saw* it. With my own two eyes. It happened right here in front of me. Why is that so hard to believe?"

Holding his temper is difficult and Turner says, "Miz Maxwell, it's eleven o'clock at night and there ain't no light here. I don't think that you could possibly make out anybody's identity in this darkness. There don't seem to be any of your neighbors coming forth to corroborate what you're saying. I'm not saying that you're lying or even that you're wrong; but I'm gonna have to have more than what I've got right now to arrest anybody. I'll talk to as many people as I can get to talk to me in the morning. Now, if there's nothing else that you can tell me about this, I'll go on over to Thad Blankenship's house and talk to him."

As he turns to walk away, he hears Eudora say, "If something has happened to him, I swear that I'll never rest until these people are caught."

There's something about the way she says it that prickles at the back of his neck.

＊   ＊   ＊   ＊

On his way to Thad's house, Jimbo drives past Cracker White's place on Red-bud Street. Out front are Thad's white Dodge truck, Swift Collins's two-year-old Chevy pickup and Cracker's new Ford F-100. Lights are burning brightly in the living room; so Jimbo stops and clumps loudly onto the front porch. Bangs on the doorframe with his big mitt and waits for someone to answer. Soon Cracker appears at the opened door and says, "Come on in, Jimbo. What are you doin' out this late at night? You wanna sit in a few hands?" Leads the sheriff into the living area where the card table is set up and the other four men are seated with drinks, cigars and dealt hands of cards.

A chorus greets him—"Hey Jimbo."

"How's it hangin' there, lawman?"

"Great. Fresh blood. Get out yer wallet."

But he just stands there. After a minute or so of silence Cracker finally asks, "What is it Jimbo? You don't look so good."

"Yeah. I reckon I'm better off than Preacher Maxwell is. I'm fine in fact. How about y'all?"

"What th' hell has Preacher Maxwell got to do with anything?" Swift Collins asks just barely able to conceal a smile.

"Well," says Turner, "his old lady seems to think that Thad here along with an undetermined number of other, shall we say, 'accomplices', came over to their house in Niggertown and kidnapped the good Reverend. Now you boys wouldn't happen to know anything about that, would you?"

Thad laughs out loud and says, "Now what in the hell would I want with a nigger preacher? I've got enough niggers working for me that I sure as shit don't need another one, especially one that can't do no heavy work."

The other men mumble their agreement and seem ready to resume their game. "So how long have y'all been playing? And why wasn't I invited to this game?" The sheriff appears not to want to leave this alone and the men are annoyed.

Cracker volunteers, "Most of the evening, Jimbo. We must've started about seven o'clock. Thad got here by a quarter after, I reckon. By then ever'body was here except Swift and he came in a few minutes later. You wasn't invited because I thought that you told me that Betty Ann was making you take her shopping in Opelika. What's this all about Jimbo? You don't seriously think that Thad kid-napped a nigger, do you?"

Turner laughs and says, "Naw. Hell, you know how Eudora can be. She makes up her mind how things are and she's mighty hard to convince otherwise. I reckon I *will* play a few minutes. Has somebody got a drink for a poor workin' man? And I want y'all to know, I didn't even notice that the hoods on all y'all's trucks are still warm to the touch. I knew that she didn't know what she was talkin' about. Hell, it was way too dark out there to be able to see anything." He pulls up a chair and accepts the Mason jar. There is general agreement with his pronouncement—and relief that this is now *official*.

✳   ✳   ✳   ✳

At 12:10 A.M. the T'Bird creeps down Mell Street, as the lights from campus fade to darkness behind. Duke's senses are hyper-alert, but he also feels a calm excitement down deep. As he approaches the intersection, the oak tree looms on his right and his heart quickens. Almost on its own initiative the car drifts off the roadway, across the verge, and toward the soft envelope that is the deeper shadow of the tree. Lights off. Coasting now to a throaty, rumbling stop. Ann waits in the darkness like a mirage. Ignition off. Silence creates a second envelope. Seals them off even further from ordinary reality.

"Hi." Her voice is little more than a hoarse whisper.

Even in this darkness she shines in his eyes. He is transfixed, unable to speak. Reaches for her hand and to pull her closer to the car. Then changes his mind and pushes himself up and over the door of the car to stand beside her. Spreads his feet and rocks back against the door for support. Again he pulls her, unyielding, toward the space between his feet. No words. Hugs her closely. Their chins rest on the other's shoulder. He is filled with an emotion that can't be accurately identified. Just when he thinks that he might burst, she says, "Thank you for coming."

"Thank you for *letting* me come. I've been sort of at sixes and sevens all night since you left."

She giggles, and he's startled—maybe a little defensive. "What?" he asks.

He can hear the smile in her voice. "I'm surprised to hear that expression coming from you. I guess I thought it was something that only my family used, or maybe that people in the North might use."

Set at ease he responds, "Oh we've got some wild expressions here in the South. Some of 'em I don't even understand myself."

Her reply is a melody falling on his ear. "Then you can imagine how I spend half my time trying to figure out what has been said to me before I answer something that wasn't asked. I'm getting accustomed to the drawl. But if I just look at you dumbly, help me out and explain."

Self-assured, he tries to be reassuring. "Hey, I'm in training to be a top-notch interpreter. No problem." Pauses. "So you really missed me, huh?"

Their faces are only inches apart. Their bodies are in full contact from knees to chest. But miraculously, there doesn't seem to be any urgency.

"Yes. I could hardly believe it when I realized that was really what I was feeling. I mean this is happening so fast. And there's a part of me that is very conservative about this sort of thing. But I kept wondering how your trip to Birmingham was going. And I was admiring that you would do something that intense for a *friend*. I even found myself thinking about your goofy sense of humor. About that time I began to realize that I was missing you." Pauses. "And I thought about how cute you are, too." Bops him on the nose with one index finger as accompaniment. Leans back to deliver this crushing blow and in consequence presses more solidly against him.

He doesn't think, but rather experiences: growing heat where their bodies touch as she traps the energy generated by his overactive metabolism, intoxication from the delicate perfume she wears, perspiration in his palms, tingling at the back of his neck where her fingers have strayed, crazy needs to hold onto and protect, and surging emotions that have no name.

He's about to respond when she moves her head slowly and deliciously forward, mouth slightly open. Her mouth is soft and sweet and at once yielding and assertive. The kiss doesn't linger on and on. Mouths tug gently. Tongues touch without urgency. Breathing is regular, punctuated with sighs. She opens her eyes just before they break apart and is startled to see him gazing at her.

Before he can think, he squints, blows the breath he's been holding, and a low groan follows, "Wow!" Her response is to giggle.

"That was *not* a joke. I'm being perfectly serious here." Mock indignity.

"I guess that I thought that only women show that much emotion. You know, that's the way it always is in the movies. Men are always the 'strong silent types' and all that."

In his best Bogart voice he says, "Welcome to the real world, baby. Maybe all those movie guys are like that, see. Or maybe most *guys* really are that way. But not me, Sweetheart." And she giggles again.

From an intensity that he has never known, the energy just keeps building. Then the awareness comes like a lightning bolt. He is stricken. "God, I really love being with you. I don't think I've ever felt this way with anyone in my life."

She can't disguise the merriment. "Well thank you. That's a really nice thing to say. The feelings must go both ways. After all, I *did* come to you this afternoon. I still can't believe I did that. I'm becoming a wanton woman—wantin' what she can't have." There's a wistful quality to her voice. "Not that I actually know what I want."

"That's a tough one. 'Fraid I can't help you on that score. Do we need to talk about this? Is this what we started talking about in the Berry?" He's willing to be truly serious for a time if that's what she needs.

"Well, maybe what I want you to know is what a struggle this is for me. I don't think that I really love the man I'm married to and I don't think that he loves me; but I have a child to think about, too. My feelings for you developed much too fast and I am suspicious of that. And I'm probably just as suspicious of your feelings. I'm pretty confused right now and think that I should be waiting for things to clear up before rushing into another relationship.

"But then on the other hand I'm here and I initiated being here. With you. In the middle of the night. And I'm not gonna be able to pretend that I'm not enjoying it. So there you have it. I'm just screwed up and trying to be honest about what's really going on with me. I think that what draws me to you is your ability to put the wants and needs of others above or at least equal to your own. That's new to me and unbelievably comforting. I really don't know much about you."

Feelings rush out of his mouth: "Whew. You say that you're confused and unsure and screwed up; but at least you've thought through things. I haven't even considered the possible outcomes. I just know that I crave your companionship. I don't know much about myself either. I know I'm a hard worker, but an unbearable idealist. I'm tough in ways too—some nice ways and some not so nice ways. And I'm good in a crisis. Other than that I don't know myself very well and haven't really thought about it."

She cocks her head and looks at him appraisingly in the gloom. "I'm glad that you're good in a crisis. Seems like you have a few to deal with. There are probably a few in my future, too. But slow down, Duke. We don't have to get sooo serious. We're just feeling each other out at this point."

An devilish grin leaps across his features. And as he pulls her closer to him, he says, "I'm glad that you reminded me of what I was supposed to be doing." Looking at each other, they simultaneously produce an exaggerated "Wow", and then break the tension by laughing.

"So here's my condition for now," she says. "I don't want to have to deal with guilt about betraying a vow that I made, so I don't want to sleep with you until the marriage thing is settled. Can you handle that?"

"I guess so. I hadn't really allowed myself to think about that yet, though I'm sure that it is leaping around near the surface in there somewhere.... Yeah, I can handle it ... I think. How about you?"

Her silence is answer enough. Soon they are deep in conversation about the events of the weekend, which for her included a phone call to her husband. Over the phone, she told him that she thinks that she doesn't want to be married anymore. His ambiguous replies left her wondering if he was agreeing or disagreeing.

CHAPTER 19

▼

Well before sunrise on Monday morning, Swift Collins awakens his son Terry gruffly and instructs him to get dressed. "What is it, Daddy? I've got classes in a few hours. I could use the sleep. Can't I do it this afternoon after classes?"

"Goddammit, son, I said to git up and that's what I meant. If it could've waited, I'd've let it wait. Now come on. Git up and git dressed. We've got a ways to go." And with that Swift goes out the back letting the screen door screech and slam shut. In the barn he gathers two rakes and a shovel, a burlap bag and a cardboard box. His eyes are red-rimmed, his white hair disheveled; but his movements are purposeful and there is no tremor in his hand. He wears worn and dirty, bib-type overalls and work boots that show permanent stains, red from the Alabama clay.

Terry joins him as he prepares to climb into the truck and together they quickly make the drive to the National Forest in silence. It is obvious that something is bothering the older man, but Terry lacks the courage to demand an explanation. He'll know soon enough. When they get to the turn that leads down to the campsite they have used to stage deer hunts all Terry's life, Swift stops the truck and says, "I'm not gonna explain anything about what we're about to do. What you don't know won't hurt you—or nobody else neither. Just help me do this and then fergit about it, and everything will be all right, understand?"

Something cold turns over in Terry's stomach, but he nods and says, "Yes sir."

The truck proceeds to the edge of the campsite but the early light reveals nothing. Swift and Terry pick up the tools and the bag from the truck's rear and Swift leads the way to the area near the fire pit. Still no sign of anything unusual except a sound—an insistent buzzing that Terry has a hard time placing. He watches as his father reaches and picks something up out of the darkness and shoves it into the burlap bag. Senses the cloud of flies that bursts into flight around them and smells the vague odor of blood, and the sickly dryness of death.

Swift roughly tosses the bag aside and says, "Let's rake things up around here." The two busily rake around in the half-light of emerging dawn. Terry can't see that they are actually accomplishing anything but continues to work alongside his father at a feverish pace. Scratching at the earth and the bushes, he hears his father's labored breathing and feels a growing nausea in his belly. The truth tries to invade his consciousness, but he repels it and focuses on trying to clear up whatever is amiss in the bushes. Shovels full of earth and twigs and unidentifiable matter are thrown into the bag.

They work and sweat until finally Swift announces, "OK, son. That oughtta do it." He throws the tools and the bag into the truck's rear and instructs Terry to sit in the truck and wait. Breaking a limb from a low growing willow tree, he then sweeps around the area with wild and desperate strokes.

Back in the truck now they drive back to the feeder road and then deeper into the Forest. At the junction with another dirt trace that meanders off to their left, Swift angles the truck into a niche. The truck would be hidden from view from the road, but there's no traffic anyway. He tells Terry to stay put and gets out.

Terry can hear him grunting as he digs. Hears him remove the bag and the box from the truck bed and then hears the sounds of refilling the hole. The shovel clangs into the truck and Swift opens the driver's side door. In the first flush of sunlight Terry sees his father as pale and drawn—sweating far too profusely for the temperature and the time of day. He knows that his father is afraid; he can smell the fear. And in his turn he becomes frightened also.

When they arrive back at the farm, Swift stops the truck out front and turns to his son, "You go on and get ready for school. If your momma asks where we've been, tell her that I had some clearing to do and nuthin' else, understand?" Terry nods. "And, son, I 'preciate that you went with me for this. I hope you never have to find out what was really going on out there, but it's good enough that you can't *really* know. No matter what happens, you can truthfully say that you don't know."

✳   ✳   ✳   ✳

At about the time Terry Collins is taking his bath at the farm, Duke is parking the T'Bird in front of the hospital. On his way in he notices Angel's Chevy sitting at the rear of the parking lot and suppresses a grin. Thinks, *How do you pay a debt to an angel?*

In through the front door and across to the elevators. Up to the third floor and turn left to the nurse's station. Ms. Whitmore greets him with a smile and directs him to Claire's room. Claire is finishing her orange juice and her face brightens as he swaggers into her line of vision. "Hello, you gorgeous woman. How're ya feelin'?"

"Weak, but I'm gonna be fine. How about you and where did you disappear to?" There is no malice in her voice. In fact, if anything she's teasing him.

"Well, I was basically told that my presence here would likely cause more problems than it would solve, so I just left. Besides, I knew that your dad would be here at some time and I didn't know what you were gonna tell him, so I thought that it would be best if I weren't around to screw that up."

He has reached her side and taken her right hand in his. She feels chilled and clammy to the touch. An IV is in place in her left wrist and clear liquid drips slowly into the drip chamber underneath the bottle. Her red hair is lifeless, her complexion pasty-white.

She scoots a little more upright in the bed and says with a bit more vitality, "Oh. Good thinking, Duke. I didn't think about that. Speaking of Daddy, he did come in and was his usual darling self. He didn't ask any questions that I didn't want to answer. He just wanted to be sure that I got good care and that everything was taken care of. I basically told him that I hadn't actually known for sure that I was pregnant and that I'd had a miscarriage. I also told him that you had saved my life. I said that I had called you, as my most trusted friend, that you had tried to nurse me back to health and then had insisted on getting me to the hospital. And just in time, too."

Reacting to the "saved my life" part Duke pleads, "Good grief, Claire. Why would you tell him something like that?"

"It made a more realistic story and one that he didn't have to worry so much about. Besides, you *did* save my life and don't try to pretend that you didn't. The nurses all know, and none of them will say anything but high praise about you. Daddy'll be here any minute and he wants to meet you."

Self-conscious now, he drawls, "Aw man, I can't believe you …"

"Can't believe what about my daughter?" The big booming voice comes from the doorway. Duke turns to face the sound finding, not a big booming man, but a short stocky man with salt and pepper hair, black rimmed eyeglasses, and a grin the size of Texas. "You must be the mysterious Duke, am I right?"

"Yes sir." Extends his hand and has his fingers squeezed tightly. "Pleased to meet you, Your Honor."

"Haw. Haw. Haw. Listen to this. And just how did you know that I am a judge, young man? I'm sure that my daughter didn't tell you. She seems more ashamed of it than proud." Without waiting for an answer, he continues, "It is nice to meet someone with manners though, I must admit. She doesn't always choose friends with that quality. It's *my* pleasure to meet *you*, Duke. Everyone tells me that you probably saved her life, and I'm grateful." From squeezed fingers to being embraced in a bear hug, Duke is supremely embarrassed. And Claire laughs out loud.

His face burning, Duke manages, "I'm glad I could help, Your Honor. I just wish that we'd gotten her here sooner and maybe it wouldn't have been quite such an emergency.... And she *did* tell me that you're a judge, though she may not remember it. Moment of weakness, I guess."

"Yes, no doubt you are right, my boy. I'm sure that I don't need to say that whatever has happened here is not a matter for public conversation...."

Claire blurts out, "Daddy!"

"Of course not, sir." Duke enjoys Claire's shock.

Leaving no doubt about the correctness of his approach, the judge continues, "Now, Claire, just take it easy. Young Duke and I will have to reach our under-standings and make no mistake about that. No offense is intended here and I'm sure that none will be taken." He nods to Duke who nods in return. "Now. What can I do to repay you for helping my daughter? Don't give me that 'nothing' crap either."

Still embarrassed Duke replies, "But you don't owe me anything. And any-way, even if you did, I can't think of anything that I really need. I'm just glad that she's OK and that I could help."

The judge rocks back on his heels and clasps his hands behind his back. "'Bout what I'd figured on. But let me say this. First, you are to call me 'Judge', not 'Your Honor' ever again unless you are in my courtroom. Secondly, I'm going to give you my card with my home phone number and my private office number on it. Sooner or later you'll need something that a poor old country judge can help you with. I want you to promise me that you'll use this card and call me when that happens. Deal?"

"Yes sir, Judge. I appreciate the gesture; and I promise that if I need some-thing, I won't hesitate to call." Duke's head is spinning a little and he's unsure of what he ought to do next. The judge has gone silent and Claire is embarrassed for Duke in the wake of her father's outpouring.

Looking at her, Duke says, "Well, I really came by to check on you and to see if you need me to do anything at the school for you—you know, like tell your department that you're sick or something?"

The judge steps forward and puts a hand on his shoulder and says, "That's already being taken care of through my office, son. The doctors say that if she'll rest today and tomorrow, she can resume classes by Wednesday, Thursday at the latest. The Montgomery federal clerk's office will be calling on her professors and gathering assignments and materials. I'm going back to north Alabama tonight and will keep in touch via telephone. I imagine that she will like to have some company, so I'll encourage you to do that part."

"Daddy!!"

"I won't need encouragement to do that, Judge … So, I'll go now and let you two visit. Need to get to class anyway. Nice to meet you, Judge." Leans over and kisses Claire on the forehead, "Take care, girl. I'll try to get by to see you tonight." And with a self-conscious grin he nods his way out the door.

As the door closes, Claire says quietly to her father, "I know what you're thinking and just don't say it. He *is* a nice man, but it's not meant to be between the two of us."

"Too bad."

"I'm just grateful for what we *do* have."

"Me, too, I guess."

*   *   *   *

Classes pass in a blur for Duke and at noon he hustles toward the Union to check out the bridge tables. In the street at Ross Square he notices that Terry Collins is trailing him from his history class and slows to let him catch up. "So how'd'ya do on your tests? You look like you've lost your last friend. I can't believe that you didn't do well. Hell, you almost always set the standards in classes. How'd ya do?"

Collins forces a smile, lifts his folded exam paper to Duke's eye and shows him the perfect "100—A". Duke snorts, "Hah! Just as I thought. So what are you so down in the mouth about? Can't be that."

"Oh just family stuff, Duke. You know how that goes. I'll be alright. How'd you do on your test?"

"Ninety-five. Barely in your league, but I'll take it and be glad of it. Going to the Union?"

"Yeah, might as well. You wanna try to play a little? That tournament is coming up in Atlanta this weekend. I don't know if I'm gonna be able to play or not, though. My daddy said something about me needing to go somewhere with him on Friday and I don't know if we'll be back. Heck I don't even know where we're supposed to be going. But if we're gonna try to play in Atlanta, we need to practice some first."

"Holy cow, Terry. I had completely forgotten about that. Yeah. The fees are already paid and obviously Pax won't be there to play, so Ron gave *us* their spot. Let's go drink coffee and talk about it. You sure you're O.K.? You look kinda green around th' gills there, buddy."

"I'll be all right." But his color is bad and there is a fine tremor in his hand as he holds up his test paper. Though the day is another hot one, he's sweating out of proportion to the heat. He feels clammy and thinks that it probably shows. He's fighting off vague anxiety and working very hard to shut off assaults of conscience. He knows that he feels guilty—but won't allow himself to think of why that might be happening.

In the Union all Duke's friends are there—Judd, Elizabeth, Ron, Leo, Teddy Bear, even Aurelia. Duke chooses an empty table and announces, "Terry and I will take on only the bravest and the brightest. We need to practice. Ron, are we still supposed to play that tournament in Atlanta this weekend?"

Ron is talking with Leo but nods in Duke's direction. Duke says, "Be right back folks. Gotta pee and get a Coke—change fluids, ya know." Drops two quarters in front of Elizabeth with the expectation that she'll feed the jukebox in Claire's absence. Asks Terry if he wants a drink and disappears for ten minutes, reappearing with two drinks and a sandwich.

He sits opposite Terry and the cards begin to riffle and fly through the air landing in piles in front of the four players. Terry's color seems to be coming back as he arranges his hand and puzzles out its meaning. The bidding is accomplished and Terry ends as declarer. Duke spreads his hand after the first lead and relaxes back against his chair to eat his sandwich. Ron is sitting as the right-hand opponent to Duke and says, "It'll be good for you guys to play in Atlanta. I'd been hoping y'all would. I talked to Pax about things and he's arranged it all. I haven't seen you for a few days. Where've you been?"

"Ah hell, I had to take a friend of mine to Birmingham this weekend and didn't really get back to town until Sunday; and then I had to work." He is aware of Elizabeth's suspicious smile. He asks, "Anybody seen Claire?"

Murmurs and head shakes all around. Finally Aurelia says, "Someone from her father's office came to the dorm and picked up her books and told the staff that Claire is sick and won't be back to classes until Wednesday or Thursday."

Duke looks up, interested. "Did they say what was wrong?"

"No. It was a woman from the local branch of the federal court offices in Montgomery and she didn't say anything else. I didn't know that Claire's father is a Federal Judge until today. Did y'all know that?" Surprised glances and more murmurs.

Duke offers, "You gotta be kiddin' me. Claire is a judge's daughter? What next? Elizabeth the daughter of a nun?"

That nets him a smack on the shoulder and, "My mom's the Virgin Mary." Laughter scatters among the friends. Everything edges back toward perspective now, and Duke begins to relax and attend to the play of the cards in front of him.

Terry has this habit. When he's about to pull some off-the-wall move with the cards, he purses his lips, puts his card in front of his mouth and waits for his victim to step into the trap. He's in that posture now and Duke notices, waiting expectantly.

When the opponents are allowed to capture a trick that Terry could have won, Duke's hand comes down on the table. "Hold it! Tell me why you did that, Terry. I know you and there's something in the wind. This hand doesn't count for anything anyway; tell me."

"Well, I just threw away my last real loser and put Leo in the lead. He's gonna have to lead into my strength or give me a 'ruff and slough'. This way I make an overtrick. That's the 'end-play' that I was trying to talk to you about the other night." He's feeling better now that his mind is occupied.

The conversation shifts to how the end-play works and almost no one notices that they are joined by Lynn. She stands near Duke and watches as Terry tries to explain the play to him. While he struggles to understand, her hand finds its way to his shoulder and he turns to see her there. "Oh. Hi, Lynn. Pull up a chair. Nice to see you. How's your dad?"

"I can't stay. But thanks, Daddy's doing better. I came by to talk to you for a minute if you can."

"Sure. Judd, will you take my hand for a few minutes?" He follows Lynn across the main floor area and into the rear section of the Union. They take a table near the cafeteria line and she looks directly into his eyes and says, "I need to know some things, Duke. George told me that he saw you at the hospital Saturday night and that you told him that you'd had to take someone to Birmingham on Friday. Is that right?"

"Yes."

"Will you tell me who you took to Birmingham and why you were at the hospital?" She is very serious and seems anxious. Her eyes are red-rimmed as if she hasn't slept well. "And where you've been since Saturday night?"

Duke pulls back from her slightly and his tone is measured. "I'll be glad to tell you, but I gotta tell ya that I don't much like the tone this is taking. Is something going on that I should know about?"

"I honestly don't know, Duke. In fact that's what I'm trying to find out for myself. *Is* there something going on? With you I mean?"

"Not really. I've just been running around in circles for a week now. My old high school friend Mitch caught up with me Friday morning and told me that his mother was going to have surgery in Birmingham around noon and asked if I could drive him up there. He doesn't have a car and offered to pay me, so I agreed. We drove up there, checked on her, spent the night at his house and went back to the hospital Saturday morning. We took her home that afternoon and came back here by Saturday evening."

He's on a roll now. "I called Ms. Posey at the library to see if I could work on Sunday, and her husband told me that she was at the hospital visiting a friend, so I went out there and waited in the Snack Bar to see her. That's when I saw George. He told me that your dad was upstairs, but that you and your mom had already left for the evening. I was sorry to hear about your dad; but I didn't see any way that I could reasonably get in touch. I figured that your mom didn't need to be disturbed by the telephone. Then I worked Sunday evening until midnight. I guess that your dad went home yesterday, right?" She nods. "So I didn't try to call—again I didn't want to disturb a home with sickness in it. Is this making sense to you?"

Very tired, she remains silent for a moment. "I suppose it does. Sorry. I guess that when I found out that you were in town and then you didn't call or anything, I just figured that you didn't want to see me or something." She's almost crying. He gathers her hands up in his.

"That's not it Lynn. I'm glad that you came over here today. I think that it's the first time that you've ever paid any attention to my friends. That's a nice gesture; I know that you don't always approve of them. I'm sure that you and your family have been under a lot of pressure with his getting beat up and then getting sick from it. Must have been scary as hell. But these are unusual circumstances and a lot of strange things have been happening. Don't get the idea that *everything's* strange now just because a few things have gone off th' track."

Lynn can hardly look at him. She feels guilty for having doubted him. "I'm sure you're right, Duke. My mom said practically the same thing to me Saturday night. Things *are* strange and I *am* scared. It's like my whole world is upside down or something. There was more trouble with the nigras in Tuskegee last night, and everybody over there is nervous. I just wish that things would be like they have always been."

Duke thinks, *Yeah I bet that you wish everything was like it always was; but it never will be again.* He asks, "What's happened now?"—not really sure that he wants to hear the answer to this question.

"Apparently somebody went over to that nigra church last night and kidnapped that Reverend Maxwell. Eudora, his big-mouthed, troublemaker of a wife swears that George's daddy, Thad Blankenship, did it, but he was playing cards at Cracker White's house all night. Now she's threatening to call in the FBI and the U.S. Attorney General, so everybody's just angry and upset."

"Why would anyone want to kidnap Reverend Maxwell—or whatever his name is?" Duke barely catches himself and feels a tingle of fear at the top of his head and the back of his throat. The mistake was too near the surface.

She goes on undeterred, and not noticing. "Exactly. And that's not all. The people, whoever they were, shot almost all the stained glass windows out of their church. How stupid. That won't help anything. It just made all the nigras mad. I guess that I don't even blame them."

Duke is more stunned than he wants to show. He wants to ask if others were hurt or anything, but stops himself. Says instead, "You're right, this is just gonna cause more trouble."

He's looking at the tabletop and avoiding her eyes, but steals a glance to assess her mood. She is limp, emotionally exhausted. Finally he asks, "Are you back to school for good now, or are you gonna commute for a while?"

"No. I'm staying. Daddy's gonna be fine and I don't want to be in that house right now. It's too depressing. Can I stay with you tonight? I think I just need for someone to hold me for a while." Her look is pleading and coupled with her dark beauty, empathy is aroused in Duke. He doesn't hesitate to welcome her.

Squeezing her hand he says, "I'm working nights and won't be home until a little after midnight, but you're certainly welcome to come over whenever you want and to stay. Maybe we can go to the Kettle and have a late breakfast. My treat for a change. How's that sound?"

Reassured by his invitation, she agrees to the plan and leaves for classes.

Returning to the table alone, Duke is greeted by Elizabeth's smirk. "So, who's the dark-haired beauty, Duke? You realize, of course, that you didn't introduce her to any of us." He rewards her inquiry with a blush and in return is rewarded by her sweet laugh.

Sheepishly he says, "Well, that was Lynn from over in Tuskegee. Her dad has been pretty sick and I guess that I didn't think this would be a good time to go through the motions. You know what I mean?"

With a little more compassion Elizabeth responds, "Sure. That makes sense. How is he anyway?"

"She says he'll be fine. At least he's well enough that she's back to school full time. She's having a tough time right now. Things in Tuskegee are kinda in turmoil. They apparently had more trouble over there last night." He directs meaningful glances at both Judd and Elizabeth.

"What now?" asks Teddy Bear. He has only peripheral knowledge of the issues that exist in Tuskegee.

"Well, Lynn says that the pastor of that colored church where those people were beaten up a couple of weeks ago was kidnapped last night." Murmurs around the table. "And not only that, apparently his wife is threatening to call in the FBI and the U.S. Attorney General."

Teddy Bear has this great grin as he speculates, "Hey, maybe we'll go over there and meet a real live Yankee attorney general." Then more soberly he adds, "I wouldn't think ol' Katzenbach would be very popular in Tuskegee, Alabama. If he shows up, he's got more balls than I would have."

Terry doesn't say anything, but his color goes pale again and he leaves the table.

As the others leave for class, Teddy Bear slips into the chair next to Duke and asks, "You ever just wanna run away?"

Duke laughs and says, "All the damn time Teddy Bear. Why? Something bugging you?"

"Yeah. Aurelia is about to drive me nuts. One day she can't be close enough and the next day she can't stand the sight of me. I've been thinking about heading to California. Is that nuts or what?"

Duke chuckles again. "Tell ya what. If you decide that you're really goin', let me know. I just might go with you. Obviously, something interesting is happening out there. Claire and I were talking about that just the other day."

Teddy Bear straightens up. "Yeah, I can't help wondering what all the fuss is about … Well I've got tests this week. Maybe week after next when finals are over. I gotta go, Duke. See ya later.

✳   ✳   ✳   ✳

Jimbo Turner is annoyed at the interruption of the telephone, and answers it gruffly, "Sheriff's Office." When he hears the grating New York voice he is surprised and a little intimidated.

"Is this Sheriff Turner?"

"Yes it is. Can I help you?"

"This is Nicholas Katzenbach, Sheriff, the Attorney General of the United States. I've had a disturbing call here from a constituent of yours—a Missus Eudora Maxwell. I believe that you are acquainted with this lady, and that she has lodged a complaint with your office concerning the disappearance and possible kidnapping of her husband. Is that correct, Sheriff?"

To Jimbo there's something really annoying about the sound of the man's voice. Not to mention that the he's meddling in the affairs of this town. His town. "That's right, Mr. Katzenbach. We are investigatin' the disappearance of her husband right now. So far I don't have any real leads on the case. I've checked out her allegations that another citizen is responsible for the Reverend's disappearance, but that individual has a good alibi for his whereabouts for several hours surrounding the time period during which the preacher disappeared.

"I've also made out a preliminary report on the damage that was done to the church at about the same time—not much to go on there either, I'm afraid. No witnesses. No real evidence except a few spent shotgun shells. Common gauge and brand. No prints that we've been able to find. Kind of a dead end. But we'll keep after it." Turner feels mostly contempt for this intrusion.

Oblivious to Turner's aggravation the Attorney General continues, "I'm sure that you'll do your best, Sheriff. I'm also sure that you know kidnapping is a federal problem. Therefore, I've been in touch with the regional office of the FBI in Atlanta already this morning. They have assured me that they can have someone to Tuskegee by noon today."

Jimbo feels the dread now. He knows that he's about to have to put up with more crap than anyone ought to have to deal with. "I appreciate the thought, Mr. Katzenbach; but we don't really need the help of people outside of our own jurisdiction. They could hardly be expected to know the area or the people as well as we do ourselves. So, I'll thank you kindly and say, 'No thanks' to your offer."

"Sheriff Turner, you misunderstand the nature of my remarks. I haven't offered you assistance in this matter. What I have done is to inform you that federal agents will be in your town within a couple of hours and *they* will be in charge of this investigation. You are to give them your complete support and any assistance that they might require. Is that clear?"

Turner explodes into the receiver. "Th' hell you say! This case happened here and the manner of its investigation will be determined by *this* office. Your boys will get *no* cooperation from me, my staff and probably not from anyone else in this community. Is *that* clear?"

Breathing hard he's thinking, *The nerve of this sawed off little shit. Who th' hell does he think he is anyhow? This county elected me to do this work and I'll, by god, do it and that's the end of that.*

Calmly Katzenbach continues. "I have a call in to Governor Wallace, Sheriff. You may want to re-think your position on this matter. Federal agents *will* be in Tuskegee soon. They *will* begin an investigation of this kidnapping. If you do not cooperate with them, you *will* be found in contempt. If you obstruct their investigative efforts in any way, you *will* be arrested and taken to the federal penitentiary in Atlanta to await trail. You may make up your own mind from where you observe this investigation—in jail or out. It makes no difference at all to me. I'm sure that you'll be hearing from Governor Wallace in a few minutes. Goodbye."

Red-faced, Jimbo inhales, ready to tell this snot-nosed Yankee a thing or two. Then he hears the click, as the connection is broken. He stares at the receiver thinking, *Hell, I was just getting warmed up.*

✴   ✴   ✴   ✴

"I tell you what, Thad, I don't like it no more than you do, but there ain't a damn thing I can do about it. Them agents will be here in a couple of hours. I just thought you oughtta know that they're comin'. I'm gonna leave it up to you to do whatever's necessary with the others. I've gotta at least pretend to cooperate with 'em. That asshole Katzenbach has done threatened to jail me if I don't. And th' guvnah's office called, saying that they couldn't stop this from happenin'." More than a little perturbed, Jimbo paces alongside his cruiser. He has come to warn his friends and Thad expects him to be able to fend off the federal government.

"Goddammit, Jimbo, that's what we pay you for. You've gotta figure out some way to keep them agents away from us—especially Eugene. He's weak. You know what our story is; tell 'em and let 'em be gone." Blankenship's emotions start with being scared of the coming confrontation and run headlong into being angry at Jimbo, the convenient scapegoat.

"I'll do what I can, Thad; but that shit ain't gonna work with these boys. Y'all might as well get ready to talk to 'em yourselves. You better get with them other boys and get your story straight. I'm just tellin' ya." In disgust Jimbo walks back to the cruiser and heads back toward town.

Blankenship drives to Swift Collins's farm minutes later and parks out front. Nell Collins calls to him from the screen door, offering coffee or iced tea. He approaches the house and asks for Swift. "He's out at the barn, I reckon. Him and Terry went out clearing some land early this morning and I haven't seen him. Terry said that he went on to the barn. If he's out there ask him if he's gonna want breakfast. You'd be welcome, too, if you want."

In the barn, Thad finds Swift stacking feed sacks on a table. He startles as he hears Thad approach. Blankenship is disgusted and says, "You're looking kinda jumpy for such a hard case kind of a man, Swift."

"Don't start a lot of shit with me Thad. I ain't in no mood to be hassled—especially by you." His tone is guttural and dangerous.

Thad adopts a mollifying tone. "I didn't come over here to hassle you; but you might as well get used to it. Jimbo just came by our place and told me that Nicholas Katzenbach called him this morning and is sending FBI men over here from Atlanta to investigate the preacher's disappearance. And the guvnah has backed him up. You know what that means, I guess."

Swift looks incredulous. His mouth hangs open for a few seconds. "Can't Jimbo do something to keep 'em away from us? I went out there this morning and cleaned up the rest of the mess at the camp. I buried th' leavin's and nobody will ever find it." He can't bring himself to say, "I buried the man's head." He's shaken but resolute in his determination to get through whatever he has to get through.

"Well nobody, 'cept maybe Terry. That was foolish, Swift. You shouldn't have involved th' boy. 'Course it's too late now, but I sure as hell wouldn't have involved my son. He's a kid.

"Jimbo can't hold back the federal government. Hell, Katzenbach told him that if he didn't cooperate they'd put *his* ass in th' penitentiary. We just have to be sure that our stories all say the same thing and we'll be okay." Thad is trying to reassure Swift, not because he cares one way or the other about Swift Collins—on the contrary he despises the man for losing control and putting all five of them in jeopardy. This is about self-preservation.

"Don't you worry about Terry. He won't say nothing. Hell, he don't even know what we was doin' out there. It was too dark. And if Jimbo can't keep them bastards off us, then maybe he *oughtta* be in th' damn penitentiary. What th' hell we payin' him for, if not for stuff like this?" The anger somehow purifies and stabilizes him. He is less anxious and more in control of his thoughts and actions.

Annoyed, Blankenship snorts, "He'll do what he can; but they've got jurisdiction since it's being called a kidnapping. That damned Eudora, she's th' one called Katzenbach. I guess just any damn nigger can call his ass; but I guarantee you that if one of us wanted something, we'd talk to some fuckin' clerk. Anyhow, the story is that you were the last one to get to Cracker's house and you got there at about seven-thirty. You lost a little money and I was the big winner. You don't know how much I won, but you lost maybe five dollars. We quit sometime after midnight, after Jimbo got there. You got all that?"

"Yeah, I got it."

Thad is dismissive as he turns to leave. "Well, I'm gonna go and talk to the others. Nell said that you didn't eat any breakfast yet. You need to be as close to normal as you can. If she gets suspicious, they might try to get at you through her—or Terry. You need to think about what might happen here and try to act accordingly."

Collins snaps back, "I'll take care of my end of things. You just take care of yours and you'd better make damn sure that Eugene don't get too skittish and fuck up th' whole deal. He'd better not mess things up, Thad. I ain't above taking *his* ass out if I have to."

"Yeah. I'm worried about him too. But we'll have to get through this together. If something happens to him now it'll look almighty suspicious. Go eat and I'll see you later."

Back in his truck, Blankenship can't help wondering if he's gonna end up in jail because of a nigger preacher and a red necked sharecropper. It's so ridiculous that it's almost funny. It never once occurs to him that the real fault is his own. He can't help laughing at himself for trying to convince Swift to be "normal". *Hell, Swift wouldn't recognize normal if it bit him on the ass.*

*   *   *   *

Mohammed sits in the living room of the church manse. He spent the night here with Eudora. She has fluctuated between anguish and anger. She paced and then, alternately, laid on the bed, racked with sobs and tears. He is helpless to change things but knows that his real mission is to stay here with her as support. There's really nothing to say, so the night passed with him thinking about what he should *do*.

When he called the denominational headquarters in Atlanta, they recommended calling the attorney general and supplied the private number that had been given to Reverend King. Katzenbach had been surprisingly available. He also had been sympathetic and had promised intervention. Eudora was splendid in making the call and talking with a man of national prominence. They had called Eudora's sister in Montgomery and she will be here soon to sit with Eudora; then he will try to get some sleep and figure out his next move.

Eudora confides to him, "Doc, I just know that those men have killed him, and in spite of what the sheriff says, I know that it was Thad Blankenship that took him off. I couldn't see the rest of 'em; but I know that I saw Thad. This not knowing how it ended up for sure is making me crazy."

"I know, Eudora. I feel the same way. We'll just have to wait until somebody with some authority gets here and then maybe the Sheriff will *have* to do something. Waiting is always the hardest thing to do, but we just have to do it."

He's been thinking for several hours now that this disappearance may in fact serve as a catalyst to get the rest of the community to register to vote. Having thought this, he almost feels guilty. Certainly he does not wish for the death of his closest friend, but if that turns out to be what happened, *some* good needs to come from it.

Maybe he could convince Stokley to do something to help bolster the community. Or maybe something will happen from Washington that will somehow help things here. At least he can call some people when he can get to his office. That's another thing, some of the men of the church are going to need to come around and board up the shattered windows, until arrangements can be made to repair the damage somehow.

When Eudora's sister Angela arrives, he sees the same iron in her constitution that he knows to be in Eudora's. Leaving the two quietly discussing things in the kitchen, Mohammed goes to the church to begin the process of bringing some semblance of order into this situation.

CHAPTER 20

▼

From the street level office at the corner of the beautiful old courthouse that stands on one side of the main street, Jimbo Turner can see the approaching traffic on the street that passes in front of the building. When the gray sedan parks out front, he knows that his company from Atlanta has arrived—even before the two men in dark suits get out. Dread sits in his belly like an anchor.

The men are stamped from the same mint—long and lean, both wear gray suits and matching hats. Each carries a vinyl bound notebook. They gaze around the perimeter of the city square, assessing things. And together they turn toward the sign identifying the sheriff's office. Casual, yet purposeful strides carry them inside—a hard look in their eyes.

When the door opens, Jimbo is looking at them with a combination of disgust, apprehension and awe. Standing near the radio, he gazes hypnotically at first one then the other, but no words come. Finally one of the men speaks, "Where can we find Sheriff Turner?"

"I'm Turner. I guess that you boys would be from the Bureau?" They nod. "Y'all here from Atlanta, right?" Nods again. "Well, come on into th' office here and I'll tell you what I've got so far. My dispatcher should be here any second now, and we can get started."

The two men walk before him into the inner office. As Turner himself moves toward the office, the front door opens and deputy Horace Banks enters in a rush. "Sorry I'm late, Jimbo. I got hung up over at th' garage. Did you know that the cruiser ..."

Jimbo raises his hands to silence the deputy and says, "I ain't got time for that now, Horace. Unless there's some kind of emergency, don't disturb me and these gentlemen in my office. Be sure that everybody on the schedule is doing what they're supposed to be doing and monitor the radio until Marcie gets here to relieve you."

He shouts into the other room, "Y'all want coffee? Made a fresh pot and it's out here with th' fixin's." They decline impatiently. Making his way back to the office, he catches Horace's eye and scowls. Shaking his big head negatively, he enters the private office and closes the door. The Bureau men are seated in front of his desk and he drops into the big leather chair facing them, opening the file that he has brought with him.

Turner looks up and says, a little sarcastically, "Since you fellows aren't polite enough to observe any of the conventions of social grace, I guess we'll just get down to business." Not one word from the federals. Jimbo waits and again looks from one to the other. Seconds pass. Tension crackles behind the silence.

Eventually the man on Jimbo's right says, "Sorry, Sheriff. We were told not to expect anything in the way of cooperation from you, so we just don't want to stir anything up unnecessarily. I'm sure that you already know that we're here about the disappearance of the preacher. Our boss is red hot on this case and pretty much told us to get it done and to get it done in a hurry. Who was this guy anyway?"

Turner thinks, *Well, that one ain't from around here. Flat sounding accent— must be from the Midwest or somewhere—Indiana or Illinois maybe. And they don't seem to know what's going on, so they weren't briefed beforehand. Seems straightforward enough.*

He nods to the other man, offers his hand across the desk and says, "Sheriff Jimbo Turner."

The man on the left accepts the proffered hand and says, "Jack Knight, this is Oscar Brandt. Pleased to meet ya, Sheriff."

This sentence is music to Turner's ears, because it is spoken in a soft Mississippi drawl. So he knows a little bit about what and whom he's dealing with. He won't expect any slack from the Yankee, but maybe the southern boy will be of some help.

"Here's what I've got. First off, the man who's missin' is the pastor of the nigger church over in th' quarter." He notices that Brandt flinches at the word "nigger" and at the word "quarter" and files this information under "buttons to push on th' Yankee".

"A little background on th' church is that recently they've been doin' voter registration pre-certification work outta the basement, and that's got the town stirred up some. We had some trouble out there at th' church a couple of Sundays back—some white kids from over at Auburn were caught over there and beat up. By the time we were called to go out there, the perps were gone and nobody was willin' to identify them. So nothin' really come from that."

Brandt moves closer to the front of his chair. "Hold on a minute, Sheriff. You mean that there was no investigation into that 'incident'?"

A little irritated, Turner responds, "Well, I tried to investigate but when nobody could or would tell me anything, I had to let it go. The boys that was hurt from th' college left town and I couldn't interview them. What was I sup-posed to do?"

"You...." Brandt waves his hand in a dismissive gesture. Shakes his head. Clenches his jaw and looks away from the sheriff.

Turner continues, "Anyhow, that's just background. Don't have nothing to do with th' current circumstances." Shuffles his papers. "Now lemme see ... Ah here we go. On Sunday night at 21:30 hours I got a call at home from my evening dispatcher sayin' that the preacher's wife had called in sayin' that some white men had come to their church and were firing into the buildin' with shot-guns. She said that her husband had gone out to try to reason with the men and they had taken him away at gunpoint. She claimed to have recognized one of the men."

He looks up from his papers and says, "I was pissed, of course at being called out in the middle of th' night like that, but figgered that since we'd had that other trouble I'd better shag my ass over there myself, instead of sendin' a deputy.

"I got to the house at ... lemme see ... 22:00 hours and interviewed Eudora—that's th' preacher's wife, Miz Eudora Maxwell. She insisted that she recognized Mr. Thad Blankenship as having been the man who held her husband at gun-point, and forced him into his truck, and drove off with him. All the other men—she didn't know how many others they was—got into other vehicles—she didn't know what kind or how many—and ever'body left.

"I looked around as best I could and couldn't really see much—there weren't no lights at the church parking lot and the power line into the church itself was shot out. So I couldn't see well enough to do a proper investigation. I told Eudora that I'd be back out there this morning. Of course that wasn't good enough for her."

Brandt interrupts again. "Did you at least post a guard? I mean, did you try in any way to protect the integrity of the crime scene?" He feels a rising sense of out-rage toward this man. He doesn't believe that he could possibly be so incompe-tent, so he believes instead, that because the victim is colored, that the sheriff doesn't feel compelled to do a professional job. Struggling to keep his temper in check, he has almost stood up.

"Protect the crime scene from what? Nobody was gonna mess with anything over there. Hell, it was the middle of the night by the time I finished there myself. Ain't nobody gonna snoop around over in Niggertown that time of night. I did find a few of the shell casings from the windows being shot out. I put those in my pocket and brought them in this morning. We dusted 'em and couldn't find any prints that were salvageable.

"I was going back over there this morning, when I pretty much got told that you boys would be running th' show, so I stayed put." His voice has taken on a harsh tone and the color is rising in his face. He looks hard at Brandt and says, "I've got my man, "Digger" Hill, posted over there at th' church this mornin'. When you boys show up over there, I'll be pullin' him back to duties in our own work place. You want the rest of my report or not?"

Knight leans forward and gently pulls his partner back into his chair. "Look, Sheriff, we don't want to cause you a lot of grief over this. We're here because we were told to come. We'd like to work *with* you, not against you. You and your men know this town better than we could in a year. It would help if you'd leave your man there to keep other people away from the scene until we're finished. Can you at least do that much for us? And, yes, we'd like to hear the rest of the report."

Jimbo slows his breathing and his color begins to return to normal. He nods in their direction and looks back to his notes. "I left the nigger church grounds at 23:00 and drove toward the home of Thad Blankenship. On the way there I passed the house of a mutual acquaintance, saw Blankenship's vehicle there and found him inside with four other men. They were playing cards and stated that they had been there and together since approximately 19:00 or 19:15. I took statements from all of them and left them at approximately 01:00 this morning. I talked to all of the men and they all said the same thing—that they'd been play-ing cards together since 19:15 at the latest."

He stops his reading and looks at the two agents. "That's all I've got. When I came in this morning at seven the phone was ringing from your boss, Mr. Katzenbach. I was told in no uncertain terms that this would be your investiga-tion. I ain't gonna pretend with you fellas that I like this. Whatever this turns out to be, it happened in my town and my jurisdiction. I should be allowed to con-duct my own investigation without interference from outside, 'specially federal interference. If either of you has worked anywhere besides federal, then you know what I mean and how I feel."

Nodding his head Knight says, "Yeah, Sheriff, I worked twelve years in Jackson, Mississippi before I joined the Bureau. I was a detective for the last six years and I know exactly what you mean.

"Hell, we didn't even like for the state boys to intervene unless we asked for help. Listen, this ain't about us thinking that you don't know how to do your job, or thinking that we're better at this than you; it's about the law stating that *all* kidnapping cases are automatically referred to the Bureau—regardless of which state or town or county they occur in. I admit that this one is getting some special attention from higher up, but to Oscar and me it's just a job we've got to do.

"Believe me, Sheriff, I'd rather be in Atlanta doing my own damn work there—I've got plenty of it sittin' on my desk. But *my* boss, who works in the same building as I do, told me that I *would* come over here and work this case. Now, Mr. Hoover, he works in Washington D. C. and I suspect that he doesn't like being told by Mr. Nicholas Katzenbach that we should be over here before noon today any more than you like our being here. But like they say 'Shit rolls downhill' and me and you just happen to be at the bottom of the hill."

Looking at Brandt he continues, "Me and Oscar are gonna have to go over to the crime scene and look around and talk to people around the area. We'll have to talk to this Blankenship guy and the men who supply his alibi, too. This is just standard procedure, Sheriff. We could use your help rounding these folks up and we'd like to use your office to do our interviews if you don't mind."

Turner looks sideways at Knight and says, "Well, I wouldn't mind if I had enough room myself, but I don't. I'll be glad to call upstairs and get them to set you up with something, though … See, I've got seventeen people working in here, on th' road and at th' jail. And this is all th' office space I've got. I 'preciate that you understand why I'm doing things this way, Mr. Knight. I'll call these men and ask them to come in … When?"

Brandt snaps, "Let's say as soon as possible—today for sure. And if you'll radio us we'll come back here when they arrive."

Knight shrugs and simply nods in agreement, then adds, "The property damage part of the case is still yours. We'll get as much information as we can find and turn it over to you. Maybe that'll help you out for leaving your man over there to help with crowd management. I expect that the press will hear of this soon, and you know how they are."

By the time the FBI men leave, the tension level is down from a roar to a hum.

＊   ＊   ＊   ＊

As Mohammed walks across the street from the Maxwell residence to the church, he sees fully for the first time the extent of the damage to the windows of the building. A deep sadness pervades his countenance and he wonders how and why a person could sink so low as to bring violence to the house of the Lord. Nearing the edge of the parking area he is approached by a uniformed sheriff's deputy. "Hold on there," drawls Hill. "Nobody's allowed on the grounds until after the investigation is completed. Sheriff Turner told me that nobody is to come into the church or onto the grounds. They's supposed to be some F.B.I. men on their way over here right now, so you'll just have to wait 'til they git here."

"But my office is in the church and I need to get in there to see about getting some of this mess cleaned up." Though annoyed, Mohammed is glad and more than a little surprised to see the deputy here.

"Like I said, you'll just have to wait 'til them federal boys git here. What you do after that will be up to them, but for now you can't go no further than the street. Hold on, this is prob'ly them coming up now. That looks like a federal car to me."

The gray sedan pulls to a stop a few feet away from the two men. Brandt and Knight get out. Knight asks, "Problems deputy?"

"No, no problems. This fella came up saying that his office is in th' church, and wanted to go inside. I was just explainin' to him that y'all would be in charge of things and that you'd have to OK him going in."

Brandt turns to Mohammed and asks, "And who would you be, sir?"

Mohammed answers, "I'm Dr. Milton Mohammed. I'm the associate minister here. I just wanted to go in and see if I could get some of the men of the church to come out and start cleaning up the mess. At least the windows need to be boarded up so that no further damage will come to the building." Inexplicably, he feels nervous in front of these men.

Brandt responds, "Well, Dr. Mohammed we need to do some things here first, but as soon as the preliminaries are done, we'll be glad to let you in to your office. In fact, if you want to come with us as we do our walk-through, we'd like to talk to you about the whole situation anyway."

As Mohammed, Knight and Brandt head toward the church Digger Hill says, "I reckon I'll head on back to the office now."

Knight replies, "Call in to the sheriff before you leave. He may have decided that you're to stay here. If you're supposed to stay, don't let anyone else onto the grounds until we get back out here." Without waiting for a response, he says, "Thanks, deputy" and continues on his way to the church.

Approaching the front door of the old building, Brandt is saying, "Man alive, this place looks like a war zone or something. What did these idiots think that they were doing anyway?" He's shaking his head in shock and disgust.

The central part of the sparkling white church is an old wooden structure. The newer addition, made of block and brick, stands to the left of the main building as you face it. Four broad steps lead up to a narrow concrete porch—all painted gray. The double doors at the entryway are tall and have small, diamond shaped, clear-glass windows at face height. The clapboard walls of the vestibule extend to a breadth of twenty feet. Inset in these walls are six-foot windows—now open into the foyer itself. Most of the glass is blown out and onto the floor inside. There are dozens of small, circular holes around the window frames and on the walls from the pellets of the shotgun blasts. Lines of lead with shards of colored glass clinging to them stick out from the sides of the frames.

A bell tower rises above the entryway with a spire at the pinnacle, topped with a simple cross. Below the opening for the bell are the remains of a round window. It, too, shows the marks of shotgun blasts. Against the clean white paint of the walls, the pellet marks seem like so many freckles. Mohammed turns the knob and the front door opens accompanied by the scratching of glass fragments being swept across the floor.

The three men stop at the entrance, awed by the extent of the damage here in the foyer. Swinging doors with small viewing windows separate the foyer from the sanctuary itself. Their steps crackle as they cross the eight feet from the out-side doors to the sanctuary doors.

Mohammed sucks in a deep breath and bravely pushes his way into the main room of the church. Here the church is open to the outside by virtue of the large rectangular holes where windows, some three feet wide by ten feet high, had graced the walls. Birds flit across the auditorium from open window to open win-dow. A breeze flutters the pages of hymnals left lying on pews. Glass is every-where. None of the three men can speak at first. Tears stream unashamedly down Mohammed's cheeks. The shock is palpable.

Brandt breaks the silence saying, "I sure hope that your insurance pays for all this." Of course all three know that even if the monetary loss is covered, the emo-tional loss can never be soothed. Mohammed thinks that since a white man's agency in town holds the insurance policy, the likelihood that the windows will be considered reimbursable losses is slight. His sadness will likely lead to anger, so he doesn't mention this to the F.B.I. men. Can't let that particular tiger out of its cage here and now.

Knight offers, "It looks as if all the damage was done from the outside in. I don't believe that any of the perpetrators ever entered the church. That would fit with what Mrs. Maxwell told the sheriff. Tell us what you know about the disappearance of Reverend Maxwell, doctor."

"All I know is what Eudora told me. I was at my own house. She called me at about ten o'clock and asked me to come over. She is insistent that she recognized Thaddeus Blankenship as the man who forced Eldred into the truck. She thinks that the truck was white, but isn't 100 percent sure of that. I feel certain that he was abducted rather than going somewhere of his own volition. He doesn't drive and it would be unlikely that he would leave Eudora alone after the trouble last night. That's all I know."

Knight nods and says, "That's fine Dr. Mohammed. You may go on to your office if you wish. We'll take our investigation back outside. If there's any way that you can find the number and a value of the windows, and the other damage to the building itself, it would help if you could gather that for us. We'll be handing that portion of the investigation over to Sheriff Turner later, but we'll also watch to see that something is done about solving that part of the crime. Thanks for your help. If you hear anything that you think we should know, please contact us. We'll be in town for at least a few days."

*   *   *   *

Mohammed's first phone call is to the chairman of the Building and Grounds Committee of the church, Willie Jones. Willie has already heard of the problems and has spoken with several committee members. They are preparing to visit the church grounds in the early afternoon to do whatever repairs they can.

The second call is to SNCC (Snick) national headquarters in Greensboro, North Carolina. He asks for Stokley Carmichael and is told that he will be in meetings with volunteers for most of the day, but that he does check in at the office periodically. Mohammed asks that Carmichael call him back at his earliest convenience, that an emergency situation has occurred at the church in Tuskegee. The secretary says that she'll give him the message.

Sitting at his desk and pondering his next responsibility leads nowhere. He's unsure as to any other move at this point, but yearns to do ... *something.* But his mind won't cooperate and the more he pushes for an answer, the more frustrated he becomes. Helplessness jangles his nerve endings. A tingling nags at the base of his spine—an itch that can't be scratched. His legs want to move, to jump up and *do* something, *go* somewhere. Rage and disgust rise up in him like bile. He feels like crying again or shouting.

Slumping back into the desk chair, he sighs and accepts that there is little else that he can do that will help to resolve the mystery of Eldred's whereabouts. At last it occurs to him that he can at least look through the church's books and find the value of the stained glass windows. Something to occupy his thoughts, some action that he can take. He calls Eudora and then opens up the file cabinets as she directed and begins looking for receipts for the payments for the windows. He's committed to staying in the church until he hears from SNCC, and then he'll plan for his further involvement.

✻   ✻   ✻   ✻

Red McKinney is on the phone with Carl Metzner, the managing editor of the *Washington Post*. Since all the trouble started with the Civil Rights Movement in the South, Red has earned a few extra dollars by operating as a stringer for the *Post* in Alabama. He's explaining to Carl that there seems to be "… some sort of major happening at the Mt. Zion AME church in Tuskegee. It's being alleged that several white men have abducted the Negro minister of the church. This is the same church where two white students were beaten recently when it was discovered that they were helping coloreds from the community gather the necessary information in order to register to vote.

"All I know at this point is that the FBI has sent agents over there from Atlanta. Th' preacher is missing and his wife is saying that she saw and can identify one of the men who kidnapped her husband. Apparently the same men also shot out all the stained glass windows from the church. Do you want me to follow up on any of this?"

"Have you been to the church? Have you talked to the minister's wife, yet?" Carl is always thorough in his filling out of the overviews given him by stringers.

"I haven't been over there yet. I did talk to the associate minister about Mrs. Maxwell though, and she's very certain about her identification. I got the tip from a student at the university here who seems to know people over there."

Red knows that his own local newspaper will not likely be very interested in printing a story that might cause any sympathy for the coloreds. He also knows that the story needs to be told and to a larger audience than he can find at home, thus his call to the *Post*.

Metzner says, "If you can get over there and talk to somebody other than the wife—you know, somebody official, like those F.B.I. people or the sheriff or somebody—and can verify that there has actually been a kidnapping, call me back with the story. I want quotes and names. No sloppy work on this now. With Carmichael and his bunch headed to Selma, this could be a hot topic. Call me and let me know what you find out and we'll go from there. Usual fees and expenses. Agreed?"

Red is pleased. "Agreed."

Rummaging around in his desk he finds Jimmy O'Reilly's phone number in Boston and calls him. After explaining what is going on and getting Jimmy's message for the preacher's wife, he hangs up and heads for his car, whistling, as he plans out the headline in his imagination.

The twenty-five minute drive to Tuskegee takes only twenty-two and Red pulls up to the church and attempts to enter the driveway to the parking area. A deputy blocks his entrance and is not impressed when Red insists, "I'm with the press".

"I know who you are, Red, but that don't cut no ice with this here situation. The feds are wandering around the church grounds and Jimbo told me to do what they asked in the way of crowd control. And they said nobody on the grounds 'til they say so."

"Yeah alright, Digger. What are their names at least? And when did they get here?" McKinney figures that he may as well start getting information as quickly as possible.

"Names are Brandt and Knight. They got here 'bout twenty minutes ago. First they talked to th' assistant preacher. His name's Mohammed—least it is now; he used to be Milton Spinks but changed his name to Mohammed a few years back. Yonder they come. You want more information, you'll have to git it from them." Hill is a little apprehensive that he may have said too much, but shrugs it off. Hell, they didn't tell him not to talk to the press.

McKinney leans out his window and shouts, "Agent Brandt. Agent Knight. Can I talk to you, please?"

The two agents approach Red's car quizzically and Brandt asks, "Do we know you?"

McKinney responds, "No. No. I just got your names form Deputy Hill here and wanted to ask you a few questions. I'm Red McKinney and I represent the *Washington Post*. Can you tell me what the exact nature of your investigation here is?"

Brandt shoots Hill a murderous glance as Knight says, "Man, you people sure didn't waste any time getting 'hold of this. How th' hell did you get here from Washington this quick?"

"Oh I'm just a stringer for the *Post*. I actually work for the *Auburn-Opelika News*. I drove here from my office in Opelika. Anyhow, what can you tell me about your investigation?"

Brandt says, "Not much at this time. We received a call this morning regarding an alleged kidnapping here in Tuskegee and were dispatched to begin preliminary investigations as standard procedure would require."

"What's the name of the person who was kidnapped?"

"We don't know yet that it was actually a kidnapping. We've just begun the investigation and can't release any names as yet. We haven't even had time to talk to the family of the alleged victim. I will say that the local sheriff will be conducting his own investigation of the vandalism and destruction of property related to someone's having shot out the windows of the church. That's about all I can comment on at this time." And so saying, Brandt leads the way for Knight and him to leave.

McKinney blurts out, "Excuse me Agent Brandt, are you the SAIC here in this investigation?"

Still walking Brandt nods to the affirmative.

"I've been told that the missing person is Reverend Maxwell. Is that true?"

Neither Brandt nor Knight looks back as they make their way across the street to the home occupied by Mrs. Maxwell. They knock and disappear inside.

McKinney looks back at Hill and says, "Is that right, Digger? Is it the preacher who's missing?"

"That's what I hear, Red; but I don't really know much about it yet. Jimbo jus' told me to stay here and keep people out of th' churchyard and away from them federals. What's that SAIC stuff mean anyhow?"

McKinney is scribbling on his notepad. "Special Agent In Charge. Somebody told me that Mrs. Maxwell says that she knows who took th' preacher off. Is that right?"

No hesitation from Hill, "Well that's what she says but it was so dark when it happened that there ain't no way she could've seen anybody."

"When *did* it happen?"

By now Hill is feeling mighty important. He straightens to full height and says, "S'posed to've been at about nine o'clock last night. She—Eudora that is—says that a bunch of white men came out here and started shootin' out th' winders of th' church and that th' preacher went runnin' out to try and stop 'em.

That's when she says that she seen Thad Blankenship throw down on th' preacher and march 'im off to his truck at gunpoint and drive off outta here with 'im."

"How'd she know it was Thad?"

"Hell, she didn't know anything of th' sort. Ain't no way anybody could see good enough to know who did what. I doubt Thad would bother with a nigger preacher. What th' hell for anyway? Don't make no sense, but you'd have to know Eudora to understand. She's a hell raiser and a troublemaker from th' git-go." Digger is enjoying being center stage for this interview. Although he's known Red McKinney most of his life, he's never been the object of attention for a newspaper story.

"You think he's dead?"

Digger seems startled, "Who? Th' preacher? I got no idea. 'Course he might be. Ya never know about these kinds of situations. But I don't have no reason to think about it one way or th' other."

"You think Thad did it?"

"Hell no. Fact is, Thad wuz at Cracker's house playing cards with my cousin Gene and Cracker and Swift Collins and Ricky Parson. Eudora's just lookin' ta make trouble and is shootin' off her mouth. Maybe she just *wants* for it t'be Thad. Maybe she's got some kinda grudge agin 'im or somethin'."

Red's got him talking without thinking now, so he presses forward, "You think Thad might've been one of them that came over to th' church back a couple of Sundays ago and maybe she's sorta angry about that or something?"

"That could be it. Or maybe even somethin' just between th' two of 'em. Ya know, Thad's had half th' niggers in th' county work for 'im over th' years. Could be somethin' like that, I guess. Who knows what it is? But Thad and Gene and that bunch was playin' cards an' they all say th' same thing, so it's prob'ly true."

"You care if I quote you about this stuff, Digger?"

"I don't know about that, Red. Th' sheriff'll prob'ly have my ass if you do. How 'bout if you call me a 'unnamed source' or somethin' like that. You know how they do in th' city papers. I don't need t' lose my job over this."

"How about 'an unnamed source close to the investigation'?"

"Yeah. That sounds pretty good. I can live with that I reckon."

"'Preciate you talkin' to me, Digger. I 'spect I'd best go try to see Jimbo. Is he at th' office?"

"Last I knew he was. Jus' be careful 'bout what you say that I said."

*   *   *   *

Mohammed closes up the files in the office as two o'clock approaches. He's lost track of time and is hungry now. Thinks, *I'll just take these figures out to those F.B.I. men and then I might as well go on home and get something to eat. If Stokley hasn't called by now, he probably won't 'til this evening.*

As he checks to be sure that he has everything in order, the phone rings. He reaches absently for the receiver and says, "Hello, this is Dr. Mohammed."

"Collect call from Mr. Carmichael. Will you accept the charges?" An anonymous operator's voice.

He stammers, remembering, getting excited. "Yes. Of course. I'll accept the charges."

"Go ahead, sir."

"Afternoon, Reverend. This is Stokley. The secretary said that somethin' has happened at the church. What's goin' on?"

Milton can't help smiling at Stokley's calling him "Reverend". They've been through so much training together that they are friends now. "Hello Stokley. Bad news here I'm afraid. We think that Eldred's been abducted by whites and the church has been shot up. I called to see what you think about this and, since you're at least headed in this direction, to get any ideas about what kind of response you think I or we should make."

"What? Are you sure that he's not off doin' church work or cattin' around or something? I mean I know how all you *knee-grow* preachers are 'bout th' ladies." Stokley is forever joking and trying to lighten up heavy and scary situations.

"No that's not it. Eudora is sure that she saw a white man take him off at gunpoint. It happened at about nine o'clock last night. No word from him or about him since. Any thoughts about a response?"

For the first time since Eudora called last night, Mohammed feels himself relax a little. It's comforting to talk with someone about these events other than white people who don't understand or care much, or local colored people who are mostly scared.

"Lemme think on this a minute, Milton." And the pause seems to stretch on for minutes. "I think that we'd best wait a bit before we do anything much. It's not like he's been kidnapped for ransom or something, so there's really no urgency to respond. If he comes back, we'll need to do one thing. On the other hand, if they've killed him—and we have to think about that possibility—we'll want to do something else. How 'bout if I call you back this evening and we'll see what the status is at that point. Meanwhile, I'll try to raise Andy or Martin and see what they can contribute. I've still got training and planning to do this afternoon, so it may be kinda late. I'll call you at home"

Milton is relieved to be sharing the burden now. "That sounds fine. What are you planning to do about overnights on your journey? You know that you won't be able to find hotels or motels that will allow a bunch of colored people to stay the night." Again Mohammed is amused, thinking that it would be just like Stokley to *make* the hotel managers refuse them service.

"Oh we're planning to stay at a church in Georgia. Some of us will stay with members of the congregation and others will sleep at the church itself. They're gonna feed us and we'll get an early start the next day. Look, I've gotta run. I'll call you at home tonight."

"Thanks, Stokley. Y'all be careful out there while you're at it."

"Always, my brother. Always."

CHAPTER 21

▼

There are students in different listening rooms in the basement of the library and Duke has started the musical pieces that they wanted to hear. Two women asked for Manuel de Falla's "Three-Cornered Hat", and a group from a Music Appreciation class is listening to "The Planets" by Holst in the largest, central room. He has the sound from "The Planets" playing softly at the control station and listens with half his mind as he absently juggles the multiple balls of his life with the other half—Claire in the hospital, Reverend Maxwell missing, Lynn, George, Terry and the bridge tournament on Saturday, Ann, classes, and a fleeting thought of Tisha—her impish smile and provocative derriere.

Ann slips in the doorway unseen. She stands and watches his body language and tries to puzzle out the thoughts that might be running through his mind.

"Problems, cowboy?" Her voice lands like a feather on his ear and evokes a smile. The muscles in his stomach relax immediately.

"Did you say 'cowboy'? Where'd that come from?" Turning toward her as he speaks, he inhales involuntarily. Shifts gears. Tries to refocus his attention and find a place to stand in this part of his world.

She chuckles and answers, "I don't really know. It just popped into my head. I hadn't actually thought about it consciously, but it fits. You *do* remind me of a cowboy—solitary, independent, sort of a do-gooder, heart on your sleeve. Not to mention those boots that you always wear with your jeans. Do you by any coincidence ride a horse?"

He's embarrassed and annoyed by it. Swallows and chokes a little on his answer, "Yeah. A little. My uncle has horses. But I really don't like it much. You can never be sure what a horse is gonna do. I'm afraid I'd be a poor candidate for the cowboy role."

Having said that much, he relaxes a little more and adds, "I'd prob'ly end up gettin' pissed and shootin' my horse. Then I'd have t'walk everywhere I went … All the other cowboys would laugh at me … I'd prob'ly end up getting' an ass-whippin' over that darn horse." They laugh together at his flight into fantasy.

Sighing, she looks away from him. "I needed to talk to you because Alex called last night." Turning back to face him she continues, "He and Melissa are coming home tonight." She frowns in anguish.

He feels gut shot—big hole in his middle. Mind blank, he wants reassurance but knows somehow that she can't give it to him. In fact, she needs something from him. He waits to respond, eventually finding a pathway in the minefield of his anxiety. "You don't look very happy about it." A fact, not an accusation. Thinks, *Give her enough room to tell me what she needs. Let her direct the conversation. This is her dilemma, although my stake in it grows every day.* Then he feels again the grinding of anxiety in his belly.

He watches as she gathers herself, knowing that she would. "I guess that for the past few days he's seemed sort of unreal or something.… I mean, I've thought of him some … And I've missed Melissa a lot. But I don't know. Suddenly he seems to be real again in a way that I had just forgotten. I don't know how I'll be able to relate to him. I think my feelings for him are gone … dead … I dread seeing him."

"Are you afraid of him?"

"No. Not physically anyway. He's big and loud but he wouldn't do anything physical. I'm more afraid of things that he might say or what he might accuse me of. He can be very hurtful that way. He's very blunt with what he thinks." Her strength returns—visible on her face and in her carriage.

Hesitantly Duke offers, "It's probably more important for you to pay attention to what *you* think and feel at this point. You don't have any control over what *he* thinks or says. You've gotta be in charge of your own thoughts and words, though. What do you want to do with your life at this point?" More praying than prying.

She looks at the floor. After a moment she looks up again and directly into his eyes. "I'm not sure, Duke. I guess I'm pretty confused about that. I know that I could be safe in a marriage with Alex, and Melissa would have everything she needs. But I've seen something now that I didn't know existed. I know that a life with him wouldn't be fulfilling, and I think I deserve fulfillment. That seems selfish on one hand—but it almost seems like survival at the same time. I just don't know what I want to do."

Fear that he wants to hide courses through him. "Do you have to decide immediately? I mean, can't you test the waters, so to speak, without showing all your cards right now?"

"I've thought of that, but I don't know if I can do it. I guess that a part of me feels like *you* is written all over my face. Part of me doesn't care that that is true, but another part of me is afraid I'll make a stupid decision … for the wrong reasons." Pausing she gathers herself … "You're right. I just need to play it cool for a few days and see what happens and how I feel about things."

Duke tries to make light of his prejudice by saying, "I'd love to advise you about this, but I'm afraid that my own wishes would keep me from being fair-minded … Besides, my instinct is you don't actually want someone else to decide for you."

Smiling uncertainly she responds, "Right again. But it's nice to know where you stand." Then with more self-assurance, "How are all the other things in your world?"

"Well, lemme see. The girl who went to Birmingham is resting and safe in the hospital at Lee County. Reverend Maxwell in Tuskegee is missing—presumed kidnapped by white men. I'm supposed to go to shoot skeet tomorrow with the son of one of the men who likely did the kidnapping. I play in a regional bridge tournament in Atlanta on Saturday. I'm supposed to see the daughter of the guy who allegedly heads the Klan around here tonight. And I've probably lost all credibility with the colored community in Tuskegee by now, since I haven't been back over there in so long. Other than that, not much is going on." Somehow rattling off all the details aloud has minimized their impact and he feels unburdened.

Concerned Ann asks, "Why is your friend in the hospital?"

"Long story. I'm gonna take a dinner break at six. If you want to meet in the break room on the third floor then, I'll tell you about it."

"I get off at five but maybe I'll hang around. Let's wait and see how things are going at that point. Meanwhile, I need to get back upstairs. Thanks for listening to my trivial little mess. You've got a lot more important things to be thinking about. See ya later."

Turning away to leave she pretends that she doesn't hear his parting comment, "Nothing's more important than your 'little mess'."

*   *   *   *

Red McKinney turns his dark green Chevy Nova left off West Main and heads toward Tuskegee and Mt. Zion AME Church for the second time today. It's mid afternoon and he is lethargic from his late lunch at Robert Earle's restaurant. He is only dimly aware that two men have crossed the street in front of him, some two blocks ahead; but as he draws nearer he realizes that they are the F.B.I. agents. He stares straight ahead to avoid making eye contact in case they look in his direction. He can't be sure if they look at him, or would recognize him if they do. Mild surge of adrenaline. He continues past their car and to the next corner. Turns left to wait and parks in the lee of a hillock covered in brush. He gets out of his car to creep through the brush and tops the rise in time to see the gray sedan headed toward West Main, presumably going back uptown.

Parking the Nova in front of the church manse, he takes his time getting out so that anyone inside can see who he is. He makes a show of gathering his notebook and pens, then heads up the walkway in the afternoon sun. As he's about to knock, the door opens a crack and Eudora Maxwell peers out at him from the relative gloom of the darkened interior.

"Afternoon, ma'am. I'd like to speak to Miz Maxwell if I might. I'm Charles …"

Her husky voice interrupts him, "I know who you are, Red. Why do you want to talk to me?" Her voice is surprisingly strong. He'd been expecting to find a grieving-widow type. His response is uncertain—not the image that he wants to present.

"Uh … Yes ma'am. I've been told that Reverend Maxwell is missing and that you believe that he was kidnapped. I was.… ."

She interrupts bluntly and forcefully, "Why do you care? Your paper never prints anything about what happens in this neighborhood. Why should you care what's happened now?" Nothing about her demeanor encourages him.

"Well, Miz Maxwell. You may be right about the local paper. But I'm actually here representing the *Washington Post*. I've been a stringer for them for a couple of years now and they're interested in hearing your side of the story. Can I come in? Will you talk to me?" His hat is literally in his hand. He fans himself absently against the stagnant heat.

Eudora hesitates, wondering if she should trust a white man with this emotional set of facts. After weighing things out, she decides that she has nothing to lose. "C'mon in. We'll see if you really want to hear *my* side of things."

As he enters the dark living room, Red is aware that he has never been inside the home of a colored person. Aside from the darkness, he can see no substantial difference in this living room and that of many of his friends, or his own for that matter. The orderliness of the home—everything in its place, no clutter, pleasant smell of cleanliness—surprises him. All his life he has heard that coloreds are lazy and not well kept.

Eudora crosses to an end table and turns on a light. The room, though still muted, is more visible and Red sees the differences between the cultures reflected in the artwork hanging on the walls. A likeness of George Washington Carver hangs near the door to the kitchen, framed religious pictures over the couch, family photos on other walls. The knick-knacks are figurines featuring colored children and African carvings.

She motions Red to a wingback chair and seats herself on the matching couch. She wears no discernible makeup and her face shows the strain of the past eighteen hours. "Where do you want me to start?"

"Start wherever you're comfortable, Miz Maxwell." He's aware of his nervousness, and doesn't want to show it. He wants her to take the initiative. Doesn't want to probe and lose his chance to get this story.

"Well, we were headed to bed around nine last night, when Eldred heard what he knew to be gunshots. At first he thought someone was shooting at the house and dragged me to the floor. Soon he realized that nothing was hitting the house and went into the living room to investigate. He crawled in there on his hands and knees ..." Her voice is breaking and Red doesn't know what he should do, so he waits until she composes herself.

"I tried to get him not to go in there, but he wanted to know what was happening outside. I guess that when he looked out he could see that there were men shooting out the windows of the church. He worked so hard to get those windows. It took him and the congregation years and years to pull together the money to have them made." Tears roll down her cheeks. She pauses again to collect herself, then struggles on. "I couldn't believe my ears when I heard him open the door. Why would he go out there when guns were being fired? I just wish he'd stayed with me ... But I know he had to try to protect those windows."

Red is scribbling as fast as he can and only notices after a few seconds have passed that she has stopped talking. When he looks up, Eudora is staring at the wall across the room. He follows her gaze to.... Nothing ... A bare wall ... He waits ... Relaxes against the chair back. He knows very little about how to respond to grief and wonders if he should do something. It's like she's hypnotized or something.

He waits.

Finally, after several minutes have passed, she speaks again, "He's a very good man, Mr. McKinney. Kind. Gentle. Caring. In fact he cares more about the people of the congregation than he does about himself. I have to stop him from giving away all our money. I still can't believe that he went out there."

Smooth as water over a rock, Red mumbles, "Yes ma'am. What happened after he went outside?"

"There was a pause in the shooting and by the time I got to the window I could see him walking across the church's lawn toward a pickup truck that was parked on the street. Thad Blankenship was walking behind him with his gun pointed right at him. When they got to the truck, Eldred just went around to the other side and got in … He just got in." There is a note of incredulity in her voice.

"Then Thad got in behind the wheel and whistled to the other men. Everybody else stopped shooting, and they all got into trucks and drove away. I opened the door and yelled at Eldred not to go with them; but either he didn't hear me or he couldn't get away. I yelled at Thad, too, but he paid me no mind. Just drove off out of here … with my husband. I keep hoping against hope that he'll be alright.… But in my heart I know he's gone." She stares at her hands, which are folded, in her lap. Her despair weighs down the very air in the room.

Red waits until he's fairly certain that she's finished and asks a little more boldly, "How many others were there, Miz Maxwell?"

Shakes her head negatively, "Don't know." Almost a whisper. "I wasn't thinking clearly enough to do the right thing. Should have looked more closely, tried to get tag numbers, counted the men, the trucks. Something." Shakes her head again as her voice trails off.

"But you're sure that it was Thad? They're gonna say that it was too dark to see anything, you know. Are you sure it was Thad?" He knows that this is a touchy area, but his instincts tell him that he needs to push a little.

Her eyes come up from her hands to meet his. Her gaze is hot/cold. The air between them crackles. "I'm sure, Red. I don't care what 'they' say. I know what I saw and Thad Blankenship forced my husband into his truck at gunpoint. I'll swear to it in court."

Red says sincerely, "Miz Maxwell, I'm not doubting you in the least; but I know what they're gonna say. In fact they're already saying it. Why do you think they came over here in the first place? And why do you think that they took Reverend Maxwell off like that?"

"It's pretty obvious, don't you think? You heard what happened over here a couple of Sundays back when the voter registration drive was being held at the church. They beat up those college kids and three men from the church that day. They don't want us to be able to vote. They believe that if we vote, their rule over the town and the county will be over. They're not going to let that happen if they can stop it. *That's* what this is all about. It's a message to the people of color in Tuskegee and Macon County, Alabama."

"Yes ma'am. I expect that you're right about that. How much of what you've told me so far can I quote you on for the paper? I mean I'm sure that they won't print Thad's name, because it would prejudice any charges that might be brought against him. But they might print that you are certain that you can identify the man who kidnapped him. Would that scare you too much?"

"Mr. McKinney, if Eldred is dead, I don't have anything to lose. Print any and everything I've told you. But tell the story and tell the truth." She is resolute now. The telling of the story has helped to move her focus outside herself and her pain. More than ever now she feels the compulsion of "the movement" to stand up for what's right.

During the ensuing twenty minutes, Red gathers personal information about the Maxwells so that he can round out the telling of the story. Then he persuades Eudora to walk with him to the church grounds and to tell him the stories of the stained glass windows, two having been handmade by congregants, another by way of a donation, others as the result of fund-raisers. Red is happy to convey Jimmy O'Reilly's message to Eudora that he will pay for temporary windows to be put in the church and for the replacement of the stained glass windows.

After two more hours with Eudora Maxwell, Red McKinney is a man transformed—a white southerner converted to the idea that justice will only exist when the rights of his colored neighbors are vested. Before today he was tepidly sympathetic. Today he has been moved—emotionally and cognitively.

✳   ✳   ✳   ✳

The gray sedan comes to a stop in front of the courthouse and Knight and Brandt exit. Brandt nods toward the line of pickup trucks across the street and says, "I guess the boys have shown up already. Why do these types always drive pickup trucks? Is it some kind of macho thing?"

Knight chuckles. "I guess that a Yankee like you wouldn't understand that men in the South have to work for a living. My daddy used to say that a man with a truck could always find a way to make a few dollars. These guys would feel naked and impoverished without a truck. By the way Oscar, be careful about that 'these types' stuff. You don't want to go into this interview with your prejudice on your shoulders. We won't get *much* information anyhow."

Looking through the manila file folder in his hands Brandt says offhandedly, "You're probably right. I'll tell you what, why don't you conduct the interview? I'll just sit in and if I think of something that you need to ask, I'll write you a note. No sense in me antagonizing them any further than need be." Knight is sure that Brandt is still smarting from the hostility that Sheriff Turner aimed at him earlier.

"Good idea." Knight is pleased to get the responsibility from a senior agent and squares his shoulders.

As they enter the front door of the building, Marcie Brooks from the sheriff's office awaits them in the central foyer and directs them to the conference room that has been made available for the interview. Behind the wooden door and arrayed around one end of a mahogany conference table sit five men.

Blankenship wears a red and gray plaid short-sleeved shirt and blue twill work pants, but, to Brandt, he looks clean and freshly showered, relaxed, not threatened.

Collins comes in dirty, sweaty overalls with an equally sweaty white tee shirt. He looks at Brandt with undisguised hatred. His frayed and sweat stained straw hat is in front of him on the table. His sunburn stretches to the hat line. Brandt notes to himself that this one was probably working at his farm. Expects hostility.

Hill wears cotton trousers and a clean short-sleeved dress shirt, no tie, black-rimmed eyeglasses. He fidgets and may feel threatened. His posture is that of a weak man, slumped forward and not looking directly at anyone, unconsciously rocking back and forth slightly on the edge of his chair. Brandt figures that he probably works in an office or bank.

Parsons's blue work uniform has his name over the logo of the Alabama Gas Company. No doubt where he came here from. He looks bemused and cocky—chewing gum and grinning.

White is in blue jeans and a black, sleeveless tee shirt. Nicks, cuts, and grease mark his arms and hands. Work boots and clothing are oil stained and well worn. He clenches his jaw and glares, first at Brandt, then at Knight, then at the floor.

Brandt hands the folder to Knight and, pulling out a chair for himself, says "Good afternoon, gentlemen I'm Agent Brandt from the F.B.I. and this is Agent Knight. He'll be conducting the interview. Thank you for coming in."

Before Brandt makes it into his chair, Parsons says with venom, "What th' hell is this all about Mr. FBI-man Brandt?" A nasal twang dragged through sorghum syrup.

Knight interrupts, "We wanted to ask you gentlemen about the disappearance of the Reverend Maxwell …"

Knight's drawl is not lost on the group. Parsons points a finger at Brandt and says, "I asked you, not him. You want me to come in here off my job to talk, then you, by god, tell me what th' hell it's all about." Bullying anger drives his words.

Knight tries again only to be interrupted again, this time by Brandt. "Unless you've got a hearing problem, Mr. Knight was just telling you what this is all about …"

Knight pushes himself into the breach, "Everybody just calm down a minute. I'm in charge of this meeting and I'll answer your questions if you'll give me a minute. Sit down Agent Brandt. Mr. Parsons if you give me a minute, I'll explain things … Last night the Reverend Maxwell was taken from his home at gunpoint and your friend Mr. Blankenship here has been accused. According to the sheriff, he was supposed to have been playing cards with you gentlemen. We just need to check that out as best we can."

As Parsons relaxes back to his chair, Cracker White leans forward and snarls gutturally, "Reverend Maxwell? You mean that nigger preacher from over in the quarter? What th' hell would any of us know about him? He ain't exactly in our social circle…. Hell, he ain't even in our damn world. This is bullshit!"

Knight tap dances, "Let's start by getting your names straight. I can see that you're Parsons. Pointing to White he asks, "Who are you?"

"Cracker." Croaked out like a bullfrog. Eyes back on the floor. Unmasked anger in his posture, his expression.

As Knight asks, "Cracker?" Brandt snickers and shakes his head in the negative.

Looking around Knight, White says, "You got some kinda problem back there Mr. F.B.I.-man? You don't like my name maybe?"

Knight ignores the comments and skipping over Parsons, points to Hill and asks, "How about you, sir?"

Still looking at the table, Hill nods and responds quietly, "I'm Eugene Hill."

Knight nods and points to Collins, "And you, sir?"

"I'm Collins." No inflection. No questions. No emotion. Blank look. Knight hesitates, then points to Thad. "You, sir?"

"Blankenship." Again no inflection. Firm eye contact. This, the accused one, is cool as a January breeze.

Parsons then says, "OK, federal man, now you know ever' body's name, tell us what you want and let us get th' hell back to work."

"Well, it was like I was tellin' you fellas, somebody has accused Mr. Blankenship of kidnapping the minister...."

Collins leans forward and in a quiet but steely voice that could cut hardened oak says, "Goddamn, son, didn't you read the sheriff's report?" It's almost a whisper and a deaf man would have heard the threat and malice.

"Yes sir, we did. We just wanted to hear what else you might have to say, and hear it for ourselves." Turning from Collins, he looks to Blankenship and asks, "What have you got to say about this, Mr. Blankenship. We have a witness who says that you did the deed."

Blankenship just laughs and shakes his head. Then fixing a cold stare on Knight he drawls, "I've done told th' Sheriff all I've got t' say about this crap. I don't know what you boys are tryin' t' pull here, or why, but I ain't got no use for a nigger preacher and I sure as hell didn't take this'n." His gravelly voice is firm, gives no quarter.

The two men's eyes lock. It is Knight who looks away first. He moves in an arc back to Cracker White at the other end of their cluster, saying as he moves, "And all of you say that he was with you from seven-fifteen 'til after midnight. That right?"

Three men answer at once but it is Parsons who is heard. "You mean that you've already read all that information an' you called us in here anyway? You sonofabitch, I've got work t' do and this here is th' kinda crap that bosses get pissed about. What th' hell d' you want? We've done told the sheriff ever'thing we know."

Brandt can contain himself no longer. Looking in the general direction of Parsons but not making eye contact with anyone, he says "We want to be sure that Mr. Blankenship got there at seven-fifteen like the Sheriff says you told him."

Collins says, "You think Jimbo got it wrong? Or maybe that he lied?" His voice is laden with mock sincerity.

Knight interjects, "No, that's not what we mean. We ..."

Cracker looks past Knight to Brandt. "How 'bout you Mr. F.B.I.-man? You think th' sheriff's lying? Or maybe you're callin' us liars. Or maybe you're callin' th' whole damn town liars. That it, Mr. F.B.I.-man?"

Before Knight can stop him, Brandt says heatedly, "The thought had crossed my mind."

Cracker White jumps from his chair, red-faced. "You Yankee bastard, if you want to leave that fancy badge in here and come outside with me, I'll show you th' real honest-to-god truth like you ain't never *seen* it before."

Brandt leans forward; but Collins is saying, "You sorry bastards come in here and waste my damn time like this ... I got a crop in th' field. That don't mean nothin' to you city boys. You just go down to th' groc'ry store for ever'thing you want; but it's my livelihood. An' if I don't git it done, I go hungry—an' so do you ... Y'all arrestin' me or not?" And with that he begins to rise from his chair.

Knight raises his hand to speak, but Parsons lashes out, "Right. Are y'all arrestin' us or not?"

"No. We just wanted information. We just want to talk. Please sit down."

At that White pushes his chair back and turns. "If we ain't under arrest and y'all just want t' talk, I got things t' do. I got customers' cars in my garage and I'm going back t' work. You wanna talk t' me, come t' th' shop. We'll talk while I work." He moves toward the door.

Brandt says, "If we come to the shop, we'll come with a warrant."

The other men are getting to their feet, but slow down to watch White, who turns and looks toward Brandt, "You do that, son. In fact, if you come to my shop, be real damn sure you've got a warrant or I might think you're trespassin' and shoot yer ass."

Brandt explodes, "Are you threatening me?"

White answers with a grin, "Hell you ain't big enough t' have t' threaten. An' too damn dumb to understand it anyhow. Let's just say it's like I'm tryin' t' do ya a favor. Your fed'ral bullyin' bullshit don't scare nobody around here. So as far as I'm concerned, you can either do somethin' or just stay th' hell outta my face."

Collins is ushering Gene Hill toward the door. Behind him Thad Blankenship asks Knight, "Am I under arrest?"

Knight says, "No." Behind him Brandt adds, "Not yet Mr. Blankenship. But we're not satisfied that we know the whole truth either."

Calming, Thad says as he passes them on his way out, "Well you just let me know, Mr. FBI-man. Y'all know where I live, I 'spect."

When they are all out of the room and the door is closed firmly, Knight turns angrily to Brandt. "Thanks for letting me conduct the interview."

Brandt's smile is self-conscious and broad. "Jack, I'm sorry. Some of that was me being pissed off and some of it was designed to push these guys a little. I don't want them to get too complacent. I don't want them to think that we buy their story and that they're off the hook. People make more mistakes when they're nervous."

Knight shakes his head in disbelief. "You think that you made them nervous? You think that you directed what just happened? Hell, Oscar, them boys just played you like a Les Paul Guitar." He laughs again and adds, "We might as well compare notes now and see what, if anything, we might have learned."

Brandt's gaze is level as he says, "I learned two things for sure. One is that they're pretty damn good liars, but liars just th' same. Second, one man only said three words, while everybody else took a stand. The three words were: 'I'm Eugene Hill'—and there's your weak point."

✳   ✳   ✳   ✳

It's almost dark by the time Red McKinney finishes pulling his notes into a reasonable order. He calls Carl Metzner "collect" from his home and tells him that he thinks that he has a good story. He gives Metzner the facts as he has recorded them and waits while Carl reads them back to him. After considering the material Carl says that the story on the windows being shot out might be something that he will want Red to expand and develop—Do it and call him in an hour.

About the kidnapping Carl is more circumspect. He says, "The story of the missing minister is really "hot". We need to get some confirmation before we get too far committed to it though. I don't want to print that there's been a kidnapping and then have this guy walk back into town unmolested.... Let me think a minute ... I'll print that he is alleged to have been abducted. And that an unidentified witness says that the abductor(s) can be identified ... That way I don't have to say 'him' or 'her' and give away the sex of the witness.

"Good job, Red. Stay on this at least through tomorrow. I'll run blurbs of both of these on our midnight edition's front page and then full play in the morning edition. Be sure that you get over there tomorrow morning. Talk to those F.B.I. agents or the sheriff. If the body turns up, call me immediately and we'll decide what to do. Listen to the news in your car on the way over, the national media boys will be waking me up tonight for details. I'll print this under a wire services by-line to protect your identity as well as I can."

When the phone is back in its cradle, Red leans back in his chair and smiles the smile of the victorious. He has always wanted to be writing to a larger audience ... Two front-page blurbs and then two full play front-page stories in the morning paper ... Wow! This is a lot of money in his pocket. He won't get a byline, but that's probably a good thing.

As this thought plays across his mind he gets his first sense of foreboding. His thoughts shift to Jimmy O'Reilly's nephew and the beating that he took. Anger and fear play tag in his gut. He owes Jimmy a lot and this could help him to square accounts and at the same time get the kind of break in his career that comes once in a lifetime. There's a certain amount of risk involved, but this is history and he's going to be the one to report it.

Leaning forward to his Royal electric typewriter, he begins banging out the story of stained glass windows that reflect the history of a community and that now lie in shards on the floor of a small colored church in Tuskegee, Alabama.

✳ ✳ ✳ ✳

Robert Earle Jackson's restaurant, Magnolias on the Square, stands at the corner where West Main Street meets the town square. It is the last building in a row of storefronts which has been painted white over brick. Directly across the square's central park is the courthouse and the four pickup trucks still stand, angled into the curb. A statue commemorating the county's Civil War dead stands in the center of the park area, accompanied by scattered benches, ancient oak trees and a few well placed magnolias. A long, green rectangular sign with yellow letters proclaims the name and establishment date of the restaurant. Thad Blankenship speaks gleefully.

"That went pretty good over there. Ricky, you sure as hell did a fine job, son. That Brandt feller didn't know which way was up. And Knight didn't ask but one question. I figure we got through th' first round of this thing without a scratch." Pauses. "I was scared you was gonna beat that Yankee's ass there for a few minutes, Cracker."

Cracker grins and drawls, "Well, like the man said, 'th' thought crossed my mind'. I reckon that if he shows up at the garage without a warrant, I'll have to figure out some way *not* to shoot him though. 'Cept I don't think he'll come. Th' other boy might show up. He seemed okay."

Collins looks at Hill with disgust and remarks, "Gene, you just sat there like you was constipated or somethin'. I 'spect they took more notice of you than anybody else. What th' hell's wrong with you anyhow?"

Hill replies with obvious anxiety, "Ain't nothin' wrong with me, Swift. I didn't say nothin' that would draw attention t' me, and nothin' that I'll have t' worry about if they talk t' me again."

Blankenship snorts, "You mean 'when' they talk to you, Gene. If I had t' bet, you'll be the first one they talk to alone, just because you took their bullshit without a protest of any kind whatsoever. When they do come around, just be damn sure that you stick t' our story—no goin' off on your own with any details that we haven't already talked about. You understand that, right?"

"Yes, dammit, I understand. I didn't ask t' be in on no killin', but y'all're just gonna have t' believe that I'll do what I'm s'posed t' do. It's my ass just like it's yours." Perspiration has formed on his forehead and under his eyes where the frames of his glasses touch his cheeks. He takes a handkerchief from his trouser pocket and wipes it away.

Collins makes no attempt to hide his contempt. Half under his breath he whispers, "You, goddamn *better* understan', you fuckin' weasel." Then aloud he says, "Thad, you need to coach him or somethin' or he's gonna screw this thing up and get us all locked up."

Blankenship tries to calm the others by saying, "Leave it be, Swift. He's gonna be fine. Ever'body ain't like you—or wants t' be. Me and Gene'll take care of Gene. I've been thinking. We might oughtta go on over t' Selma an' let this thing blow over for a few days. Stokley Carmichael and that bunch oughtta be there by Thursday or maybe even Wednesday. We was gonna go and help th' others turn 'em back anyhow. Maybe we oughtta just go on over there tomorrow, or Wednesday at the latest."

Blankenship is less certain of Hill's ability to stay quiet than he let's on. "What d'y'all think about that?"

There is general agreement and all pledge to make arrangements by noon of the following day and to meet back here at the restaurant for lunch, prepared to go in tandem to Selma, some fifty miles away. That decided, they disburse to their jobs and homes. Hill turns right out of the restaurant and walks down four doors to the insurance agency where he works. As the other four cross the square's central area, Parsons says, "You reckon Gene's really gonna be alright, Thad?"

Before Blankenship can reassure him, Swift Collins interjects, "One way or another, he ain't gonna screw this up, Ricky."

Parsons tries to stop but is pushed along by Blankenship. "What th' hell you mean by that, Swift? You threatenin' Gene now?"

"Naw, Ricky. I'm just sayin' that he ain't gonna put us all in jail, that's all. One way or another. I won't go t' prison because he's a coward."

✳   ✳   ✳   ✳

At six-thirty Mohammed has finished his dinner, and the dishes are washed and put away. He tries to read his Sunday School lesson, but gives up, unable to concentrate. His thoughts ricochet from Eudora and Eldred to stained glass windows, to Stokley, to shouldering the responsibility of the church if Eldred can't continue with it. He would like to feel more positively about Eldred's chances, but isn't kidding himself. He fears the worst, feels it in his heart somehow. Forces himself to consider how the immediate future will have to play out and what his role will necessarily have to be. Pacing the floor, he feels guilty that he dreads the church duties.

Engrossed in his own thoughts that he answers the phone distractedly. "Hello."

"Good evenin', Reverend. This is yo' friend Stokley. How're you this evenin'? And has our brother Eldred returned from his wanderin' ways?" Caramel tones from the telephone. Mock formality leaves the sweet taste of familiarity.

"Hello, Stokley. We haven't heard anything about Eldred. Eudora has talked to the F.B.I. I can't tell yet if they're gonna do anything, but at least they're here." Somehow the sound of Stokley's voice has calmed Mohammed, and his mind snaps sharply into focus. "When are you and your group leaving North Carolina?"

"We'll be leaving before first light in the morning. I talked with Andy earlier and let them know what's going on. Martin, of course, is very upset. Andy said that they want to be kept informed and that they'll try to help in any way possible. He said that if you have a plan or idea, let them know and they'll help with planning, or even with money if that's what you need."

Mohammed hears the facts and the tone in Stokley's voice behind the facts. "What else, Stokley? Are you leaving out something?"

"No. That's what they said. I put in that maybe we oughtta think about doing more than waiting, but they're content to let things play out a little further. Personally, it doesn't seem like enough. I said that I thought that they oughtta say something to the media, but they want all of it to come from down there."

Mohammed considers this and then asks, "What would you do in my place? Have you got any ideas that I could be working on?"

"Well, I've thought about it, and if it were me in your place, I'd go talk to the deacons of the church and tell them that if Eldred is dead, they should join together and make a big push to register voters as soon as the news is out. There will be media, F.B.I. and other federal agents all over the place, and it should help getting folks registered. How's that sound to you?"

Although Mohammed had started thinking in this direction, he hadn't put it all together as Stokley has. "Good idea. I hadn't thought to get the deacons primed to strike *before* we're sure about Eldred; but it makes perfect sense.

There's nothing to lose. If he isn't harmed, we'll all be so happy that the extra alert won't have mattered. On the other hand, if we start talking about it now the emotions will grow and be ready to explode, if and when his body is found." Mohammed's mind is racing. His depression from a few minutes earlier is dissipated. Cogs turn. Energy rises like a thermometer at midday. "Thank you, Stokley."

"Uh ... Tell you what. Let's say that this was your idea. I mean, it'll be better if my name isn't brought into this right now. You know me and Andy don't always see things the same way. Atlanta'll probably be upset if you start doing things that I suggest. You dig?" There's more here than he's saying.

"That'll be fine—at least for now. I didn't know that you and Andy were arguing. I'd like to hear more about that sometime. Are you gonna stay in touch during the next couple of days?"

"Yeah. I'll call you at our rest stops until we hear something definite about Eldred. I'll call the church number first and if you aren't there, I'll try this number and if you're out actually doing some work, I'll call Eudora and leave you a message. I've got to try to get some sleep now. I'll talk to you tomorrow.... And as a friend of mine said to me earlier—'Be careful'."

"OK, Stokley. As a friend of *mine* said, 'Always my brother'."

As he places the phone back into its cradle, Mohammed pauses a moment to say a prayer for Stokley's safety and for those who are traveling with him. Then he gathers his hat and a notebook and goes outside to his car. Absently, he wonders how the deacons will respond to the suggestions that Eldred might be dead and that in response to that eventuality, the church needs to rise up—under their leadership. The shiver along his spine could be excitement, or just plain fear. Whichever, it's more welcome than the gloom he was enduring an hour ago.

✳   ✳   ✳   ✳

At a quarter to ten Duke is counting the minutes until he can leave. Ann had stayed until six and had sat with him in the break room on the third floor, while he ate a sandwich he'd brought from the Union cafeteria. He told her as much as he could remember, and she helped him by asking the right questions, to draw out things that were hazy. She gave him permission to ask another student worker to cover for him after ten o'clock, so he can now leave a little early.

When the relief worker shows up at exactly ten o'clock, Duke expresses his gratitude and heads upstairs. Out the door and into the humid summer night. His spirit takes flight—released from the drudgery of hours of sitting. Dogtrots to the T'Bird in the lower parking lot. He takes down the top, saddles up and the T'Bird eases out of the lot, rumbling toward the hospital.

Peeking into Claire's room, Duke sees that the head of the bed is raised but that she seems to be sleeping. He turns to leave and spies a bouquet on the nurse's station desk. Wandering in that direction he sees Miz Whitmore approaching from an intersecting hallway. With his biggest smile he asks who the flowers are for. "You know, Duke they came in around eight o'clock and the woman they were intended for went home at seven. She's gonna have her husband pick them up in the morning."

"Think she'd miss one flower? Just one? I mean she hasn't seen them or anything." Lena Whitmore barely pauses, returns the smile and nods her assent. Duke carefully chooses a red carnation and redistributes the remainder … Not noticeable. Takes the pocket knife from his jeans and cuts the stem to the length of a water glass. Steals back into Claire's room and puts the flower into her water glass. As he's leaving, Claire sleepily commands, "Stop. Where do you think you're going?"

He turns to face her and says, "Aha. Sleeping Beauty awakens. And without the requisite kiss."

"Damn right. I don't wanna sleep through that. Come over here and do your duty." Big drug-induced grin on her pretty face. Her hair is combed and a little more alive than this morning. A pale hand extends toward him weakly. And he takes it. Moves closer and leans in to kiss her lightly on the lips. She strains toward him. He pulls away and looks deeply into her shining eyes. "Whoa. I'm a sucker for a vulnerable woman. You seem to be feeling better."

"Yeah, I am now. I had some pain earlier, but the nurse gave me a shot and it's all gone away. I was sure that you'd come by. You said so this morning, so I was trying to stay awake for that. But I'm not gonna be able to visit. I'm really out of it."

Eyes half-focused. Slurring her words. He can only grin and feel love for her. She does seem so vulnerable right now. The invisible side of Claire Hollister. Her eyes close involuntarily. Smile playing across her lips and cheeks. Her hand limp in his. Duke scribbles a note on the pad near her glass and quietly leaves the room, the hospital, the parking lot.

Back on the parkway the T'Bird growls, prowls like some big hungry cat after his supper. Streetlights flash past overhead and Lloyd Cramer's piano wafts through the radio's speakers. He's almost sure that if he would just accelerate a little more, the T'Bird would take flight. Exuberance wells up in him as he slows through the main part of the campus. Few people wander the streets at this hour on a Monday evening. Turns into his street and suddenly remembers ... Lynn. The Sting Ray is parked out front. The front door is open to the screen. Soft light leaks out through the door and the window.

Duke turns the T'Bird into his parking space and exits. Approaching the front door he sees Lynn emerging sleepily from the bedroom. Her short skirt clings to her perfect thighs. Dark hair slightly disheveled. Make-up mostly gone. Buttoned blouse pulled high and tight across her chest. Barefoot. And out of the mouth of this sensual apparition comes, "I'll be ready in a minute. Sorry. I fell asleep." At that point he remembers that he promised breakfast.

CHAPTER 22

▼

As Red McKinney saunters into the sheriff's office in downtown Tuskegee at seven-thirty, Sheriff Jimbo Turner is hanging up the telephone. Turner shakes his head, bemused. He looks up, sees Red, and turns back toward his private office without speaking, nodding as he goes.

Marcie Brooks, the daytime dispatcher and secretary sits at a table near the radio, writing something into an open file. She turns and recognizing Red says, "Oh my God. Th' Press has shown up already."

"Whaddaya mean 'already'?" Red responds with a smile. "You expectin' somebody else later on?"

Marcie, a twice-divorced, slightly overweight bottle blonde, is very relaxed in her relationship with the world. Since most of the community sees her as a fallen woman anyway, she figures she doesn't need to try to make people believe any different. She does her job and goes home to take care of her kids. Jimbo has done her a favor by letting her keep this job in the face of public criticism—divorce doesn't sit well with the upstanding female members of the white community. But then most of them didn't go through the abuse she got from her two worthless ex-husbands. She has given up on being accepted by those women, and is realistically, bitterly aware of the hypocrisy that they live by.

"Well, I just meant it's god-awful early to have to deal with reporters." With an exaggerated sigh she adds, "I imagine that we'll be hearin' from a lot of you fellas before too much longer. If there was a missin' white man, I doubt anybody but his family would care much; but let one colored preacher go missin', and it's literally a federal case." Like most white people in the area, Marcie has grown weary of the seeming unrelenting attention paid to anything having to do with the colored population. She has no idea how many reporters actually will descend on tiny Tuskegee, but fears the worst.

"Yeah," Red says, "I guess that it's just the sign of the times, Marcie. 'Ever' dog has his day', as the say. Speaking of 'federal', how does the sheriff feel about them F.B.I. boys bein' here?" The question rolls easily off his tongue, the drawl more pronounced when he deems it prudent.

Marcie snorts and says, "He prob'ly feels about like you'd think—mad as hell. You know how Eudora is. She called the *White House* fer Chrissakes. Now we've got federal people in our county doin' our work for us—and *somehow* the national media reported on this story this morning." The accusation is unspoken, but clear all the same.

In a voice as free of sarcasm or threat as he can make it McKinney says, "Well kidnapping *is* a federal crime, you know."

"Oh yeah, it is; but if this was a white man gone missin', we'd have to *beg* for assistance from the F.B.I. But since it's a colored man, the feds are gonna crawl all over this county 'til they find some way to blame white people for it. How'd you find out about it anyhow? I meant to ask you yesterday, but you were gone before I remembered to."

"I got a phone call telling me that something had happened to Reverend Maxwell and that Eudora was saying that she recognized Thad Blankenship as the man who took Eldred off. Is that the way it's playin' out?"

The pause and eye contact between them seethes, verges on boiling over, when the radio crackles and a voice cuts through the static: "Ranger Rollins calling Sheriff Turner. Rollins to Sheriff's Office."

Marcie looks again at Red and says, "Hold on a minute." Grabs the stainless steel microphone. Pulls it forward, near her mouth, pushes the button on the base and says, "Sheriff's Office, go ahead Roger."

"Hey, Marcie, is Jimbo around there?" His voice sounds far away and the static makes it difficult for McKinney to understand.

"He's back in his office. Whaddaya need?" You have to get past Marcie to get to the sheriff.

"I ain't sure about this, but I think I've got a body out here at th' bottom of that ravine off Deer Creek Road. I saw buzzards circlin' around out there this mornin' and went out to see if I could see anything. I'm pretty sure that there's a body down there." He doesn't seem alarmed. Just matter-of-fact, reporting on this like he'd report on a new pothole or something. "This kinda thing ain't in my job description, Marcie, so I was wonderin' if maybe Jimbo could come out here or send somebody to check this thing out."

Marcie and Red share the same thought—Maxwell. She pauses a moment and says into the microphone, "Hold tight Roger. I'll get Jimbo to get back to you, OK?"

"Ten-four on that, Marcie. I'll be right here at the office. Rollins, out." And the radio goes silent.

As Marcie turns to go to the sheriff's private office, she sees that Red is headed for the front door. She can do no more than to sigh and say under her breath, "Oh Lord, here it goes."

✳   ✳   ✳   ✳

Knight and Brandt are eating breakfast at The Grille in Auburn. They stayed the night at the Heart of Auburn Motel on College Street in the middle of downtown and walked across and down the street for food. The early national TV news had reported the "alleged abduction" as having been reported in the midnight edition of the *Washington Post.*

Knight says, "At least they didn't give out our names yet. Maybe we can get in another full day of work before we have to build the press into our schedule. That reporter didn't waste any time, did he?"

Brandt responds, "I'm not surprised. Like you said, though, at least he hasn't given up our names yet. I'll remember that when the time comes to have to deal with the rest of those headline-hungry assholes. He did us a favor. Never can tell when we might need another one."

With a sideways glance at Brandt, Knight continues, "I'm more concerned about going the rounds with you today after what happened yesterday. You gonna be able to keep yourself under control?"

"Don't be ridiculous, Jack. Most of that was show and you know it. Besides, we'll be talking to a completely different sort of person today." Brandt's displeasure at the admonition from the junior agent is obvious.

Knight is less than convinced. "Why don't we split the duty today and see if that works better? I mean, maybe it would be better if you do the interviews over near the church and I'll check out the neighbors of the suspects. How's that sound?"

"Well.… I guess we can do it that way. Might save us some time at least. But that's the only reason I'm agreeing to this. I don't think there'd be any problem if I went with you into the white neighborhoods."

Relieved, Knight sighs and says, "Good enough. I'll drop you over by the church then, and I'll drive around the areas where the others live. I'll pick you up near the church at noon, and we'll eat at that restaurant out on the highway and compare notes."

Brandt struggles between mild indignation at Knight's near insubordination and feeling genuinely self-chastened. "Let's get finished and get out there. I'm sure we're gonna see a lot of reporters before this day's done."

They finish breakfast, quietly thinking their own thoughts.

✳   ✳   ✳   ✳

Red's green Nova sits at the roadside and he paces back and forth along the verge of the pavement. A dozen turkey vultures glide into the chasm below. He can't quite make out the details from this vantage point. His view suggests that there *is* a body at the bottom, but there's something wrong with how it looks. Brush and outcroppings block his view, so he can't be 100 percent certain. He gets the 35mm camera that belongs to the paper and snaps half a dozen pictures and then hides the camera away in the trunk of his car. He's still pacing when Jimbo Turner and his deputy Horace Banks arrive.

"Red, you're gonna have to evacuate the area. This is a potential crime scene and we can't have civilians around here." Jimbo's bulk is threatening and his scowl says that Red shouldn't argue.

"When can I get in to find out what you found down there? How far back do I have to stay? Looks like a body down there, sure enough, Jimbo. Do you think it's Maxwell?" All this is said as McKinney moves toward his car. He opens the door to the driver's side and stands waiting for Turner to respond.

Turner nods toward Banks and says, "Horace, escort Red back to the intersection with the main road in and set up a police line there. Nobody passes without my say-so, understan'?" He gives no answers to any questions—no further acknowledgement to Red. He turns back to begin checking the same area that Red was looking at. "Get him outta here. *Now.*"

As Banks and McKinney clear the area, Turner calls Marcie on his radio and says, "Marcie, we need to get the Rescue Squad out here. Tell them they're gonna need ropes and rigging. It's a body OK, and it's gonna be a bitch to haul outta there. And Marcie … nobody knows about this 'til I say they know. Understand?"

Banks and McKinney approach the intersection that will define the crime scene, as Brandt and Knight flash past on the main highway. Unseen. Unseeing.

＊　　　＊　　　＊　　　＊

At noon Knight arrives at the church and finds Brandt sitting on the steps, which are now swept clean of the debris. Plywood sheets cover the windows. Seeing Knight approach, Brandt stands and moves to meet the sedan at the curbside. Both men look dejected and annoyed. Brandt initiates the commiseration, "You don't look any more successful than I was."

Knight shakes his head and replies in kind, "Nobody knows anything. Nobody saw anything. Nobody knows when any of the suspects left home or arrived at White's place. It's like everybody went blind and deaf for that one night." He accelerates slowly and heads the sedan toward the restaurant on the south side of town.

"Same with me," says Brandt. "I gotta admit that I'm surprised. Seems like the colored community would want to come forward with information, doesn't it? I mean if they're ever gonna get out from under the boot heels of these yahoos, they're gonna have to stand up and be counted. I don't get it. Nobody saw anything. Nobody even heard the damn shots. Why do you think that is, Jack?"

Knight chuckles, "You really *don't* get it. These people have lived in fear of their white neighbors forever. This goes across generation after generation since the days of slavery. Whites have always held the dominant hand in this part of the country and they've enforced their dominance with violence. Taking the life of an occasional colored person means very little when it comes to preserving the established order—meaning that whites rule and coloreds obey. Challenging that order means a threat, a beating, a lost job, a rape, or a killing."

As Knight angles the car across the highway and into the parking lot of the nondescript cafe Brandt asks, "I know all that, but how are they ever gonna even move *toward* equality if they're too afraid stand up? I don't see how it can ever happen."

Knight kills the engine and answers smugly, "I'm sure that the good white citizens of this and every other community in the South are counting on that holding true. But I'll tell you something, Oscar, this King fellow has the answer. Every demonstration that's held and then reported, every senseless act of violence committed on defenseless victims and seen on TV, every overreaction by officials and civilians that is seen on the evening news—all these things are taking a toll on the status quo."

"Sure, Jack."

Knight presses on, "Even white southerners are having to reevaluate their positions. I'm tellin' ya, Oscar, all these good Christian folks are caught in the dilemma of proclaiming themselves to be adherents of Jesus Christ and then having to justify the violence that gets brought on the colored population in the name of white supremacy. Before TV, they could pretend that it wasn't real. No more.

"Whites now have to question the disparity between what they say they stand for and the reality of what is actually being lived out in their communities. Slowly but surely the power is weakening; but they're not there yet."

Brandt doesn't like this answer. "So it boils down to this kidnapping won't be solved—at least not in this decade, right? How th' hell do we make any progress if nobody will stand up and tell the truth?"

Knight ponders for a moment, then says, "I'd bet th' mortgage that nobody goes to jail over this. But the publicity that the press will generate? At the very least it will bring this sort of vigilantism out in the open. People are gonna be shocked and outraged—especially if the preacher is dead."

"Nice philosophy," snorts Brandt. "How many lives get ruined to guarantee a man his God-given rights?"

Knight grins and drawls, "Philosophical answer: As many as it takes. Practical answer: Probably quite a few more."

"Where th' hell do you come from with that phony Mississippi drawl? You're no southerner."

"Oh yeah. Born in Mississippi. Daddy was in the Air Force and I was a late kid—prob'ly a mistake. So he'd made some rank and we lived all around. He retired when I was in junior high school and we moved to Jackson where mom had relatives with money. I was born there, but had only been back for visits since I was two years old." Looks to Brandt and with deliberate over-emphasis says, "BA in sociology and philosophy." Shrugs. Opens his door. "We gonna eat or talk?"

✳   ✳   ✳   ✳

Duke and George listen to the radio as the T'Bird cruises down Highway 14, west out of Auburn. Top down and the sun feels fine. Each has a cold beer open and sitting between his legs. The shotguns are in the trunk. A large box filled with clay pigeons sits on the back seat. The Skeet and Gun Club has leased a twenty-acre field five miles outside of Auburn from the uncle of one of the members. A pond, stocked with fingerling catfish and over which the club members throw and shoot the pigeons, lies at the end of the dirt road.

Duke slows and turns into the dirt road, crosses the railroad track, and follows on around the stand of pines to the club's shooting area. He pulls the T'Bird up on the levee that dams the creek and forms the pond. "The thrower is in the storage building over there, George. Why don't you get that and the birds while I get the guns?" Duke opens the trunk and takes out, first, the old Army blanket that he lays folded on the T'Bird's hood. The three guns are placed with near reverence on the blanket—a Fox, double-barreled, over-and-under, 16-gauge, a Winchester Sweet 16 automatic, and a Stevens, double-barreled, side-by-side 20-gauge. Four boxes of shells follow.

George has dragged the box of clay pigeons or, "birds", as Duke calls them, forward of the car, and examines the thrower—a spring-loaded, metal and wood device that looks like the letter "Y" with the wooden handle being the base and the metal tongs the upraised arms. Both men have practiced with the thrower so many times that they are facile with it by now. "You wanna shoot first?"

"Sure." Duke selects the Fox and opens the box of number 6 shot shells. "You really need to shoot this Fox, George. It's about the sweetest gun you've ever held."

As he fits a disk between the metal arms of the thrower, George replies, "Yeah, I'd like to. 'Fact, ever' since you won the shoot-out last fall, I've thought I'd like to shoot it. Where'd you come by it anyhow?"

"Hell, it's like ever'thing else I've got. I traded for it. I had an old Stevens double, side-by-side and a CB radio that a friend of my cousin wanted. That and $20 got me this baby. What a deal. Some people just don't know the value of the things they own. 'Course it helped that I didn't care anything about that radio and he did."

"You mean like that Stevens over there on th' hood of th' car?"

"Yeah he needed money more than he needed th' gun and I bought it back for $30. So I got th' Fox for th' radio and fifty bucks … I'm ready when you are … PULL!"

George holds the thrower low and with a sweeping motion flings the clay disk out across the pond. It seems to hang in the air for the longest time, floating ever further across the expanse. At last the Fox fires and the disk shatters into untold pieces.

Over the course of the next two hours the men engage in that male dance of tacit competition. At last, with ten shells left in the last box George says, "Tell you what. We'll shoot the best of five for a beer. One single and two doubles, deal?"

Through his "Duke grin" he's says, "You wanna shoot first or throw?"

"I'll shoot."

When Duke throws the first bird, George shatters it no more than twenty feet from the thrower. Duke sees no malice in George's demeanor and says, "Nice … Quick." He loads the thrower carefully with a double which George breaks easily and again quickly. While George reloads for the final throw, Duke says that he'll throw less horizontal—more 'long' and 'away' from the shooter. George breaks the first, hesitates and then breaks the second barely above the surface of the pond.

"Well, at least I don't have to worry about losing." George's pride at his own performance bubbles over in spite of his efforts to contain it. Big self-satisfied smile as he replaces the Sweet 16 on the blanket.

"Hey, no press, man." Duke catches the single within a second of release and reloads as George looks back at him. The first double is taken almost as quickly.

"I'll throw a long one for you, too." George coils and flings the two birds with all the force he can muster. Duke blasts the first immediately and shouts at George. "Double or nothing on the last one? Hurry!"

A surging thrill springs up in George. "Yeah. OK. Do it!"

At the last possible moment Duke shoots. The bird settles gently on the surface of the pond and in total silence sinks out of view. Both are struck dumb—mouths open, energy racing unbound and without focus. "Missed? I fuckin' *missed*? This isn't supposed to happen. What the hell did you do to that bird George?" Same big easy grin as if he'd just won the club championship again. "Hell, what good is having *one* beer anyhow. Good shootin', George. Let's go to th' Plainsman."

An hour later the two men are having their third beer at the concrete block bar with the tin roof that sits off the highway atop a red clay hill. They have transferred the competition to shuffleboard at the table that stretches along the back wall away from everything and everybody on a Tuesday afternoon. George half-whispers, "So I guess you heard about th' missin' preacher over home, huh?"

"Yeah, Lynn mentioned something about it to me. Any idea what happened?"

George is uncertain about telling his suspicions but needs to talk to *somebody*. "I'm not for certain, but d' you remember me tellin' you that there was gonna be hell t' pay over Lynn's daddy's gettin' beat up?"

Duke nods, afraid to speak.

George continues, "Well, I think that th' guys probably got th' preacher. Nobody's said anything, but something's really wrong with th' whole damn bunch of them anymore. You know that th' preacher's wife said that my daddy did it?"

"Didn't know that for sure." *Don't interrupt—let him talk.*

"I don't know if he did it or not, but I know that him and Swift Collins are barely talkin', and my daddy's mad as hell all th' time. He told me this morning that they're all going over to Selma today and they're gonna stay for at least th' rest of th' week. They've probably left already. I think they're just gettin' out of the reach of those FBI guys in town. Hell, I don't know anymore, Duke. Somethin's fucked up about this."

As George slides the heavy disc down the hardwood table Duke's thinking: *Careful. Don't rush here.* Then he says, "Sounds scary as hell, George. You going with 'em?"

"Naw, hell, somebody's got to look after th' farm and Momma. We've got calves to get to market later this week. I'm just as glad m'self. This worries th' hell outta me, Duke. I don't want to think of my old man as a killer or anything like that … I just hope that I'm wrong about it." Explaining his fears he stares at his hands, his words come out forced and uncertain.

With empathy Duke says, "Yeah, I hope so too, man. You need any help with the gather of those calves? I could get out there easily enough." The offer is sincere enough but the thread of duplicity runs down the center—too obvious to Duke, but unnoticed by George.

George waves off the offer and says, "Nah. Terry's gonna come over and help. Y'all still playin' that tournament in Atlanta on Saturday?"

Duke nods.

"I may go over and watch, if y'all don't care."

Another nod. "Sure."

Finally George closes the circle in Duke's mind, saying, "I wonder if Terry's thinkin' th' same as me on this. I know he's got to have seen the difference in his old man … Well maybe not. Swift's such a pain in th' ass all th' time. Might seem normal if you had to live with him. I'll find out Thursday I guess … Look, I need t' go, Duke. Take me to my car, OK? Momma's at th' house by herself."

*   *   *   *

The green Nova rumbles onto the square and Red scans the scene ahead. Two vans bearing the logos of TV stations sit near the Sheriff's Office. A small group of men cluster across the street in the park, surrounding the two F.B.I. agents. Late afternoon in August is stifling in Tuskegee, Alabama. No breath of a breeze. No rain expected. The air heavy with moisture. Brandt sweats and notices Red approaching the group. Quickly he closes up the interview.

McKinney looks at Brandt questioningly and teases, "So y'all see me comin' and just close up shop, eh?"

As the other newspeople drift away, Brandt indicates that they should talk privately. They walk together toward the gray sedan. "Mr. McKinney, we appreciate how you handled your reporting of this thing yesterday. Appreciate that we weren't identified until this afternoon and then it was by the Sheriff's Office. If you want what little information we have at this point, I'd be glad to summarize it for you. You wanna have dinner with us in Auburn this evenin'?"

Red is tickled to hear this. "Maybe later, but right now I'm gonna stay around here and see if the Sheriff will say if the body they're takin' in to the morgue is th' preacher. Guess y'all haven't heard about it yet, huh?"

Knight reacts with curiosity, Brandt with outrage. Brandt speaks first. "You mean that they've been working on a 'found body' and they didn't fill us in? How long have they been working this? Where was the body? How did you find out about it?"

Red looks at Knight, grins, angles his head toward Brandt and says, "Not a patient man is he?" Turning back to Brandt he continues, "It started this morning at about eight. The ranger at the National Forest called and said that he thought that he had a body down in a ravine near a road in the Forest. It has taken most all day to get the body up out of there and to complete a search of the surrounding area. Jimbo sent Marcie over to get Miz Maxwell. They're gonna meet up at the Lee County Hospital 'cause that's where the morgue is, but Jimbo is coming by here first to get his paperwork."

Knight says, "So the sheriff is coming here in a few minutes, right? Why are you here?"

"I'm here to try to get a statement from him about identity. I'm hopin' to get an exclusive from him."

Brandt quickly interjects, "We'll give you an exclusive if you want it. As far as I'm concerned, I'd rather not talk to anybody else but you about things. Does Sheriff Turner ever go into his office through the back?"

Red leads out immediately saying, "Yep. Didn't think of that. I bet he's in the office right now. C'mon. Let's catch him before he gets out of there." As the three men start across the square, the sheriff's brown sedan powers out of the side street and leaves the square at speed.

*   *   *   *

Knight and Brandt cross the parking lot and meet Red at the side entrance to the building. A discreet sign—"Morgue"—includes an arrow pointing to the left. They hustle down the hallway and arrive at a small waiting room next to large double doors. Miz Maxwell sits erect on the one chair. Another dignified-looking colored woman stands at her side with a hand consolingly on her sister's shoulder.

Eudora notices and acknowledges the agents' presence. "I think they must've found him. I knew that nothing good could come from this. They've killed my Eldred, Mr. Brandt, Mr. Knight. I haven't seen him yet, but I know."

The doors swing open from the center and Jimbo Turner strides out into the waiting area. He scowls at the F.B.I. men and signals toward Miz Maxwell. She stands and says to Brandt, "Would the two of you come in with me? Angela, you come too, please." Red takes her place in the waiting room's chair.

Turner starts to protest until Eudora silences him with a look that is three parts rage and two parts widow. The room is cold and smells pungently of chemicals. A body lies on a stainless steel stretcher covered completely with a white sheet. Turner picks up the foot end of the sheet and Eudora catches her breath as she recognizes Eldred's shoes and socks. "It's him. Oh Jesus, my Eldred's dead. I knew it." She reaches for the sheet but Jimbo stops her hand.

"You don't want to look any further, Eudora. If you recognize the clothing, that's good enough."

Her glare has steel in it. "No, Sheriff. I have the right to see what you have done to my husband."

In response and with a shrug, Turner releases his grip on her hand. She pulls the sheet higher. Sees blood on the shirt front. Trembles and pulls still higher. Abruptly the body ends at the shoulder. Nothing beyond. The scene is surreal. Everyone in the room—including the doctor who was to do the autopsy and the sheriff who had worked all afternoon with the Rescue Squad to retrieve the body—recoils with shock.

The head, of course, is missing.

Eudora's legs collapse. She falls directly to the floor as Brandt steps in to try to soften her landing. Too late, her head hits the stretcher as she plunges downward. Knight bends to assist Brandt and together they lift her and get her seated in a chair. The doctor steps into a small office near the main room and returns with smelling salts and a gauze bandage. Eudora moans as she revives. Brandt snarls at Turner, "Cover him up."

Turner turns and walks through the double doors saying as he goes, "Cover him up yourself. When she's able, tell her that I need some papers signed and that I'll be upstairs at the chaplain's office." Brandt watches in disbelief as Jimbo turns down the hallway and disappears.

✳   ✳   ✳   ✳

Digger Hill heard of the possibility of finding Preacher Maxwell's body at nine that morning and went immediately to a phone booth to call his cousin Gene with the news. Gene sounds pretty weak on hearing him and only asks, "Did you say they're lookin' on Deer Creek Road? Alright."

Digger snorts as he thinks, *That's it? Not a "thank you"? Not a "howdy-do"? Not a "kiss my ass"? Nothing? Just one question and he hangs up.*

The men cancel the meeting at the restaurant and go to Blankenship's farm instead. Tempers are again close to the surface. They finally agree to go on to Selma as planned. They will meet and stay at a motel owned by one of the brotherhood. Hill, White and Parsons ride together in Hill's sedan. Collins rides in Blankenship's truck.

Blankenship, hoping that he can defuse some of Collins's fury about Hill, says, "You know, Swift, you may be making things worse with Eugene. If you're right and he's weak, and you criticize him too much, it'll just make him more nervous and he'll be more of a threat. Why don't you take it easy on him?"

After a long pause, Collins answers, "That's possible, I reckon; but my thinking is that if I put pressure on him and he doesn't crack, then he's safe. If he cracks from pressure from me, then he'll sure as hell crack with them agents. I just need to know what to expect from him."

Blankenship is quick to add, "Well, so far he's done all right. I mean, he ain't calm and in charge of hisself like the rest of us, but people are different, you know. If you'll take it a little easy on him, I'll try to coach him some, like you suggested the other day. I think he trusts me and would take advice from me."

Collins nods and says, "Yeah, I can try that. I just get so pissed when he acts like such a baby about this stuff. What th' hell did he expect? This ain't no church picnic we're dealin' with here, Thad. If we don't do something, th' niggers will take over th' whole damn town. You talk to 'im and I'll do my best to stay th' hell away from 'im." He delivers this with more calm than Blankenship had credited Collins with possessing. Thad thinks, *Maybe this can be worked out after all.*

*   *   *   *

Mohammed sits in his car curbside at Eudora's front yard. The sheriff's patrol car stops in front of him, headlights temporarily blinding him. He gets out as the woman deputy is opening the rear door to allow Eudora and her sister to get out. Eudora is ashen gray and seems disoriented. Angela has fully taken charge and guides Eudora to the front door. She motions for Mohammed to follow and dismisses Marcie with a curt "Thank you."

Inside the house, Eudora stares ahead fixedly. She won't or can't respond to questions from either Mohammed or Angela. Angela maneuvers her into the bedroom and changes her clothing. Back in the living room, Eudora sits in silence. Angela motions Mohammed to the kitchen where she makes coffee. "What do you think, Reverend? Is she gonna be alright? Do I need to do something for her?"

Mohammed considers for a moment and says, "I think she's in shock. I'll call Doc Jemison at the school and see what he thinks we should do."

So saying, he places the call to the Infirmary at the Institute. Dr. Jemison is a member of the Maxwell congregation and agrees to come to the house.

Still in the kitchen, Angela explains that Eldred's head was missing and that the sheriff's men had been unable to find any sign of it. She tells Mohammed of Eudora's collapse and that she hasn't spoken since seeing the body. "The sheriff tried to stop her from looking, but she wouldn't have it any other way. She's always been stubborn like that."

"Did the sheriff have any ideas why they couldn't find his head?" Mohammed's color has gone chalky gray. His stomach turns over and threatens upheaval at the thought of his friend's head being missing. The idea seems unreal. *Why would anyone do such a thing?*

"He said he thought Eldred was probably killed somewhere else and that the body was dumped out at the National Forest. He said that unless they could find out where the killing happened, there isn't much hope of finding the—uh—rest of him."

Dr. Jemison arrives and administers a sedative to Eudora, and sends her back with Angela to the bedroom. While Angela changes Eudora's clothes again, this time to sleepwear, the two men sit at the kitchen table and drink coffee.

Jemison is likewise stunned at the insult to the body of his friend and pastor. "No wonder she's in shock. It's bad enough to hear about it. I can't imagine how she must have felt when she saw it. No telling how this will affect her in the long run. My God, Milton, why would anyone decapitate the man?"

Mohammed is pensive as he answers. "I don't know; but all I've been able to think about since Angela told me about it is the old saying, 'Cut off the head of the snake and the whole thing will die.' Maybe it's supposed to be some kind of message or sign or something. I don't know, Doc. I just don't know."

✳   ✳   ✳   ✳

As George's taillights disappear around the corner at the far end of the street, Duke shakes the fuzziness from his brain. He decides to shower before doing anything else. And in the cold sting of the shower he realizes that he needs to get this new information to Judd for dissemination to Mohammed. Climbing into clothes he remounts the T'Bird. Anticipation builds as he re-thinks the things that George told him.

In the gravel-covered space near Judd's apartment, the T'Bird growls to a halt. Duke is still a little light-headed from the effects of the beer, but manages to navigate the stairs without falling. As he approaches the screen door, Elizabeth opens it before him. Cut off blue jeans. Halter top. Hair swept back. An earthy scent titillates. The sweet smile of friendship—and a little more. "Hi. I saw you through the window. Come on in. Judd's in the bathroom."

A hug. A brief kiss on the cheek. Mostly sterile but not without a certain amount of heat. "What's wrong, Duke? You look upset."

"Nah. I'm all right. Just a lot going on, and I need to bring Judd up to speed on some things. How 'bout you? Damn! You look so fine, girl."

From further inside Judd's voice belts out, "Watch yourself, Liz. I think I hear old wolfman Duke out there … Aha! There you are. How goes it Duke?"

"Fine. Fine. You busy or can we talk for a few minutes?"

"Sure we can talk. What's happening?"

The three friends array themselves around the table—a huge, empty, wooden spool from the rear of the electric company. Elizabeth has brought the Chianti bottle and pours a little for each of them as Duke spins the tale of his afternoon with George. Judd reaches across to his books and retrieves paper and a pen. "Let's go through this one piece at a time." And writes down each point that the three agree needs to be passed along.

He folds the paper and searches out a key from a drawer. "I'm gonna go over to Pax's place and call Mohammed right now. None of this could be used to convict anybody, but it sure goes a long way toward saying where to look."

Duke looks around the room and sees the phone sitting on a bedside table. "Why are you going to Pax's? Doesn't your phone work?"

"Yeah, it works. Mohammed and I decided that since it's long-distance, I should use Pax's phone. Besides, if there were to be anybody tracing calls over there or anything like that, it's already known that Pax was involved in the voter registration project. No sense implicating myself unnecessarily, right?" Grabs the keys to the VW and heads out the door.

As Judd is leaving, Elizabeth says, "So he *beat* you?"

Off guard, Duke asks, "What? Beat me? Oh, you mean George? Yeah, he beat me fair and square."

"You sure you didn't *let* him win? You know just to cozy up to him? C'mon, tell th' truth."

Duke grins—"I'm pretty sure that he won outright. But I'll tell you what, on the way over here a while ago, I wondered if I had subconsciously thrown the match … Nah. I just missed."

They sit, turned with arms on the back of the couch, looking out the window to the parking courtyard below. She says, "You are the most dangerous man I know. You don't even know how you do the things you do half the time. If you ever get all that harnessed and focused, I don't even want to think about it."

Genuinely surprised he responds, "Me? You gotta be nuts. I'm just average. I might work a little harder than everybody else. I'm not all that special. But keep talkin'. I like hearing nice things from beautiful women."

"See? That's exactly what I'm talking about. I'm sure that you don't realize that you just made a major league pass at me, do you?" To his puzzled look she explains, "The whole business of self-deprecation with you is a hook—drags people in. Of course, you're special. People are drawn to you and they even don't know why. And when they get there, you absently throw compliments at them and they're helpless—caught up in the Duke web."

"You're scaring me, Liz." Trying to laugh it off.

"Good. Assholes who get all the breaks should at least have to be responsible for it. I know that you're taking this like it's some kind of joke, but I'm totally serious. You'll figure it out. Hope I'm around when *that* day comes … Hey. I've got a roach. Wanna catch a buzz?"

"Yeah. OK. Sure." Duke is grateful for the change of subject. There was in her words a sense that others have tried to evoke in him. Too close. Too much responsibility. Too far out of his range.

She finds the aluminum film canister and unscrews the top, tips the contents into her hand and skewers the tiny half-inch nub of a joint with surgical hemostats. She heats the nub with a match held an inch or more below until it begins to glow. Sucks the smoke in greedily and passes the smoldering jewel to Duke, who copies her movement and passes it back. Each gets two passes at the coal before it falls into the ashtray—spent.

By the time Elizabeth refills their wineglasses and returns to the couch, Duke is beginning to relax. She puts the wine on the sill of the open window next to where he continues to sit. She asks, "What're ya thinkin' about? Was it hard getting the information from that guy George?"

"No. He really wanted to talk to somebody and I guess that there aren't many folks that he would trust with that sort of stuff. See that whole 'be responsible for what you do' thing is very real for me, Liz. I'm not sure exactly how I feel about betraying George. Hell, he's a nice guy … Well at some level or other he's nice. Anyhow, you're right. He's sure as hell not expecting that the stuff he tells me will get back to the coloreds in Tuskegee. He's 'in the web', sort of. I don't like this feeling much."

"Yeah, I can believe that, Duke. You're in a tough position." With that devilish smirk that defines who she is with Duke, she adds, "I'm guessing that it's a little easier with that girl, though. What's her name again? Lynn?"

Duke hesitates. "Right. Lynn. Why would you think it's easier with her?"

"I'm sure there are certain—uh—distractions with her that you don't have with George." Mirth dances in her eyes and turns up the corners of her pretty mouth.

"That's taking on a whole other set of complications, Liz. I'm almost afraid to tell you this, because I know you'll tease me; but I think I'm in love."

Elizabeth's eyes go wide. "With her? You've gotta be kidding. That's just too dangerous, Duke."

"No, not Lynn. Worse. I've been talking with a woman who works at the Berry and she's like no one I've ever known. I mean she's smart and pretty and mature …"

Liz exhales, "Thank god. You scared me there for a minute. So, another one on your string, huh? Can't say that I'm too surprised by that. Why should this one complicate things any more than the others?" She's grinning again now, relieved.

"No. This is different, Liz. Her name is Ann, and when I'm with her I'm like a totally different person. She brings out a calm in me that I didn't even know existed. We can talk for hours. She always asks the right questions that help me get things straightened out in my head. She's funny. And very, very smart—probably smarter than I am. I think about her all the time."

"Another secret woman. You know, none of us had even seen Lynn until she came to the Union the other day. We've never met your supposed girlfriend from your hometown. So when do we get to meet this one?"

Color rises in Duke's neck. His ears burn. "I don't think you get to meet her at all. There's a problem ... She's married."

"Oh my god, Duke."

"And has a child."

Liz flops on the couch beside him. "Nothing comes easy for you does it? This is serious stuff, Duke. People could get hurt from this."

"Yeah, I know. We both know. It's just happening, Liz. Neither of us seems to be able to stop it. I'm not sure either of us really *wants* to stop it. Anyhow, knowing her makes it very hard to play the game with Lynn." After a poignant pause the old Duke grin spreads across his face and he says, "But I'm gonna keep tryin'. I get all the tough jobs."

Elizabeth smacks him on the shoulder and says, "Have you been putting me on with all this?"

As Duke responds that he hasn't been kidding, the VW putters into the parking area and Judd gets out—shoulders slumped, head down, gait slow and unsteady. The two friends turn to greet him. He is pale and shaken.

"Reverend Maxwell is dead. They found his body out at the National Forest. He'd been decapitated." That burden off his shoulders, Judd collapses into a chair. Elizabeth is immediately at his side.

The three sit in silence. Tears trickle down their cheeks. Duke recovers first and asks, "What did Mohammed say about the information?"

"He said to tell you 'Thanks a lot' and that the suspicion is already there. He was glad to hear that the main players were gonna be out of town during the time of mourning and the funeral. That's a very sad bunch over there this evening."

As Duke thinks of things in Tuskegee, he realizes with a jolt that Lynn is due at his apartment—looks at his watch—*now*. "Oh shit, guys. I've got to get outta here. Lynn is probably waiting for me at my place. I completely forgot. Look I hate to leave in the midst of this kind of news, but I'd better go."

Judd says, "It's fine, Duke. I'll be alright. Do what you need to do."

Elizabeth teases, "I'm flattered that being with us—well actually me—made you forget that 'other woman' for a few minutes." Secret smile between the two.

In the T'Bird Duke realizes that he can't tell Lynn anything of what he has learned. He has to get a grip on his own emotions. And he's gonna be facing her while he's under the influence of the marijuana. Anxiety and amusement. Rumbles his way up Mag Avenue, and on to the apartment.

*   *   *   *

Alone in his small, neat home, Milton Mohammed nee Spinks at last gives full vent to his pain at the loss of his best friend, mentor and advocate. This was the first man with whom he had had a real relationship—from whom he had learned to believe in himself and to love others. This quiet, gentle soul who had encouraged him to go on to school, had interceded with the denomination to provide scholarship money; had helped find him a job at the college; had periodically dipped into his own pocket so that Milton could have a little spending money— *is gone.* The wise, experienced clergyman/teacher, who had guided Milton's own theology and explained the politics of the church to him, has left his pupil alone.

The ache is of a depth that is wholly new to Mohammed. Gut wrenching. Physically sickening. Unexpectedly, he is reduced to tears and weakness of limb. He moans, convulses involuntarily and is, first, almost embarrassed, and then blessedly relieved as he allows the pain to find its own course. At some point in the process he becomes aware that no matter how much he hurts, it will pass and that when he needs to perform whatever tasks, he will be able to function.

The idea forms suddenly in his mind: *No one can bear my pain for me. It's for me to do. So I need not expect that some one should. I can accept this—another piece of myself.*

Like a mantra from his pastoral training he remembers, *Calm grows from within, like a small spark growing into a brighter light. Grief—one of the great levelers—is like so many powerful emotions, you only overcome it by giving up to it. You gain control by giving up control.*

His emotions run their course and he becomes calmer. Then the phone rings. "Hello."

"Good evening, Reverend. Sorry to be so late getting back to you. How are you?"

Stokley's voice jerks Milton into reality. "Ah, Stokley, it is good to hear your voice, my brother. I'm afraid we've had the worst kind of news. Eldred's body was found out at the National Forest this morning. And, Stokley, his head had been … blown off." Explosion in his ear:

"GOOD GOD. THOSE BASTARDS! Oh no! Dammit, Milton, what happened?" His anger is pure, and pristine, and raging red.

As calmly as possible Mohammed says, "Looks like some Klan men took him off and shot him. The medical examiner says that it looks like he took a double barrel blast to the throat and it just ripped his entire head off. The sheriff thinks that he was killed in one place and then the body was dumped down a ravine in the Forest. He doesn't have much hope of ever finding the … uh … rest."

When Stokley speaks again, his voice is transformed … and frightening. "You told me that Eudora knows who took him off, didn't you?"

"Yes, but … Look, Stokley, don't get carried away about this now. Don't react until the shock wears off. Come and talk to Eudora before you decide to believe her."

Stokley asks with steel in his tone, "Meaning that you don't?"

"I didn't say that. I do believe her, but you need to make that kind of decision for yourself. And besides, if you're thinking of retaliating, she should have some input into that. Both she and I believe that Martin's non-violence is the real answer to these kinds of things. You know how strong-minded she can be. She's earned the right to be heard, don't you think?" Milton waits breathlessly for Stokley to respond.

"I'll give it some thought." Cold as the grave. "I'll call Andy right now. You gonna stay around?"

"Yes, I'll be here."

"I'll call you back." In the silence of the phone lines Milton can hear the intensity of Stokley's need for action of some kind—any kind. This time his prayer is for Stokley to keep himself safe. As he considers the difference between his last two prayers for Stokley he can't help smiling. Stokley, if he survives, will make a difference.

Milton replaces the phone in its cradle and leans back in his favorite chair. Silence threatens to implode his eardrums. He can almost hear, can certainly feel, the beat of his own heart. He's aware that mortality is such a thin thread in God's huge universe, aware that he trusts his God to be and to do the necessary things. Then silence becomes peace. The wait bearable.

The phone rings.

He answers with a smile, "Good evening. This is your pastor speaking."

"Doc? Is that you?"

Alien voice. Not Stokley. Mind warp. Spin. Settle. "Yes, this is Dr. Mohammed. Who's calling, please?"

"Hey, Doc. Sorry to call so late. This is Judd over in Auburn. Look, Duke just came over and had some things that we thought ought to be passed along." And Judd goes on to explain about the info that Duke got from George. Mohammed thanks him and hangs up feeling pensive and, for unknown reasons, excited. The Klan will be out of town during the services. Good. The congregation will be less afraid to come out.

The phone again.

"Hello."

"Well, Reverend, the brass thought your idea about proceeding immediately with a massive voter registration drive was a good one. Using the killing of one of God's representatives is an emotional draw—oughtta work, they say. You might get a promotion outta this. Don't forget us peons when they move yo' puny ass to Hot-lanta." Stokley has calmed down, at least somewhat.

"Great. I knew they'd see it *my* way. I just found out that there is even some suspicion in the white community that what Eudora said is true. Nothing that amounts to anything yet, but it's better than I would have expected. And I got another piece of interesting news too. The Klan men from here are in Selma waiting for *yo'* puny ass. So they won't be here to disrupt the funeral and services. So thanks again, my brother. You do too much."

Mohammed permitting himself a small verbal swagger.

Stokley, ever one to surprise, says with great sincerity, "You know for a fact they're going to Selma, Milton?"

Mohammed is curious. "Yes. Very reliable information. I'd bet th' farm on it—if I had a farm. Why?"

"Just hang tight. I'll call you right back."

And this time Mohammed spends the intervening minutes puzzling over what could possibly be going on in Stokley's wild mind this time. He didn't have to wait long. But if he'd had all night to speculate, he would have never stumbled onto the idea.

The phone rings.

"Shoot, Reverend, I'll prob'ly get to Hot-lanta before you do. Have you got your congregation organized yet? If you haven't, you'd best get up bright and early tomorrow morning, because me and my two busloads of volunteers and th' U. S. Marshals *protectin'* my puny ass will be in Tuskegee by early evening tomorrow. We're gonna register the whole county in two days."

"What? You've gotta be kidding, Stokley. It's not humanly possible to be ready that quickly. There's been some work done, but nowhere near enough. What are you doing?"

Completely assured, Stokley says, "You just get the people together, Milton, we'll get it done. Even Andy and Martin thought that this was a real opportunity."

"But if you don't show up in Selma, they'll come back home and ruin everything. This is too dangerous, Stokley." Mohammed's sweating now. This is front line stuff Stokley is talking about here. And another thought comes—again from the unknown: *Nobody can handle my fear for me either.*

Mohammed hears the amusement in Stokley's answer. "I don't think I'll be missed in Selma. Martin and Andy will have a little surprise for all the good citizens of the planet tomorrow in Selma, Alabama. Martin's gonna announce that he and anyone who will follow him will march again from Selma to Montgomery in protest of the lack of progress in voter's rights in the state. He's making calls from New York to Washington to Hollywood right now. This is a major pop, Milton. And we're both getting a top job in it. Our piece will be relatively invisible but very productive. While everybody's storming th' front door, we'll sneak in the back."

Again Mohammed's mind reels trying to wrap itself around the size of these ideas. But in the end he sighs and accepts it. "Okay, Stokley. How many people do you have with you as volunteers? We'll need to house and feed them. Good god, how's Martin gonna feed that kind of crowd that will surely follow him on his march?"

"There'll be about a hundred and twenty-five of us altogether." Then Stokley laughs, "Oh and the other part'll be easy. Martin will just break out th' loaves and th' fishes, and everything'll be fine."

CHAPTER 23

▼

By the time Stokley notices that the sky is lightening in the East, dawn has crept up on and over him. It lingers there now—a promise of the spectacle that will be sunrise. He had tried once again to be aware of that exact moment when night surrendered to dawn on the way to daylight. Distracted, or perhaps having even dozed off for a second, once again he missed it. *Probably not an "it", but a process. Martin would like my thinking that way, now wouldn't he?*

Maybe what roused him was the sound of the big charter buses rounding the corner and heading into the parking lot. The Ebenezer Tabernacle AME Church is on the edge of the city of Greensboro, NC. The parking area is ragged pavement with weeds growing at random intervals. The founders of the church had the foresight to locate the church out of the main traffic area of town and near the neighborhood where the largest concentration of colored families lives. After the flurry of phone calls between, first, himself and Mohammed, then with Martin in Atlanta, then again with Mohammed, Stokley spent several hours rounding up the volunteers from the various homes and churches in and around Greensboro.

He has answered the same questions over and over, as groups trickle in. "Yes, we are leaving earlier than previously expected. No, we will not be waiting for the last few stragglers to show up. Yes, it is necessary to leave at six. No, breakfast won't be served at the church grounds. Yes, we will stop for food as soon as practical. Yes, the denomination will be paying for food along the way. Yes, everything will be explained to *everyone* at the departure area. Yes, I do have a little money for gas for those transporting volunteers to the church ..." And so on.

Then to himself: *I swear, as good as these people are and as pure as their intentions, they are a stone pain in the ass to deal with sometimes.*

Now, as he approaches the first bus, he notices two more automobiles approaching the parking lot—the arrival of the volunteers is also a process, not an event.

The bus door whooshes open and he steps up onto the first step to greet Alonzo. "Mornin' Zo. Sorry to get you up so early and on such short notice."

"Not a problem, my brother. I been ready to get this show on th' road for three days. When you wanna leave?" Alonzo and George, the only names Stokley has, are here from New York to drive the two buses that have been chartered by an anonymous benefactor in New York City. The benefactor had to sell the charter company that he was providing his own drivers. He also had to send them copies of the drivers' commercial licenses and then buy expensive insurance to cover the buses. He promised to preserve the anonymity of the charter company. That promise hinges on whether there is trouble at the church this morning—anonymity needs to go both ways.

Stokley jokes, "I'm ready right now, but we'll have to wait for these sleepy-eyed 'tourists' to show up I guess. Like I been tellin' you, this could turn out to be a rough ride and it's about to begin in earnest, brother. You all set for that?"

Stokley doesn't know what to expect for the next few days; and he wonders what thoughts might occupy the minds of these others who will ride with him into the furnaces of hell.

Zo is unprovoked. "I s'pose so. I never been to Selma, so I'm lookin' forward to that part. My momma's people are from around there someplace. If things ain't too bad, I might try to look them up. I know what happened the last time colored folks tried to get into these Alabama towns riding on buses with white people, but we'll just have to wait and see how it goes this time."

Then Stokley drops his first bomb of the morning. "Well, if we survive the first stops, we'll get to Selma by and by, but we've got some other work to do before that. We're gonna stop short of Montgomery and go to Tuskegee first for a couple of days. That's not a problem for you is it?"

Zo is still unperturbed. "No sir. I go where you tell me you want to go. That's my job and it don't make me no difference where that might be. What's in Tuskegee?"

Stokley eyes him as he answers, "For one thing Tuskegee Institute is there, founded by Booker T. Washington and the home of George Washington Carver's research. You've heard of those men, I guess. But we're not going to the Institute; we're gonna start us a revolution in Macon County, Alabama. It's been needin' one for a century or two now."

Zo's eyes open wide and he asks, "How you gonna do that, Stoke? We ain't carryin' guns on this bus, are we?"

"No, Zo. This is a much bigger revolution than that. I'll be tellin' the whole group about it in a few minutes, so hang on 'til then and it'll all be clear. Wish I had some coffee or something to offer you, but it's just too early for that."

After a long pause he asks, like he's trying something on for size, "You ever get tired of being called 'colored'? I mean we ain't really colored, ya know. Look at me. I'm black as coal tar. Science says that black is the *absence* of *all* color. I think from now on we oughtta call ourselves *BLACK*, like we've got some definition or something. I've been thinking about this for a while now; what do *you* think about it?"

Zo pauses and considers. "Be honest, Stoke, it just don't matter that much to me. I mean, I don't wanna be called 'Nigger', 'cause white people been callin' us that for centuries in a nasty kind of way. 'Colored' has a little more respectful sound to it. I never thought about being called 'black' ... Seems kinda harsh to me. I'll have to think on that some."

As Stokley waves and exits the first bus to head for the second, he hears Zo praying: "Lord, just get us through this mornin'. I'll be askin' about other times as we go along; but for right now, Lord, just get us loaded up and on our way ... And, Lord, please let this young man know what he's doin', 'cause I sho' can't figger it out myself."

By the time Stokley has traversed the twenty steps between the buses, George has opened his door and is standing on the step with his hands locked behind him, looking out at the parking lot and the church. "Good mawnin', boss. I hear we're goin' to Tuskegee, this fine day. You know, my daddy went to school there back years ago. I've always wanted to see the place, but I've never been this far south before."

Stokley's stomach turns over. How could George know this? Is there a leak in the organization? If so, it would have to be very high up, because no one knows the plans but himself, Martin, Andy and Mohammed. "Excuse me for askin', George, but how did you know we're goin' to Tuskegee?"

George rocks and grins, "Scary stuff ain't it? I mean me knowin' that and all. It's like magic or something ..." Big, lazy grin on his face. "Nah, actually it's jus' radios. These buses come with CB radios and Zo just told me about it. I'm lookin' forward to the trip."

Cars arrive and depart. People of various ages and racial backgrounds mill about in the parking lot—about half white and the other half black with a few mestizoes in the mix. The sun still has not punctured the horizon, but threatens to do so at any moment.

Stokley makes an executive decision: "Folks, let me get your attention please." He stands on the slight rise between the verge of the parking area and the church lawn. The buses have been shut down and early morning silence washes over the entire area.

"I know that most of you are wondering what happened to cause us to leave earlier than advertised. So be patient and I'll tell you the story. Then we'll have a few minutes for questions after which we're gonna get these buses rollin'. First of all, we're going to Tuskegee, Alabama today. We'll drive straight through, stopping only for gas and food. Our white brother, Mr. Anderson from Pennsylvania, and his fellow travelers have agreed to buy the gas and the food at our stops." Murmurs from the crowd.

"I know what you're thinking: That we should go into restaurants and 'sit in' along the way; but that's a battle for another day. The battle for today and tomorrow and Friday is much more important and maybe a lot more dangerous.

"It was learned yesterday that the chief members of the KKK in Tuskegee, Alabama—where Reverend Eldred Maxwell was killed and decapitated this week—are in Selma, awaiting our arrival. I'm sure that they have a warm welcome planned for us and are very excited to have us visiting their state." Chuckles across the crowd. "The local black churches in Tuskegee have been working diligently to get our brethren ready for voter registration and they have all their documentation in order. The next step for them is to show up at the designated registration place in the county with a witness, present their documents, and sign the official papers to be fully registered voters in Macon County." Louder murmurs now. Excitement begins to build in the crowd as the message sinks in.

"Reverend King and his associates in Atlanta have secured assurances from the President that a contingent of federal marshals from Montgomery and Atlanta will accompany us to the county offices in Tuskegee. Once there, the marshals will direct the clerks of the county to complete the proper registration under threat of arrest. If the clerks refuse, the president has authorized the marshals to do the registration themselves. In this way the people of Tuskegee will have the right to vote."

Applause begins to ripple across the crowd. "Our job will be to provide support and witness to this process. We won't let them be turned away. We've gotta get this whole project movin' now.

"We are certain that this registration will be challenged in court; but we are just as certain that the old adage works as well for black people as it does for whites: 'It's easier to ask forgiveness than permission'." Laughter.

Stokley stretches a hand heavenward and says, "'Scuse me, Lord, just this one more time." More laughter. Applause. Whistles. There are no sleepy eyes now. No grumbling. Heads nod and smiles adorn faces. Feet shuffle with the need to move.

"Today's trip will be long and boring. We won't take much time to stop for niceties. When we get in to Tuskegee tonight we'll be fed by the local people and housed in homes and churches. This is the real deal here, folks. If you've got cold feet, now's the time to do something about it. If you get on the bus, you gotta go where it goes and take the consequences of being there. I won't be able to help you later, but right now you can help yourself. If you have *any* doubts about your commitment to this project, by all means drop out now. Once we're on the road, it'll be too late. Remember what happened last time black folks and white folks took buses into Alabama together—'course that's what they want you to remember.... In spite of that—no, maybe *because* of that, *these* buses are about to get rollin'."

Amens from the crowd. No questions asked. Everyone is poised to board the buses. Stokley adds as a final note, "I'm gonna ride in the trailing bus until we stop for fuel, then I'll switch to the lead bus. That way I can answer any question that you have ... Providing that I *know* the answers. Thank you all. Let's all try to be safe and to look out for each other. Now, let's load up and get movin'."

*　　　*　　　*　　　*

Duke wakens to the smell of food. Coffee gurgles in the pot. He has a mild hangover from the alcohol and the roach. No headache—more a lack of energy. He got to the apartment as Lynn was pulling up in the Stingray. She drove as they went for burgers at the Varsity. He had been tired and thought that he would surely go immediately to sleep. Lynn, however, had other ideas. He was surprised to find that he had enough energy, interest, and stamina.

And now breakfast. *Th' lady is trying really hard. Give her credit.* Rolls out of bed and goes to the bathroom. Slips on a pair of shorts and hugs her from behind.

"Smells good, Lynn. Sorry that you had to go out to find food—I haven't been around much to keep anything in the fridge. Oh my, you feel nice." Hands slide under her shirt to find her breasts unencumbered. "Hah. You went to the convenience store without a bra? Bet ol' Johnny got his jollies from that."

Around her smile she says, "I doubt if he noticed. I just didn't want to wake you so I slipped out without dressing completely. But I'm glad that *you* noticed."

"Believe me. Johnny noticed. He's an old fart, but looking at you young college girls, he thinks he's died an' gone to heaven. Since you were nice enough to go out for food, at least sit down and let me serve it." He reaches for plates, then flips on the stereo and chooses the radio setting while she sits at the small table. The Lettermen croon while he finds flatware, sets the sweet rolls on the table and pours coffee.

As they finish their food, the radio broadcasts the seven-thirty news. The lead story is that Reverend Maxwell's body was found in Tuskegee National Forest. Duke watches Lynn's face as the story unfolds and is surprised to see compassion in her expression. His surprise is short-lived however as she says, "Oh no, this is going to upset my momma and daddy. He's been very emotional since they beat him up. I hope they're OK."

Hiding his disappointment Duke says, "Me too, Lynn. I wish I had a phone so you could call them."

"I'll call later from the Union. Speaking of which, let me get dressed and get out of here. Mr. Shorter is giving me a break and letting me make up some work in my history class. I sure don't need to miss that class again."

She fiddles with her food then adds pensively, "I enjoyed last night." Dreamy-eyed, dark-haired beauty. More purring than speaking.

Duke plays his part. "So did I. Are you coming back tonight?"

"Yes. I'll come by the Berry after lunch. You're working aren't you?"

"Yeah, I have to work at least through the afternoon. Guess I'll dress and get outta here too. See ya this afternoon." Pecks her cheek, slides on his weejuns, grabs a T-shirt and, leaving her to dress, climbs into the T'Bird, and leaves.

✳   ✳   ✳   ✳

Mohammed's day started very early. He hardly slept, tossing and turning with the ideas of Stokley's proposed coup tap-dancing across his consciousness, alongside plans of whom to see and how to get his part of the program organized. Now after his shower, two cups of coffee and the short drive to his office at the church, it's eight o'clock and safe to start calling on some of the congregation. He has the list on the front seat beside him as he pulls up to the Abney home just a few doors down from Eudora's house. Mary Ruth Abney has been a pillar of the church for decades. She is the perennial president of the women's auxiliary, and a chief organizer of all church events. In her late sixties she has known Mohammed all of his life.

Cheerful, as always, she answers the knock on her door. "Well you're surely out early this mornin' Brother Milton. Come in. Come in th' house. What can I offer you? What brings you to my humble kitchen this fine mornin'?" Even at this hour her gray hair is perfectly coifed, her dress clean and freshly pressed. The breakfast dishes dry in the rack on the counter. The coffeepot stands on the stove, its smell lingering in the air.

Milton follows her into the kitchen area and sits at the table. Sister Mary has been widowed for twelve years now. To combat the loneliness, she works—at her home, her church, her grandchildren's schools—at all sort of projects. "I'd love coffee Sister Mary, but I probably should ask for milk instead. I already had two cups this morning." He sits in Caleb's former spot at the head of the table. "As usual, I've come to beg for help. I have a big and important project that has to be done, and done very quickly. I know that you have been working very closely with Eudora on voter registration."

An affirming nod from Sister Mary as she pours his milk and replaces the bottle in the refrigerator. She sits as Mohammed begins.

"Do you know who this fellow Stokley Carmichael is?"

Sister Mary smiles and says, "Why, of course I do. He's that young man up in Carolina who organized all the lunch counter sit-ins, isn't he?"

"Yes ma'am, that's the man I'm talking about, except he's actually from New York and is living right here in Alabama now."

"Isn't he supposed to be bringing another group of Freedom Riders to Selma in a day or two?"

"Yes ma'am. That was the plan until last night." Watches the curiosity spread across Mary's face. "Last night he heard that all the main men in the KKK 'round these parts are all in Selma waiting for him and his group. 'Course he and Reverend King know about the voter registration here and they decided to act on this information." Sister Mary looks puzzled.

"How do you mean 'act on', Milton? What can *they* do that we aren't already doin'?" Almost a touch of anger there. Her brow wrinkles and she's thinking hard.

"Well that two busloads of colored and white folks will be *here—tonight.*"

Sister Mary Abney is aghast. "Why on earth are they coming here? Oh my word. This is terrible timing. Eldred isn't even buried yet and the congregation is in shock. We're not prepared. You must stop them, Milton."

"It's too late, Sister Mary. They left before sunrise this morning and will be here before midnight. I've talked with Brother Cleveland at the Red Hill Baptist Church and we agreed that they would put up signs that they are having a 'Homecoming' celebration this week. The buses will go directly to the church and we have to be ready to feed and house 125 people." Sister Mary starts to protest but Mohammed holds up a quieting hand.

"Then tomorrow morning—Thursday—we have to be ready to send all those people we've been working with down to the Court House with these volunteers as witnesses and accompanied by—are you ready for this?—Federal marshals."

While Mary's eyes grow large and before she can interrupt, Mohammed continues, "Reverend King has said that we should try to register every colored person in the entire county on Thursday and Friday. The president of the United States is behind this and is the one who sent the marshals. Stokley says that if the clerks don't cooperate, the marshals will arrest them and do the job themselves."

Tears threaten Mary's eyes. She says, "Milton, this is all well and good, but what's Eudora gonna think about it? Doesn't it seem a little disrespectful to Eldred? Won't this hurt her and the rest of the congregation?"

Milton is quiet in his response. "I'm going over there as soon as you and I are finished. I don't know how she'll feel about it. The funeral is scheduled for tomorrow at two. If she agrees to this, we have an awful lot of work to do. Can I count on your help, Sister Mary?" As she looks at him she sees the concern but he cannot mask the excitement behind his respectful countenance—an excitement he cannot control, and one that is building in *her* as well. She sees vestiges of the little boy she watched with pride grow into a man of substance.

"If she'll agree, we'll do it. And you can tell her that I'll be helping—*if* she agrees. Be sure that she knows that I won't do anything if she doesn't agree."

*　　　*　　　*　　　*

The are buses rolling now. Growling and blowing black smoke. Eating up th' roadway. Southbound. Staying on the speed limit. Seeking no attention. Just rollin'. Nervous quiet in the passenger section. Drivers all focused and tight-jawed. Future uncertain. Determination grows. Charlotte has disappeared out the back window. High Point fades in the distance. Greensboro just a memory now.

✳   ✳   ✳   ✳

Thad Blankenship awakens to the sound of pounding on the door of the cheap motel room that he and Gene Hill occupy. Sleepily he hobbles across the few feet from the bed and opens the door a crack to reveal Swift Collins standing in the early morning sunlight.

"What is it, Swift? What time is it?"

Collins' grizzled jaw is cracked with a grin. "Y'all gonna sleep all day? Ya need t' get up and let's find some breakfast somewhere. There's news from home that you'll be interested to hear. Get dressed and let's go eat. Y'all're burnin' daylight." And with that he turns and walks next door to his own room.

Closing the door Thad heads to the bathroom. Hill grumbles, "What's wrong with him now?" His distaste for Collins is obvious. So is his fear.

"Hell, I don't know, Eugene. It's always something with Swift. He said something about news from home, but I don't know what he meant. It's nearly eight though and I guess it's time to get movin'." He closes the bathroom door as Hill drags himself out of bed.

In a few minutes the five men sit in a greasy spoon cafe drinking coffee and talk about the fact that Maxwell's body has been found already. Collins offers, "I'm glad the news is out. Maybe some of these agitators will think twice about sendin' more people into places where they got no business."

"I wouldn't count on that, Swift." Cracker White is not as happy about the world getting the news already. He had hoped for a few days reprieve from the pressure. "I 'spect those F.B.I. boys will be up our asses when we get back home for sure now. An' these agitators comin' in here today will just use this as more fuel to fire up th' rest. Naw, I don't see no good comin' from it."

"That's what I've been sayin' all along." Hill risks Collins's displeasure yet again by voicing an opinion suggesting the imprudence of the killing. Collins glares, but says nothing.

Blankenship says, "You may be right, Cracker; but we dealt with it on Monday and we'll do it again if we need to. We'll be fine as long as we all stick to our story. Right now we need to figure out what we're gonna do today. That demonstration is supposed to be at noon at the courthouse. I say we go up there and listen to what they've got to say and when the so-called Freedom Riders arrive, we just join in with the local boys and crack a few heads. If we keep kickin' their asses, sooner or later they'll learn and quit comin' down here. How's that sound t' y'all?"

As the eggs and grits arrive, the men nod their agreement. Collins adds, "Eugene, if you can't stand the idea that somebody might get hurt, you oughtta just stay at th' damn mo-tel. I sure as hell don't wanna have to nursemaid you through another incident. I don't even know why you bothered to come over here in th' first place."

Impulsively Hill explodes, "Go t' hell, Swift. I've got as much right to be here as you do. I just ain't as damn stupid about things as you are." Bold words from a man eroded by fear. Collins looks sidewise at his cohort. No words. No expression. Danger crackles in the air. Hill feels anxiety like something alive crawling in his belly.

When the men leave the café an hour later, Thad notices gloves in Collins' back pocket and asks about them. "Thad, I ain't gonna bust up my knuckles on some worthless outsider. Besides, you ever see the kind of cuts a glove makes on a man's face? Split him like a ripe watermelon."

∗   ∗   ∗   ∗

Red McKinney's enters the Magnolia restaurant quietly. When his eyes adjust to the difference in the light, he notices Brandt and Knight sitting in a booth near a window. "So what do you FBI boys have on your minds this morning? Are y'all gonna make an arrest today?"

Brandt looks up from his personal reverie and says earnestly, "I doubt it, Red. Right now we only have Mrs. Maxwell's word on our only suspect, and he's got four men who'll alibi for him. You got any news for us?"

Sitting next to Knight in the booth Red grins and says, "Maybe. For instance, I know that you won't be arresting that particular suspect this day unless you travel to Selma. Thad and that whole bunch are over there waiting for Carmichael and his Freedom Riders."

Brandt looks first at Knight then back at Red and says, "Well, they're gonna be disappointed, because the Freedom Riders are probably coming in *here*." He pauses to allow this to sink in. "You need to wait about reporting this, Red; but our national office called us this morning and told us that Carmichael and his group are coming to Tuskegee to register the coloreds of the county tomorrow and Friday. I wanted you to get this first because you've helped us out, but you need to wait until tonight at least before you let it be known." Brandt and Knight are smug as they watch the surprise in Red's face.

Red whistles softly. "Man, it's really gonna hit the fan now. It won't work, you know. The clerks will just refuse to do it and Jimbo may even arrest them for trying. But this is really great stuff. Why do I have to wait until tonight?"

Knight answers, "I wouldn't count on its not working because there will be federal marshals with them. And those marshals will be empowered to arrest the clerks if they refuse and then do the job themselves. Secondly, since this is a federal matter, Sheriff Turner is out of the mix. And you have to wait because if you report it now we could easily have a bloodletting on our hands. So just let it play out. When they get here, you notify your pals in Washington and then we'll see how the scene plays. Alright?"

Red's drooling. "Sure. What can you tell me about it? I mean how many are coming? Where will they come to? How did your national office find out? When will they get here?" He literally rocks as he asks these questions. Enthusiasm bubbles up and bursts out of him.

Knight answers, "Whoa, Red, slow down. I'll answer you under the condition of its being off the record for now. And the answer to the question about 'how' will *forever* be off the record. Deal?"

McKinney nods. "There are about 125 of them all totaled. They'll be coming to a country church somewhere in the county and should get here some time before midnight. We got this information from headquarters and we suspect that they got it from wiretaps in Atlanta."

Red looks puzzled. "Atlanta? What's in Atlanta?"

Knight responds, "This is permanently off the record too, Red. We think that King's people are headquartered in Atlanta."

"But I thought he was from Montgomery."

"Maybe so, but it would hardly be safe or advisable to try to run this thing out of a town as small as Montgomery. They wouldn't last a week before they were found and burned out, or worse. It'd be much harder to find them in a city the size of Atlanta."

Red is impressed. "Well I'll be damned. Who knows about this locally?"

"We don't know for sure but you can't talk to anyone here about this until tomorrow, Red. Don't screw us up or you'll never see another exclusive piece of information." Knight's voice is edged with threat.

"Yeah, OK, Jack. I won't betray you. Thanks for the scoop. I think I'll go write a draft and come back this evening and watch for the landing of the freedom birds. This is great. I'll figure out where to wait. Don't worry about that. See y'all later."

McKinney backs out the front door into the brutal midmorning heat. Brandt and Knight share a smile and soon leave the restaurant themselves.

*   *   *   *

Silver buses roll through the late morning swelter. Diesel smoke belches. First generation air conditioners hum and blow semi-cooled air. Appalachia's foothills etch a saw-toothed silhouette out the right-side windows. Tension grows as the border, that artificial demarcation between North and South Carolina, appears in the windshields. George and Zo are determined. Greenville, South Carolina looms like a specter. A quiet stop at a truck stop for diesel fuel and sandwiches wipes out the restaurant's cooked food supply. A dirt road in the woods serves as a "pit stop". Then the buses roll again.

*   *   *   *

At noon in the park near Selma's center, Miss Julia Alexander, the city's best-known activist for civil rights and change, stands on the temporary stage at the bandstand. Hundreds of black faces sweat in the heat and slowly quiet themselves to hear Sister Julia's words.

"I know that we were all expecting that Stokley Carmichael and his brave group of Freedom Riders would be arriving here at about this time." Murmurs throughout the crowd. "But Stokley and his people have been unavoidably detained. They may arrive tomorrow or Friday or maybe even on Saturday." Moans and sounds of dismay echo throughout the expanse of grass and bodies.

Swift Collins stands under a tree at the outer most edge of the crowd along with a couple of hundred other white men strung out along one side of the square. With a laugh he says to Cracker White, "Guess they thought better of trying to come in here, after all." Cracker and the other men within earshot chuckle and mumble agreements.

As the crowd again grows silent, Miss Julia continues, "The committee has decided that we should all meet here again tomorrow. And again on Friday and even Saturday, if necessary, to greet these brave travelers. We don't want them to arrive at an empty square, do we?" Scattered applause and halfhearted cheers from the congregated blacks greet her plea. The white men are gleeful and grin at each other in triumph.

With all attention focused on Miss Julia, no one notices the doors of the black sedan parked behind the bandstand opening. Nor does anyone notice the four men in suits as they make slow and deliberate progress toward the stage.

Miss Julia continues, "I'm sure that all of you are as disappointed as we organizers are about this turn of events."

"Thass right"—from the crowd.

"Sho' am." Another voice stands out over the growing clamor of the assembly.

Louder now Miss Julia insists, "Knowing that you'd be disappointed, we have arranged for another speaker to come and share a message with you this afternoon." Groans from the crowd. "And as certain as I am of your disappointment, I'm equally certain that this speaker will more than make up for the failure of Stokley to get here."

A few people near the front have now noticed the four men approaching the bandstand. Finally one woman recognizes King and turns to her sister and says, "Look, it's Dr. King."

Miss Julia continues to soothe the ruffled feathers of her constituents, "This speaker is known in this nation from Atlantic to Pacific, from Canada to Mexico." More people at the front are now recognizing King and a swell of shouts and applause begins. Those at the rear strain and stand on tiptoe to try to understand the reason for the increasing noise from the front. The white men stop congratulating themselves and also search the area to see who this well-known speaker might be.

"Coming all the way from Birmingham to be with us today...." Her words are drowned out as the sparse groundswell erupts into mass recognition of a modern day hero. The cheers are deafening. People jump up and down, twirl in the air, and hug each other. Applause. Whistles. Shouts. Arms wave jubilation.

At the fringes of all this, the small group of whites looks incredulously at the spectacle and at each other. Thad Blankenship leans to the man next to him and says, "I'll be damned; if it ain't the HNIC."

"What's that supposed to mean?"

"It's King, the Head Nigger In Charge. If this don't beat all. We come angling for a goldfish and end up with a goddam whale."

By now King and his retinue have reached the steps leading to the stage. He reaches out to touch the hands of numerous well-wishers. Just when the welcoming roar can be no louder, it crests again as King climbs the four steps and walks onto the stage. Pandemonium. Tears run freely in the audience. In the din individual voices can occasionally be heard: "Brother Martin." "Reverend King." "Praise God."

Even King himself, who is accustomed to hearty greetings, is moved by the intensity of this Selma outpouring. Raises his hands. Approaches the microphone but backs away as the ovation continues and rolls back and forth across the square.

"Good afternoon, brothers and sisters.... ."

Several people begin shushing the others. "Shh ... Shh ... Quiet ... Be quiet so we can hear what he has to say.... Shh ..." until there is enough calm to allow King to be heard.

Cracker White drawls to his friends, "This oughtta be good."

"I appreciate that you will accept me as the poor substitute for Stokley and his brave followers this afternoon." Again the crowd erupts with applause, shouts, laughter and whistles. And again they have to be shushed so King can continue.

"I know that Stokley wanted to be here today and I want to convey to each of you his apology. Do not think that this means that he and his group won't come. They'll be here. Perhaps tomorrow. If not tomorrow, then Friday. If not Friday, then certainly no later than Saturday." Scattered applause. King raises a hand for silence and the crowd quiets as one. "I hope that all of you will join me here tomorrow and again on Friday and even Saturday, if necessary, to welcome these dauntless and weary travelers." More and enthusiastic applause.

"I don't have to tell anybody here today about the struggle gripping us as a people. The forces aligned against us are numerous and powerful. Those forces would keep us in the grip of poverty and ignorance. Would keep from us even the smallest of life's bountiful advantages. Would keep the minds of our children imprisoned in darkness. Would keep us from exercising the most basic rubric of freedom—the right to participate in choosing those who govern."

The huge crowd has been almost reverently quiet until this last sentence, but with those words a mighty roar erupts. Standing alongside Thad Blankenship, Eugene Hill feels the hair rise on his arms and neck.

King goes on. "Yet the colored peoples of America do not seek preeminence. We do not wish to control the lives of others. We do not want more than our neighbors have. The things we want are simple. We want the same things that our white neighbors want." Another great cheer.

He continues, almost singing, "We want good jobs. We want decent homes. We want a good education for our children."

Frenzied cheering.

Waiting just long enough, King again raises his hand to quiet the crowd. "We believe that until the men and women of color in the South have the right to participate in choosing our governing officials, there is no hope of earning the other benefits and responsibilities of a free society. Notice, brothers and sisters, that I said 'earn' those benefits. We must be willing to work for all those blessings. But we're not afraid of work. We all know how to do that."

"That's right, Dr. King," heard from several places in the crowd. A smattering of applause and affirmations.

"We have worked and struggled all these years, just to survive. We'll pay the price."

"Yessir, Brother Martin; we'll do that work." A loud voice in the audience rings out.

Things are relaxing a little now. The talk and response set a tone of intimacy. People begin to notice each other and share in the understanding of the message. Scattered hand-clapping. Men sway with concentration. Women shade their eyes against the sun and almost hum in sympathy with the words spilling down upon them.

"Our work has built this nation. We plucked the harvests from the fields—we've done that work. We built the roads and railroads that we travel on across America—we did that work too. We've done the most basic and brutal work in the history of this great land. We've dug ditches and laid brick and built houses. No, we're not afraid to work."

Applause and shouts of agreement are heard across the crowd.

"Knowing that we have to work for everything is all well and good, but what work must we do to earn the right to vote? What must we do in order to have what is granted as a birthright to our white brethren? I have thought long and hard about this question and have finally come to the conclusion that we must show the legislators of the state of Alabama that we are *sincere* in our desire to participate in our government."

An uneasy quiet settles over the gathering.

"You may wonder how we can demonstrate this to men who will hardly talk to us. I have given this much thought also and have arrived at the understanding that we must go to Montgomery *again*—and *tell* the legislature that we are sincere."

The crowd hangs in mute thrall. Will going to Montgomery a second time make any difference?

Among the whites at the fringes of this meeting, suspicion and distaste are beginning to sprout into anger and hatred, fear and defensiveness.

"Therefore I am announcing today that I will lead a second march from Selma, Alabama to the state capitol in Montgomery. We will walk *again* that fifty miles. I invite everyone here, and anyone else in America who wants to join us, to leave with us next Monday morning. I have received promises from numerous others from around the country who will be arriving between now and our departure time. I'll also add that if you can't get here by the time we leave, you may join us at any time along the way and do as much of the journey as you can. Our route will once again be straight down Highway 80."

The crowd buzzes in shock and anticipation. The whites begin shouting curses from their side of the square. Confusion is the order of the moment.

Sensing the need to cut short any further embellishment of the plans, King faces the crowd and says, "Again I invite you to join me here tomorrow at noon to greet Stokley and his Freedom Riders. Until then, remember: WE ARE NOT AFRAID TO DO THIS WORK." King walks steadily to his three companions at the stage's rear and they make their way in good order to the sedan and exit the square.

The cheers of the crowd swell and then die as King leaves the square. It is only then that the jeers and threats from the whites at the square's edge can be heard. Preston McCormack stands at Rube Townsend's side as Rube shouts, "Y'all better stay out of th' highway. You fuck with a truck, you just might get run over. We ain't puttin' up with that shit again"

A group of teenage blacks hear the taunt and shout back, "We'll be there. We'll do th' work." As the crowd disburses, the going is slow and more shouts and insults are thrown back and forth. Finally the whites can stand no more and charge into the milling remnants of the great crowd. Fists flail and panicked blacks run here and there causing terrible confusion. Screams and curses. Red blood flows from black and white alike.

When the fracas gets warmed up and confusion is at its highest, Collins, who is wearing his gloves, positions himself near Hill. While Hill scuffles with two black men, Collins pulls a rusty old .38 revolver from its hiding place in the small of his back. Grabbing one of the smart-talking teenagers, he maneuvers him next to Hill. Placing the old pistol against Hill's rib cage just above his heart, Collins pulls the trigger with one hand while holding the teenager firmly with the other. The sound of the shot causes a delayed reaction and in that brief moment Collins forces the gun into the hand of the terrified, squirming youth and pushes him away.

As the mixed crowd reacts to the shot by withdrawing from the direction of the sound, Hill lies gasping and bleeding on the ground in a spreading pool of his own blood. The black teenager stumbles away from Hill with the pistol clutched reflexively in his hands.

At that moment the sound of sirens fills the air as the local police force, riding in slow moving cars, pushes its way into the crowd with full lights and sirens. People of both colors run in every direction.

By the time the ambulance arrives, Hill is dead. The police take the teenage boy into custody. The contingent from Tuskegee has regrouped a few blocks away and returns to their motel. Thad Blankenship asks Ricky Parsons to go the hospital to see about Hill, and then accuses Collins of somehow being complicit in the shooting. Collins indignantly denies it and no one can really dispute him. Parsons returns after dark and says the ER staff sent him away, but that he believes Hill didn't make it. Even the Sheriff's deputies sent him packing.

＊   ＊   ＊   ＊

Afternoon heat overwhelms the air conditioners. Now the sun slips down the other side of the sky. Glare and leg cramps bedevil the passengers. Everybody wants to stop but can't. The tanks are full and they all ate a little. Atlanta will be under the buses' tires soon. They just keep on moving. Rest will come tonight. But for now, they keep rolling.

＊   ＊   ＊   ＊

Duke came into the library at two o'clock and busied himself with the work left undone over the past few days. By four he has things in pretty good order and sits down with his Spanish novel, and begins the struggle of reading for content and trying not to translate each word as he goes. At first his concentration doesn't hold well and anxiety rises like a fine mist. But as he calms himself the storyline takes over and the task becomes pleasure.

The phone jangles at his elbow and he answers to hear Ann's sweet voice. "Hi. I'm glad you're still down there. I had thought that maybe you'd be up here at some point this afternoon. I'd like to talk to you. Are you busy?"

"No, not anymore. Want me to come up there?"

"No, I'll be down in a minute."

He's grateful that the music rooms are empty right now. He hears the click of her footfalls as she comes down the concrete stairs and looks in anticipation until she rounds the final corner and, like an anthem, suffuses the air around him with her presence. Her smile like sunshine on his face.

They sit at the desk in the office that adjoins the front desk of the small department. His spirits are high but he senses that she is troubled. She explains that she and Alex had pretty well decided the night before to end the marriage. She is relieved and saddened. She worries that Melissa will somehow be harmed in all of this. And after a few minutes she says, "So I've decided that I really need to get out of Alabama for a while, maybe for good. I have a sister in California who told me this morning that if I want to come and stay with her and her family for a while, that I can. And I think I'm going do that."

*   *   *   *

Sometime after nine p.m. the two busloads of weary travelers turn off U. S. Highway 29, which they had been following all day, and onto Alabama State Road 49. Five miles out of town a few small signs on the roadside announce the homecoming services for the current week. A dirt driveway leads to the ancient frame structure that sits aglow in light, nestled in a pine grove. Red clay shows through the rough grass of the parking area. Headlights catch children running back and forth in the night, playing tag or hide-and-seek even at this hour.

Half an hour after their arrival, the visitors sit and stand at various places in and around the church building, eating, chatting with their individual hosts and growing excited at the prospect of tomorrow's engagement with history.

*   *   *   *

The dark green Nova sits invisibly on the logging road across Highway 49 from the church. Red scribbles furiously on his pad by the light of a penlight in his lap. His smile spreads as he writes. He hadn't believed that Brandt and Knight could have possibly been right about the busloads of Freedom Riders coming to tiny Tuskegee, but there they are. He was certain that if they *did* come, they would come here to Reverend Cleveland's church. Cleveland is the only other minister in the county who has publicly expressed any inclination to stand up for his people. Red arrived at eight, noticed the signs proclaiming "Homecoming" and knew that his suspicions were correct. He waited patiently and at nine the buses rolled in without ceremony and disgorged their human cargo.

Without headlights, Red eases back onto 49 and quietly makes his way back toward his Opelika home. All the way home he thinks about the enormity of this story and how pleased Carl Metzner at *The Post* will be. He knows that he has already missed the midnight edition of the paper, but anticipates his story leading the early morning edition.

*   *   *   *

At midnight Duke drives leadenly to Judd and Elizabeth's apartment. Lynn called late this afternoon to report that her father was ill and that she was meeting her mother and him at the hospital. She called again around eight and said that apparently Robert Earle was having heart problems and was being moved to Montgomery. She would call him tomorrow. He hardly heard her and showed very little in the way of compassion.

His mind and heart are elsewhere, both heavy from Ann's decision to go to the west coast. She had explained that Alex had agreed for Melissa to stay with her, but that she doesn't trust him or his family to stick to the agreement. She wants to be out of striking distance. Understanding her rationale didn't stop the pain. And the pain is more intense than anything he has ever known. Maybe the company of his friends will soothe him.

CHAPTER 24

▼

On Thursday a loud banging at the door of his motel room again awakens Blankenship. Hung over, his head throbs and he feels nauseated. In this sorry state, anger flares that Collins would again awaken him at this hour. Flinging open the door he is shocked to find two uniformed officers standing in the awful morning sunlight. The brown-clad sheriff's deputy holds a yellow sheet of paper and asks, "Are you Thad Blankenship?"

"That's right, deputy. What's the problem?"

"Well, no problem really. I understand that this Eugene Hill fella who was killed yesterday was a friend of yours. We need for you and the rest of your party to come with us down to 'the County'. Where are the rest of them?"

Fighting through the hangover, Blankenship replies, "We're all stayin' here. What do you need us for?"

Before the deputy can answer the city police officer in black and silver says, "They's several things that's got to be done, Mr. Blankenship. We've got to notify his kin, and with all these federal people here for the Carmichael doin's, we've got to at least make a show of investigatin' this killin'. Some of th' nigras are sayin' their boy didn't do th' shootin', even though he was caught red-handed with the gun in his hand. Anyhow th' federals will be watchin' pretty close. Y'all need to come on down to th' courthouse and go through th' motions."

With rising anger Blankenship storms, "Are you sayin' we're *suspects*?"

The deputy answers, "Not as far as we're concerned, but you know how these federals are actin'. How long before y'all can get down there?"

"Give us a couple of hours to clean up and eat something and I'll make sure that we're all there."

"That'll be fine. Ask for Deputy Clarke or Officer Daniels." The two lawmen nod and go along to their cruiser.

I ain't believin' this shit. Thad walks next door to wake up the others.

✳   ✳   ✳   ✳

Activity makes the Red Hill Baptist Church resemble an anthill. Dozens of older, ramshackle cars and a few shiny, newer ones, as well, arrive and depart. Excitement suffuses the air. Sister Abney and a group of other church women check names off lists and direct potential voters to ally themselves with members of the group that arrived last night. The locals are now referring to the Freedom Riders as "the Cavalry". Fear and excitement mingle indistinguishably. A contingent of government automobiles arrived at seven o'clock and twelve U. S. Marshals have positioned themselves at the corner of the parking lot talking, smoking, and planning.

Stokley Carmichael is in his glory. His sometimes-controversial positions, even within the larger controversy of the civil rights movement, seem on the brink of vindication this day. From the steps of the white frame church he surveys the chaos that is slowly organizing itself into a campaign. With him stand the Reverends Cleveland and Mohammed.

Mohammed says, "I sure hope this thing works, Stokley. I feel guilty staying back here while these brave souls walk into what is sure to be a storm of fear and anger. Why can't I go with this first group and let Sister Abney deal with the second wave?"

Unmoved, Stokley responds, "Doc, I need you a lot more here than I do out there. I'm sure that Sister Abney is plenty qualified, but someone with an official tie to the movement has to be responsible for these outcomes." Then he adds with a smile, "Besides, you're too pretty to risk being in harm's way."

Reverend Cleveland chuckles. "I don't know 'bout too pretty but we sure don't want to risk both leaders in the first foray. I'm no military man, but seems to me that we need to have something in reserve. How's this supposed to work anyhow, Stokley?"

"The first carload of marshals will arrive at the clerk's office five minutes before the first busload of voters. They're just gonna show the clerk the first order from the U.S. attorney general requiring him to produce the official list of registered voters for the county. Once that is accomplished and while the marshals are looking over the list, the first bus will arrive. A second carload of marshals will be directly behind the first bus and will hold off any interference that may try to block progress.

"If the clerk complies, the initial progress should go fairly smoothly. If not—which is more likely if you ask me—two of the marshals will take the clerk into custody and will try to have him held at the county jail. The other two will then begin the registration of the applicants.

"When half these applicants are registered, the driver of the first bus will radio the second driver; and the second bus will load up and head into town. With the radios we can time it so the second bus will arrive at the square at the same time that the first busload is finishing up. It will be escorted by two more carloads of marshals. The remaining four marshals in reserve will be used to deal with the detention of the clerk and any other interference that may occur, including the sheriff's office, or just as a visible presence on the square."

"Sounds easy enough," says Mohammed with a wistful grin. "Wonder what's really gonna happen?"

Grinning back, Stokley says, "We're gonna play it like it's a done deal. What-ever comes up other than that, we'll just have to cope with it at the moment. I gotta admit that I don't expect these white folks to just roll over. First busload might catch 'em off guard, though. If it was just me and I was wantin' to register, I'd wanna be in that first bus rather than any other one. We'll see. It's gonna work out."

✳   ✳   ✳   ✳

At six in the morning, Lynn sits in the private hospital room and watches the endless "blips" crossing the small rounded screen near her father's bed. He hasn't been awake in hours, but the blips continue and with their progress her hopes are not lost. Her eyes burn from the lack of sleep and she is annoyed at the soft snores that emanate from her mother, who sits in another chair near the window. Lynn's head aches from clenching her jaw. She doesn't contemplate life without her father, in fact she hardly thinks at all. When thoughts intrude on her mes-merized stare, they represent a growing red rage toward the coloreds who caused her father's problems.

The door opening startles both her and her mother into alertness. A tall gray-haired man in white medical garb approaches and explains that Mr. Jackson needs open heart surgery. Both women sit down from the news to consider the implications. When the doctor explains how the surgery is performed, the fear is almost too much to bear. Finally, Mrs. Jackson says, "If it's going to save his life, then we have to try it."

Arrangements are made to transfer Robert Earle to a hospital in Birmingham. As the Wilkins women walk woodenly toward their automobile in the parking lot, Lynn says, "Mother, we don't have any clothes or toilet articles or anything. Don't we need to go by the house first?"

"No, we'll just buy what we need in Birmingham. You drive, honey, I don't think I can manage it."

Looking to her left Lynn sees an ambulance leaving the rear of the hospital, imagines that her father is in the back on a stretcher, and finally the tears come.

From the passenger's seat her mother whispers, "Hush, baby; you'll just make it worse."

*   *   *   *

Knowing that *his* story will be big news, Red McKinney is up early with both the TV and the radio tuned to Montgomery stations ... Nothing. No mention of Freedom Riders heading to Macon County ... Nothing about colored citizens massing to register to vote in Tuskegee ... No story about federal marshals escorting those coloreds ... *What's going on here?*

Instead the airways are pulsing with the story that Martin Luther King Jr. has announced that he will lead a second march from Selma to Montgomery in protest of the lack of progress in registering colored people to vote in the state of Alabama, that he has invited notables from around the country to join him in this march, that the march will begin a week from this Monday, that local reaction has been outrage and covert threats. *Holy cow! That's almost a week away* ... Still. No mention at all of the events that should be about to unfold in Tuskegee—*today!*

Picking up the phone he dials the number at *The Post* and asks for Carl Metzner. When Carl comes on the phone Red's concern tumbles out disguised as anger: "What's th' big idea? Why isn't my story being aired? What happened? Aren't you gonna use it?"

As always, Carl is patient. When Red's outburst slows for a moment, he says, "Take it easy, Red. We're going to use the story, but this story on King and his proposed march is just bigger. Also the managing editor decided that if we wait until the afternoon edition, the registration thing will already be in progress. If we had gone to press with it last night, we would have unnecessarily endangered the lives of those people. Does that make any sense to you?"

Red is slow to respond, but after considering these ideas he reluctantly agrees that the managing editor has a good point. "But the story will come out this afternoon, right?"

"Yes, Red, it'll hit the streets at one o'clock and I mailed your checks out this morning. Now get back over there and stay on top of this thing. There's a lot popping down there this week. Stay in touch."

Before Red can say he's on his way, the phone goes dead. Carl is on to other things. Red dresses hurriedly and heads for the Nova, a cup of coffee, a doughnut and Tuskegee.

∗   ∗   ∗   ∗

Duke, too, has his radio on as he tries to coax his percolator to finish making the coffee. When the announcer cuts to the news and tells the story of King's announcement of a second march from Selma to Montgomery, he marvels, admiring the creativity, courage, and audacity of the man. The announcer goes on to mention that there will be a closed-casket funeral for the Reverend Eldred Maxwell in Tuskegee at two this afternoon. Duke wonders about going to the funeral, but knows that he can't. Oddly, that thought depresses him even more than his sleepless night had done. Once again his thoughts turn to Ann and the fact that she will be leaving in a matter of hours, and that he won't even be able to say goodbye.

∗   ∗   ∗   ∗

At eight-fifteen two men in light gray slacks with crisp creases, matching gray shirts with epaulets at the shoulders and dark ties step into the office of the clerk of Macon County. Their faces are pleasant enough but their demeanor is serious. The office occupies half of the first floor of the Macon County Courthouse. In the large rectangular room, a white vinyl counter top extends from one wall into the larger room. Behind the counter are rows of file cabinets, two desks, map cases and several chairs. An older man with sparse white hair and glasses, dressed in baggy pants, white shirt and tie, sits at one desk and looks up from his newspaper at the unexpected visitors. Each man shows his badge to Billy Wayne Banks, who has been the county clerk for thirty-seven years

The taller marshal speaks: "Good morning Mr. Banks. I'm Marshal Tolles and this is Marshal Davenport. We have an order from the attorney general of the United States for you to produce the official list of registered voters for Macon

County." Saying this, Davenport pulls the folded order from his back pocket and opens it.

Startled, Banks hesitates behind his spectacles, his red tinged skin turning a brighter shade of pink. "What's this all about, boys?" Shuffling toward the counter top where the two marshals stand, he cursorily examines the badges. "Y'all shouldn't need any order from anybody to see that list. I'll show it to you and you can keep your paper." He reaches for a legal sized brown folder underneath the counter and plops it down onto the vinyl top. "There you go. Now, what's this all about?"

As Tolles examines the folder, held together by an aluminum fastener, Davenport says, "We've been ordered to look over the list and report back to the attorney general as to what we find."

Tolles has flipped all the way to the back page and seems to be reading each individual name. Banks, still baffled, asks again, "Well what do you expect to find? I mean it's just a list of names."

Tolles looks up and asks, "How does the process work, Mr. Banks? I mean, how do you get added to the list? And if someone dies, how does their name get removed from the list?"

"Well, these new rules and all are going to make getting on the list pretty easy. All's ya have to do is prove who you are, that you're a resident of the county, fill out the form, and sign in or make your mark in the presence of a witness. Used to be a lot different, but that's it now. Getting off is a whole another thing. We're supposed to check over the list every couple years or so and take off the names of those who have moved or passed away …"

The front door opening interrupts Banks's recitation. Startled for a second time this early morning, he looks up A crowd files into the room, most of them colored. The longer Banks looks, the more people appear. "What 'n the world is going on here? You people can't come in here. Y'all're gonna have to go back outside." He starts to move toward the end of the counter as if to physically intervene; but Tolles puts a restraining hand on his shoulder.

"Mr. Banks, these residents of Macon County have come to register to vote. You just told us how easy it is and now it's your job to see to it that they are registered. Please step back over here and do your job." All this in a measured voice, free of threat and malice.

As Tolles removes his hand, Banks recovers from his shock and edges toward the desk. He reaches for the phone as Davenport moves to go around the counter. Banks mutters, "I'll not do it. These people ain't registerin' in here. The sheriff won't stand for this." But Davenport reaches the phone before he can dial the number, breaks the connection, and places himself between Banks and the desk.

Tolles says, "Mr. Banks, I'm afraid that your choices are pretty limited here." Reaches to his own back pocket and draws out another folded order. "I have another order from Mr. Katzenbach which is, in effect, a warrant for your arrest in the event that you refuse to carry out your sworn duty and register these citizens. Not only that, Mr. Banks, if you refuse, I am further authorized to register them myself, so you'd be going to jail for nothing."

As Banks stands dumbfounded and confused, the room fills to capacity. Tolles turns the folder around toward Banks and says, "We're going to make carbon copies of these records, Mr. Banks. So let's get started."

$$* \quad * \quad * \quad *$$

When Sheriff Jimbo Turner arrives at his office at ten 'til eight, the night dispatcher says, "Sheriff, there was a call for you about half an hour ago from Washington, D.C. Somebody named Katzenjammer or something like that. He'd forgot about the hour difference in time. Anyhow he said that he'd call back at eight-fifteen"

Jimbo stops at the door into his inner office and with a pained look says, "Well, hell, did he say what he wanted? And it's Katzenbach, you ninny. He's the U. S. attorney general."

"Yeah, that's th' name. I knew it was something like that … Nah, he didn't say what he wanted. Sounded funny though, even for a Yankee. Why d'ya think he'd be callin' us anyhow?" Gary "Spud" Wagner, lean and balding, isn't very smart, but he's dependable and loyal. He either ignores the Sheriff's jab at him or just doesn't get it.

"I don't know, Spud, but whatever it is, it won't be good." Holds up a brown paper sack and asks, "You wanna sausage biscuit? I bought an extra one. Did you hear about Robert Earle being in the hospital?"

Spud nods to the biscuit and adds, "Yeah, I heard 'bout it. I reckon he's all the way to Montgomery this mornin'. Too bad. Hope he makes it."

Jimbo hands over a biscuit wrapped in wax paper and says, "Naw, he's in Birmingham. I got these at the Magnolia, and they said that he got worse. He's gonna have to have open heart surgery this mornin' sometime. I'm gonna look over th' paper in my office. Tell Marcie about the phone call, so she can let me know when it comes through." He sits at his desk and agonizes over the story that King is planning another march to Montgomery. With a smile he wonders how

Blankenship, Collins and the others reacted to the story. He vaguely hears Marcie arrive to relieve Wagner. Soon Marcie shouts that the call he's expecting is on the line.

With dread and disgust Turner picks up the phone. "Sheriff Turner."

The voice at other end is calm and businesslike. "Good morning, Sheriff, this is Nicholas Katzenbach. The president has asked me to call you to brief you about a situation that is about to take place in your jurisdiction."

Jimbo is puzzled. "What situation are you talkin' about? I don't know about any situation. Is this something about the preacher's funeral?"

"No this is something quite different."

Even as Jimbo listens he is aware that Spud Wagner has come back into the outer office, and is exclaiming to Marcie, "They's niggers all over th' place out-side."

Turner interrupts Katzenbach saying, "'Scuse me Mr. Katzenbach, my deputy is tryin' to get my attention." Puts one hand over the end of the phone and shouts out to the outer office, "Spud, come in here. What are you saying?"

Wagner enters, wide-eyed and obviously excited. "Sheriff, they's niggers all over th' square. They's a whole busload of 'em and they're goin' into Billy Wayne's office upstairs. Must be a couple of hun'erd of 'em." Turner holds up a hand to silence him and redirects his attention to the phone. "Sorry Mr. Katzen-bach, I think some people have arrived for the funeral and may be lost. What were you sayin'?"

"Yes, Sheriff ... sounds like I called just in time. As I was saying, the president wanted me to call because there are going to be a number of your colored citizens registering to vote there this morning, and we wanted to head off any trouble that might occur otherwise."

Jimbo's blood pressure immediately skyrockets. "What? You mean that whole busload out there is gonna try to register to vote today? Here? What's this all about? We'll just close the clerk's office down."

"Hold on, Sheriff. Yes, that whole busload is going to register, today. When we finish on the phone and you go outside to check this out, you'll find that there are twelve U. S. Marshals accompanying the colored citizens. The marshals were approved by the president and are there to make absolutely certain that legal citizens in Macon County, Alabama are not denied the right to register to vote. I hope that the presence of the marshals is enough to convince everyone that this registration is *going to happen*. We would not like to utilize any further safeguards."

Turner can barely speak through his rage. "What d' you mean 'further safeguards'? Are you threatening me now? Or maybe the town of Tuskegee?"

Katzenbach interrupts calmly, "Sheriff, this is not a threat. I'm simply warning you that the president of the United States has authorized me to activate, if necessary, a National Guard unit from New Jersey that is at summer camp at Ft. Benning in Columbus, Georgia. I can have these men in your town square in forty-five minutes if I have to. They are on alert right now. We'd like to avoid that if possible. That's why I called you.

"The marshals have federal court orders to inspect the county's voting list, and to arrest the county clerk if he refuses to register citizens. Further, they are empowered to register any applicants who present themselves, in the event that there is no local agent to do so, and to make and keep copies of the records of any citizens who register themselves today. Finally, they will arrest any other person or persons who attempt to obstruct the enforcement of the laws of the United States."

Jimbo feels emptiness in the pit of his stomach. *Federal troops. My god. What am I gonna do? The county commission is gone ... Robert Earle, Thad, Eugene. Hell, they're all gone. Twelve marshals? I've got seventeen people—eighteen counting myself—and most of them are idiots.* Finally he says aloud into the phone, "I'm gonna have to talk to the commissioners about this and maybe to th' guvnah too. I can't promise you anything at this point."

"I'm not asking for any promises, Sheriff. I'm merely advising you, as a professional courtesy, of the scope of the federal government's commitment to this undertaking. And by the way, I have already spoken to the governor this morning. He made no comment about his intentions to me, but I don't believe that there are very many options open to either of you at this point. I have other duties to attend to, Sheriff, so I'll be saying 'good morning' to you now." And after a brief pause, in which Jimbo says nothing, the connection is broken.

"What're we gonna do, Sheriff? What are all them spooks doin' up there?" Spud Wagner is agog at the edge of Jimbo's desk.

Turner hangs up his phone and shouts for Marcie to come into his office. He tells Wagner to shut up and directs Marcie to contact the governor's office. Then turning to Wagner he says, "Spud, we ain't gonna do nothin' 'til we hear from the guvnah." So saying, he walks to the front window to survey the scene outside for himself. The hole in his belly just gets worse when he sees the line of coloreds and others coming out of the front door of the Courthouse, trailing down the steps and along the sidewalk. A few smiling pairs walk toward the waiting bus, apparently finished with their task. Jimbo Turner's jaws and fists are clenched in frustration. He has no one to turn to.

*   *   *   *

Deputy Rusty Clarke meets Blankenship, Collins, White and Parsons at the entrance to the Dallas County sheriff's office in downtown Selma, Alabama. Ignoring their complaints, Clarke ushers the four into a small interrogation room on the second floor and leaves them there saying, "Somebody'll be with y'all in a minute."

When Sheriff Grady Womack comes into the room a scant few moments later, he is accompanied by a tall, strongly built man, identified as the Dallas County District Attorney, and by another tall, thin man in a suit, identified as an F.B.I. Agent from Atlanta. All take turns introducing themselves.

Cracker White growls, "Another F.B.I. man? We've got these people crawlin' outta th' damn woodwork all of a sudden. What does this one want?"

Womack says, "He's been asked by the U. S. Attorney General to sit in on and observe this part of the investigation of this murder. You boys are friends of the deceased, Mr. Hill, right?" They all nod and mumble affirmation. "Well we've got two sets of witnesses that claim they saw someone other than the colored kid shoot Mr. Hill. One of these groups says that the real shooter was a white man—tall, gray, wearing overalls and a baseball cap. The other group says that the shooter was medium height, bald and wearing blue twill work clothes. What do you fellas say to that?"

Parsons speaks immediately, "What th' hell do you want from us? None of us fits that description any more than a hundred other people. Why would any of us wanna kill Eugene? He was our friend. Why are we here?"

The DA, Johnny Mack Webster, says, "Well the five of you were together. What did y'all see? How did it happen that your friend got shot dead in broad daylight, and none of you has offered any sort of explanation?"

Blankenship answers, "Mr. Webster, Sheriff, we was just standin' there on the street watchin' th' festivities when them nigras attacked us. We were all pretty busy defendin' ourselves and only knew that Eugene was hurt after the shot was fired. We sent Ricky here up here to the office yesterday to talk to y'all, and somebody told him that y'all was too busy to talk to him then, and to come back today. I guess that since the witnesses have only said that white men did the shootin', they're all colored, right?"

When Womack nods, Collins says determinedly, "If y'all ain't arrestin' us, I think I'm gonna leave now. This is just another bunch of bullshit to harass us."

Andrew Harmon, the F.B.I. agent, says quietly, "We would like for you men to stay in town and take part in a line up tomorrow or Saturday—just as soon as we can get it organized."

White drawls, "I was planning on going back home tonight myself. Y'all can prob'ly handle that without me."

Harmon snaps, "Johnny Mack, do you have that order drawn up requiring that these gentlemen stay here for the line up?" Webster nods and produces a sheet of paper with the appropriate order on it and passes it across the table.

Womack adds, "We ain't gonna hold y'all or nothin'. You can go back to your motel or wherever you want to in town. Agent Harmon has assigned two of his men to accompany you until this is resolved. Sorry 'bout th' trouble, boys; but y'all understand that we've gotta do this."

Blankenship asks, "What about th' body? Are y'all gonna send it back home without us goin' with it?"

Webster responds, "Well, the body's being held for an autopsy by the medical examiner. That probably won't get done 'til Monday. We do need to know about his family. Who do we need to contact and how?"

"Just call the sheriff's office in Tuskegee," says Blankenship. "His cousin, Digger, is a deputy over there. Far's I know that's all the family he's got. He's been divorced for years and there ain't no children. We're all gonna need to call our families and let 'em know about this, and that we won't be home for a day or two."

✳ ✳ ✳ ✳

At nine o'clock Red McKinney walks into the sheriff's office in Tuskegee. Jimbo Turner is pacing in the outer office, muttering and red-faced. Marcie Brooks shoots an accusing look at Red and Turner demands, "What d'you want in here, Red? Can't you see that I've got enough trouble today without havin' to put up with you?"

Taken aback, McKinney stammers, "Hold on, Jimbo. I'm just here doin' my job. What's goin' on anyhow? What're all the coloreds doin' out there?"

"I don't have to hold on to a damn thing, Red. And I don't need th' press in here right now. Now I'm askin' you real polite-like to leave. I got nothin' to say to you. I'm about half-way convinced that you're in cahoots with these people anyhow."

Prickles of fear dance down Red's spine, but he says, "What th' hell is that s'posed to mean? In cahoots! Hell, I don't even know what's happening. Don't accuse me of nothin'. I *am* th' press though, so I've got th' right to be here and to ask you questions about what's going on and what you're gonna do about it."

"I've got no comment. Now get out of here...."

The jangling of the phone interrupts the exchange. Marcie says in a low voice, "Sheriff, it's the governor's office." Without looking at Red, Turner stomps off to his inner office and closes the door behind him.

Inside at his desk Turner hurriedly picks up the receiver and says, "Sheriff Turner speakin'."

A familiar voice responds. "Yes, Sheriff. This is Guvnah Wallace. How's it goin' over theah this mawnin'? I understand that you're havin' a few visitors in your fair city today. Have they arrived yet?"

Jimbo says flatly, "If you're talkin' about a busload of niggers accompanied by U. S. Marshals, then yes sir, they're here. In fact they're upstairs right now registering to vote. The marshals have threatened to arrest the clerk if he doesn't let them register, and me if I try to interfere. I called because I don't know what to do. Have y'all got any ideas about that over there in Montgomery?"

Wallace answers, "Not very many and not *any* good ones. The state attorney general has been in here with me most of the mawnin' and these boys have kinda got us over a barrel. I expect they called you from Washington. They told me they were goin' to tell you the same things they told me. I've been tryin' to find some legal way to call out our own National Guard to seal off the county offices, but I'm afraid that would lead to bloodshed. And Sheriff, there'll be *several* busloads to deal with.

"The best that we've been able to come up with at this point is to let the registration go on, and then we'll strike it down as illegal—take it to court if we have to. But I don't think that it's wise to allow this to go on unchallenged."

Turner is fretful, "Neither do I, Guvnah. What do you suggest? Our entire group of county commissioners is out of pocket today and I don't have anybody to help me decide about this."

Wallace says, "We've talked about it and I think you need to get yourself arrested by these marshals. They'll have to take you to jail, but we'll get you out immediately. How do you feel about that? Are you willing to go along with it?"

Jimbo's back pedaling now. He's remembering that the F.B.I. agents told him that he'd end up in the Atlanta federal prison and implied that he'd stay there. So he hedges. "I don't want to leave the county without *any* elected officials,

Guvnah. And what if they don't let y'all get me out quickly? Are y'all sure this is a good idea?"

Wallace's drawl is as smooth as butter. "It's all worked out, Jimbo. I talked to the president myself just a few minutes ago. He understands these things. He has agreed for you to be brought to Montgomery and has arranged for you to be released on your own recognizance. This way we look like we're at least doin' *somethin'*. Will you do it?"

Slowly the political wisdom of this approach dawns on Turner and he agrees. "OK, Guvnah, I'll go do it right away."

His enthusiasm is curbed however when Wallace says, "No I want you to wait until two o'clock. Nobody knows about this yet and the news people won't respond to it 'til this afternoon. We're takin' care of that part too right now; but you don't want to make this gesture without havin' some of those boys around to report it. We'll have local TV people in Tuskegee this afternoon at 1:30. You can make your move around two and it'll make the evenin' news. You'll be back home in time for supper tonight.

"I'll ask the attorney general to have you brought by my office when you get out of court, and we'll talk about what happened and maybe look at the news together. How does that sound?"

For Jimbo Turner to meet with the governor of the state, either at the Capitol or at the governor's mansion would be to have climbed higher than he had ever dreamed possible. Quickly he answers, "I'd be much obliged, Guvnah. Two o'clock. I'll do it then."

"That's just fine, Jimbo. We'll see you later this afternoon."

As the line goes dead, Turner stands with the receiver and stares at nothing, while his understanding of his world undergoes rapid and necessary reorganiza-tion. Part of him is filled with a kind of joyful anticipation. To meet the gover-nor! His status in his town, county and in his own mind soars. But somewhere along the fringes of his awareness, a terrible thought niggles at him. *It's all "worked out". What does that really mean? Does the governor make deals with the federal government? Is this what happened in Tuscaloosa? Was that all "worked out" too, before Wallace stood in the schoolhouse door? Have I ... have the people of the state been duped into thinking he was defying the government when it was really all "worked out"?* These are worries for another day.

Back in the outer office, McKinney asks, "What did the governor have to say, Jimbo? Y'all got a plan?"

Again the phone rings and Marcie says, "Sheriff, it's the sheriff from Dallas County."

Turning back to his office, Turner says, "I got no comment, Red. I thought I told you to get out of here."

∗   ∗   ∗   ∗

By a little after nine o'clock, fifty-seven new voters have been registered in Macon County. The news of what's going on has circulated throughout the town and a few white citizens have gathered at various places to discus these events. The chief rabble-rousers haven't made an appearance, so the indignation and frustration haven't risen to the level that might have occurred otherwise. All the same as the last few of the first busload walk toward the bus, a handful of curious and angry onlookers mill about in the square. Stokley is on the radio with the second bus. Zo prepares to vacate his parking space to make room for the next wave.

On his signal, Zo revs his engine and as Stokley steps off, the bus departs. Stokley stands alone and sees the hatred in the faces of those few whites gathered among the trees. Before the next bus arrives, a young black child approaches Stokley and says, "Miz Maxwell wants you to tell Reverend Cleveland to come over to her house. She said it's about the funeral."

The second bus appears and parks in the place vacated by the first. Stokley steps aboard and says to the anxious passengers, "So far everything is fine, no problems. But be alert." The new batch of applicants files out of the bus in an orderly fashion and into the courthouse. Stokley takes the radio from George and tells Zo to ask Reverend Cleveland to go to Miz Maxwell's home. He then steps out of the bus to speak to individuals and to keep things organized.

The arrival of a second busload of coloreds causes an uneasy stir among the few gathered white citizens. Some shout across the square to the new arrivals, "Go on back home." But no organized threat materializes for the moment.

∗   ∗   ∗   ∗

Ricky Parsons turns from the phone in Sheriff Womack's office looking pale. Blankenship asks, "What's th' matter with you Ricky? You look like you've seen a ghost or something."

"Worse than that, Thad. A whole lot worse. Melinda says that busloads of niggers are showin' up at the courthouse back home and that they're registerin' them to vote. She said that there're hundreds of 'em."

Blankenship is dumbfounded. "You gotta be shittin' me. What th' hell is Jimbo doing? Twiddlin' his damn thumbs? Gimme that phone. We'll see about this."

Collins, White and Parsons stand and listen as Blankenship talks with Jimbo Turner. At first Thad is belligerent and forceful. But as the conversation continues he becomes firm and demanding, then quiet, and finally resigned. Before he hangs up the phone though, he says, "Jimbo, you tell th' guvnah that this damn sure better work. Our whole way of life depends on it workin', an' if it don't, he'll see th' results in th' next election."

White asks, "What'd Jimbo have t'say for hisself?"

Blankenship answers with disgust in his voice, "Well, it's true. Th' federal marshals are over there with court orders registering ever' sonofabitch that walks in th' damn door. Most of 'em're with some Yankee that's signin' as a witness. He says there's already been almost sixty of 'em to register, and that th' guvnah says there's nothin' that can be done about it except to let it happen, and then throw it out as illegal. Says th' guvnah will take it to court if he has to. And Jimbo is goin' to get hisself arrested by th' marshals so it looks like he's tryin' t' do somethin'. Th' feds are gonna take 'im to Montgomery and the judge there is gonna release 'im. I'll tell you what, boys, I don't like this worth a damn. Let's go find something to drink."

CHAPTER 25

▼

Miss Julia Alexander received her briefing from the King camp on Wednesday evening. The briefing took place at a motel in Atlanta, owned and operated by and for Negroes. Miss Julia, as everyone knows her, was made to understand that Stokley and his Freedom Riders would not be coming to Selma until Friday evening, but that she was to keep the crowd of supporters in Selma ignorant of this fact. As King put it, "If it becomes known that Stokley and his group are in fact registering colored people to vote in Macon County, all the violent hatemongers who are here, awaiting his arrival, will go there, and people will be hurt."

Approaching the central square in downtown Selma now on Thursday near noon, she feels alternately proud at being in the inner circle and anxious that she might somehow do something wrong and people will be hurt. A crowd of coloreds already mills around, searching for shade. White men and boys stand in scattered groups along the sidewalks bordering the square. Memories of the brief fight yesterday stab at her and intensify her anxiety. There is some small comfort in knowing that by now more than three hundred colored citizens of Macon County have been registered to vote—a fact unprecedented in the history of this state. With less than an hour to wait before noon, she calms herself and plans out how she will announce that Stokley and the others won't arrive in Selma until tomorrow at the earliest.

＊   ＊   ＊   ＊

The sparse but growing number of whites collecting along the sides of the square represents overt members of the Ku Klux Klan, curious bystanders drawn by the violence from the previous day, others who are angry but lack direction. A few plainclothes F.B.I. agents and federal marshals will watch carefully to see who initiates violence, if anything actually happens. The coloreds, gathering in the square's center, are less vociferous today than yesterday, more reserved and tentative. Police officers and deputies are strung out sparsely along the gutters of the four sides of the square. Police cruisers drive by slowly at intervals.

Thad Blankenship and his friends stand near Rube Townsend from Montgomery and Preston McCormack from Gadsden. Townsend, recognizing Blankenship, asks, "Thad, did ya'll ever find that Windsor boy that was supposed to be working for th' niggers over there?"

For a moment Blankenship doesn't even remember that a man was killed over this very question. "Naw, hell, we tried to find out about 'im but didn't get nowhere. We got worse problems than that now, though. We got niggers by th' damn busload registerin' t' vote in Tuskegee right now."

Townsend is shocked. "What? If that's so why in th' hell are you here, an' not over there kickin' some nigger ass? They wouldn't be registerin' in Montgomery without a fight, I'll tell ya."

Cracker White speaks up to say, "Yeah, well, we ain't gonna be there for a day or two at least. The fuckin' sheriff and the feds've got us stuck here because of that killin' yesterday. They've even got F.B.I. men watchin' us so we don't leave town."

With the Mason jars passing back and forth among the few men gathered there, Blankenship explains that the coloreds have convinced the feds that maybe the black teenager didn't actually shoot their friend Hill, and now the investigation includes the four of them.

After hearing as much of the story as he could bear listening to, Townsend volunteers, "Tell you what. Me an' some of these boys will go over there tomorrow morning and see if maybe we can't at least slow things down a little. Sheriff Grady Womack ain't gonna keep me in this town if I don't wanna stay. There ain't no marshals watchin' my ass." Turns to McCormack. "How 'bout y'all Preston? You and your boys wanna come with us over to Tuskegee?" Preston is slow to answer, but when the silence becomes uncomfortable he agrees.

Later that afternoon, when Blankenship finally reaches his son at home and explains the situation. He tells George not to worry about the coloreds registering to vote, that the governor is gonna fix all that. He also says that help is on the way in the form of some of his buddies from around th' state who'll be over tomorrow to crack some heads.

*   *   *   *

The living room at Eudora Maxwell's home is dark and heavy with the overly sweet smell of flowers. Reverend Joe Lee Cleveland sits in respectful silence as Eudora makes her wishes known to him. His heart is at once saddened and filled with respect for the strength of this woman—brotherly love overflowing.

"Joe Lee, you and Eldred have been friends for forty years. You know that he would understand the importance of what is going on downtown today. If he had to make a similar decision, he would agonize over it just as I am sure you will; but he *would* make it and he'd make the right one. I'm sure that when you take time to think about it you'll do the same.

"We don't need to interrupt this work to honor the dead. This work is for the living and for the unborn. What happens today and tomorrow far outweighs anything that could happen at a funeral. I'm proposing that we have the burial today and that we keep the service very short and private. We'll hold it at the cemetery. On Sunday, after the work at hand has been completed, we'll have a memorial service and a celebration. That would make Eldred proud, certainly prouder than if we somehow cut short this opportunity for the people of color in Macon County."

Cleveland knows that she is right. Knows that his lifelong friend would agree with her. Knows in his rational mind that this is the right thing to do. But the idea of shortchanging his friend in this, his last hour, almost overwhelms him. The conflict between the rational and the emotional strikes him dumb, and he just sits. Hot tears track in streaks down his cheeks.

Eudora goes on, "I'd like for you and Milton to come to the church with me and help me tell those who show up, and then to accompany me to the gravesite. We can invite them, and everyone else, to join in the effort downtown today and tomorrow. That'll give us Saturday to prepare for a real memorial service on Sunday, and a feast. We can all gather together and eat and tell stories of Eldred's life. We can console each other and gain strength from each other. I need that too, Joe Lee; but I need even more for his death to mean something." She has no tears as she presents her wishes to Cleveland, but his heart breaks for her. He knows that he can't refuse her this wish. And so he agrees.

*   *   *   *

Lynn feels like throwing up. She can barely stand the strain of sitting in this waiting room with all these wretched people. She's learning, however, that she not only has to stand it for herself, but also for her mother who has slipped into a frightening state of mind. Tilly Wilkins has never been particularly strong. Her husband has not encouraged that trait in her and she has not wanted the responsibility. The threat that her husband might no longer be there to take care of her is so powerful that she cannot even acknowledge the possibility that it might occur. She talks of things that she wants to do with the house, and of new business ventures that Robert Earle plans to start soon. She refuses to eat and instead sleeps—in the car, in the waiting room, at the motel room that was rented this morning. Her face is taut, her eyes a little wild. Lynn can only try to console her and to agree with even her most irrelevant ideas.

And now this waiting room. Beige walls and tile floors. Straight chairs with so little padding. Old tattered magazines dating from a year previous. How Lynn wishes that she could retreat to the comfort zone of last year's oblivion. Tilly sleeps on, unaware, blessedly unconscious. Others in the room are similarly stressed. No one would be here given the choice. No, here one comes to stand vigil. Here existence is reduced to its simplest terms—life or death. One finds the profundity of this inevitable duality in these chairs. Even sudden death is easier than this. Here you must confront your own weakness and find strength, or you must, like Tilly, slip into the protective arms of sleep.

A green-clad nurse comes to the open door and calls, "Wilkins family?"

Lynn looks up anxiously and approaches her. Tilly sleeps on and Lynn decides to let her. The nurse looks serious and Lynn feels a flood of fear in her throat.

"Are you Wilkins?"

Lynn nods. "Daughter."

"It looks good, Miss Wilkins. We can't be sure, of course, but the operation went well and your father is a very strong man. He's in the recovery room now. He'll be there for a couple of hours and then they'll transfer him to a private room. If you want to go up to third floor, they'll probably allow you to go in and see him."

Gently shaking her mother awake Lynn says, "Mom, come on. We have to go up to third floor."

Tilly rouses slowly and stupidly. "What is it? Is he OK? What's wrong, Lynn?"

"Nothing, Mom. They think he's going to be fine. The operation went well and he's in recovery. They'll let us see him upstairs. Come on with me." Tilly's eyes flash wildly for a moment and at last she begins to cry.

Lynn supports her arm as they move toward the elevator. Relief is like a warm room on the coldest night. Her mother cries and leans. No matter now—he's gonna make it. Thank God for that.

∗   ∗   ∗   ∗

Driver George's voice forces its way through the static and crackle of the bus' radio, "Tell your folks that lunch is waiting for them when they get back to the church." The near-full bus buzzes with approval as the last of these, the fifth group of new voters, crowd back into place for the return to Red Hill Baptist Church. "And tell Stokley that I've got a box lunch for him, too. We're less than five minutes out, are you about ready to leave?"

Zo keys his mike and says, "I gottcha, George. And Stoke's lookin' like he's definitely ready for that food. We'll be pullin' outta here in two minutes. I see the last of my bunch comin' out th' door right now. They's lotsa white folks out here now, George. They ain't doin' much, 'cept hollerin' and stuff, but you'll wanna let yo' people know 'bout 'em. Don't take no chances. Stokley says that the total is runnin' right at 300 now." Zo's eyes continually scan the crowd that still stands well back from the bus. His senses are on alert and his feelings hover somewhere between fear and anger.

"I hear you loud and clear, Zo. We're on the edge of town now and we're gonna keep this thing movin'. Not to worry—me and these folks are takin' no chances. They can hear you just like your group can hear me. By the way, please tell Stokley and the others that Miz Maxwell has canceled the funeral this afternoon in favor of a memorial service on Sunday. She and the two reverends will be doing a graveside service today and are keeping it to the three of them and Eudora's sister." Another buzz echoes in the bus.

As Zo's bus pulls out and the next one pulls in, a few shouts and curses are heard. Something rattles on the top of George's bus and he realizes that someone has thrown a rock. Rolling to a stop, he says in a loud voice, "You folks heard what Zo said now. Don't even look at these white folks in the square." He whooshes open the door and Stokley steps inside.

Carmichael addresses the group. "As y'all know we've been incredibly lucky so far. But th' white folks are startin' to get restless now. They're cursin' and threat-enin' and shoutin'. That was a rock that you heard that skittered across th' top of th' bus; but it was just a little rock. Couldn't've hurt a flea. But just because that one was small don't mean that y'all shouldn't be careful. Here's how we're gonna do this now. Ever' body on this side will get up and walk single file across to the clerk's office. Then as one pair finishes up inside and comes back to the bus another pair from inside will get out and take their place at the back of the line. This way nobody will have to stand in line outside. No sense antagonizin' these people any more than we have to. But first things first, where's that food y'all promised me?"

Nervous laughter accompanies George's handing over the box with a flourish. Those on the driver's side of the bus stand and make their way to the door. Their appearance precipitates another round of shouts and threats from the growing crowd. The would-be voters and their companions walk with heads held high but without making eye contact with anyone in the surrounding crowd. Fear and resolve. This act of assertiveness is at once selfish and selfless. Those who register themselves now pave the way for generations that will do so later, hopefully without the threat that exists here today.

Several reporters, some with TV cameras are making their way to the square. The crowd reacts variously with jeers and by preening, wanting for different reasons to be seen on TV.

✻   ✻   ✻   ✻

Across the square at a booth in the Magnolia Restaurant, Marshal Claude Davenport sits with the two F.B.I. agents, Jack Knight and Oscar Brandt. Knight wavers at Davenport's request that the two agents provide transportation for Sheriff Turner whom they will arrest dramatically in a few minutes on the steps of the courthouse. Knight says, "I don't know about this, Oscar. We don't really have any jurisdiction. And we're supposed to be investigating the kidnapping and murder of the preacher anyway."

Brandt laughs sarcastically. "Right, Jack. Like we're gonna get anything done here today with all this other stuff going on. Besides, I'd like to be around while the sheriff squirms a little. He's been such a prick about our being here, it'll be fun to see him being arrested—a little comeuppance for the fat bastard. Hell, if you don't want to come, I'll do it myself." Brandt still smarts from the treatment he has received as the Yankee intruder.

Knight's resistance evaporates. "OK. OK. I don't dare leave you alone with anybody down here. I'll go." Then to Davenport: "When are y'all gonna do this, Claude?"

The marshal looks at his watch and replies, "In about fifteen minutes. He's supposed to come out and try to arrest the next person who tries to enter the clerk's office. We'll be standing by and when he moves on that person, we'll move on him. He won't resist. This is all cleared, all the way to Montgomery and then on to Washington. It's not what I'd like to see happen, but I guess the boys upstairs know what they're doing."

Brandt snorts, "Huh … I can't wait to see this martinet act in public like the puppet he is in private. He's just a puffed up redneck. This will be a much-needed lesson in humility for him. I'll be sure that he doesn't miss the point."

Knight rolls his eyes and says, "See what I mean, Claude. The sheriff wouldn't be safe alone with him. All right, let's go on over there and get this over with. It'll be kinda nice to see Wallace. I've read a lot about him. We've got a pretty good-size file on him, but I've never seen him in person."

The three men make their way across the square that is growing more crowded by the hour. Sheriff Turner stands at the door to his office, preparing to make a grand entrance. People in the crowd begin calling for him to do something to stop this influx of people into Billy Wayne's office. As the marshal and the two agents near the courthouse, Jimbo hitches up his pants, steps out onto the sidewalk, and approaches a black man and his white escort who are at the curb.

He reaches out and grasps the arm of the black man saying in a loud voice, "Hold on. We've had enough of you and your friends' crap here for one day. You're under arrest for trespassing and unlawful assembly." He was just saying whatever came to mind. He hadn't thought and no one had told him what the charges were supposed to be.

Davenport at once steps in and removes the sheriff's hand from the man's arm. He tells the man to proceed to the clerk's office and says quietly to Turner, "You're under arrest for obstruction of justice, Sheriff. Please come with me and these two gentlemen."

The crowd, which had begun to cheer Jimbo's actions, now voices their displeasure with these intruders:

"Leave 'im alone and let 'im do his job."

"Git outta here. Y'all ain't got no damn business here anyhow."

"Attaboy, Jimbo. Give 'em hell."

The furor increases in volume and intensity until Turner lifts a hand to quiet the crowd. "I 'preciate it folks, but y'all don't have to worry 'bout it. Th' guvnah will take care o' this. Y'all just leave it alone. It's gonna be all right." And the jeers toward the officers turn to cheers and whistles for the sheriff.

*   *   *   *

Red McKinney approaches one of the reporters, who is accompanied by a cameraman and asks, "Who're y'all with?"

The reporter looks surprised and says, "Channel 12. Haven't you ever seen the evenin' news? Who're you?"

"Oh yeah. Sure. Sorry, I'm Red McKinney from the *Opelika News*. I didn't recognize you. You look a lot different in person, but now that I know, I can see that it's you. Has the report about the coloreds registering to vote here hit the TV news yet?"

"Oh yeah. It was reported at noon. *The Post* put it out at noon their time, which gave us an hour to get it into our broadcast. Why d' you ask?"

"Well, I work for *The Post* part-time. I sent them the story. Somebody called me about it and I just came on over. What's th' deal with Jimbo … er … the sheriff?"

"I don't know for sure but I do know that he's going to Montgomery, because another of our guys is gonna be at the federal courthouse there to cover him going in and coming out. How do things look here?"

"So far there hasn't been any violence, but the natives are restless, if you know what I mean. It's almost three more hours 'til the clerk's office is supposed to close down for th' day. What are y'all gonna do? You gonna stay here or are you leavin' now that Jimbo's in custody?"

The reporter looks to the cameraman, who shrugs. "I'd like to stay long enough to see how many they actually get registered, but that's a long wait doin' nothin'."

"There was supposed to be a funeral at two for that preacher, but I've heard that it was been canceled. They're having a graveside service for the wife and her sister. If you want to go over there, you might could get some pictures or something. Maybe even talk to her if you want to." Red hands over his business card. "Call me and I'll tell you about the number that gets registered."

When the cameraman shrugs again, the reporter says, "Thanks. Maybe we'll go over there. I don't know if we'll take footage or not, but maybe I'll try to talk to her, if she has anything that she wants to say. Here, you take my card. I need the information in time for the six o'clock news. I'd appreciate it if you could call me as soon as you can."

*   *   *   *

Duke looks at the clock for the tenth time in the last fifteen minutes. *Four—oh—five. Time's creeping by like a tortoise on the uphill. Dull. That's what this is. Just damn boring. Nobody here. Most folks are out getting ready for the weekend and I'm stuck here at this desk. I've got work to do—but to hell with it. Got no energy for it. Got no interest in it. I don't wanna be here but don't really want to be anywhere else either. I just can't believe she's gone. Weird how I let myself get so caught up in her. Strange how little day-to-day life seems to matter without her being around. Stupid. I mean, I didn't even see her everyday. I never got to spend more than a few of hours with her at any one time. How can this be happening? What do I do? Not a damn thing—that's what. Get through th' day, then get through th' night. Endure—go through th' motions, and endure. Have I eaten yet today? Hell no. What's wrong with me anyhow? Wonder where she is right now. On a train somewhere. The Zephyr. What th' hell kinda name is that for a train anyhow?*

He glances again at the clock: Four—oh—eight. Gets up and paces around the desk and the area behind. Absently picks up the novel he's supposed to be reading and glances at the spine, Calderon de la Barca. Thinks, *To hell with it. Not today.* Tosses the book to the desk and watches as it slides over the edge and drops to the floor. *Who cares?* Sighs and sits again. Drums a pencil on the Formica desktop. Feels energy welling up under his diaphragm. Wants to shout. Or run. Or hit something.

Just as it seems as if he'll explode, he hears faint footsteps coming down the stairwell. He immediately thinks of Ann, but knows almost simultaneously that it isn't possible. Almost laughs aloud at himself. Claire appears, pale and haggard looking. She carries a notebook and a thin volume that is likely a special reading assignment. Even though she is pale, her eyes blaze with intensity. Her smile is at once warm and wicked. "Hi, sailor. How are ya?"

Duke's mounting stress dissipates. "Hi yourself. It's great to see you. And what do you mean 'sailor'?"

Her smile triggers his smile expands her smile. "You know, a girl in every port and all that. What's wrong with you? You look wrung out or something. Come hug me."

His smile grows as he rounds the desk to hold her semi-tight. "God you feel good. I'm OK really. A little down maybe, but happy that you've started healing. How are *you*? You're looking a little on the pale side."

"I feel good, but I haven't been outside for five days. I need a beer and to talk to someone who isn't in the medical field. Are you taking me out tonight or do I have to get really brazen and go to a bar alone?"

Teasingly, Duke looks at her sort of sideways. "So you think it's less brazen for a pretty woman to go out alone than to come right up and demand to be taken out? I mean this is pretty damn forward, don't ya think?"

Not missing a beat she turns and starts for the door, saying, "Oh well, if you don't want to take me out, I'm sure I can find somebody. I'll go hang out by the door to the men's room." Bats her eyes. Cocks her shapely hip and says, "Pick me up at the dorm at 7:30 sharp, or I really will find somebody else. Leave th' top down, Duke. I need fresh air."

"Wait." But she's gone without another word. He hears her climbing the stairs.

*   *   *   *

A gray sedan pulls away from the rear of the Macon County Sheriff's Department. Knight drives with Brandt beside him. Jimbo Turner sits silently in the back seat. Highway 80 is practically deserted this afternoon. Their exit from town is mostly unnoticed after the drama and formality of Turner's "arrest". The sun bearing down through the windshield makes Brandt glad that Knight insisted on driving.

"So how do you like riding in the backseat, Sheriff?" The mockery in Brandt's voice grates on Turner. He hadn't counted on having to put up with being harassed.

"It's a new experience for me. But I 'spect you've been back here a few times. That's how they recruit F.B.I. agents, ain't it? Find crooks that's got a little education and slap a ugly suit on 'em?" Jimbo relishes dishing back the sarcasm from Brandt.

Brandt is quick to respond though. "Yeah it's the total opposite with you sheriffs, I guess. You know—too dumb to be able to read and too fat for a decent suit of clothes. I'm guessing there's a pretty good reason that your uniform is brown."

Anger rises red to Jimbo's neck and face. He can think of no suitable rejoinder, so he stays quiet until Brandt begins to laugh, then he says, "Wait 'til th' smoke settles, old son. This little story ain't half told yet. You'll be back in my town before all's said and done. Then we'll see who's laughin'. I've tried to treat you as well as possible under the circumstances. But bein' a damn Yankee, you ain't got enough sense to understan' that. When things git tough by and by, you just remember what I'm sayin'." Eyeing Knight in the review mirror he adds, "You're a good southern boy; what'd you do so bad that you got stuck with this asshole?"

Knight chuckles and says, "Well somebody had to do it I guess. Maybe it's just my turn in th' barrel. He's OK most of th' time, but like you said, he just don't understand."

*   *   *   *

Following Miss Julia's announcement that the Freedom Riders and Stokley Carmichael are still en route and should be in town tomorrow, the separate crowds of Negroes and whites slowly disperse. As more and more people exit the area, the tension that had crackled in the air diminishes. Colored talk quietly among themselves and, keeping eyes averted, return to their homes or churches.

Preston McCormack says to those nearby, "He ain't comin'. This ain't nothin' but a big rigmarole, and now he ain't comin'. Him and that bunch of so called Freedom Riders are all scared to come back into this state."

Rube Townsend shakes his head. "Naw, he'll be here all right. He's done run his big mouth on national TV, so you can bet he'll be here. He wouldn't miss an opportunity for a little more camera time. He might've had trouble findin' enough volunteers this time around though. Maybe that's what's holdin' up th' show; but don't you worry, he'll turn up. An' when he does, he'll get th' same reception that th' last bunch got. Me and Lester Cogburn set th' torch to that 'un up in Anniston ourselves. I ain't got no compunction 'bout doin' it again."

McCormack and Townsend huddle and make their plans to meet the next morning to drive to Tuskegee. They plan to disrupt the attempts at registration by mobilizing the locals in the absence of their leaders. Blankenship supplies them with the names and phone numbers of several people who might be persuaded to join them. That done, the three separate groups gather at the motel where the men from Tuskegee are quartered, and spend the evening drinking and talking.

*   *   *   *

When Lynn and Tilly Wilkins come out of the recovery room on third floor, several relatives who have gathered at the waiting area welcome them. After telling of the horror of seeing her father with various tubes and electrical wires running into and onto him, Lynn allows the family to take over some of the responsibility of the vigil. She returns to the motel room and falls into an exhausted sleep.

Tilly, who is now the center of family attention, braces up and stays at the hospital. She's back in control now, wearing the sympathy of her sisters and Robert Earle's family like a mantle for her pain. Suddenly she is the essential strong southern female, bearing her fears with grace and dignity.

✳   ✳   ✳   ✳

The few who had not heard of the funeral's cancellation have been turned away. Four figures in black stand hunch-shouldered at a fresh grave. The casket bearing the remains of Eldred Maxwell has already been lowered and the Reverend Milton Mohammed is speaking.

"Those few of us gathered here know the worth of this man better than all others who knew him. We have been his constant companions over these many years. Even his children who are in missions in far off lands don't know him as we do. He was a quiet man, but his quiet demeanor should never be confused with weakness or a lack of enthusiasm. He was a man who prized action over words, deeds over promises, results over fanfare. We know of the generosity of his heart, and the amazing depth and richness of his spirit.

"Eldred, my friend, my brother, you gave far more than you ever took. You left each and every place and person you touched better than before you came. You saw the future and took steps to influence it. You created opportunities for others to let their lights shine. You fed the hungry. You gave shelter to the less fortunate. You ministered to the sick and infirm. You gave comfort to those who were in pain. For all the gifts that you gave and for the opportunity of having walked along with you for this short time on earth, we are grateful.

"You are lost to us now on this physical plane, but you will live forever in the hearts and minds of those whose lives you touched. Your influence on others will carry on down through the generations from mother to son and son to granddaughter. Your spirit dwells among us even now as we commit your body back to mother earth.

"Ashes to ashes and dust to dust. We bid you goodbye, our friend and companion."

The four figures bend and scoop handfuls of dirt to toss into the open grave. As they turn to leave, Mohammed signals to the two men seated under a nearby oak tree to complete the task of covering the grave. Then the four walk slowly toward the entrance to the cemetery adjoining the church.

From the window of the Channel 12 news van, the reporter asks if Miz Maxwell has any message that she would like to deliver. Eudora grimly shakes her head and continues toward her home across the street. Then she stops and approaches the van. "Phrase this any way you want to, but I want it to be known that I do not intend to rest until those responsible for my husband's death are brought to justice. This was a senseless and ruthless murder. I have identified the abductor to the authorities and nothing has been done; but I *will not rest* until justice is done—no matter how long it takes, no matter what I have to do."

The reporter then says, "I'll report it just like that Miz Maxwell. We took a few seconds of film while the four of you were at the gravesite; do you mind if we use it on the air tonight?"

"That will be fine, young man. Thank you for asking. Your mama raised you with good manners. That's becoming all too rare these days."

When the four mourners have disappeared into the church manse, the reporter looks at the cameraman and says, "I've lived in these parts all my life and I don't believe a killing like this will be solved; but I'd sure hate to be the man that pulled the trigger on the good Reverend Maxwell, because that lady means what she said."

*   *   *   *

The gray sedan bearing agents Brandt and Knight along with Sheriff Jimbo Turner glides up the drive to an antebellum home in Montgomery. The grounds are immaculately kept and expansive. Ornamental trees and plots of flowers interrupt the acres of closely cropped grass.

Jimbo's head still spins from his appearance before Judge Frank Johnson. He had expected his time there to be simple and that the judge would go easy on him. Not so however. In the courtroom he had to formally plead "not guilty" to the crime of obstruction of justice. Judge Johnson had looked down on him from his lofty perch and explained the seriousness of the crime. He then went on to state the possible punishments if he was found guilty, which included up to two years in the federal prison as well as impossibly high fines. In very stern terms the judge said overtly that he was disinclined to release Turner before his hearing date. At that point Jimbo had begun to sweat. But in the end the judge relented. On the advice of the federal prosecutor, he released him with the warning that should he miss his trial date or fall further into noncompliance with federal laws, this release would be revoked. He would, the judge said, go to Atlanta until the time of his trial.

Rarely had Oscar Brandt enjoyed an appearance at court. Today was a special occasion, however. The longer Turner stood in front of Judge Johnson, the more unsettled he became. Brandt could see the perspiration pop out on his forehead and could almost feel the effect of the judge's words on the country sheriff. Seeing Turner's hands shaking from the tension almost made Brandt feel sorry for him—almost.

Now the sedan comes to a crunching halt underneath the porte-cochere. A tall liveried black man steps forward and opens the passenger doors. He directs Knight to park the sedan in a designated area. When Knight returns to the doorway, the three are escorted inside and then down a hallway to the library.

Governor Wallace sits in one of two leather armchairs that face a large mahogany cabinet that holds a TV. Looking up he nods toward the two F.B.I. agents and says to Jimbo, "Come on over here, Sheriff, and sit with me. The news should be startin' any minute now."

He waves to the agents, "There's a couple of chairs there if you'd like to sit." Brandt and Knight make their way to straight-backed chairs sitting against the wall across the room.

Wallace returns to the armchair and another liveried black man appears with a silver tray that holds two old fashioned glasses. The servant sets the tray on a table between the chairs without comment. Wallace says, "Bourbon and water. I s'pose that's agreeable to you, Sheriff?" Jimbo nods, elated.

Wallace adds to the retreating servant, "Willis, see if these other gentlemen would care for a drink." They ask for water and the servant disappears.

"Sheriff, I hope that your time in front of Judge Johnson wasn't too unpleasant. He doesn't care much for me, you know."

After a sip of the governor's excellent whiskey, Jimbo replies, "I gotta admit, Guvnah, the man scared th' hell outta me. I thought he was gonna lock me up for sure."

Wallace's laugh is like a stone in a matchbox, dry and without inflection. "I'm sure he enjoyed makin' you sweat. He and I don't see eye to eye on most things happenin' these days. He seems to want to do anything that will make me look bad or even just make my life miserable. But I'll tell you something, Sheriff. I'm gonna have the last laugh on 'im … Hold on here's th' news comin' up now."

The Channel 12 anchor states that informed sources in Tuskegee, Alabama report that 637 coloreds have registered to vote today, making this the largest number of voters to register on any day in any county in the state's history. As he is reading these statements, film footage of Negroes being escorted by whites or others Negroes from buses into the courthouse at Tuskegee plays on the screen.

Then the reporter's face appears on the screen and he says, "Sheriff James Turner attempted to halt this process by seeking to arrest the would-be voters at the base of the steps to the courthouse." His face is replaced by footage of Jimbo's approach to the colored man and his white escort. Davenport, Knight and Brandt then appear to intercept Turner and to lead him away.

"Sheriff Turner was subsequently arrested by federal agents and charged with obstruction of justice. He was removed from the area and transported to his indictment before Judge Frank M. Johnson in Montgomery. At broadcast time Sheriff Turner was still in custody, though sources close to these events have stated that he will be released on his own recognizance at some point this after-noon or evening."

As he watches the images of himself play across the screen, the words being spoken are largely lost on him. Jimbo is excited and awed at being the focal point of such a story. He looks across at Wallace who nods and says, "Good job, Sher-iff."

With their attention drifting from the TV they almost miss the reporter's shift into: "In other news from Tuskegee…." Then the footage of four solitary mourn-ers at a gravesite, as the reporter drones on about Miz Maxwell's pledge to stay the course in pursuing justice in her husband's murder.

Wallace turns abruptly to Turner and says, "Sheriff, you hafta find the killah of that preacher. If you don't, this is gonna cause more harm than good. How is that investigation goin'?" Hearing this Brandt is at once attentive.

Jimbo stammers, "Well, Guvnah, we ain't got much to go on … Eudora, that's the preacher's wife, she's sayin' that she saw a local man, a Mr. Blanken-ship, at the scene; but he has four witnesses that put him across town at a card game for a long time before and after the preacher got took off. It was dark and she was a good ways away from where she claimed to have seen 'im. She couldn't identify what color of vehicle, a license plate number, how many others there might have been. Nothin'. I don't see how I could arrest a member of the County Commission on that kind of evidence. I questioned him and the others in that card game myself and their stories sounded legit to me. There was a bunch of windows shot out of the preacher's church and we picked up some of the shells, but couldn't get much from 'em."

He nods toward Knight and Brandt. "These fellas here tried to question 'em too, but only succeeded in pissin' 'em off. They were callin' it a kidnapping. Now I guess they're callin' it a kidnap/murder. We just ain't got no evidence right now. Nobody else in that neighborhood has agreed with Eudora about what she's sayin' that she saw."

Wallace looks skeptical but says only to keep him informed. He then thanks the sheriff for his help in this matter and assures him that state's attorneys are already at work to have the registration of the coloreds declared illegal. As he ushers the three men to the door, he says he's certain that this will stand the test of legal scrutiny.

Crunching across the driveway toward the sedan, Turner is reeling with the stimulation of the day. He can't help feeling prideful at being this close to the center of power in the state. But at the same time, doubt nags at the recesses of his subconscious. Wallace, who had always seemed so much on the side of the common white man, today allowed 637 blacks to register to vote in Turner's county, without so much as lifting a finger to stop it. He allowed the federal officers to arrest Turner, and stand him before Judge Johnson for a reaming out. He even admitted to "fixing" things with the feds. And now he's pushing for Turner to pursue solving the killing of this colored preacher. Jimbo allows himself the unthinkable thought: *Whose side is he on anyhow?*

CHAPTER 26

▼

Seven—fifteen and the sun is almost down. Duke has showered and shaved. White jeans and a sleeveless black T-shirt feel good in the warmth. The T'Bird, full of gas, wants to roar off into the night. He can almost feel it tugging against inertia, sucking his weejuns down toward the floor. He won't need his dark sunglasses much longer, but will wear them anyway. Since Claire left the library, this afternoon he has felt a little better. He needs to shake off the darkness that had settled over him—shackled spirit straining to be free.

He cranks the radio. The Beach Boys' harmony infects him and, as he cruises slowly along Roosevelt Drive, music seems to echo off the walls of the buildings. Something almost holy about that sound. Pulled along now. Anticipation takes hold and his eyes dance. Hungers just to hold someone and to be held. Claire, once unapproachable, now connected to him inseparably. The thought of her sweet intensity pulls at his heart. The memories of her so multi-faceted now— physical, visual, tactual, and … the taste, the smell of her. Sweetness and sensuality. And, perhaps known only to him, vulnerability.

He pulls to the curb and before he can open his door to collect her, sees her walking toward him, hand out, palm up. The unspoken message: "Don't get out, I can get there by myself." He wonders where her insistent independence comes from. Even pale from being inside for so long and from whatever effects of the trauma, there is still a radiance about her that he has only rarely known. The short skirt doesn't hurt either.

"What are you grinning about? Did I do something unladylike?"

"No. I just like looking at you. You look great. That's my favorite skirt."

Deadpan she says, "It's brand new. You've never seen it." Leans across and pecks him on the cheek. "But I like your taste in things.… like this car. Let's just ride for a while, OK?"

He agrees happily. "I was thinking about that very thing on the way over here." Drives out to College Street and turns left. Through town and across the railroad tracks. Hammering down, the force pulls their heads back to the headrests. The power of the pull is a thrill all to itself. She reaches for the radio and turns the volume up even more. A few houses and then open farmland flash past. Hills and flats. Scattered cattle in verdant fields. Ponds. No traffic—just blasting along with the music and the wind. He can sense her relaxing as they get to the edge of town. At 80 mph the fourth gear overdrive shifts out and he backs off the accelerator. Leans back and relaxes himself. Thinks, *Thank you, Claire.*

As he's about to give voice to that thought she turns and says, "Thank you for this. I was about to burst to get out. Before you ask, I'm fine—fully functional and healthy. Being fussed over for almost five days is not my idea of a good time. The nurses meant well and all that; but really, they were just afraid of my father. Speaking of whom, he said to tell you hello and thanks again. How'd you like him?" Her flat, almost sardonic, voice is pleasant to hear.

"To be honest, he was a little scary at first. But after I got over that, I liked him. He's a straight shooter and I don't know many adults who do that with people our age. Pretty clear where your take charge spirit comes from."

With mock incredulity she says, "Hah. He's a teddy bear. All bluster and fake indignity … Well, maybe not all fake. I guess he's pretty tough in the court room, but at home he's just a pushover."

"Maybe for you. I doubt very many people can get anything over on your dad, though. I know I wouldn't want to tangle with him … Now you on the other hand …" Wolf grin.

They approach the intersection with Highway 280 and he automatically begins to turn right. Her hands on the dash, she sits bolt upright. "No. Don't go that way. Go back through town."

Slowing down he turns back to the left into a lazy, swooping U-turn, coming back to face the sinking sun. "Whoa. What?"

She crosses her arms and looks perplexed. Brow furrowed, jaw clenched. She waits a moment before answering. "I just didn't want to go back past the hospital. Too many fresh memories … It's gonna take some time to get over all that's happened."

Duke squints and asks, "What do you mean get over what's happened? I thought you said that you were … uh … let's see, 'fully functional and healthy'."

Going easy on the accelerator now. Cruising instead of blazing. Not even outrunning the quiet rumble of the V-8.

"Get over th' guilt, you idiot." Stops. Looks astonished at herself. Turns to Duke. "Sorry. I didn't mean you. Me! I have to. Nobody can understand how I feel about all this. It was a terrible thing to go through, Duke. I feel so many things at once—like I did something wrong, like something is somehow missing in me, like I'm no good anymore, like I violated some basic rule, both getting pregnant and then going through with the abortion." She's shaking her head and staring into middle space.

Embarrassed, he manages only, "I'm sorry, Claire. I didn't understand—and I guess I still don't. I thought that you had decided it was the best thing ... and so that was it."

"It *is* the best thing. But that doesn't mean that everything about it was OK. I don't know, Duke. There's just so much emotion going through me that I hadn't expected. I don't know what to do. Somehow, knowing *about* something is incredibly different from experiencing it."

Nodding he agrees, "Yeah. I think that we talked a little about that before. Do you want to find something to eat? ... Wait. Look at the sunset before you decide. We won't get to see this one again."

That brings a smile. "You're such a corny romantic. But I love that about you ... Yes, I'm ready for food. How about the War Eagle Supper Club? They have a good steak and daddy sent money for us to go out on."

Duke is past feeling self-conscious about being broke. "Sounds good. That's nice of your dad, especially with my next paycheck being a week away. I've never eaten there."

As they bump over the tracks coming back into downtown, Duke spies Teddy Bear standing on the corner at Glenn. He coasts over to the curb and says, "Hey Teddy Bear. How are ya?"

Teddy Bear looks at Claire and then back at Duke and says, "Y'all ain't gonna believe this. Aurelia dumped me. Twice. This week. *I* can't believe it."

Claire laughs aloud and says, "You don't really look all that broken up about it. Do you wanna come with us to eat at the War Eagle?"

"Can't. Gotta big quiz in 442 tomorrow. I haven't even read the theories yet, much less worked any of the problems. Gonna be a looong night. I still can't believe that she dropped me in favor of some fraternity puke. All I can say is that he deserves what he's gonna get. Gotta go." Grinning a bearish grin, he crosses the street in front of them, headed to his apartment. From the other side of the street, he yells back at Duke, "I'm ready for California whenever you are." Waves and turns back toward home.

The T'Bird eases back out into the traffic lane and up the slight hill near the Heart of Auburn Inn. Duke says absently, "I'm glad he didn't come with us."

"Me, too; but asking him was the right thing to do. What was that about California?"

"Oh just a joke about something we teased about one night. You're right though, ya gotta take care of your friends. Sooner or later they'll have to take care of somebody, too … Might even be you. But for sure if we all keep doin' that, it'll come back around."

Claire's brow furrows as she responds, "I feel like I've got a big debt to pay."

"I don't think it works that way, Claire. I don't think there's an accounting. Mostly we're just in this thing together and help each other out as we go along. The easier I make it for you, the more likely that somewhere down the road someone will make it easier for me."

By now the T'Bird has eased through town and out past the Casino. Still further out Highway 29, the War Eagle Supper Club sits on the left-hand side of the road. The place has always seemed vaguely mysterious to Duke. Inside it's outfitted like a down-home restaurant with wooden chairs and tables for four scattered across a large open space, but with a bar against the wall on the left-hand side. Linoleum over concrete floor A jukebox sits on the right against the far wall, some bluesy kind of music playing. An opening, like a window, leads into what must be the kitchen in the back right-hand corner. Two private rooms and three booths are arrayed in front and down the wall to the kitchen. Dim lighting reinforces the mysterious atmosphere.

Claire shows the doorman a card and they go in. They sit at a booth across from the jukebox and order steaks and beer. The stub of a candle on the table softens her features and casts a golden glow. Her eyes are dark pools that draw him down and down—into her magic. Flecks of red fire glitter as her hair catches the candlelight. He leans forward on elbows and says, "Are you better now?"

"Well, some better at least. I probably won't really be better for a long time— maybe ever. It's not something that I would have ever expected to go through. Now it's done and I can never un-do it. There's so much difference between what I think and how I feel. Sometimes it hits me out of the blue and I just get sad. Other times I don't think of it at all for hours … I'm sure that in time I'll be fine, but I'm not very pleased with me right now."

Their food arrives and conversation lapses for a while as they eat. Her appetite is ferocious for such a little thing. Distracted by thoughts of Ann, Duke wishes he could talk about it, but it doesn't seem appropriate. Wonders about Claire's true feelings toward him.

With a piece of steak impaled on her fork, Claire asks, "What do you think about all the stuff going on in Tuskegee?"

Interested, he replies, "What stuff? I mean, I know about the funeral, but that's it. Something else going on?"

"I'll say. You remember Stokley Carmichael saying he was gonna bring a new wave of Freedom Riders into the state? Well, instead of going to Selma, like he said they would, they went to Tuskegee. They've been escorting all those people we know into the county clerk's office, and registering them to vote. The news said that over 600 people registered today. The Sheriff over there was arrested when he tried to stop them. Then Miz Maxwell closed the burial of Reverend Maxwell, and has announced that there will be a memorial service on Sunday instead. She looked pretty bad on TV."

Duke whistles soft and low. They share a smile and the feeling that their efforts, however small, helped a little in this turn of events. Claire continues in a conversational tone, "The news on TV showed a shot of the square and there were a lot of whites milling around and yelling things, but they didn't report any violence today. I guess I'm kinda surprised about that. Aren't you?"

He considers for a moment and then says, "A little maybe, but I know that most of the white opposition leaders are out of town. In fact, most of them are over in Selma waiting for the Freedom Riders to show up. That's hilarious …"

The front door opens and George Blankenship walks unsteadily into the room. He looks around and heads to the bar where he gets a beer. Turning to survey the room again, he spies Duke and weaves his way to the table.

"Duke, where th' hell've you been? I went by the Union a couple of times lookin' for ya. Wanted to get set for that bridge thing in Atlanta on Saturday. We're still going ain't we?"

Duke can smell the alcohol on him. "As far as I know we are. I haven't seen Terry for a couple of days either; I've just been busy as hell. Sit down and join us. You know Claire, don't ya?"

George looks at Claire and says, "Nope. I don't believe I've had the pleasure." Extends his hand and moves to sit at their table. "George Blankenship. Pleased to meet ya. You're a pretty thing. Duke's got a way of turning up with pretty women." He turns toward Duke and says, "I'll sit for a minute, but I've gotta get outta here and back to th' house pretty quick."

He speaks to Duke, completely ignoring Claire, saying, "Big doin's in 'Skegee, my friend. Busloads of niggers troopin' in an' out of the county clerk's office, claimin' they're registered to vote, good as any white man. Federal marshals all over th' damn place. Th' sheriff's been arrested and hauled off to Montgomery to stand in front of that bastard Judge Frank M. Johnson. And nobody's doin' a damn thing to stop all that shit. It's amazin'." Nods to Claire, "'Scuse my language, ma'am."

Duke says, "I just heard about all that myself. Hard to believe. Never thought I'd live to see the day when that many coloreds would register to vote in this state. So folks over there are just leavin' them alone and lettin' them do it, huh?"

George leans in a little closer to the table and semi-whispers, "You 'member when I told you that my daddy an' 'em was goin' to Selma? Well, without them being around, most ever'body else is too scared to do anything. 'Course with all them federals over here even daddy might not be able to do anything. I talked to him this afternoon an' one of his buddies got killed over there in Selma. There was apparently a big fight and Eugene Hill got shot an' killed by some nigger kid. Th' damn sheriff and more federals over there are makin' daddy an' 'em stay in town 'til there's some kinda lineup or something."

As George drinks, Duke glances quickly at Claire, then back saying, "That doesn't sound good, George."

"Ah hell, it ain't nothin' to worry about. Daddy said that th' guvnah's gonna fix the votin' list; so all this registerin' don't mean nothin'. An' he told me that some of his friends from other places around th' state are gonna come to town tomorrow and crack a few heads in Tuskegee. We can't let these people get away with this shit whether th' guvnah fixes the voters list or not. They'll run us out of our own damn town if we let 'em get started with it."

Trying not to seem overanxious Duke says, "I hear ya, George. What d'you think they'll do?"

"Prob'ly just beat th' hell out of a few of 'em and that'll more than likely put th' qui-e-tus on th' whole thing. They're comin' in th' mornin'. Oughtta be a sight t'see. I'm gonna go down there myself an' watch 'em."

Duke finishes his beer and makes to get up for another. "You want another one of those, George?"

Blankenship looks at his bottle and thinks the better of it. "Nah. Thanks though. I gotta be goin' home ... Wait. Tell ya what, I'll take one in a go cup. Momma's at th' house by herself an' she gets scared; so I better go on."

Duke says, "Let's meet at the Kettle Saturday mornin' at about seven-thirty. Th' mornin' session over there is for the pros. The Open Session's th' one that

Terry and I are playin' in an' it doesn't start 'til two. That'll give us plenty of time. We might even get to watch some of th' big boys play a little. Sound all right?"

Getting up George says, "Yeah. That'll be good. I'll pick Terry up on my way in."

He turns back to Claire. "Nice to meetcha, pretty lady. Sorry that we got all caught up in our own talk and I didn't get to know you better. Maybe another time." With that he joins Duke at the bar, takes the cup he offers, and walks out the door and into the night.

Duke returns to the table with a beer that he divides between their two glasses. "Well, now you've met my friend George. He's actually a pretty nice guy—at least some of the time. Interesting about the plans for tomorrow, don't you think?"

Under a level gaze Claire says, "I'll tell you what I think. I think that we need to finish this meal and call Doc Mohammed and let him know that there's gonna be trouble there tomorrow."

Duke nods. "Sure. We can go and let Judd know and he can make th' call."

"I have the key to Pax's place. We can make the call ourselves. The sooner the better."

✳   ✳   ✳   ✳

Milton Mohammed trudges from his car to his front door just after nine o'clock. It has been a long and emotional day. He is weary and longs for the bed, knowing that tomorrow may be a little easier or may be a little worse—but it will be just as long. Hangs his jacket in the closet. Loosens the tie and pulls it through the collar. Unbuttons the white shirt. Sits on the edge of the bed to untie his shoes.

The phone jangles in his ear. The temptation is to ignore it, pretend that he hasn't come through the door yet. But he reaches for the receiver. "Hello."

"Hello, Doc, this is Duke. How're you this evening?"

"I'm bone weary, Duke, but otherwise fine. Have you heard about the good news here in Tuskegee today?"

"Yes, I just heard this evening. Congratulations. In fact, that's part of the reason I'm calling. I guess that your folks are intending to continue with their registration tomorrow, right?"

Mohammed pauses, as if he dreads hearing what's to come. "That's right. We're gonna go on with this tomorrow and then Stokley and his bunch will head out to Selma to join the big rally. Why?"

"Doc, I just heard tonight that a group of whites from other parts of the state are intending to come there tomorrow morning and, as they said, 'crack some heads'. I thought you should know about it."

Another pause as Mohammed processes this information. Finally he says, "Oh my ... You're right, Duke. It's good that you called. I don't know exactly what to do right now, but I'll figure it out. Thanks for calling me. If you don't mind, where did you hear this?"

"George Blankenship told me at the bar. He'd been drinking before he got there and was pretty loose with his information. Hold on a second. Claire's here and wants to say hello."

In his mind Mohammed can picture Claire's pixie face as she chirps her hello and congratulations. He knows nothing of the recent troubles in her life. In the end he thanks her and asks her to pass his appreciation along to Duke again as well.

After the conversation is finished, he sits and ponders what to do next. In a few minutes he calls Atlanta and turns the problem over to those higher in the chain of command. Then he turns out his light and embarks on a largely sleepless night.

*   *   *   *

Claire hangs up the phone and says impulsively to Duke, "Let's stay here tonight. There's no food, but there is a TV and I can make coffee. I don't want to go back to the dorm. In fact, why don't you go to the Sani-Freeze and get some ice cream while I make coffee and wash my face."

They try to stay up for the late news, but after the ice cream and coffee, the intensity of the week sends them quickly and soundly to sleep.

*   *   *   *

The phone startles Reverend Joe Lee Cleveland awake, his heart pounding. Before picking up the receiver at the third ring he realizes that it is probably Andy calling back from Atlanta. The young Atlantan had called earlier to report that Mohammed had informed them that there was to be trouble tomorrow in Tuskegee. He said that Washington had promised "assistance", but he hadn't been clear what that meant. He was probably calling back to tell Joe Lee what form it would take.

"Hello."

A harsh voice growls, "We know your church is bein' used by them outsiders."

Cleveland stammers out, "What? Who is this? What do you want?"

"It don't matter who I am. What matters is that you know we know what's goin' on. If more niggers show up downtown tomorrow, you'll be sorry. One nigger preacher's done found out th' hard way—one more won't matter much to us."

"I don't have anyth …"

"You been warned."

The line then clicks off. Dead. Joe Lee sits for several minutes regaining some little bit of composure. The man left little doubt that his words were not threat, but promise. Joe Lee does what he knows best to do. He slides off the bed and onto his knees and asks God to help him and his people to have the strength to do the right thing.

CHAPTER 27

▼

With the morning sun in his eyes, Ruben Townsend pilots his 1960 Chevrolet Impala at the front of a three car caravan headed toward Tuskegee. Three of the men he trusts most ride with him in the Chevy. Another four men from Elmore County follow Rube, and trailing along at the rear, Preston McCormack drives the other three Gadsden men. McCormack isn't enthusiastic about this venture, but fears retribution from his friends and neighbors if he doesn't go along. Townsend specifically invited them on this foray and though McCormack imagines that there is a certain amount of honor in being selected, he can't get excited about the project.

When the twelve men assembled to leave Selma, there was some laughing about being the twelve disciples headed for a Come-to-Jesus meeting. Secretly, McCormack wonders if he is the Judas of the bunch.

They've been on the road for over an hour and a half, edging around the early morning traffic of Montgomery by using back roads and shortcuts known to Townsend, and are now, at nine o'clock, only a few minutes from the city limits of Tuskegee. Looking ahead, Townsend notices two olive green jeeps sitting, one on either side of the highway. He waves as his car passes them and wonders aloud, "Why are these Army vehicles sitting out here in th' middle of nowhere?"

Soon the caravan approaches the downtown area and a roadblock looms ahead. Rube rolls his window down and creeps up to the enlisted man who is directing traffic away from the square. "What's goin' on? Why can't I drive on into the square?"

The sergeant's answer is curt. "The square's closed to traffic today, sir."

"Yeah, I can see that. Why?" Rube is annoyed at the inconvenience and even more annoyed at the Yankee accent of the sergeant. Color shows on his face and bald head.

"Don't know, sir. Just doing my job. Please move along, there's more traffic behind you. Parking for downtown is 'off-street' and behind some of these buildings." Steps back. Blows his whistle and waves to Townsend to turn left and continue.

Muttering, Townsend leads the other cars down a block, turns right and finds parking in a vacant lot immediately behind the Magnolia Restaurant. The twelve walk together toward the square. As they approach, they notice a couple of armed soldiers standing in the intersection of Main at the square. Nearing the corner they can see nothing but soldiers and Army vehicles. With their weapons slung, soldiers are arrayed at fifteen-foot intervals in the gutters all around the square, leaving the sidewalks free. Jeeps and two-and-a-half ton trucks line three of the streets with one side of the square left open. At the curb on the open side sits a bus, engine running. A stream of mostly black men and women walk from it toward the courthouse in single file.

As the group from Selma prepares to cross into the square, several soldiers unsling their weapons to the port arms position and face them. A young corporal says, "Sorry, gentlemen. The square is closed to foot traffic. You may use the sidewalks to access businesses or government offices, but the streets around the square are closed."

Townsend grumbles, "Who says the square is closed?"

"Sir, my commanding officer told me and the president of the United States told him. That's all I know and all I need to know." No menace in the corporal, but no give either.

Over his shoulder Townsend says to the others, "Let's get some coffee." The twelve enter the Magnolia to discuss what, if anything, they might accomplish here today.

Marcie Brooks is walking toward the entrance from within as the men sit down. Townsend calls out to her, "'Scuse me, deputy. Do you work at the Sheriff's Department?"

Marcie surveys the group and answers. "That's right. I'm the daytime dispatcher. Can I help you?"

"Prob'ly so. What th' hell's goin' on out there? Where'd all them soldiers come from and what're they doin' here?" Rube leans back and waits for an answer.

"All we know is what th' guvnah's office told us. The soldiers were here when we got in this morning. Th' night dispatcher said that they showed up at about six o'clock and told him that the guvnah's office would be callin' to confirm their orders to seal off the square. 'Parently there's supposed to be some kinda violence planned for th' coloreds."

Townsend feels a cool breeze of anxiety. "What kinda violence?"

Marcie shrugs, "We don't know. The captain in command of th' troops said that he was told to expect men tryin' to disrupt th' voter registration. I guess Washington got antsy about things and activated this National Guard unit. Th' attorney general told th' sheriff earlier this week that he'd do that if there was trouble."

"Oh, I see," says Rube. "So did y'all have trouble over here yesterday?"

"That's just it; there wasn't no trouble at all. When the sheriff called Washington a while ago, they just said that they *heard* there was gonna to be trouble, and decided to head it off by sending these Yankee Guardsmen over here from Benning." Her body language suggests that the whole thing disgusts her.

McCormack asks nervously, "Reckon where they heard there was gonna be trouble? Did th' sheriff say?"

Marcie nods knowingly, "He asked, but they wouldn't say nothing. Don't matter much, I guess. Like th' sheriff says, 'We've got occupyin' troops right here in our own county.' He's not too pleased with th' whole deal … Look, I gotta get back."

*   *   *   *

Red McKinney sits unseen in a booth with his back to the front door of the Magnolia. When Marcie goes past him toward the front exit he offers her an air kiss, but she just rolls her eyes and walks on by. He eavesdrops on their conversation and his suspicions are aroused. The impulse is to go over and try to interview this new group, but he thinks better of it. Sits and listens instead.

What he hears from their low tones suggests that these men had come here today to cause trouble. Now they are frustrated and unsure as to how to proceed. He overhears them decide that after their breakfast they will spend the morning watching, and then go to Thad Blankenship's farm in the afternoon to await his return from Selma. The lineup there has been scheduled for one o'clock and he should be home no later than three-thirty.

＊   ＊   ＊   ＊

Stokley Carmichael stands in the center aisle of the bus. The side of the bus behind the driver is empty, but the others remain silent. Those on the bus still anticipate something happening, although they can only see military men on the square. Looking out the windshield, Stokley remarks to no one in particular, "I wonder how those guys out there feel about being sent here to guard us. I mean, they don't know us and for all we know, they might not even agree with what we're doing here. They're just white boys from the North caught up in this thing."

They have taken care to send mostly males on the first busload this morning. The warnings conveyed by Mohammed seemed serious. Seeing those Guardsmen there was great relief. Stokley radioed back to Mohammed and Sister Abney to send most of the remaining women on the next loads since no trouble has yet materialized.

From somewhere near the rear a voice replies, "Just doing their job. I surely hope we don't have to test their commitment though. Who knows what would happen then." All the passengers seem to hold their breath with the tension that lurks near the surface.

Across the square from them, a cluster of men enters the Magnolia. A few minutes later, the female deputy exits the restaurant and makes her way across to the courthouse. Stokley comments again to no one specifically, "Sho' is quiet out there. Maybe all these soldiers made whoever it was change their minds. We just might pull this off."

The first pair from the courthouse returns across the street and steps back into the relative safety of the bus. Questions bombard them from all quarters.

"What was it like?" "Who was in there?" "Was there any trouble?"

Stokley holds up a restraining hand. "Hold on a minute. Let 'em tell us." Then to the returning pair he says, "Tell us what it was like. Was it any different from what people said after yesterday?"

Alfred Anderson says in his flat Pennsylvania accent, "I was here yesterday and there was no difference in how the process was handled. The only difference I could tell was that there are six marshals inside the registration office instead of the two who were there yesterday. It was all very quiet and efficient."

His partner, Willie Williams of Tuskegee, smiles, nods and rasps, "Umm-hmm. Sho' was easy. Nuthin' to it."

Stokley feigns relief and says, "Great."

Underneath his expression however he's thinking, *Too damn quiet and too damn easy.*

*   *   *   *

Duke and Claire have put the ragtop up on the T'Bird in the early morning. He checks the tension on all the fasteners and opens the door for her. As she swings her legs inside, he grins and says, "I'm tellin' ya, that's my favorite skirt."

She smirks at him and he rounds the car and gets in, and backs out of the parking space. His glance crosses her and he asks with no little apprehension, "So how are things really between us, Claire? I mean where do we really stand with each other?"

She bats her eyes comically and in her best southern drawl says, "Why, Duke, whatevah can you mean?"

"No, seriously Claire. Like I've said to you before, I just wanna stay straight with you and for you to be straight with me ... I mean are we a couple now or something?"

The wistfulness in her face is so quickly gone that he can't be sure that it was actually there. She smiles, then laughs as she says, "Don't worry, Duke. I don't have my talons in you. I know that what goes on between us is a lot of things, but it ain't love, sweetie. I'm still engaged and you're still playing the field. Why do you ask? Gettin' scared?"

He fingers the switches that raise the windows and moves out of the parking lot and into traffic. "No ... well maybe. I don't know if 'scared' is the right word. It does seem a little strange to be so close without being committed. I don't know how you feel about things. We have such a good time together."

She settles back into the seat and staring ahead says, "Yeah. Being with you is special; but I don't have any illusions about who you are and who I am. Circumstances have sort of thrown us together in this crazy tangle. You were there for me when I had no one to turn to and I'll always be grateful for that. The sex has been great fun but it probably happened because of other needs. I was vengeful for a while. Then I was lonely and scared and in need of closeness. You? You're just a man, and I don't mean that in an ugly way. Men are just different—always looking to score. Don't look so surprised. Women know that about men."

As she speaks, Duke nods and relaxes, clearly relieved. When she stops, he says, "Well I gotta admit this is the best friendship I've ever had, or hope to have. I guess that's what you're sayin', right? That we're friends?"

"Yeah, Duke. It's the best friendship—and a lot more … By the way, I don't want to insult you or anything, but my dad sent an envelope for you."

He looks questioningly at her. "What sort of envelope?"

She holds up a white envelope that is sealed and marked with his name in a bold cursive hand. "This one. I'm sure that it has money in it. And I'm sure that you won't want to take it. I really hope that you won't be insulted or that you won't insult him by refusing his offering. It's all that he knows to do, and surely you can find a use for it.

Truly a dilemma. Duke lives on the edge of poverty, but he makes it—barely. He could certainly use the money. At the same time, he doesn't want his willingness to help Claire to be cheapened. He drives in silence and struggles with these conflicting ideas

"Before you refuse, take a day and think about it. I'll keep it and we'll talk tomorrow. Will you at least do that much for me?"

As she prepares to get out of the T'Bird at her dorm, he says, "Yeah, I'll think about it."

*   *   *   *

George drives into town around ten, anticipating seeing some real action this morning. The sight of armed troops in the downtown area is at first shocking, then infuriating. The sound of the SuperSport tearing around the periphery is loud as it echoes off the buildings. He parks at the rear of the sheriff's office and walks around to the front entrance. Inside the front door he sees the sheriff, Marcie, and Digger Hill. Nodding his head in Digger's direction, he says, "Real sorry to hear about Eugene, Digger. You goin' over there today?"

Hill returns the nod with an expression of disgust on his face. "Naw. Won't do no good to go over there 'til they finish the autopsy. Can't for th' life of me figger out why they'd want or need a damn autopsy. 'S pretty damn clear that he was shot and killed. Th' sheriff over there says that the federals always want a autopsy in a murder case, though. I reckon I'll go on Monday mornin'. They're 'sposed to be done by then. 'Preciate your kind words."

Then to the sheriff, George asks, "What's with th' damn Army out there, Jimbo? Who are they and where'd they come from?"

"Them's National Guard boys from New Jersey. They was activated by the attorney general on the order of yo' president. We was just talkin' about it when you came in. Katzenbach told me yesterday that if there was trouble here that he was gonna activate this bunch that was at summer camp at Bennin'. When I called his office a while ago, they'd only say that they'd heard that there was gonna be trouble here today and that they weren't takin' no chances that these people might get hurt. Wouldn't say how or who they heard that from; just said that it was done and that these boys would be here all day." Turner's frustration is apparent in his demeanor.

Marcie speaks up then, saying, "Oh, Sheriff, I forgot to tell you that there was a bunch of strangers over at th' Magnolia a while ago. They were askin' about th' troops, too. I haven't ever seen them before, but they seemed nice enough."

Jimbo shakes his head and responds, "I 'spect they's lots of strangers here today wantin' to see what's goin' on with these niggers an' their escorts. Prob'ly just a bunch of rubberneckers."

George's interest is piqued. At first he simply takes in the information and tries to absorb it. Marcie's input reminds him that his father's friends haven't been accounted for as yet. But something about the attorney general's having "heard" that there would be trouble bothers him. He can't quite grasp what it is but knows that something seems strange about that. Who would have told the federals? Who knew, for that matter?

Looking back toward Turner, George asks, "Is there anything you need me to do, Jimbo?"

"Just to be honest about it, George, I don't know what to do myself. 'Preciate th' offer though."

George turns to leave and, still puzzling, says to Hill, "Digger, come walk 'round th' square with me. I don't expect they'll bother me none if I'm with a deputy, and I'd like to check this out up close."

✳   ✳   ✳   ✳

In Selma Thad Blankenship, Collins, White and Parsons arrive at the sheriff's office after eating a breakfast meal for their lunch. They all have red, rheumy eyes and conversation has been sparse among them. Deputy Clarke escorts them to the now familiar conference room. After they arrange themselves around the table, Clarke says to them, "We got a little more news for you boys. Th' sheriff is gonna let that colored boy loose this afternoon. Th' medical man found gun powder residue on your friend Hill's shirt and even on his skin under th' shirt, but there wasn't no residue on th' boy's hands. Th' feds all agreed that if there was that much on Hill that there'd have to be some on th' boy. I 'spect they're gonna ask y'all to take a test for gunpowder, too."

White growls, "Why should we; we ain't done nothing."

Collins contradicts him by saying, "Naw, Cracker, if we don't it'll just make 'em that much more suspicious. I'm ready to get this over with an' get back to th' house. I got work to do. An' since these so-called Freedom Riders ain't comin' anyhow, I'd just as soon go tend to my own business."

This surprises Blankenship, who has never heard Collins be compliant about anything, but he agrees readily that being finished with the current difficulties will get them back to Tuskegee. They need, somehow, to cope with events there. "Swift's right. Let's try to get outta here and back home before they give th' whole damn town to th' niggers." Turning to Clarke he adds, "Deputy, you can tell whoever's in charge that we'll take th' test for th' gunpowder; but let's get things goin' here. We need to get home."

✳   ✳   ✳   ✳

Back in Tuskegee, George and Digger Hill spy Townsend and the others from Selma standing at the corner of East Northside Street at the square. George recognizes Townsend and approaches him saying, "Hey, Mr. Townsend. I'm George Blankenship. I think we met one time before, maybe in Montgomery or Union Springs. Nice to see y'all. Did y'all talk to my daddy over in Selma?" He pauses and nods toward Hill, "This here is Digger Hill, brother of th' fella that was shot over there."

Townsend has no recollection of George, but nods to Hill and says, "Sorry 'bout yo' brother. That's a crazy situation goin' on over there. I mean that kid was layin' there in th' street with th' gun in his hand and now the feds are questioning about who actually done th' shootin'.... Yeah, son, I talked to yer daddy, but he didn't say nothin' 'bout there bein' troops here." Knowing that the deputy is brother to the man killed in Selma is enough credentials for him to speak freely in front of him.

"We were gonna talk to some of the local folks here about trying to do something to stop this voter registration stuff; but we've been out here for an hour or more an' there ain't hardly nobody around. Where th' hell is ever'body, and why ain't they tryin to slow this down some?"

Hill speaks for the first time, "I'll tell ya. People are scared off by these troops. They figger they'll get shot if they even come out here today. Mostly folks are lookin' for somebody to lead them and all our leaders are gone right now."

Rube turns to George and says, "We told your daddy that we'd meet him at your farm around three-thirty. Why don't we meet somewhere for lunch and you can take us out there?" George agrees and they make arrangements to meet at the

Torch café for lunch on the way to the farm. George hurries back to the sheriff's office to call his mother and warn her that they will be coming this afternoon, and that there'll be a crowd for supper tonight.

Later, as he's winding along the narrow two-lane road headed home, George can't seem to let go of the fact that the attorney general somehow found out that there was supposed to be trouble in town today. He doubts that the information would have leaked from Selma—his dad and his friends are too careful for that. Who else knew?

A sickening dread creeps into his stomach along with the idea that he had told Duke about his father's friends coming to Tuskegee. He also remembers that he told Duke that all the community leaders were going to Selma and then these outsiders had mysteriously shown up the next day. He thinks ... *Nah. That's crazy. Duke's not connected to those kinds of circles.*

*   *   *   *

By three o'clock the last of the registrants have been processed and the two buses stand at the Red Hill church. A few from the last group linger still, talking quietly. Reverend Cleveland and Mohammed are in deep conversation with Stokley. Carmichael remarks, "I guess you gentlemen have just scared the local population into submission or something. I would have never believed this could happen in any town in Alabama, yet we've finished registering everybody who had been processed at the church, and a few that hadn't as well. And nobody's been hurt. I wish we could all stay for the memorial Sunday, but we need to get to the rally in Selma. Push our luck a little further, I guess."

The three men embrace. Mohammed looks into his friend Stokley's eyes and says, "Stoke, you know these white folks won't let this slide by this easily. I don't know what tricks Governor Wallace may have up his sleeve about it, but at least we struck the first blow. They'll have to undo it now. That's a position of strength, and it feels mighty good. Thank you for your courage and your bold idea in coming here."

Carmichael beams. "Why thank you for sayin' so, my brother. Don't forget that your information about the local Klan members bein' gone was what spawned the idea in the first place ... Better make sure that y'all say something to these folks that came with me as well. They didn't really even have a stake in this thing; well, at least all them white people out there didn't. Y'all really need to speak to them."

"Way ahead of you, Stokley," says Cleveland. "Our people here have kept up a constant stream of gratitude with those folks. We also have all their names and addresses and will be staying in touch with them as time goes by. Families here will adopt them and report to them as different things happen. But I'll echo Milton's words and say that we're especially grateful to you, and proud of your ideas. Thank you."

The three men move toward the waiting buses and Carmichael cautions, "Don't let that list get away from you Reverend. In fact you probably need to give one name to each of your families and keep no consolidated record. That could be way too much temptation for our pale-faced brethren."

Cleveland nods and the Riders are called to the buses. Hugs all around. A few tears. A lot of heart-felt emotion. The buses ease toward the highway and spontaneous applause breaks out. Then as the buses turn the curve everyone turns to the task of cleaning up. This is a time of small triumphs in rural Macon County, Alabama after lifetimes of defeat.

✳   ✳   ✳   ✳

The four Macon county men, free from their obligations in Selma, pull into the square just as the last of the National Guardsmen is leaving. The roadblocks are down. They passed two charter buses rolling out of town as they approach the city limits. Collins growls, "What's all that shit about? Where'd th' troops come from? Let's get over to Jimbo's and see what's goin' on."

Turner stands at curbside with his hands behind his back rocking back and forth slightly, his jaw locked in rage and frustration. When Blankenship and the rest get out of their trucks, and before they can ask any questions, he says snidely, "Well if this don't beat all. 'Bout time y'all got here. Actually it's a damn sight late to be draggin' your asses in here now. While y'all was over in Selma drinkin', th' damn president, th' attorney general and th' guvnah have just about give th' whole town away. Glad y'all could find your way back."

Rankled Collins snaps back, "Don't start no whole lot of shit with us Jimbo. We've about had a bait of law enforcement th' last couple of days. What th' hell you talkin' about—th' guvnah givin' th' town away?"

"I'll tell you what, Swift, you had plenty to say about how I dealt with them two F.B.I. boys before y'all sneaked out of town an' left me with it. I don't much give a damn how hard a time you've had. I got arrested by the federals and am just out here on my own recognizance. That asshole Judge Frank Johnson has threatened to put me in jail if anything else happens around here.

"Th' guvnah made a deal with the federals to let that registration business go on without doin' a damn thing to stop it and, of course, ever'body in town thinks it's my fault. He even staged me gettin' arrested, so it'd look like me and him was doin' somethin'. He pretty much demanded that I find out who killed th' preacher, too. I've had National Guard troops here all day keepin' me and th' rest of th' townsfolk from walkin' around in our own town. Now y'all wanna come in here and start a bunch of shit with me. I ain't gonna put up with nothin' from th' likes of you, Swift."

Blankenship quickly intercedes. "Whoa, Jimbo. Take it easy. We're not tryin' to start anything with you. We just want to know what happened. How deep is th' hole? What did th' guvnah say about the registration thing? How come th' troops were here? We're not mad at you. Not yet anyhow."

Turner isn't much mollified by Blankenship's words. "Th' guvnah says that him and his fancy lawyers will get these registerings declared illegal but I don't see it. Judge Johnson hates his guts and *he's* th' Federal judge 'round here. Th' 'hole' as you call it goes slap to China. They registered over 1100 people in two days accordin' to Billy Wayne. An' th' troops were here because th' attorney general called me and said that he had *heard* that a bunch of men was comin' over here and *crack a few heads* to stop them from registerin'. I'll tell y'all what, th' guvnah cut a deal and it's got me to wonderin' exactly which side he's really on."

Ricky Parsons laughs aloud and jibes, "Goddamn Jimbo, you're gettin' kinda worked up ain't ya? The guvnah? I'm pretty sure we know which side he's on."

Turner's thumbs are hooked in the belt that holds his holstered pistol. "Is that right? Lemme ask you somethin', Ricky. What exactly happened to them coloreds that went to Tuscaloosa and wanted to register to go to school? You know, when the guvnah stood in the schoolhouse door? What happened to them?"

Parsons looks confused. "Well, you know as well as I do that the feds sneaked them around to th' side of th' buildin' and got 'em registered anyhow. What's that got to do with anything?"

Red-faced Turner says, "Don't ya see? It was all just a big damn show. It was gonna happen like that all along and th' guvnah just did all that so's people would think that he was tryin' to stop 'em from goin' in. It was a put up job. Same shit as what happened here yesterday. Them coloreds are still in school at th' University, and I'll betcha that all our newly registered voters will, by god, be votin' next year, in spite of what th' guvnah says right now ... And yes, I am worked up. We've been had. Especially *I've* been had. I'll have to go back in front of Frank Johnson and he ain't gonna take kindly to me now that I'm lined up with th' guvnah."

The force of Turner's discontent silences the men as they consider the implications of what he has said. Blankenship breaks the spell asking, "Did you say that the attorney general actually said that somebody was gonna come over here and *crack some heads*? Did he use those words?"

"Yep that's what th' man said. What the hell difference does it make what words he used?"

Blankenship feels a surge of apprehension. "Maybe none, but it's got me to wonderin'. Seems kinda strange. Prob'ly don't mean nothin' though … Unless … You don't reckon they'd have my phone tapped, do ya?"

*　　　*　　　*　　　*

By nightfall, the ten-foot wide barbecue grill at the Blankenship farm is glowing red and the steaks and chops from the freezer are marinating in big aluminum pans. Several of the men have chipped in to buy cases of beer, which are iced down in the bed of Swift Collins's truck. The men have been drinking for a couple of hours now and the conversation is loud and becoming boisterous. George approaches his father, as the latter is assaying how and when to begin cooking.

"Daddy, I need to talk to you."

Thad casts a sideways glance at his son and grumbles, "What is it, son? I got work to do here. In fact, come on over here and help me start puttin' th' meat on th' grill."

George picks up the first pan and holds it while his father forks steaks sputtering onto the grill's surface. "I think I might've screwed up."

Thad doesn't even look up. "Hell, that ain't unusual. What'd you do this time?"

"This might be serious. 'Course it might not be anything at all, but I need you to know." The pan trembles in his grasp.

Half annoyed Thad says, "Spit it out, son. Don't take all night tellin' me that you've gotta tell me somethin'. Just say it."

George continues, "Well remember when you called home yesterday an' told me that y'all was gonna have to stay in Selma? And that these men were comin' over here to try to stop th' niggers from registerin'? Well, last night I ran into a buddy of mine and we got to talkin' and I told him that some people were comin' here. We laughed about it and I didn't think nothin' about it until today. A few days ago when me and him was out shootin' I mentioned that y'all were going over to Selma, too. Now with ever'thing that's happened with those buses of people comin' in here and then today with th' National Guard bein' here, I just got to thinkin' that maybe I shouldn't've told him."

Thad stops and looks at his son. The same bad feeling that he'd had at the square this afternoon returns. "Who was it?"

Flustered, George stammers, "D-Duke. It was Duke. He's that boy that's been datin' Lynn. You met him over at Robert Earle's one night."

"Is he from Gadsden?" Blankenship is alert now.

"Yeah, I think he's from up that way somewhere. Why?"

"'Cause we've been told that some boy from Gadsden was workin' with th' niggers here, and we've been tryin' to find out who th' hell it is. Now it turns out it's some damn friend of yours? I swear t' God, son. I've gotta think about this a few minutes. Don't say nothin' to nobody else about this just yet. Goddammit, George, you may've really screwed th' fuckin' pooch this time." The perspiration on Thad's brow is not from the heat of the grill.

"Maybe you should've told me y'all were lookin' for somebody from Gadsden …"

"Well it don't matter. Th' thing's done. We just have to figure out how to deal with it now. We'll talk about it after while." Thad turns away from his son and busies himself with moving the rest of the meat onto the huge grill. George heads for the pickup/cooler near the driveway.

A gloom has fallen over George as he snaps off the tab on a can of Pabst Blue Ribbon … *I guess I'm just a screw up. How could I know? Daddy's mad at me now and I deserve it. There's gotta be a way to make this right. I've got to figure out a way to make up for what I've done. Dammit Duke, I could kill you for puttin' me in this position … How could he be workin' for the other side in this? Doesn't he even care about his own kind?*

The cold beer feels mighty good on his tight throat.

* * * *

The mood in the buses is exuberant as they roll toward Selma. By sundown the excited talk has given way to naps and quiet conversation. Now they plan to enter town quietly; and then to circle back tomorrow and enter again, coordinated with the massive rally that has been waiting to kick off for several days now. Though tired, Stokley's mind won't let him rest. Surprised that things have gone as well as they have, he still worries that their run of luck might end tomorrow. Still, that's tomorrow, and he wants to enjoy the good feelings from the current triumph.

And the buses are rolling again.

CHAPTER 28

His work at the library finished for the week, Duke heads outside and the warm, clear evening. Though restless, he doesn't know what to do about it, where to go. At last he decides to go to Judd and Elizabeth's place to see what they're up to. In town, he spies Terry Collins walking along, head down, his stride purposeful. Beeps the horn and throws up a hand as Terry turns toward him. A smile breaks out on Terry's face and Duke coasts to the curb.

Duke asks, "Where're ya headed?"

"I was gonna try to catch a ride with a buddy of mine up town. Momma had to have the truck today and dropped me off in town." His slicked down, dirty-blond hair is damp from the exertion of walking. Perspiration trickles down a cheek fuzzy with a faint beard. He explains that he's been at the library for hours trying to get a paper finished. "We'll be gone a lot of the day tomorrow, I guess. And I might not be able to get in here on Sunday. How 'bout you? Where're you goin'?"

Duke pauses for a second then replies, "You know Judd and Elizabeth don't you? From the bridge tables at the Union?" Terry nods. "I was headed over to their place. Why don't you go with me and we can talk a little bridge, maybe even play a little if they're up to it. I'll take you home later. Wanna do that?"

"Sure, if you think they won't mind. Maybe we can discuss some of those conventions I was talking about the other night." He grins enthusiastically, and Duke wonders if he has any friends on campus. Suspects that he goes to his classes and then hustles back home to work on the farm.

"I'm sure they won't mind." He wheels the T'Bird out onto the Parkway to the ABC store for a bottle of wine, and then back to the parking area in front of

Judd's place. As he's pulling into the driveway, he wonders if it might be possible that Judd and Elizabeth are smoking pot and is suddenly less certain that they will welcome visitors.

When he stops the engine, he blows the horn a couple of times until Elizabeth's pretty face appears at the window. He shouts up, "Can Terry and I come up and thrash you and Judd at a few hands of cards?" Then aside to Terry he whispers, "Didn't wanna interrupt them if they were screwing or something"

Elizabeth is cheerful, "Sure. Come on up, but Judd can't stand losing in his own house."

Duke, Terry and the bottle of Chianti go upstairs to find Judd and Elizabeth sitting at the big round table/spool finishing off an early meal of spaghetti. The smell of garlic is heavy on the air. Behind it Duke fancies that he can detect that unmistakable scent of marijuana, and realizes that Terry wouldn't recognize it anyway. He hugs Elizabeth. Touches hands with Judd. "Y'all know Terry, don'tcha?" They acknowledge that they do and welcome him.

Over the next four hours the friends play cards, and Terry instructs Duke in the use of Stayman responses and the Blackwood convention, explaining that these are basic and standard in club and tournament bridge. They share the wine and when that bottle is finished, another appears from somewhere. Terry obviously enjoys his role as teacher and the others learn these new methods together. Duke is constantly aware that Terry is walking on new ground—probably has never been in this kind of social situation before.

As eleven o'clock approaches, Duke says, "Guys this was great but I need to get out of here. By the way, Judd, I was gonna ask you guys if I could leave my car here tomorrow. We're meetin' George at seven-thirty at the Kettle and goin' to Atlanta in his car. It'd be easier to leave it here than to drive all the way out to my place and then back again. I'll leave the keys under the front floor mat in case you need it for any reason." They agree and Duke and Terry take their leave.

✳   ✳   ✳   ✳

The feast is over at the Blankenship farm. The men have all chipped in and cleared the massive mess, right down to taking the remaining twenty-seven beers (somebody counted them as the came out of the bed of Collins's truck), putting them into a No. 2 washtub, and then scooping in enough of the remaining ice to cover them.

In a somber mood the men sit in a group around the two picnic tables. Ricky Parsons, speaking carefully as those who've had too much to drink sometimes do, says, "I just wish there was something we could do about this voter registration bullshit. It's humiliatin' that they could just come in here and do whatever they wanted to do and nobody did nothing to stop them."

Digger Hill snaps, "They didn't just come in here. They had help."

"What d'you mean they had help?" asks Cracker White.

Feeling important, Hill stands and says "They stayed with some of the coloreds around the county, and even a few of 'em in town. They'd meet up ever' evenin' and mornin' at that nigger church out at Red Hill and eat, and go back and forth to town."

Blankenship is interested by this. Several of the men in that area work for him at various times during the year. "How do you know that, Digger? Are you sure?"

"I know it 'cause I seen it with my own eyes. I live out that dirt road behind th' church and when I was goin' out to Three Notch on Thursday, I drove right past 'em . There was one of them buses out there in the church parkin' lot, and people was sitting around on the tables and such, eatin'. I got curious and went back out by there that night after I got off, and they was havin' a big time. When I headed back home late that evenin', I passed again and there wasn't nobody there."

Blankenship swears and says, "I can't believe that Joe Lee would get hisself involved in somethin' like this. He's always been easy t' get along with. Never a word out of line. A bunch of th' boys in that church have worked for me for years in th' gatherin' times. This is a bitter pill."

Swift Collins is less phlegmatic in his response. "I say we go out there and burn their damn church buildin' to th' ground. If we don't do somethin', next thing you know they'll be movin' in next door to us, goin' to our schools and marryin' our daughters."

The men grumble, generally supporting the idea. Soon a plan emerges, and excitement grows. They gather kerosene in cans and buckets. They tie rags to a pair of cane poles, and then pile into two trucks for the trip around the edge of town to Red Hill. They have agreed that they will park on the dirt road behind the church and walk the thirty yards through the woods.

The parking lot is empty. Collins says, "There ain't a light on in the church anywhere and it's way past midnight now. Let's just go do it."

At the edge of the clearing the men divide into prearranged teams and circle the building. No word is spoken. They splash the fuel noiselessly onto the walls of the church and copious amounts are poured along the entire perimeter of the building. Two men light torches and set the puddles on the ground ablaze giving everyone time to back into the edge of the woods to admire their handiwork.

Fire creeps along at a snails pace at first. Swift Collins is about to take one of the torches and set it in more places, when a slight breeze picks up the flames and speeds them along the wood frame building. The church's left-hand corner catches first and moments later the same thing happens at the opposite corner. Fire reaches upward until the fuel-soaked timber walls ignite.

The speed with which the pinewood catches and becomes wholly involved is astonishing and the men gathered at the edge of the woods stand in awe of the terrible beauty. In seconds the fire is roaring and within minutes flames engulf the entire building. Soon the flames roar like a jet engine. The men can barely hear themselves talk. In no time at all flames reach the small cross at the top of the cupola-style steeple. As the cross catches, Collins says almost reverently, "Long live the brotherhood."

Behind him Digger Hill whispers, "This one's for you, Eugene."

*   *   *   *

The night is clear and warm. Duke and Terry have the top down and are cruising along Highway 29 toward Tuskegee. Terry says, "I appreciate the ride home. I had a real good time tonight. I don't get to do this too much. None of my friends have their own place like y'all do. Must be nice to live on your own like that." Underneath this he's thinking: *'I don't even have any real friends, much less friends living on their own. I felt really out of place in there for a while tonight. That was the first time I ever drank wine. It was more bitter than I would have thought. I hope to God Momma ain't still awake, she'd be mad as hell, and tell Daddy too.'*

"No problem, Terry. It was fun. This is my first time living on my own; and I'll tell ya, it's not easy. Judd and Elizabeth are good people. I'm sure they learned a lot and enjoyed our being there."

They turn right a several miles before the square and drive almost two miles out into the country before Terry points out the driveway leading to the house. Duke creeps along the potholed drive and leaves Terry at the unpainted frame house. They salute each other and agree that tomorrow they'll meet again at seven-thirty.

*   *   *   *

Red McKinney guides the Nova carefully along Highway 29 returning from Union Springs, where he had been visiting with a widow woman of his acquaintance. As he approaches the outskirts of Tuskegee, he sees a red glow in the sky and wonders if some farmer has been burning off brush and let the fire get out of control. Through his fatigue, he remains a reporter and heads in the direction of the glow. His path soon becomes obvious and he knows that he is going to end up at the Red Hill Baptist Church.

Swinging around the last curve, he sees the church ahead in full flame. The steeple has fallen and the roof blazes. As he arrives at the driveway, the roof gives up at last and crashes inward and downward. Sparks fan out and fill the night sky—like a congregation of fireflies. A wave of nausea washes over him. Only when the sparks seem to have settled does he think to report the blaze. He turns with the lump still in his throat and speeds back to town.

Spud Wagner is asleep at the desk in the sheriff's office when Red shows up. The door crashes against the wall as he rushes in. Wagner jolts awake reaching for the pistol at his hip until he recognizes McKinney. "Goddamn, Red, you scared th' livin' daylights outta me. What's th' big hurry? What th' hell time is it anyhow?"

McKinney tells Wagner of the fire and together they decide that both the county fire marshal and the sheriff will have to be called. Wagner reluctantly picks up the phone and mutters, "Jimbo ain't gonna like this."

Red has his notebook out and is rapidly scribbling his recollections. Lost in thought, he doesn't hear what Spud says.

*   *   *   *

At the Blankenship farm, the men finish the twenty-seven beers. When the last beer is drunk, Townsend announces that he and his men are going to head back to Selma. "I reckon that the 'Freedom Riders' will show up over there tomorrow for sure now. I guess ole Stokley will be struttin' about this on TV tomorrow in Selma. Y'all got a mess to clean up over here and I wish you good luck. Thanks for th' bonfire." There is general laughter and the *disciples* get into their cars and leave.

George approaches his father after the rest are gone and says, "I don't know if this will help or not, but I'm supposed to go to Atlanta with Duke and Terry Collins tomorrow. Is there anything that you want me to say or do?"

Blankenship's first impulse is to forbid his son's going with Duke, but slowly a plot hatches in his mind. "Yeah, there is something. You bring that boy out to th' Temple when y'all get back from your business. When you think that might be?"

His father's wish for him to bring Duke to the Temple shocks George. This is the place where the Klan holds the most serious of its ceremonies. Located three miles out a logging road beside a wide stream, the hollow has probably been used for centuries by one group or another. The Klan has used the place for ceremonies as long as George can remember. To take a traitor there seems unusual to him—almost sacrilegious. "I'm not sure how long these things take, but prob'ly it'll be around eight or nine. You want me to bring him there that late?"

"Yep. That's just th' last place he needs to go, and you need to get him there. Don't fuck this one up, son. This is your chance to make up for a lot of things you've done."

"You want me to bring Terry, too"

"No, just bring that bastard Duke. Terry's got no business in this."

"OK, daddy, I'll do it."

*   *   *   *

The T'Bird swings around the corner onto Ann Street and for the first time Duke makes the connection to *his* Ann. He immediately feels depressed. Looking down the street a few feet, however, he spots Claire's car sitting streetside just beyond his apartment. He can't stop the smile on his face or the tingle in his belly. He'll be glad to see her.

A candle burns on the table. A note is propped against a cup:

> Duke,
> I couldn't face the weekend at the dorm.
> Hope you don't mind too much. See ya in the morning.
> C-

As he's reading he hears her pad up behind him and sticks out his butt to touch her. Her hands are soft on his taut shoulders and she asks, "Want coffee or something?"

"No it's after midnight and I have to meet Terry and George at seven-thirty. I just need to sleep. It'll be nice to have you here with me though." Turning, he reaches for her and holds her close against his chest. Her hair smells fresh and clean. He thinks … *I could get used to this, but I'm not gonna.*

"You mad at me for coming here?"

"No, not even close. I'm tired though. You O.K. to sleep now?"

"It'll be back to sleep for me … Sure that's fine."

Soon they are asleep, tangled but chaste.

*   *   *   *

At 2:15 a.m. Red is on the phone with Carl Metzner. "It looks like the church was burned down in retaliation for being used as a base of operations for the voter registration effort earlier this week."

Carl mulls over the report and says, "I'll write this up based on what you've told me and call you back in an hour or so. This will certainly make the paper on a slow news night. You're in a damn hornet's nest down there, aren't you?"

"I guess you could say that. I hadn't really thought of it that way, but I guess that's about right." Rage drives Red to the edge of losing control. While not a deeply religious man, he can't countenance the desecration of a church in any way.

*   *   *   *

The Reverends Cleveland and Mohammed stand in the cool of the early morning in the parking area that had so recently been a place of rejoicing and clench their jaws in anger and despair. The families of the church have gathered. Tears and anger waft across the evening air from the different clusters in the parking area.

The Rescue Squad has set up two floodlights in the parking area, illuminating the remains of the church building. Two pumper trucks are throwing streams of water onto the embers of what had once been the Red Hill Baptist Church. Steam rises into the sky along with the final failing sparks, as the fire burns itself out. Soon the men, all volunteers, will be rolling up the hoses and heading back into town and their own families.

CHAPTER 29

▼

At 6:55 a.m. Terry Collins hears the horn from George's SuperSport in the driveway. A hangover attacks his head and eyes, but he's dressed and ready to go. As he walks through the living room, his father speaks from the kitchen, "I can't believe you're gonna waste a day on this foolishness. You better get your fill of it today, boy. This'll be th' last of it for you."

Terry says evenly, "I worked while you were gone. It oughtta be all right for me to go somewhere too."

Swift appears, head cocked to one side and hands at his side, from the door to the kitchen. "You sassin' me, boy?"

Terry keeps moving toward the front door and says over his shoulder, "No, Daddy, I'm not. I'll see you tonight or in th' mornin' if it's too late tonight." The screen door creaks open, then slaps closed as Terry trots toward George's car.

"Let's get outta here, George. I swear, you'd think I never did anything around here."

George gives him a crooked smile and says with a chuckle, "Swift on th' warpath this mornin'?" Gears the SuperSport and eases down the rough drive.

"Like every morning. I'm tellin' ya, George, one of these days I'm just gonna pack my stuff and leave. Only problem is I've got nowhere to go and no money to get there with." This last lightens the conversation as Terry accepts the inevitability of his current situation and chuckles at his own impotence regarding it.

George responds in a like vein. "Know whattcha mean. Seems like I never do anything right according to the honorable Thad Blankenship. But maybe I'm about to finally get the chance to fix a long series of fuck-ups. You won't believe what's goin' on now."

"What's that?"

Turning onto the highway, George asks, "Has Swift said anything to you about there being a traitor in our midst—some white guy working with th' niggers, tellin' 'em when things are supposed to be happenin', where people are and so on?"

Terry's brow furrows as he tries to remember any such rumblings in his father's rants. "No. I don't remember hearin' anything like that. What's it mean."

"I hadn't heard it either 'til yesterday. Seems that 'the honorable' and his buddies, your daddy included, have been lookin' for some guy from Gadsden, because he had told his ex-girlfriend that he was helping with the voter registration stuff here in Tuskegee. She told her new boyfriend, he told Rube Townsend in Montgomery, and it all got back to 'the honorable'…. Guess who it is." George has shifted into fourth gear and is picking up speed, the roar from the glass packs deafening.

Terry draws a complete blank. Shouts over the noise, "I don't reckon I even know anybody from Gadsden. I've got no idea. Who is it?"

"Let me put it this way. We're gonna pick him up in a few minutes." George lets this statement hang in the air until Terry grasps the meaning and reacts.

"You mean Duke? You gotta be kiddin' me. Duke is workin' for th' nigras? Why would he do that?" But beyond the shock, Terry knows it might be true. He sees in Duke a kind of compassion that just might lead him to work for the underdog. He thinks back to last night and how he had spent the evening with Duke and his friends, having a social life for the first time ever that didn't involve being out in the woods with guns. He knows that Duke went out of his way to include him and then drove twenty-five miles late at night to bring him home. Finally it registers that Duke said that he is from north Alabama.

Calming himself, Terry asks with a forced chuckle, "So how is it that you're gonna fix things. What're you gonna do to him?"

"Me? Hell, I ain't doin' nothin' but deliverin' 'im to daddy and his friends. Th' kicker, though, is that daddy told me to bring him to th' Temple. Does that make any kind of sense to you?"

At cruising speed the noise from the car is lessened. As the implication of George's daddy's request sinks in, Terry feels chilled even in the warming morning air.

Quietly he says, "Do you think they'll kill him?" The question is almost too frightening to ask, but Terry has laid it out there and both young men are now forced to look at it.

Staring down the highway, George answers soberly, "Hadn't wanted to think of that. Could be, I guess. I think they're capable of it, and they're sure as hell mad about it. They'll prob'ly just scare th' hell out of 'im though." He hesitates before adding, "All I know is that I'm finally gonna do something right that my daddy wants me to do. What happens after that remains to be seen." He doesn't mention the late night foray to the church. He's sure that that act was only to scare folks as well.

Terry recalls an unspeakable early morning trip with his own father into the Tuskegee National Forest, scrabbling around in the dirt, and Swift's admonition to never mention it again. He knows that these men are capable of, probably practiced at, murder. For the first time in his life, he faces a dilemma of such magnitude that it will affect him forever—and he has no one to advise him. They are discussing the impending fate of someone he calls his friend. On the other hand, they are also talking about the judgments and decisions of their fathers, men who have raised and supported them. George seems clear about what he wants to do, but *he* isn't. Very soon Duke will be with them. Terry wonders if he can look him in the eye, knowing what lies ahead.

*   *   *   *

Duke wakes up early and showers. Claire looks groggily at him, until he tells her to go back to sleep. He makes instant coffee and scribbles a note to her, that he leaves on the kitchen table, saying that he'll see her tonight, around eight o'clock. He selects casual pants, a golf shirt, and even shaves his light beard for the occasion. Excitement flutters in his stomach now and he is eager to prove himself in the larger world of bridge in real competition. As he leaves the relative darkness of the apartment, he looks in on Claire sleeping in his bed and feels a twinge of something that he can't quite put words to. Whatever its name, it feels nice.

Driving to the Kettle, he can't help laughing at getting so worked up over a card game after so many years in athletics. This, he reasons, is a time when he'll use his brains, rather than his body, to try to win at something. He occupies himself with an unsuccessful attempt at sorting out the philosophical differences between the two, until he arrives at the Kettle. Within a few minutes he hears the SuperSport approaching the corner a block away, grins at the noise and gets out of the T'Bird.

Breakfast passes uneventfully, but Terry seems unusually quiet. Duke figures that he is also nervous and thinks no more about it. Wonders if he might have a little bit of a hangover. Terry wears khakis and a madras shirt that has been starched and pressed. As usual he's wearing too much cologne and Duke decides to mention that to him at some point. George rattles on and on about gathering the cattle and getting them to the auction—how hard it had been, but then how much he enjoyed getting the money and taking it straight to the bank. Everything seems normal when they drop the T'Bird at Judd's place

On the road Duke watches from the back seat. With the radio playing and the rumble of the glass-pack mufflers, the efforts of Terry and Duke to talk bridge one last time prove impossible. Thoughts of Pax and the death of Reverend Maxwell ping at his mind until he eventually decides to nap. The vibration from the exhaust soothes him and he drifts off. He awakens when they stop at traffic lights in the small towns they pass through, then drifts back off again until they hit Peachtree Street in Atlanta.

It is the first visit to the city for Terry. Duke has visited there many times with his father and friends for Atlanta Crackers baseball games at Ponce De Leon Park. George knows town as well, and between them they locate the Downtowner Hotel in the maze of Atlanta's city streets. They have to park in a parking garage, a new experience for all three. The attendant explains that if they take the ticket that he has given them to the desk in the hotel, the hotel will pay their parking fee. Excitement bubbles over in Terry and Duke, all other thoughts temporarily displaced.

Entering the hotel lobby, the three are awestruck for the first time today. Highly polished marble floors extend to distances that the three have never experienced indoors. Stairwells go up one floor to the mezzanine and banks of elevators line an interior wall. Men in red, black, and gold livery lounge at the doors and near the expansive front desk. Dark paneling gives the interior a rich, dignified look and feel. Conversation groupings of expensive furniture and plush area rugs dot the huge lobby.

Duke approaches the front desk and asks the older man for directions to the bridge tournament. Although the man looks as though he doesn't think these three belong there, he points to the mezzanine and says the tournament is being held in ballrooms A through D. He adds that the players have broken for, lunch and Duke remembers the one-hour time difference between here and Auburn.

Duke reports his findings to the other two and they decide to wander around the lobby and take in the new sights. Terry says, "I feel like 'country comes to town'."

They laugh at themselves and George replies, "Well, that's exactly who we are. This is fantastic. I wish my momma could see it; she'd be amazed ... She'd love it."

Behind the stairwell, visible from the front door, the three find a secluded bar and beside it an escalator—another first for them. Beyond the bar a small café is jammed with people. The men are all dressed in suits and the women in semi-formal attire drip with jewelry. Duke stops in his tracks. "Look at how they're dressed. Oh man, we're gonna stand out like flies in th' buttermilk."

George snickers, "Too late now. Unless y'all wanna just turn around and go home."

Terry is vehement, "Oh no. I've waited too long to do this to leave now. They can think what they want to, Duke and me are gonna beat their asses at their own game and without th' discomfort of th' neckties ... Besides, we're just impoverished college students; what d' they expect? You still game, Duke?"

"Oh yeah." But his confidence was checked at the door.

✳   ✳   ✳   ✳

When the suit and jewelry group begins to move back toward the mezzanine, Duke and Terry, followed by George, take their maiden trip on the escalator. They're grinning like kids at the Good Humor man's truck. When they step off the moving stairs at the top, a long hallway lies ahead. Following the crowd, they see tables set up along one wall with officials sitting behind them. Duke approaches with Terry and they present the paperwork that they had received from Pax via Ron. The lady who helps them looks at the papers and says, "Oh yes, Mr. O'Reilly called us about the change in his plans. I do hope that his health has improved."

She sorts through a cardboard box in front of her and finds two plastic badges with the names Duke Windsor and Terry Collins printed in bold script. She also hands them blank bid sheets to fill out, wishes them good luck, and directs them toward a double door entryway.

Duke looks at Terry and says, "Well, you warned me about these cards, but I have no idea how to fill one out." Inside the tournament area, he sees that floor to ceiling vinyl dividers between the four rooms have been pushed against the walls, creating one continuous, long rectangular room. The floors are parquet and gleam with a dull luster. At each end, tables line the width of the room and are covered with pitchers of water and tea, sodas, huge aluminum bowls full of ice, stacks of paper and china cups with saucers, rows of coffee pots, condiments, and trays and trays of snacks. Four-person card tables are arranged around the room with plenty of room between. Each table has a placemat in the center with a number and the four directions, North, South, East, and West, delineated.

Terry leads him to an unoccupied table and says, "Give me your card. I'll fill out both of 'em. Don't worry about all this, Duke. It's no different from playin' at th' Union. Th' people are just older, that's all." This does not soothe Duke's nerves.

Soon the pair is seated at an assigned table and to Duke's amazement and horror, twenty or thirty "watchers" are gathered around them. A tall dignified gentleman and his female partner approach. The man extends his hand toward Duke and says, "Good afternoon, my name is Omar. This is my partner, Amanda."

Duke stammers his name and indicates his partner, Terry. The director delivers three, pre-dealt, aluminum boards—eighteen inch rectangles with slots cut out for cards, and labeled "N, E, S, W", to each table. After a brief explanation, play begins. Duke's hands shake so much that he can hardly read the cards. He pushes himself back slightly from the table and rests his forearms on his knees to calm himself. He's relieved to have such a poor hand that he knows he won't have to bid. The bidding proceeds around the table with Duke mumbling "Pass" in his turn on each round.

The opponents eventually arrive at a contract of 6 no-trumps. Omar, on Duke's right will play the hand, so Duke must lead first. Again he is assaulted by nerves, and pauses to look over his cards, trying to decide what to lead. Nothing seems right. Finally, almost in panic he pulls the eight of clubs from his array and places it face up in front of him. Omar glares at him and pauses to decide how to react. When he asks the jack of clubs instead of the king, Terry quickly produces the Queen, takes the trick and plays the Ace, which also wins a trick and sets the contract. After this play, Omar holds his cards face up in the center of the table and says, "I claim the rest." Terry acknowledges his right to do this and grins at Duke.

The next two hands go by in a blur for Duke. When the final card is played from this three board set, Omar says, "Pleasure to meet the two of you." As he walks, away he turns to Duke and asks, "Out of curiosity, why did you choose the club lead on the first board?"

Duke blushes deeply. He stammers, "Mostly it was just eenie-meenie-miny-moe."

To his complete mortification Omar roars with laughter, drawing unwanted attention to the table. Duke feels like a bug under a microscope.

While the pairs change tables as directed, Terry sidles up to Duke and asks, "Do you know who Omar is?" Duke shakes his head. "That's Omar Sharif, the movie star and a world renowned bridge player. We made a good score there. Nice play."

That one moment represents all the glory the friends will know today. Over the next three hours Duke makes mistake after mistake. After Terry suffers the humiliation of reneging on a play, and having the director called over to make a ruling, he also gives in to the pressure. The two muddle through and feel relieved when the end comes.

George has been bored for the last hour of the meet and waits for them in the hallway outside. He has already had the parking ticket stamped. The three gladly retreat to the car, and flee Atlanta.

As the SuperSport pulls out of the parking garage, Terry remembers that in a few hours they will be in Tuskegee and George will take Duke to an uncertain fate. After a few words of consolation to Duke, who is again in the back seat, Terry lapses into an anxious silence that lasts all the way home. Duke takes the opportunity to sleep off his depression and embarrassment, as they roar through the failing light.

✳   ✳   ✳   ✳

Midafternoon in Auburn and the Stingray crunches to a halt in the gravel in front of Duke's apartment. Lynn and her mother have deposited Robert Earle in the master bedroom of their home in Tuskegee and Lynn feels relieved to escape for a while. Instinctively she headed for the only safe haven she knows. Now she notices that the apartment door is open and that the T'Bird is nowhere to be seen. An unknown vehicle sits parked a few feet down the street, but she pays it no mind.

The screen door creaks as Lynn opens it. A smile, accompanied by a shake of the head, indicates her amusement at Duke's chronic carelessness about the security of his apartment. The creak startles Claire awake from her nap and she gets up, hoping that Duke is back early. She turns the corner to the living room and the two women stand facing each other. Fire flashes in Lynn's dark features. "Who are *you* and what are you doing here?"

Claire responds sardonically to the woman's obvious anger. "I'm Claire and I was invited. Were you?" Although she's barely awake, Claire just doesn't take bullying.

Claire's brusque response shocks Lynn and she can't think of a rejoinder. In a moment, Claire figures out who she is and says, "Oh wait, I know you. You're the girl from Tuskegee that Duke has been seeing, right?"

Lynn nods, still mute.

Claire relaxes and says, "Come on in. He's in Atlanta playing in some bridge tournament or something. I'm Claire Hollister and I just needed a place to stay for the weekend. Duke and I are friends. He let me stay here so I could study. He'll probably be back sometime around eight o'clock. Do you wanna stay? Or come back? Or leave a message?"

The casual manner with which this woman has spoken shocks Lynn anew. After a pause she asks, "So are you staying here *with* him? I mean, did you stay here last night? Are you gonna stay here tonight? What's going on with the two of you?" These possibilities don't exist in Lynn's world. A strange woman spending the weekend *with her boyfriend? Crazy.*

Though she feels a certain compassion for this woman, Claire can't stop herself from laughing. "Well, I *did* stay here last night, but nothing happened. Look, we're just friends. I'm sure that this looks pretty bizarre to you, but really it's not as bad as it seems. Duke has just been there for me through some very hard times … He's maybe the best friend I have. I'm not a threat to you."

That's what she said out loud. Inside she's thinking, *Sister, I'm the absolute least of your worries. This guy's way too big for the likes of you.*

Lynn walks woodenly to a chair and sits. The stresses of the past two weeks come tumbling down on her and she stares at the floor, not knowing what to do. Claire remains silent while Lynn's internal drama plays out.

Finally Lynn says, "Just tell him I came by, will you? Frankly, I don't know what to think right now. I'm gonna go back to my dorm room if he wants to contact me." She stands and, without looking at Claire, she walks out the door, gets in the Stingray, and drives away. Claire stands in the small living room and doesn't know whether to cry or laugh.

*   *   *   *

Duke awakens as the SuperSport slows to make the turn into the driveway at the Collins farm. He recognizes the turn from the previous night and says, "Man, I really slept back here. What time is it anyhow?"

Terry looks at the dash-mounted clock and reports, "Quarter 'til eight. Looks like my daddy's gone again. I hope Momma's got something left for me to eat. Y'all wanna come in and see?"

George looks hard at Terry and says flatly, "I can't. I've gotta do some things. I'll see you in a few days. Daddy wants us to cut that hay down by th' creek. You up for that on Tuesday or Wednesday?"

"Yeah. Just lemme know when." Looking back at Duke Terry says, "Take care of yourself, Duke. Don't worry too much about th' beatin' we just took. Those folks are supposed to be that much better than we are. We'll get 'em next time." He holds the door as Duke transfers from the back seat to the front. As Duke passes close to him Terry whispers under the noise of the SuperSport, "Shh. Be careful, Duke. And pay attention."

Even groggy from sleep, Duke comes instantly alert. He almost asks what he means but Terry's posture warns him not to. Instead he sits, reaches for the door and says, "I'm all right, Terry. Thanks for puttin' up with my lousy play today. They won't intimidate me so much next time. See ya Monday at th' Union."

George slips the SuperSport into first gear and begins easing out of the driveway. When they get to the highway, George turns left and says, "Duke, I've gotta run an errand for my daddy. You won't mind going with me will you? It's kinda on the way but I have to turn off the main road for a ways."

Duke answers quickly, "No, I don't mind. I appreciate that you drove us over there today. You must have been almighty bored. What made you decide that you wanted to come with us?" While waiting for George to answer, he thinks, *What the hell did Terry mean? George? Surely not; but, what th' hell else could he have meant?*

George shifts into fourth gear and accelerates. Over the engine noise, he replies, "I was just needin' to get outta town for a while. Me and Daddy haven't been gettin' along too well lately and I needed an excuse to be out from under him for a day. Heck, I 'preciate y'all lettin' me tag along. Sometimes Daddy can be a pain in th' ass."

By now the SuperSport is fairly flying along. Duke continues with his conversation but is beginning to wonder about this "errand". What kind of errand could be run out in the middle of nowhere, and at night? "So, do you even play the game? I mean did you follow what was going on at all?"

Through a clenched jaw, George says, "Oh yeah, I've played some. I'm not as good at it as y'all are; but I've played some at the Union. I thought y'all were gonna have a big day after that first hand. I guess it just got harder, huh?"

"I'll tell ya th' truth, George. I was so nervous that I couldn't figure out what I was supposed to be doin' most of th' time. It's a wonder that it wasn't even worse than it was." The car begins slowing as they approach a dirt road ahead, and

Duke asks, "Where in th' hell are we goin', George? What kinda errand takes you out here at night anyhow?" He feels very anxious now.

"There's a nigger man that works for daddy who lives out this road a ways, and Daddy wanted me to bring him his money. Th' guy worked at another farm today, and wouldn't've been home this mornin', so I agreed to bring it out here to him if we got back before nine o'clock. It's a little ways out this road; maybe a couple of miles."

After driving several more minutes, they pass a shack of a place with light burning dimly in the windows and open door. George says, "They ain't even got electricity out here. I don't see how they can live like this, but … well you know how they are."

The chert road narrows and Duke can see a bridge ahead in the glow of the headlights. Alongside the bridge on each side steel girders rise, ten feet high and painted a dull gray. George slows as they approach the bridge and comes to a stop. Only when they are a few feet from the bridge does Duke notice the road, or track more accurately, that turns right and into the woods. It is an abandoned logging trail and George puts the SuperSport into to narrow space that passes for an entryway. Immediately in front of them is a huge dip and George has to stop completely and ease slowly into the dip to keep from bottoming out.

Duke starts to protest when out of the woods on the passenger's side of the car, a figure emerges from the trees. At first Duke thinks that his eyes are playing tricks on him, but quickly he realizes that the bizarre figure is a man in a sheeted robe and with a white mask fixed across the top of his face. The word leaps terrifyingly to Duke's mind: KLAN!!

*   *   *   *

Terry Collins was in turmoil when he turned away from the SuperSport. Now as he heads toward the house the muscles in his body twitch with stress. He has to do something to help Duke, but he can't think of anything. Instead of going onto the porch, he angles toward the barn. Inside sits the work truck that they use around the farm. Swift lost the driver's side door one day when he was backing out of a wooded area pulling the tractor that had quit in the field. With the door open he had seen that the pine was too close, but when he mashed the brake his foot slipped and hit the accelerator, full to the floor. The truck bolted backwards and ripped the door off its hinges.

Now the old truck only has one headlight. The license plate is long out of date, but the truck still runs. Terry gets in without knowing what he'll do or where he'll take the truck. He starts the engine and with the slipping clutch complicating his efforts, lurches toward the highway. By the time he reaches the highway, he has decided that the only hope he has is to go to Auburn and finding Judd. He doesn't know him well, but if he's really Duke's friend, he'll have to help someway.

Avoiding any place that might likely have a sheriff's patrol or any other law enforcement presence, he takes the back road to Auburn and drives as fast as the road and the old truck will allow him. In town he follows alleys and drives through parking lots to avoid city or university police. Thanks to his custom of walking around town, he finds a relatively short route to Judd's place. As he pulls into the parking area at Judd's place, he notices lights and music playing.

The old truck doesn't sound so bad when it moves along over 10 mph, but at the slow pace required to enter the driveway at Judd's, the engine sounds like a pea thresher. Terry wonders, at first, seeing the T'Bird sitting there, but then remembers dropping it off earlier. By the time he gets the rattling, wheezing truck stopped, Judd is peering out the window upstairs. Terry steps out and, seeing Judd, motions for him to come down, all the while shouting, "Come down here quick. Duke's in trouble and we've gotta go help him."

As soon as he understands what Terry's saying to him, Judd flings himself out the door and down the stairs. Elizabeth isn't far behind. At the bottom of the stairs Terry begins telling them what's happening, and what his fears are. Judd grasps immediately the gravity of the situation: Duke has been found out and they're gonna make him pay.

Terry says, "I know where they're gonna take him. There may be a way out of it, but I'll need a lot of help. It'll take timing and we still might get caught, but we've gotta try to do *something*. Bring his car and I'll explain to you when we get underway from my house."

Elizabeth gets the keys from underneath the floor mat and hands them to Judd. "I'm going with you. Don't even think about saying that I can't."

The couple backs out of the driveway and follows Terry as he sneaks out of town, toward Tuskegee on the back road. At the farm Terry pulls the truck into the barn and whispers for Judd and Elizabeth to wait for him. When he opens the door to go inside, his mother speaks to him from the darkness. "What are you doin' with that old truck, son? Who is that out there? Is it that same boy that brought you home last night?"

"Momma, you need to go back to bed. Don't turn on any lights. There's things goin' on that I can't even tell you about. I'm gonna do somethin' tonight that will make Daddy hate me for th' rest of my life, but I gotta do it. I'm not comin' home tonight, or tomorrow night either. On Monday I'm gonna join the Army or the Marines or somethin'. I love you, Momma; but I've gotta do this."

After a brief, gut wrenching silence, she replies, "Go pack what you can in that old suitcase from the hall closet. I'll come in and help you in a minute. He hears her retreat into her room and wastes no time grabbing the old beige and brown suitcase, and stacking in his few clothes from the rickety dresser. While he packs, he hears her fumbling around in the small closet in her bedroom. As he is closing the suitcase, she returns to him and presses a wad of paper into his hand. "Take this money with you. I guess I've always known that this would come. It's not much, but it'll help you get started. You be careful, he's a hateful man, son."

"I can't take this, Momma. I'll be fine. What will you do now?"

"No you take it. My life has to stand for somethin' and if you don't take it, I'll have come to naught after all. I'm prob'ly not gonna stay here long neither. If you're gone, there ain't no reason to stay with a man like him. Take th' money. I've got people that'll help me if'n I need it."

Emotion wells in Terry, but he knows that he can't afford emotion right now. Stuffing the money in his pocket and picking up the small suitcase, he hugs his mother close and kisses her hair. "Bye, Momma. I'll let you hear from me through Reverend Walters at the church. I love you."

Out the door, his heart thuds in his chest. He motions Judd to follow him to the barn, where he retrieves a five gallon gas can, heavy from recently being refilled, an oily rag, and a carpet knife. With the trunk opened at his request, he wedges the gas can upright against the spare tire with the suitcase. He slams the trunk and jumps into the T'Bird. Then Judd drives him out of this phase of his life and onto the next thing. By the end of the driveway he has left his mother behind and is explaining to Judd and Elizabeth what they are going to try to do during the next couple of hours. He also gets permission to sleep on their couch for the next few nights.

When Judd turns left out of the driveway, Terry pulls the wad of bills from his pocket. By the light of the dashboard he counts it … Thirty-one dollars, all singles.

*   *   *   *

"I'm tellin' you, Carl, this story just keeps gettin' bigger and bigger." Red McKinney has finished his latest report to the night editor at *The Washington Post*. "I'm absolutely sure that the trail of this thing is gonna lead straight to the local Ku Klux Klan. I mean, all the evidence is there to publish that this is the work of the Klan, or at least to say that Klan activity is suspected. Give me one good reason why we can't say that much at least."

"Red, let's not get ahead of ourselves. One of my cardinal rules is that I don't publish what I *suspect*. I might as well publish fairy tales and call it the news, if I start doing that. No, we'll go with what we *know*. We *know* that the fire marshal believes that there was arson. That's enough of a story for today. In fact, it's a hell of a story. When we know more, we'll report more; but not until. Is that good enough for you?"

"OK, Carl, you're gonna do what you want to do anyway. But I'm gonna keep after this. Am I still on th' payroll?"

"Story by story, Red. If it's good enough to print, I'll pay you for it. You know the deal. Be careful out there. I'll send your check in the morning. Good night."

Red doesn't want to agree, but how can he argue with that reasoning. Nevertheless, he knows in his heart that the Klan caused these troubles. Instinctively, he wants to expose them. The magnitude of his anger about the fire and the events of the previous weeks surprises him. Two months ago he felt pretty much neutral about the whole matter of desegregation and civil rights. Two years ago he had leaned toward segregation himself. But tonight he finds himself righteously, indignantly angry about how life is being conducted in his hometown.

CHAPTER 30

▼

The white-clad figure opens the door at Duke's side, grabs him roughly by the arm, and yanks him out of the car. "George, yore car won't make it through them ruts up yonder, so you drive th' truck. I'll take care of our friend here."

He half pulls and half drags Duke toward a pickup truck parked around a bend in the track. He opens the door, and shoves him roughly onto the front bench-seat, climbing in beside him and never letting go the grip on his arm. "You know where th' Temple's at, George. Ever'body else is waitin' on us."

The gruff words contain no hint of mercy. They also confirm what Duke has feared from the moment the word 'KLAN' occurred to him back near the bridge—he's going to be brought to trial in front of the Ku Klux Klan. He struggles to control his runaway fear. Fights the panic rising inside him. Tries vainly to slow down his thoughts, to think logically. He can see no advantage to reach for and slowly relaxes, accepting his fate—for the moment. Maybe when they get to wherever they're taking him …

George drives at a snail's pace with the truck rocking wildly side to side across ruts and deep depressions. The trees tilt in the windshield as the rocking headlights dance—now high up in the limbs, now down at the trunks' level, even sometimes splaying across the ground. Duke can only brace his feet against the floorboards and his free hand against the dash trying to keep from flopping out of control.

When he feels a little more in control of himself, Duke asks, "George, why are you doin' this?"

The Klansman backhands him with a closed fist near his right eye and says, "No talkin'."

Duke feels the swelling begin almost immediately and the three continue in silence. Although there are periods when the drive is smoother, it takes a full ten minutes for the truck to ease to the right and pass a second pickup, this one gleaming white in the milky moonlight. They roll another thirty feet and come to a stop. The logging track has roughly followed the creek bed. They are deep in the woods, more than three miles from the turn at the bridge.

The Temple, sitting ahead and off to the left, is a natural, shallow amphitheater, twenty feet across at the bottom, or "stage" section. Tall pines and hardwoods form an irregular ring around the upper boundary of the area. From where George parks the truck it is a short walk around well-worn boulders to center stage. A pungent odor grows stronger as the trio approaches. Two small fires burn in the stage area, one warming a black cook pot, the other simply providing eerie light. Sitting on crude benches of boards set on boulders, three men in complete Klan regalia—robes, hoods or masks, and tall pointed hats—wait. Duke can't help thinking that if he weren't in so much trouble, these men would seem absolutely, absurdly comical. George sits on a rock, apart from them.

The man who escorted Duke to the Temple now leads him to the base of a squat oak tree located at the back edge of the stage, near the creek bank. Duke can hear the water gurgling behind him. He doesn't know it, but the creek runs deep and wide at this point. A length of rope lies on the ground near the base of the tree. His escort forces Duke's hands behind his back and around the tree and binds them there. The rest of the rope he wraps around the tree and Duke's chest twice, then once around his neck before tying it off against itself. As the man is wrapping the rope, Duke expands his chest as far as he can and holds it there, hoping to create some slack for himself. The man inspects his work cursorily, retrieves his own hat from a nearby bench, and joins the group of his friends, twenty feet away. Present, though unrecognizable, are Thad Blankenship, Digger Hill, Swift Collins, and Ricky Parsons.

One of the men, clearly the leader, stands and begins to recite what sounds like a ritual of some sort. Duke can't make out the words, but there is a singsong quality to his droning voice. Another of the men shouts loudly enough to be heard, "We don't have to go through all that. We're here for a purpose; let's get on with it." Duke observes the argument that ensues and hopes that it will stretch on longer, or that the two men will fight, taking the focus away from him. After several minutes of heated discussion, however, the leader begins anew with his incantation. At intervals the others make some verbal responses to whatever he says. To Duke it resembles some bizarre play.

After several minutes, the ritual clearly finished, the men begin a more relaxed discussion. Occasionally one or the other will point in Duke's direction. There doesn't seem to be universal accord among the four. One man in particular, the one who opposed the ritual, seems animated and more demonstrative than the others. Finally they all turn together and walk toward Duke, until they face him from six feet away. He senses their anger. Smells the sour stench of alcohol. Imagines that he can smell his own fear. Believes that harm and maybe death inhabit the minds of these men. The figures are less comical, more fearsome now. Duke trembles, his stomach rolls.

The leader, Thad Blankenship, points a finger in Duke's face and announces, "We know what you and your friends have been doin' here in our county. We know that you have funneled information to the niggers about our whereabouts and plans. We know that you have betrayed your friendship with George and prob'ly with Lynn Wilkins as well. What do you have to say for yourself before we pass judgment on you?"

Duke can barely speak from fear. He feels himself shaking violently against the rope. "I—I don't know what you're talkin' about. Why are you doin' this to me?"

The oppositional Klansman, Swift Collins, surges forward and slaps Duke hard across the mouth. "You son of a bitch. You know goddamn well that you've been helpin' them niggers get registered to vote. You're tryin' to destroy our way of life. If I had my way we'd hang you and both them damn preachers on the town square."

Duke tastes blood and sucks at his swelling lip. The slap has served to awaken his anger. He says with vehemence, "Those people voting won't have a damn thing to do with your 'way of life'. That's just stupid talk."

Collins lands a punch to Duke's jaw that stuns him and rocks his head back against the tree, before Blankenship intervenes. "Back off, Swift. We've all decided now what we're gonna do. Keep your hands to yourself. The pain of this tar and the humiliation of these feathers will be enough punishment for 'im."

Turning back to Duke, Blankenship continues, "Swift's tellin' th' truth. What you and your outsider friends have done here is gonna change how we're able to live. The majority of these coloreds don't have any idea what it takes to run a town or a county. They'll never be able to keep things goin', and they'll waste our money on all th' wrong things. You've got no idea what you've done to th' white people of this county!"

Incredulous, Duke blurts out, "That's just foolish. They don't have any candidates. And if they did, they couldn't be any worse managers than those in office now."

Now Blankenship's anger overflows. He punches Duke hard in the stomach and Duke collapses against the restraining rope, gasping for breath. He feels the hair on his neck tingling. His knees are weak. Trickles of sweat run down his sides. He's having trouble feeling his hands.

Blankenship regains his self-control and steps away, still facing Duke. "We've decided that as punishment for your crimes against our people, we will give you a little something to think about … for the rest of your life. The tar in that cookin' pot over yonder is almost down to the right consistency. In a few more minutes, we're gonna cover you in it, throw feathers on it while it is still hot and then turn you loose out on the highway. If you survive, this will mark you for life as a traitor to your supposed friends and to your race. Prepare yourself to reap the consequences of your treason."

Duke's mind muddles, horrified. He has heard of this punishment as a boy; but thought that no one practiced anymore. It was done in the 1800's, not in the twentieth century. He knows that it will burn terribly and that he will carry the scars for life, if he survives it at all. "Don't do this to me," he pleads. "I haven't done anything to hurt you."

But the men turn their backs on him and walk away. Duke looks pleadingly at George; but the younger Blankenship won't look at him. On this stage in these woods, Duke stands alone.

＊　　　＊　　　＊　　　＊

As the T'Bird approaches the bridge, Terry Collins notices that George's SuperSport is nosed into the logging road. "Judd, stop th' car. This is perfect."

He gets out and kneels beside each of the four tires of the SuperSport. A hiss of escaping air can be heard in the stillness of the evening. Elizabeth giggles at the thought of the noisy SuperSport sitting with four flat tires.

Grinning widely, Terry leaps over the side of the T'Bird and back inside the convertible. He says, "OK, Judd, drive across th' bridge and switch off the headlights. There's a hard dirt road on the other side that runs right alongside the creek. It's about three miles down that road to where the place is on the other side of the creek. We don't want the headlights to give us away. Go real slow, so they don't hear us."

The T'Bird glides along in the moonlight. Even at their slow pace, it takes only a few minutes to arrive at the place that Terry explains is directly across the creek from the Temple. The glow of the fires can barely be seen, reflected off the branches of the trees. Quietly, Judd and Terry open the trunk and remove the can of gasoline, the rag, and the razor sharp carpet knife that Terry had grabbed on his way out of the barn. He instructs Judd to keep his shoes on, and the two young men ease themselves into the water.

Keeping the gas can afloat between them and the rag balanced on top, they sidestroke across the thirty yards to the other bank, where they quietly exit the creek upstream of their target and pause to catch their breath. They have discussed what they want to do and how they want to do it; so nodding to each other, they go their separate ways. Terry takes the gas can and the rag, and sneaks through the woods to the logging track.

Judd, crawling on hands and knees, makes his way along the creek bank, until he can see Duke tied to the tree. As he nears the tree, he hears Duke pleading, saying, "I haven't done anything to hurt you." He believes that the danger Terry feared is imminent. Duke's life very likely depends on them.

Ahead of him now, Terry can see the white pickup, sitting behind his father's darker truck at the edge of the narrow logging track. He quietly opens the truck's gas cap and lays it on the ground. Next he unscrews the small cap from the funnel spout of the gas can that he's carrying. He stuffs the rag into the exposed mouth of the tank and soaks it with gasoline from the can. The towel soon reaches saturation and gasoline spills down the side of the truck. Terry continues to pour until he is certain that the side of the truck is sufficiently soaked, and that the ground underneath is, likewise. Next he pours a trail behind himself as he backtracks carefully and quietly to the edge of the creek.

Judd works his way silently and invisibly directly behind Duke. As the four Klansmen turn away to attend the melting tar, he hoarsely whispers, "Duke! Duke! If you can hear me, wiggle your fingers."

At first Duke thinks he's imagining that he heard a voice. When he hears the voice say to wiggle his fingers though, he decides to respond. He'd rather be wrong than to ignore possible salvation and be lost. He wiggles his fingers.

Judd whispers again, "I'm gonna cut the rope. Don't move yet. There's gonna be a big explosion in a minute. Watch the others and when they react to the explosion, I'll help you get free of the rope. The creek is right behind you. We'll have to swim across. If you understand all that wiggle your fingers again."

Wiggle.

Judd cuts the rope that binds Duke's hands and then slips the sharp knife under the part that is around his neck.

They wait.

A few feet upstream, Terry fumbles nervously with a cigarette lighter. At last it lights. Fire races across the woods from the creek bank to the truck, up the side— *Whoosh!* The rag catches, there is a momentary pause, and then—*BOOM!!!*

The white pickup explodes violently, rocking over to one side without turning over completely. A ball of fire roils up past the treetops. Sheet metal and secondary fireballs blast outward toward the Temple. The four Klansmen and George gasp and duck reflexively. As one they all run toward the truck. Thad Blankenship yells at the top of his lungs, "My truck! My fuckin' truck!"

Judd cuts the rope from around Duke's neck and they quickly untangle it from Duke's chest. No one has looked in their direction. All attention is on the burning truck. Secondary explosions begin to sound as the shotgun and the box of shells under the front seat reach critical temperature and begin exploding. As they slip into the water, Duke has the satisfaction of seeing the man identified as "Swift" grabbing his shoulder and staggering in apparent pain.

When the truck goes up, Terry pushes back into the water at the edge of the creek and strokes to where he knows Duke and Judd will be coming shortly. When they do, he asks quietly if Duke can make it alone or if he needs help. Assured that he can make it on his own, the three paddle furiously across the creek. They pull themselves out of the water, and head for the T'Bird.

Duke insists, "Let me drive. Just tell me where I'm going. I know this baby better than anybody else."

Terry says, "Leave the lights off for a minute and just go straight. This will come out on Highway 14 in about twelve miles. Turn right and that'll take us through Loachapoka and on into Auburn. Don't wreck us. They're gonna be a while gettin' out of there."

Around the first curve Duke switches on his headlights and picks up speed. Only then does he remember to say, "Thanks Terry, Judd. I thought I was dead meat. How did you know where I was? I sure as hell didn't."

✳   ✳   ✳   ✳

Once again Miss Julia Alexander prepares to face the huge Selma throng, this time at the park at the foot of the Pettis Bridge. On Friday the King camp had suggested, as a compromise to local businesses, that the next day's gathering take place at the park. Saturday in Selma has been hectic and joyful. Early this morning a National Guard unit that had been in Tuskegee the previous two days arrived and set up a perimeter around the small park. By eight-thirty, the official announcement that Jonas Baker, the colored teenager who had been accused of the Hill murder, had been freed came to the temporary King headquarters. Then at ten o'clock, Stokley Carmichael and two busloads of people from all parts of the country had arrived to the jubilant cheers of the assembled crowd.

These new Freedom Riders had been celebrated and practically deified by grateful citizens. The triumph of 1100 new voters in Macon County was revealed and the crowd had cheered loud and long. After brief speeches by Stokley, Martin, and local officials, the crowd sang and rejoiced together. The lyrics of "Ain't Gonna Let Nobody Turn Me 'Round", "Hold On", and "We Shall Overcome" were sung over and over in the bright sunshine.

As the morning's frenzy died down, Miss Julia announced that Dr. King had asked her to invite everyone back to the park at seven o'clock this evening for special messages to be delivered by himself and Stokley Carmichael. By noon the crowd dispersed peacefully. Miss Julia and her committee gathered at the church to contact those same people they had spoken to only a few days earlier, canceling the proposed second march on Montgomery.

Sometime in the early afternoon, the local TV station reported that the Alabama Bureau of Investigation in conjunction with the U.S. Marshals, announced the arrest of Rueben Townsend of Montgomery for the murder of Eugene Hill. He had been positively identified by four separate eyewitnesses as having been the one who shot Hill, forcing the weapon into the hands of Jason Baker. Townsend, of course, proclaimed himself innocent to the TV cameras and to anyone else who might listen. He remains in custody.

Now as seven o'clock approaches Miss Julia peeks around the corner of the temporary stage. A large crowd fills the park. A few workmen are still setting up lights that will be turned on as the natural light fades. Her spirits sail, light and hopeful. After a lifetime of dejection and defeat, of pain and impotence, she and her brothers and sisters can sense a new beginning. Her emotions hover between purest happiness and the underlying anxiety that says, "Don't trust this; it can't last."

As the sweep-second hand of her watch crosses the twelve at seven o'clock, she steps onto the stage. The roar of the crowd moves like a wave—applause, cheers, whistles, shouts … Deafening … Thrilling. Goose flesh tickles her all over. At the podium she thinks, *Let them shout and cheer. After all this time, let them have this moment of exhilaration. How I love them.* Tears well up, but she suspends them. Raises her arms in victory, and the crescendo breaks anew across the crowd. She brings her hands down in a quieting gesture, and slowly, reluctantly the crowd hushes.

In spite of her nerves, her voice through the speakers is strong and unwavering. "Those of you who know me know that my job is behind the scenes—organizing, making phone calls, getting volunteers. I'm a gopher; go fer this and go fer that." The crowd chuckles with her. They love her too.

"These last few days I've been pushed up here on stage to make announcements and give instructions. I want to warn all of you, I'm startin' to like it up here." Applause, laughter, and cheering. "Who would have ever thought that a woman of color in Selma, Alabama would be able to say that?" Cheers greet this statement. Exuberant and enthusiastic.

"For now I'm gonna stay in the background like always; but I see better days coming in *our* city." More applause. "Tonight two of the leaders of the movement which is responsible for bringing us these new feelings are here to speak to us. I don't know what their messages will be, but I do know that whatever they have to say, I want to hear ... Without further hesitation, let me introduce tonight's first speaker—the man who organized and then brought to us today's new Freedom Riders, who bravely stood with our brothers and sisters in Macon County as 1100 people of color were finally registered to vote. Ladies and gentlemen, Mr. Stokley Carmichael."

As the crowd goes crazy, Stokley makes his way up the stairs at the rear of the stage. He saunters to the podium and glares at the assemblage. They cheer. And he stares. They whistle and clap. And he gazes impassively at them. Soon his lack of response lets the air out of the balloon and the crowd assumes an uneasy quiet. People whisper. A buzz swirls around the park. Finally with the suspense almost unbearable, Stokley speaks.

"I know y'all are thrilled to death about havin' a few new voters in Macon County." As the applause starts, he shouts, "Stop it! Hear me out! Yes, I'm happier with 1100 more, but I ain't happy that *you're* not registered to vote. Are you happy that it took these same soldiers that are standin' out there tonight protectin' us from God-knows-what to get those 1100 people registered? Are you happy that white kids from Auburn University had to come to Tuskegee to teach *our people* how to fill out a bunch of forms? Are you happy to know that we are gathered here in this park only because those white soldiers out there are protectin' us?" He's got their attention now.

"If you think for one minute that because 1100 people in Macon County registered to vote it means that life is gonna be easier for *you*, then you've got a very serious shock comin'. If you don't believe me, then you just waltz on down to the Dallas County Board of Registrars on Monday and tell them that you've come to register to vote ... Those white people aren't gonna let you register. You're gonna have to do what the folks in Tuskegee did. You're gonna have to *take* that right to vote.… For yourself."

A few nods can be seen in the crowd now. "That's right," comes from the front row. Another voice from the center says, "Amen, Brother Stokley."

"On our way down here from Carolina I was talkin' to one of the bus drivers and I asked him how he felt about being called 'colored'. All he could think to say was that it was better than bein' called 'nigger'. I've been thinkin' about this ever since. Why should we be called 'colored'? Look around you. Do you see any color? I don't know what you see, but I see beautiful black brothers and sisters. Ain't no color in a damn one of 'em." The crowd chuckles, amused but also a little anxious at these words.

"One of the white men who was allowed to buy fuel for the buses on the way down told me that an attendant at one of the pumps was astonished that 'one of them colored boys could drive a big ole bus like that'. Are you happy being referred to as '*one of them colored boys*'?"

Murmurs from the crowd. They're beginning to warm to these new ideas.

"I'll tell you what, my *black* brothers and sisters, I'm no longer willin' to be one of their '*colored boys*'. Used to say in my neighborhood, 'See a boy slap 'im'. I'll say to you tonight that we need to stop callin' ourselves by these dishonorable names. We need to have an identity that *we* have chosen—not something that our oppressors have pushed onto us and that we just weakly accept."

Applause ripples through the gathering. A few men are rolling their fists in the air. Shouts and yells of approval surface and gain strength. Stokley speaks loudly over the growing roar.

"There are other things that this community of *black* brothers and sisters must address. We must stop relying on liberal whites to do our work for us. Yes, we must appreciate what has been done, but we must start doin' this work for ourselves. If your brother can't read or write, then *you* must help him fill out his forms to register. If your children can't read and write, then *you* must see to it that they go to school and learn. We cannot rise on the backs of whites. We have to stand on our own."

The approving applause that began earlier is now at a fevered pitch. Black men and women begin to understand the strength of standing on their own. This man speaks of *dignity*.

"None of the things that we want are gonna come easy, and if history is our teacher, more *black* lives are gonna be at risk, more *black* people are gonna be beaten, more *black* teenagers are gonna be falsely accused of things.

"I'm growing weary of standin' still and takin' it, while these things go on. I don't know how much longer I can just allow myself, my friends, my family, and my children to be harmed. I'm on the edge of needin' to fight back." These words are met with tepid applause. Most of those gathered here are followers of King's non-violent philosophy. "At some point we may have to fight fire *with* fire. We cannot expect respect from others if we don't respect ourselves first."

The crowd is confused. No one can fault the idea of self-respect, but this business of fighting fire with fire—of repaying violence with violence—doesn't resonate with the tactics of recent history. Still …

I'll sum up my message to you in this way: Let us not be ungracious to those who have helped us; but let us cease to be constantly in need of someone else's help in order to do the ordinary things required of ordinary citizens. Let us not continue to allow excellence to be withheld from us through complacency; but let us demand access to the pathways to success. Let us not wait for others to protect us from the slings and arrows of those who would keep us in submission and ignorance; but let us learn how to, and be willing to, protect ourselves. When we can achieve these things—and we *can* achieve them—*then* we can call ourselves free."

With one last glare at his audience Carmichael turns to exit the stage. The applause begins slowly and sparsely, but spreads across the great throng. There are no whistles. No shouts. Just the clapping of hands in earnest appreciation, if not universal acceptance, of this message from a man who has demonstrated the courage to stand up, and who now asks the same courage of all those present.

✳   ✳   ✳   ✳

When the shotgun blasts stop, they examine Collins's wound and find it to be superficial. Only then do the men finally notice that Duke has disappeared. George rushes over to the tree and says, "Th' rope's been cut. Somebody got 'im outta here. How can that be? Where could he have gone?"

Thad roars at him, "Who'd'ya tell this time? Goddam you George. You're the only one that knew where we was comin' besides us. Who'd'ya tell?"

"I didn't tell nobody. I swear. There wasn't nobody *to* tell." He realizes suddenly that he told Terry, but decides that he'll lie forever to protect him.

Digger Hill says, "It don't matter nohow. What we need to do is get outta here and go find th' son of a bitch before he turns us in to th' goddam feds or somethin'. You know where he lives, George?"

"Not really, but it's in Auburn somewhere and his car ain't exactly easy to hide. We can find him. I know the parkin' lot where we left his car. We can start there."

Ricky Parsons says, "Yeah, well first we've gotta be able to get outta here without burnin' up Swift's truck too."

When the fire in Blankenship's truck dies down enough that they can squeeze the other vehicle around it, all five men pile in and begin the laborious ride back to the main road. As with the drive in, the going is slow and uncomfortable. By the time they reach the SuperSport almost half an hour has passed since the explosion.

Thad says to his son, "George, move your car and let's figure out how we're gonna find your buddy."

As George reaches for the door handle, he stops. Feels the air go out of him. "Hey, my back tire's flat."

His father shouts, "I don't give a damn about your fuckin' tire. Get that thing outta the way."

George then sees that the rear bumper of the SuperSport is resting on the upslope of the big dip that he's parked in. "It ain't gonna move. Th' bumper's sittin' on the ground."

Enraged, Thad rushes to the SuperSport and pushes his son out of the way. Then he sees that the front tire is also flat. The stress of his truck burning, the disappearance of their captive and now the inability to pursue him combine to drive Thad over the emotional edge. He begins hitting George with his hands—slapping, punching, and cursing all the while.

Seeing the spectacle in the glow of the headlights, Parsons jogs up and pushes Thad away. "You can beat him 'til your hands hurt and it won't change nothin'. Just calm down and let's figure out what th' hell we're gonna do. We can't get this truck outta here with th' car in th' way. We're gonna have to move it somehow."

From inside the truck Collins says, "I've got a hand pump in th' back of th' truck, but it'll take forever to fill all four of them tires."

"Maybe so," says Digger Hill, "but we might as well get started, 'cause that's th' only option we've got right now unless somebody wants to walk the eight miles into town."

When Parsons tries to attach the pump to the front tire, he turns to the others and says, "Y'all ain't gonna believe this. There ain't no valve cores. They've all four been taken out. The tires won't hold air."

This revelation spawns another round of cursing. Digger Hill strips off his robe and flings it angrily into the back of the truck. The he begins the longs walk toward town. After he leaves, George suggests that they take the valve cores from Collins's tires and use them in the SuperSport. Grumbling they agree and set about doing it. By the time the remaining four men get into the SuperSport and head toward town midnight has passed. They pick up Digger about five miles into the eight-mile hike and stagger into Tuskegee to search for Cracker White, who refused to join them earlier. His house shows no lights and his truck isn't there. They knock but get no response. Nobody at his shop either. Disgusted, they give up and get Parsons's truck, and the two vehicles head for Auburn.

*   *   *   *

On the way into town Judd and Terry give the details of the rescue to Duke. Terry explains that his idea of how to set the fire came from years of burning brush on the farm and having to make a trail to a safe place before igniting the fire.

When Duke and friends pass the first intersection in town, Judd asks, "Where're you headed, Duke?"

"Gotta stop by Teddy Bear's place. We've been talkin' about goin' to California for a while, and I think the time has come."

Turning left off Glenn, Duke follows a driveway that leads behind a substantial house. At the rear is a small house; in fact it has only two rooms and a bath. Light glows in the windows. The T'Bird rolls to a stop a few feet from the stoop. Before anyone can get out of the car, the door opens and Teddy Bear's smiling countenance beams at them. "Come in. Come in. This is great. I never have company. Good to see y'all."

Maneuvering his long legs around the steering wheel, Duke scoots himself into a sitting position atop the driver's seat. "We can't stay but a minute, Teddy Bear. I just came by to ask you if you still want to go to California with me. I'm gonna leave in an hour and if you wanna come, I'll be back to get you then. I mean unless you're hiding Aurelia in there somewhere."

The four friends watch disbelief play across Teddy Bear's features, but when no one laughs or moves to finish the joke, he asks, "Are you serious?"

"As a heart attack."

"Why? I mean why now? Why in an hour?" Only now does he notice that the clothes of all three of the young men are wet, their hair disheveled. Then the knot near Duke's eye. "What th' hell happened to y'all?"

Duke runs his fingers through his hair, straightening. "Don't have time to explain it now, but I'll tell ya on th' way. Make up your mind and I'll be back by here in an hour, give or take fifteen minutes. If you're goin', be packed and ready. If not, hey, no hard feelings; but I gotta go. See ya in a few." With that he slides back down into position, starts the engine and backs around to leave.

As the T'Bird eases forward after turning around Duke hears Teddy Bear say, "No shit?"

The farewell at Judd and Elizabeth's apartment is much more emotional than Duke expected. They exchange the addresses and phone numbers of their parents so they can try to keep in touch. Duke hugs first Judd, then Elizabeth. Elizabeth cries a little and clings to Duke. By now Duke is aware that Terry has saved his life and shakes his hand firmly, saying that if Terry ever needs him, "Just holler." With a grin Terry agrees that he will.

At Duke's request, everyone pitches in to put the T'Bird's top up. With consideration emotion Judd says, "I hate this. Just when you get to know someone, they walk out of your life. Be careful out there, Duke. Let us hear from you."

With a heavy heart Duke gets back into the T'Bird, waves, and heads to his apartment and another dreaded goodbye.

Claire's car is in the same place as when he left this morning. Lights burn brightly in the living room. He stops out front and steps from the car almost directly into the doorway. Claire sits with her feet up on the worn couch. Looks up. Pixie grin. Sparkling eyes. Swings her legs around to stand and flashes him for maybe the last time. Notices his wet clothing, the bad eye, and says, "What on earth happened to you?"

"Come into the bedroom while I change and I'll tell you."

"An invitation no sensible girl would refuse." She follows him into the bedroom where he peals off the slacks and golf shirt, while explaining that the Klan had found out about his role in the recent events in Tuskegee. Then he tells her what had happened with George taking him out into the woods.

She hasn't noticed yet that he has pulled out his one and only suitcase and is packing clothing into it. He then recounts the events at the Temple, her eyes growing wide and fear reaching down into her stomach. And at this point she notices that he's not dressing anymore, but packing. "What are you doing, Duke? Are you leaving?"

He stops dead still and their eyes meet. Nods his head. "I've got to go, Claire. Those men know who I am now, and they were planning to hurt me pretty bad tonight. They'll be even more pissed now. I can't fight them by myself. If I stay and they want to kill me, they'll find a way … No doubt. I've definitely got to go."

Pain crackles in the air between them. When she speaks, her voice is, as always, strong. "I can't argue with you about it. I just wish that things weren't happening so suddenly. I'm not prepared for this. I don't know how to react."

Holding her gaze he replies, "I don't know how to react either, Claire. I just know I've gotta go."

Her face has gone pale now. "I feel like I'm going to throw up. I'm just sick … What can I do to help you?"

The impulse is to stop and cling to her, but better judgment propels him onward. "If you really wanna help, shove as much of this stuff as you can into pillow cases and help me get everything that'll fit into the T'Bird. There's a road atlas somewhere in the living room. I'll need that. Hell, I don't even know where California is, except that it's west of here."

Activity helps both of them to avoid dealing with the hurt until the final moment, but that moment does arrive. She finds the atlas and suggests that he take Highway 14 around to Montgomery, in order to avoid passing Tuskegee and possible trouble. As she plots his route for him, she remembers the envelope from her father and retrieves it from her purse. Holding it up between two fingers she says, "I don't think that dear old Dad had any idea that his gratitude was going to be so timely. This certainly works out well, though, don'tcha think?"

By now Duke has packed everything that he needs from the scant existence he's been living. The envelope brings relief and a big smile. He takes it from her, folds it, and crams it into the back pocket of his jeans. Claire comes collapsing into his arms. It's one of those hugs that is remembered for a lifetime. Bodies melding together. Spirits spinning, spiraling around them … Tears want to, won't do.

Leaning backwards from the waist they share a last smile. She says, "Thank you for so many things."

He says in kind, "Thank *you* for being in the absolute dead center of my life these past weeks. I'm sure you know that I'm gonna go out there and find Ann."

"Yes. Lucky girl … Oh, I forgot. That other girl, Lynn, came by here earlier today. She said that she'll be at her dorm if you want to reach her." Coy smile.

"Pass."

"Yeah, I figured. Be safe, my best friend. I'll love you forever."

"You, too, Claire. Umm … you probably better leave here. I don't think any of them know where I live, but if Lynn gets into the mix, and she very well could, you could be in trouble. You be safe too."

She follows him to the front door and watches as he climbs in and starts the engine. With a wave he accelerates to the end of the street and turns right. Standing alone at the doorway, Claire whispers, "I'll miss you."

✱   ✱   ✱   ✱

After the applause for Carmichael's message has died down, a buzz of anticipation rolls around the crowd. Soon a man who would need no introduction, and accepts none, walks up the stairs at the back of the stage and approaches the podium. The crowd recognizes him instantly and the thunderous roar goes on and on, until he finally pleads for them to stop so he can speak. Even this plea succeeds only partially, the roar continuing at a slightly moderated volume. Then Martin Luther King, Jr. begins his message in that mellow, universally recognized voice.

"Thank you for joining us on this momentous evening here in Selma. I'm certain that all of you share our joy at learning today that Jonas Baker of Selma was released by the authorities as not being guilty of shooting Eugene Hill from Tuskegee.

"The arrest of Mr. Ruben Townsend for that crime gives us no pleasure, but if he is found guilty and punished, at least justice will have prevailed." The roar increases in volume for a few moments until King once again asks for quiet.

"As you all know, the original purpose of this rally was to mark the five month anniversary of the first march to Montgomery, and to send yet another message." The roar surges again and King speaks over the sound. "That first march was held to protest that people of color in the state of Alabama were, and continue to be, disenfranchised. Negroes and whites alike made a statement in that march. Negroes and whites alike suffered hardships, even death. That statement, made at such grave costs, was, and is still, that continued disenfranchisement based on the color of one's skin is no longer acceptable."

The noise behind his words resembles the constant roar of the sea. "As recently as three days ago, we were not convinced that the legislators of this state believed in the sincerity of our intentions. As recently as three days ago, we believed that it would be necessary to repeat our statement." Another great surge in the noise level. They know where he's headed with this now.

"However, since that time three days ago when we felt the despair of failure, young Stokley Carmichael and one hundred and twenty-five other brave supporters of this great cause came to us. They demonstrated that with courage and perseverance, long-standing obstacles *can* be overcome." The crowd's roar is so loud that only those nearest the speakers and to King himself can actually hear all the words.

He shouts over the crowd's continuing clamor, "How stirring is the slogan under which these brave souls traveled to us here: 'Freedom Rides Again'." Although it had seemed that the sound could be no louder, a fresh crescendo rises to a higher level.

"We are grateful for these wonderful blessings. And we are grateful to those who bravely stood against the threat of physical harm to do the right thing … This afternoon I spoke with Governor Wallace on the telephone. We agreed to postpone the second march on Montgomery. We do this in the hope that the officials of the various counties and towns across this state are now aware of the intent of our people." This draws another burst of cheers—a sustained, deafening clamor.

"Certainly we hope that 'postpone' in this case will mean 'cancel', and that we won't have to reinstitute our commitment to keeping Montgomery apprised of our intentions." Those who are able to hear this last statement smile at the underlying meaning.

"Earlier tonight young Stokley Carmichael stood before you and issued a series of challenges: to pursue self-help, to insist on education for and of our youth, to reach for excellence, to have an identity that we choose for ourselves, to learn to protect ourselves and our children from harm. These are honorable, even necessary goals." The noise of the crowd subsides somewhat as many strain to hear how King will react to the firebrand rhetoric of Carmichael. He seems to be endorsing Stokley's point of view.

"I want to remind you that thus far in our struggle, nonviolence has triumphed over violence. Love has triumphed over hatred. Patience has triumphed over haste. Fighting fire with fire only produces a wasteland. No, I do not believe that we will overcome wrongs inflicted upon us by inflicting more wrongs on others. I believe that we will overcome those wrongs by enduring them *together*. There is no strength in individual violence. But the power of unified nonviolence is overwhelming." The crowd again bursts into a clamorous ovation.

"The only fire that I agree will defeat oppression is the fire of commitment *in each* of us *for all* of us. Let us go forth from here this day *not* with the rampaging fires of vengeance and hatred; but with the burning desire to endure all things together." Raising both hands in blessing and farewell, King turns and retraces his steps to the rear of the stage.

The crowd continues its exhilaration until they see him walk across the grassy area behind the stage, get into the waiting car and leave. Slowly, happily, the great gathering disperses.

✳   ✳   ✳   ✳

At twenty minutes after midnight Duke arrives back at Teddy Bear's place. The front door stands open and when Duke looks in, he sees stacks of books and clothing. He hears Teddy Bear rustling around in his bathroom and calls out, "Teddy! What's th' word, bud?"

Teddy Bear's head appears around a doorfacing and he says, "I'll be ready in a minute. I called Ron over at the AEPi house and he and Leo are gonna come over here tomorrow and clean this place out for me, sell my books and send us the money." He points to a stack of bagged clothing, a shaving kit, and one medium sized suitcase and says, "That's all I'm takin'. Is there enough room for it?"

Duke suppresses a groan. "Yeah, I guess so. But we'll have to repack some and we need to hurry. No questions right now, OK? Just trust me on this and let's get it together as best we can and get th' hell outta here. I'm startin' to get nervous."

Together they push and cram things into the remaining space in the T'Bird's backseat. The trunk is already full. Duke asks if Teddy Bear has a flashlight and then asks him to get it. The two friends shake hands in unity and back the T'Bird around to head out the driveway. They turn right on Glenn Ave. and drive to its intersection with Highway 14. As they turn onto Highway 14 on the northwest side of town, a pickup truck and George's SuperSport pass the Casino on Highway 29 from the south headed toward downtown Auburn.

In the darkness five miles out of town, Duke feels the tension leave him and begins telling Teddy Bear his wild and crazy story, starting with his being recruited to spy on the Tuskegee group and moving forward to today's events. The telling carries them past Montgomery and, after picking up Highway 80, lasts through Selma and on into Mississippi. Teddy Bear punctuates different parts of the story with exclamations, but otherwise makes no comment. At the end of the story Duke lapses into a prolonged silence.

"Duke?"

"Yeah, Teddy Bear."

"Did you really meet Omar Sharif?"

The end

Epilogue

▼

On the Monday morning after Duke and Teddy Bear left for California, Lynn Wilkins was found unconscious in her dorm room from an overdose of pain pills that she had stolen from her father. She survived and eventually married George Blankenship.

On that same Monday Terry Collins joined the US Army. He tested 'high' on the language section of the screening exams and went to the Army's language school at Monterrey, California. After 3 years in Germany he re-enlisted to go to OCS and served a tour in Viet Nam, where he earned a Purple Heart. He retired from the military as a Colonel after 25 years of service.

George Blankenship joined the US Marine Corps a few days later, after suffering much abuse from his father. He was wounded in action in Hue, RVN during the Tet offensive of 1968. He returned to Alabama and sold real estate, including the family farm.

Pax O'Reilly recovered completely from his injuries and finished his degree in 1966. He went on to teach at Washington and Lee University in Virginia and served for several years as the editor of the prestigious *Suwannee Review.*

Claire Hollister finished her degree, and then took a Master's Degree in math at Vanderbilt. She married her fiancé in 1967 and had three children, but never held a job.

Judd and Elizabeth finished their respective degrees in History and Secondary Education. They married and moved to Denver, Colorado in 1968. Judd finished his law degree in 1975. They were unable to have children.

Rueben Townsend was convicted of the murder of Eugene Hill and was sentenced to life imprisonment. He was killed in a prison riot in 1971. His appeal was scheduled to be heard the next month.

Robert Earle Wilkins lost his restaurant when it was discovered that he owed thousands of dollars in unpaid taxes. He never fully recovered from his heart attack, but lived a long, unhappy life, dying at age 85 in a nursing home.

Raymond T. "Swift" Collins was arrested in 1987 for the murder of Eldred Maxwell. The police, operating on an anonymous tip, located the buried head of Reverend Maxwell and were able to match the DNA to that found on an old shovel that was hidden in the loft of the barn on Collins' farm. The tip that provided the location of Rev. Maxwell's missing head also revealed where the shovel was hidden.

Emma Collins moved to Texas to live with her cousin in 1966 and was never heard from again.

Ricky Parsons became Chairman of the County Commissioners of Macon County in 1972. He retired from his job with Alabama Gas in 1998.

Thaddeus Blankenship had a stroke and died in 1970. His farm passed to his wife and was sold off piece by piece to fund her expensive lifestyle in Montgomery.

Timothy "Cracker" White was never heard from again after fighting the fire at the Red Hill Baptist Church. Some believed that a body found in a shallow grave near Highway 80 was his.

Charlie "Red" McKinney won a Pulitzer Prize for journalism as a result of his investigative work in the Civil Rights arena. The unpopularity of his views forced him to move north to Cleveland, OH in 1970.

Eudora Maxwell lived long enough to see Swift Collins indicted for the murder of her husband; but had a heart attack a few weeks later. She died satisfied.

Reverend Milton Mohammed became a driving force in the Southern Christian Leadership Council. He never married, but was instrumental in many of the gains made in the Civil Rights movement.

Reverend Joe Lee Cleveland retired shortly after the fire that destroyed his church. He and his wife moved to Florida to live out their remaining days.

James "Jimbo" Turner was defeated in his bid to remain the Sheriff of Macon County by a young black man who was the first elected black official in Macon County, Alabama since the nineteenth century.

Tisha Jemison graduated summa cum laude from Tuskegee Institute and taught for several years before being appointed Superintendent of Schools for the state of Alabama by Governor Wallace in his fourth term.

978-0-595-46525-5
0-595-46525-0

Lightning Source UK Ltd.
Milton Keynes UK
26 May 2010

154763UK00001B/167/A

9 780595 465255